The Riddle

of

Alabaster
Royal

OTHER NOVELS BY PATRICIA VERYAN

Lanterns
The Mandarin of Mayfair
Never Doubt I Love
A Shadow's Bliss
Ask Me No Questions
Had We Never Loved
Time's Fool
Logic of the Heart
The Dedicated Villain
Cherished Enemy
Love Alters Not
Give All to Love
The Tyrant
Journey to Enchantment
Practice to Deceive
Sanguinet's Crown
The Wagered Widow
The Noblest Frailty
Married Past Redemption
Feather Castles
Some Brief Folly
Nanette
Mistress of Willowvale
Love's Duet
The Lord and the Gypsy

PATRICIA VERYAN

The Riddle
of
ALABASTER
ROYAL

ST. MARTIN'S PRESS
NEW YORK

THE RIDDLE OF ALABASTER ROYAL. Copyright © 1997 by Patricia Veryan. All rights reserved. Printed in the United States of America. No part of this book may be used or reproduced in any manner whatsoever without written permission except in the case of brief quotations embodied in critical articles or reviews. For information, address St. Martin's Press, 175 Fifth Avenue, New York, N.Y. 10010.

Library of Congress Cataloging-in-Publication Data

Veryan, Patricia.
    The riddle of alabaster royal   /   Patricia Veryan.
        p.   cm.
    ISBN 0-312-17121-8
    I. Title.
    PS3572.E766A79   1997
    813'.54—dc21   97-23035
                                        CIP

First Edition: November 1997

10 9 8 7 6 5 4 3 2 1

For Nancy Eads,
who has given so much time,
effort and enthusiasm to
being the President of my
Fan Club

The Riddle

of

Alabaster
Royal

1

Spain
June 1813

Desperate to find shelter from the hail of shot, Captain Jack Vespa crawled on doggedly. Even if he still had the strength to call for help, it would have been pointless; the French cannonade drowned out all lesser voices. He was finding it increasingly difficult to see now, and when his groping left hand slid over an edge, for a heart-stopping moment he thought he was going to plunge down the high crag above the river Zadorra.

"Hey! A new arrival, my Tobias!" The voice that came through a lull in the uproar was strained but undeniably British.

Another voice said an unsteady, "Ain't wearing red or green. I say—this shell hole is under British occu-occupation, Monsieur, so you'd best surren—"

"Don't be a dolt, Toby. It's a blue coat! We're visited by a mighty Staff Officer, no less!"

"Oh, egad! One of his lordship's famous 'Family'!"

A shell screamed overhead.

"Best not hang about, sir," urged the first voice. "Come on in."

Vespa lowered himself cautiously, then rolled and for a minute or two lay still, pain causing him to curse faintly. The cannonade resumed but seemed less ear-splitting. Hands were touching him; something was wiping his face and he could focus again. A youthful, smoke-blackened countenance, framed by curling light brown hair, bent over him. "Lieutenant Tobias Broderick, sir. Forty-fifth."

Vespa blinked at him stupidly. "You're Third Division. What the hell . . . are you doing up here?"

Broderick bent lower so as to hear the gasped-out words. He clutched his side painfully, but roared, "Old Picton properly got his nose out of joint when his lordship sent word we were to support the Seventh. So we charged like the devil at the French centre. My poor hack was hit and bolted, and I—er—rather tumbled in here."

"I see. Who's that?"

"Oh, yes. I'm binding him up. Musket ball's smashed his shoulder and broken his collar-bone by the looks of it. I'll help you first, sir. You're all blood. Can you see?"

"Not well enough to see your friend, but . . . finish with him. I'll do."

Watching this member of the select few chosen by Wellington as his personal aides, Broderick thought it more probable that he would die. He started to crawl back to his first patient, then remembered, and half-turned to shout with a quivering grin, "You likely know him, sir. Lieutenant Manderville."

'Manderville?' thought Vespa. It must be some other Manderville. The tattered casualty lying huddled in a rain-swept shell hole atop a Spanish crag couldn't possibly be . . . ? Reality melted away.

He opened his eyes and started up, swearing. Broderick was wrapping a torn piece of shirt tightly around his leg. Catching his breath, he lay back. "Sorry. Good of you, Broderick. Is—is the bone severed?"

"No, sir. But your leg's pretty damned riddled. I'll get to your arm in a minute. What happened to your head?"

He'd been returning from delivering a despatch from Lord Wellington to Colonel Cadogan when a shell had killed his horse under him and sent him hurtling against a boulder, rendering him senseless. "I dismounted on it," he said wryly. He heard a faint laugh. "You wouldn't be *Paige* Manderville?" he enquired, peering mistily.

"The debonair Dandy of Mayfair," said Broderick, with a gallant attempt at a chuckle.

"The devil!" exclaimed Vespa.

"I think I resent that. Sir," complained Manderville.

"I was reacting to—to Broderick's—efforts," gasped Vespa. "Do I mistake it, or is the cannonade fading? Are you badly mauled, Lieutenant? Can you shin up there and have a look?"

"Horse rolled on me, sir," said Broderick. "Think he snapped a couple of ribs. Or something. I'll make a try at it."

Manderville drawled, "You'd best tie up the Captain's arm first, Toby, before he's bled white."

Broderick investigated. "A piece of shell-casing, by the look of it. I think I can—" He gave a tentative tug.

Vespa shouted an anguished "No!"

Aghast, Broderick recoiled. "No. I think I won't." He moved in a sideways crawl to the edge of their shelter and returned to announce that there was "the devil of a fight round Arinez Hill. I fancy his lordship means to chase King Joseph all the way back to Paris."

He completed his first aid, then settled himself between the other casualties, looking from one to the other anxiously.

Manderville said with a sigh, "I don't imagine either of you has a canteen?"

They hadn't, but the wish had been in all their minds.

"Open your mouth," panted Vespa. "You might . . . catch some rain."

"I might, sir. Except that it's stopped raining."

"Never mind," said Broderick. "We'll have help here in a trice, I don't doubt."

His optimism proved unfounded. The action that was to be known as the Battle of Vitoria raged on, and the three young officers lay in their damp and chilly sanctuary hour after weary hour. They endured their misery in silence, until Vespa, his mind wandering, muttered, "The crocuses will be in bloom."

Broderick argued wearily, "Can't say that, sir. It's cro-ci, not -ses."

"No, it ain't," said Manderville. "Lay you a pony it's -ses."

With difficulty Broderick reached Manderville's outstretched left hand. "You're on! Will you be a witness, sir?"

Vespa gathered his wits and said, "Let's forget rank for a while, shall we? What are you wagering on?"

The other men exchanged a quick glance.

Broderick said, "You were talking about flowers, Cap— Jove! We don't know your name."

"It's Vespa."

"Jack Vespa?" Manderville dragged himself to one elbow. "Aren't you the fellow who hauled Tim Van Lindsay out of the Esla last month?"

"Tim's a clumsy fellow." Vespa shifted painfully. "Always falling down something, or—or into something. Was I really talking about flowers?"

"You were," confirmed Manderville. "Like to garden, do you? I've seen your Richmond house from the river. Beautiful grounds. Do you mean to live there when we get home?"

It was an effort to talk, but Vespa knew it was as well to try and keep their minds off things. He said, "No. I've inherited an estate in . . . Dorsetshire. Never have visited the old place. I rather fancy country life. My . . . my father won't like it, I fear, but . . . "

Manderville waited, but the sentence went unfinished. "Sir Kendrick don't approve of me, I fear." He grinned irrepressibly. "Jealous, probably. He's quite a Non-Pareil."

Vespa's dulled eyes brightened. "Yes. He is."

"Sir Kendrick Vespa!" Broderick exclaimed. "Now I know who you are! Jove! I'd never have taken you for *his* son!"

Vespa could not keep back a laugh, and then had to smother a groan. "I don't have his . . . good looks, is . . . is that what you say?"

4

"If he does, it's because he's a clumsy clod," grumbled Manderville. "My nurse came from a hamlet called Pudding Park in Dorsetshire. Anywhere near your place?"

"No. Alabaster Royal's farther north."

The name struck another chord with Broderick. "Alabaster Royal," he muttered frowningly. "I've heard something about it. Can't remember what. Except that it wasn't good."

Manderville gave a moan of exasperation. "And there goes the other foot into his mouth!"

"Please . . . " whispered Vespa. "Don't make me laugh! . . . Tell me—Broderick, what you mean to do when . . . when we get home."

"I shall go back to Oxford. Lead the exalted existence of a don amid minds equal to my own."

Manderville gave a crow of derision.

Vespa peered at the young lieutenant curiously. "You must have done very well at school."

"Oh, he knows everything," said Manderville, cradling his hurt arm tenderly. "Except how to come in out of the rain!"

Before Broderick could retaliate, Vespa asked, "What about you? Certainly, you have the pick of London's Fairs at your feet."

"Of course. I've also a comfortable fortune, thank heaven, so I can take my time about selecting a lady worthy of becoming Mrs. Paige Manderville."

"I am going to be sick," announced Broderick. "Vespa, how can you listen to such— Vespa?" He leant closer and scanned the captain apprehensively.

"Is he gone, poor devil?" asked Manderville.

"Not far from it, I'm afraid. Likely he's got a concussion. That's a beast of a head wound."

"It'll scar him for life, to say the least of it. Pity. He's a good man from what I've heard." With a sigh, Manderville closed his eyes.

"Paige?" Dismayed, Broderick called, "For Lord's sake, don't you go and die, too!"

"Wouldn't dream of it," said Manderville weakly. "Toby, do you

5

really know something about that inheritance of his—Arabesque something?"

"Alabaster Royal." Broderick hesitated, then muttered, "If only half of what they say about the estate is truth, it's no place for the faint-hearted."

"Well, if only half of what I've heard about—about Jack Vespa is truth, faint-hearted's what he's not! Even in his present state, poor fella. Can't help but be sorry for Sir Kendrick. Sherborne, the elder son, was—was the bright hope of the family. He fell at Badajoz last year, as I recall. Splendid fellow. Almost as good-looking as I am."

Broderick's scornful retort was cut off by a shout from the cliff path. A moment later, a dragoon sergeant beamed down at them and howled exuberantly, "Here we are, Captain! Praise God, we've found you!"

"All th-three of us," said Manderville.

"He won't like it," whispered Vespa, his mind far away. "He'll think . . . I'm ripe for Bedlam. . . . "

England
September 1813

"You're stark, raving mad!" Tall, trim, and at fifty still strikingly handsome, Sir Kendrick Vespa was flushed, and the fine dark eyes so much admired by London's ladies were wide with consternation. Gazing at the drawn features of his younger son, he gestured as if grasping at invisible straws, causing the two great bloodhounds that lay on either side of his chair to sit up as one and eye him anxiously. "Those damned Frenchies have done more than reduce you to—to a physical cripple," he sputtered. "They've made swill of what was left of your brains!"

The young captain's hand tightened on the papers he held, but he said calmly, "Very likely, sir. But you have to admit, I won. I didn't come home from Spain in a box. You owe me a pony."

6

Sir Kendrick grunted, rose from behind the desk and crossed the sun-splashed study escorted by the hounds who waited as he unlocked an armoire chest and took out a cash box. "Aye, well, I'm glad enough to be paying this," he grumbled as he counted out the twenty-five pounds. "But there'd have been no need had you not felt obliged to go haring off after Sherborne. Compounding folly with folly. It's not bad enough that my first-born must lie buried somewhere in Spanish soil. I came perilously near to losing you as well!" He dropped the bank notes into his son's lap and leant back against the desk, frowning down at him.

The baronet not only loved animals but seemed to possess the ability to awaken an answering affection in any canine he encountered. His bloodhounds, Solomon and Barrister, were seldom far from his side, and today was no exception. They took up their flanking positions and watched the younger man, so that when Jack glanced up it appeared to him that three pairs of eyes were regarding him sternly. He slipped the notes into his purse and pushed away the hurt that accompanied any mention of Sherry— the brother so loved; so missed. "Oh, I don't think it was ever that desperate, sir," he said. "I can still ride, and—"

"And limp like an old man! And do not be telling me that gouge down your temple adds to your appeal, 'cause it don't! You never were a beauty, John!"

"Lord, no. Sherry had all the looks." Striving for a lighter note, he managed a grin. "I got the brains."

Sir Kendrick was not to be diverted. "Oh, did you? One would never guess it! To move into that desolate, draughty old pile is scarce an indication of mental acuity. You've a home here and another in Town that most young fellows would be proud of. If you don't choose to share my company—"

"How can you say that, sir? You know I've always felt . . . I mean—I could not be more grateful and—and proud to be your son, but—"

"But not sufficiently grateful to allow that I keep you by me for a spell! John, you *must* know how I—we've worried, your mother

7

and I. You did but now get out of hospital. Old Rickaby warned us that you'll be subject to extremely violent headaches, and perhaps hallucinations, for months to come. It is the height of folly to choose this of all times to go off and live miles from anywhere. You are *ill,* boy! You need rest and care. You'll get both at Richmond."

Jack avoided his eyes. It was ironic really. All his life he'd been in awe of this splendid gentleman. He'd pitied other boys because their fathers were dull and ordinary and fell far short of Sir Kendrick, the very model of what a British diplomatist should be. He'd said as much once to Sherry, who had laughed and argued teasingly, "Silly gudgeon! How are you qualified to judge? You scarcely know the guv'nor." It was true that Sir Kendrick's duties kept him away from Richmond for much of the year, but absence had not dimmed Jack's affection. As a boy he had dreamt of performing some deed of valour that would win the approval of his idol; saving him from a runaway coach, perhaps, or leaping between him and a would-be assassin, or plunging into a raging torrent and dragging him safely to shore. And now he must refuse one of the few requests ever made of him. Nor could he put his reasons into words. He knew only that he could not endure this house. Not yet. And the London mansion would be as bad.

In Spain he'd been too busy to have much time for reflection, but here, everywhere he looked brought memories of his brother: some childish prank, or youthful endeavour, or one of their furious battles that had so quickly dissolved in laughter. He could hear an echo of that laughter still; see the blaze of mischief in those magnificent near-black eyes. Sherry . . . tall and graceful and as darkly handsome as their famous sire. So different from himself, with his average height and nondescript light brown hair and hazel eyes. Sherry, who should have been the one to inherit the title. Sherry, a careless scamp and hothead, who hadn't given a button for rank or property; whose quick wits and endearing smile could extricate him from the most flagrant violations of academic, civic or paternal authority, and behind whose merry insouciance had dwelt the warmest heart and the deepest loyalty any brother could wish for.

Given time, he would have mellowed and acquitted himself with dignity, as a Vespa must. But the time had been denied. Afire with patriotic zeal, he had rushed off to join his hero, Lord Wellington, and his precious young life had been snuffed out during the terrible third siege of Badajoz. Sherry . . .

As if sensing his distress, Solomon padded over and pushed a cold nose under his hand, and Jack stroked the great head absently.

"I see that it *is* too much to ask," said Sir Kendrick, irritated by the long pause. "Well, if you're too damned high-in-the-instep to dwell under my roof, you can at least stay in Town. Take up residence in that scruffy club of yours. No need to retreat to the wilderness and lick your wounds!"

Bristling, Jack stood, and leaning heavily on his cane, said, "I do not care to reside in Town, sir. Either at the Madrigal or under *any* roof! As for retreating—" He broke off and took a deep breath. "I think I'd best do so, Papa, before I say something I'll be sorry for!"

The steel in voice and eyes was unfamiliar. The thin, scarred face was grimly set. Disconcerted, Sir Kendrick stared at this unfamiliar stranger, then said with his brilliant smile, "Longing to give me a set-down, are you, my boy? Well, and I deserve one. I shouldn't have said that. I ask your pardon. Now say I'm forgiven, and sit down, do."

Jack's stiff shoulders relaxed. He sat down again, his answering grin banishing the resentment from his face. "Of course I forgive you, sir. And I respect your opinions. But you'll not change my mind."

"Just remember that I tried." Sir Kendrick pulled Solomon's ear and was obliged to repeat the caress for Barrister. He murmured, "I—er, don't suppose a certain Miss Warrington could have anything to do with your decision?"

Again, Jack tensed. Like any healthy young man, he enjoyed feminine companionship. During his undergraduate days he'd entered the 'petticoat line' and for several months had been favoured with the affections of a vivacious little opera dancer. But while finding a seat at a musicale one evening, he'd accidentally stepped on someone's toe, and turning to apologize, had looked into the loveliest face he'd ever seen. From that moment, Miss Marietta Warrington had been the lady of his dreams. Mama had not approved of his choice, and Sherry, himself as good as betrothed, had teased that there were so many 'fish in the sea' and it would be years before Jack must confine himself to only one. His devotion had not faded, however, and the passing years had served only to deepen his love. He'd lost Marietta, and he had accepted that sad fact. He said quietly, "So Mama told you of my hopes in that direction."

"She did. And I'll confess I was tempted to take my horse-whip when I called on Warrington."

"Good Lord! You didn't—"

"Call on him? Yes. The man's a fool. He's whistled most of his fortune down the wind since his wife's death, and I've no doubt the rest will follow. If he's to send his boys to University and provide for his daughters, he'll likely have to sell up. Or—Miss Marietta Warrington will have to find herself a rich and indulgent husband."

Jack stared at his papers and said nothing.

"Have you called on her since you came home?"

"No, sir."

"But you did offer, I understand."

"Five times."

"Indeed! You must be extreme fond! Does the lovely Miss Warrington return your affection?"

"I—I believe she does. Perhaps not as fully as— But we have both accepted that it is hopeless. Marietta is still under age, but even if she were not, she has a strong sense of duty, and Sir Lionel will have none of me. He has no choice, I suppose. Certainly, I couldn't provide for the whole family."

"No more could I. As you know, my fortune is comfortable, but while it enables us to enjoy the luxuries of life, it would not stretch to support that brood!"

"I am aware, sir. And the responsibility would be mine—not yours."

"Well said! Then so soon as you're fully recovered, you must start to look about. There are plenty of sensible females who will not be put off by a limp and a few scars. Find a well-dowered wife and we can all live here together very comfortably."

'Heaven forbid!' thought Jack. "Perhaps," he said. "But I've a fancy—for a while at least—to just live quietly."

"Very quietly! That blasted great barracks of a house would cost a fortune to repair and bring up to style, and another fortune to maintain. You'd need a staff of twenty inside servants at a bare minimum, to say nothing of gardeners, gamekeepers— Now why do you laugh?"

"Your pardon, Father, but I'll only require a kitchen and one bedchamber, and I can—"

"*One* bedchamber? You'll take your man and a groom with you, surely?"

"No, sir. Pence has no taste for country living. At least, that's what he says. I suspect there's a pretty parlour-maid lurking in the picture somewhere."

"Hmm. I wonder." Sir Kendrick pursed his lips. "Very well, I'll send one of the grooms along with you. Don't be too proud to admit you're in no condition to care for your hacks."

"No, I'll own that." Jack took up his cane and limped towards the door, his father and the dogs accompanying him. "But I prefer to hire a local man to serve as groom or major domo. Someone who can acquaint me with the area. And, have no fear, sir. I don't mean to be a recluse, if that's what troubles you."

"What troubles me," said Sir Kendrick gravely, "is that you may have no choice. Now go on up and see your mother. She's waiting for you."

———— ⚜ ————

"I lay the entire horrid business at your brother's door." Reclining on a white velvet chaise-lounge in her private parlour, Faith, Lady

Vespa, took a scrap of cambric and lace from the bosom of her pink satin negligée and dabbed it at her large blue eyes. She waved her other hand to silence her son's response and went on, "No, pray do not at once leap to his defence as you always do. Sherborne was my first-born, and I loved him. But he was selfish and inconsiderate and never gave one single thought to the inevitable consequences of his ridiculous escapades. With a fine future ahead of him, he chose to throw it away! When I think of how many disasters he dragged you into . . . "

Seated beside the chaise, Vespa argued gently, "Now, Mama, you must not hold Sherry's patriotism against him. He died bravely, for his country. And as for his pranks, you know he never intended—"

"Oh, but of *course*! He never *intended* that my horse should bolt that day in Hyde Park when he came thundering out of the trees for all the world like one of those dreadful Tartans or whatever they're called. Had you not ridden to rescue me, I dread to think what might have happened! He never *intended* that we should lose tutor after tutor because of his silly practical jokes, and reduce my delicate nerves to shreds. He never *intended* . . . "

Jack resigned himself to the inevitable recital of Sherry's faults, and watched his mother patiently. She really was a fine-looking woman, he thought, and had managed to keep her figure. It was unfortunate that her nature was so pessimistic. She doubtless couldn't help it, but it was her maudlin tendency to whine, and to dwell upon tragic events and the shortcomings of others, that had long since driven her husband into less tiresome arms. The knowledge that her famous spouse had a mistress only a year or two younger than herself exacerbated Lady Faith's sense of ill usage. She complained to all who would listen that Sir Kendrick seldom visited his Richmond house, but when he did come she sniped at and reproached him, with the result that his visits became less and less frequent.

When she removed to Town for the Season, Sir Kendrick was unfailingly sent on 'a diplomatic mission' elsewhere. The efforts of

friends and family to support her dwindled when they were re-
galed with long and tearful accounts of the ills of her situation,
and even the reminder that she had two fine sons could not allevi-
ate her gloom. Sherborne's strong resemblance to his father irritated her, and although she would grudgingly admit that her
younger son favoured her own side of the family, Jack's efforts to
cheer her usually ended in failure, just as an amused Sherry pre-
dicted.

Bringing her grievances up to date, Lady Faith wailed, "But for
Sherborne, you would never have got into the war, you know you
would not." She stretched out a hand to him pleadingly. He had
been holding his cane, and discarding it hurriedly, he brushed
against a bowl of sweet peas on the table beside her, sending it
tumbling to the floor. "Oh, no!" she wailed, ringing the bell for her
abigail. "My new bowl! Is it chipped? I so seldom receive gifts any
more! Oh, my poor nerves!"

He rescued the heavy and charmingly enamelled bowl, and
scooping the blossoms inside, told her soothingly that it appeared
to be undamaged. "It's a pretty thing," he said, attempting to turn
her thoughts. "From Papa, or one of your cisisbeos, love?"

"Cisisbeos, indeed! At my age?" Despite the dismissing tone,
she looked pleased. Her maid hurried in and brought a towel to
wipe up the floor. Jack limped aside and the abigail gave him a
sympathetic glance that was not lost upon Lady Faith so that before
the door had closed behind the woman she moaned, "My poor
boy! Barely able to totter about, and—your *face*! Whatever will my
friends say when they see you?"

"I hope they won't faint," he said with a whimsical grin. "Cheer
up, it's not that bad, surely? And this scar will fade, so the doctors
tell me."

"Doctors! Who can believe one word those quacks utter? You
are thin as a rail and will never regain your full health. Only to
think"—the tears started to flow—"of how proud I was when you
were small and I would go with Nurse into the park. All the ladies
would so admire your curls, and say how much you took after me.

13

And you did, for you have always had beautiful eyes, John, even if they are that unfortunate tawny colour. Sherborne cast everyone into the shade, of course. But you grew into such a good-looking boy. And now . . . !" Her voice almost suspended, she sobbed, "I can scarce bear to—to look at you!"

He took a deep breath and said lightly, "Well, you will not be obliged to do so for very long, Mama. I have decided to live down at Alabaster Royal for a while, and—" He drew back, his ears ringing to her horrified shriek.

"*What?* You cannot be *serious*! No, no, you must not! It is a dreadful, *dreadful* house!"

"How so? It has walls, and a roof. And it stands in beautiful grounds, so I hear. If it is somewhat run-down, why, walls and ceilings can be repaired."

"I do not speak of such mundane things as *bricks* and *mortar*!" Lady Faith sat up straight, her face pale and her manner so agitated that he took her outstretched hands and held them firmly. "It is *evil*!" she declared, her eyes wide and frightened. "Even as a child I hated going down there in the summer-time. And your dear Grandmama Wansdyke loathed it also. I was never more pleased than when she told my father she would sooner stay in London's heat! There are *spirits,* John! Drifting about—*everywhere*! And that dreadful cat! Ugh!" She shivered. "It was always so . . . cold! And I saw . . . " Her voice trailed into silence.

He said teasingly, "You're surely not saying you believe in ghosts and goblins and such nonsense?"

"I am saying I *saw* something in that horrid old place! Something terrifying. To this day I often wake in a panic, just to recall it. Ah. You choose to laugh at me! So why do I trouble to warn you?"

"No, really. I only—"

"Never mind. I am accustomed to being slighted and ignored. It is my lot in life. You are a typical male and will go your own way, no matter what I say, or how my poor nerves are overset. Well, go then, and be done! Abandon me in this l-lonely house w-with no one to care about me!"

Dismayed, he said, "But Mama, even when I am here, you seldom have time to see me. You have Cousin Eve to keep you company, and all your charities and bazaars and card-parties, and your friends. I'd not thought you were lonely. Perhaps you should move to the town house, where there is so much for you to—"

"There is no call to pretend you care about poor me," she declared, dabbing at her eyes again. "*Go* to your country monstrosity! It is all of a piece. You are every bit as s-selfish as Sherborne was, and so I tell you! When I look back, I wonder why I wasted my youth . . . c-caring for the pair of you, for all the affection I was given in return. If ever there were ser-serpents' teeth . . . "

Among his friends Captain Jack Vespa had the reputation of managing to surmount any obstacle with cheerful persistence, seldom allowing his temper, which could flare unexpectedly, to get the best of him. He persisted now, soothing his mother's lamentations and attempting to win her to a happier frame of mind. But in the end, perhaps because by then his head was aching fiercely, he promised to stay by her side for at least another week.

Sir Kendrick was "called away" that very evening. Solomon and Barrister, of course, escorted him.

⌑

Ten days later, Jack rode through the gates of the Richmond house and breathed a sigh of relief. It had not been easy, but he was free at last.

The word of his return had spread like wildfire, and friends and neighbours had flocked to welcome him home. Lady Faith had been in her element. She had presided over luncheons, teas and dinner parties with the air of an inwardly heart-broken mother struggling gallantly to present a brave face to the world. Her martyrdom, and the sympathetic glances that came his way as she recounted ever more dramatic tales of his narrow escape from death, had tried his patience to the limit. His attempts to leave had been blocked with what he had to admit were superb tactics. He was grateful to those who had come to see him, but that the constant society functions might prove exhausting to a semi-invalid had never seemed to occur to his mother.

The promised week had stretched to nine days, and yesterday afternoon he'd told her he must depart. She had dismissed this with a merry laugh and a list of upcoming events and invited guests whom he "simply could *not*" disappoint. He'd done his best to please, but he was beginning to feel worse than when he'd left the hospital, and he was not such a fool as to endanger his health only to provide his mother with an excuse for a continuing round of parties. Accompanying her up the stairs after a particularly tiresome evening, he had told her politely but with determination that he would drive out for Alabaster Royal first thing in the morning. This had precipitated a flood of tears and reproaches, but the fact that Lady Faith had not once enquired as to his own well-being had helped him to withstand her demands, and he had left instructions that his curricle was to be at the door early in the morning, with Secrets, his black mare, tied on behind.

Lady Faith was nothing if not determined. When he came down to breakfast, he was informed that the curricle would not be available due to the fact that my lady had driven out in it to visit some friends in Purley, but that she would return shortly. In view of the distance involved, this was unlikely, and since her ladyship had never in living memory been known to leave her suite before noon, or to be driven in a sporting coach, there could be no doubt but that this was a deliberate attempt to further delay his departure.

Irked, he'd ordered out his phaeton, only to be told it was at the wheelwrights. His rare temper had flared and he had instructed his man to fill a valise with immediate necessities and send his curricle and two trunks to Alabaster Royal the following day. The valise had been strapped to the saddle, he had said his farewells to his dismayed and protesting valet, the butler and the housekeeper, and with the aid of an equally dismayed groom had mounted Secrets and ridden out.

Now, he looked about him, his spirits lightening. The day was bright, with a warm breeze blowing and the old Thames threading like a diamond-studded ribbon through the low, rolling hills. It was England at her best, and as he skirted the town and entered open country he was warmed by the beauty of his native land.

Like all Wellington's aides-de-camp, he was a splendid horseman, but he was shocked to find that he now tired quickly. He was obliged to rest at a wayside inn near Farnborough, and not until late afternoon did he reach the outskirts of Andover. He acknowledged to himself that he'd been too sanguine about his state of health, and gave up, taking a room for the night at a pleasant hedge tavern where he ordered dinner sent to his room and fell asleep twice while eating a plain meal of fish soup, roast chicken accompanied by overcooked vegetables, and a gooseberry tart. He grinned drowsily, knowing that Sir Kendrick would have been appalled by such a menu, but compared to the roots and berries that had often been the only food available in Spain, he'd found it satisfactory.

In the morning he awoke to leaden skies and a chill wind. His injured leg was making it clear that a day in the saddle had been unwise, and getting down the narrow stairs became a painful and difficult task. He was short of breath by the time he reached the ground floor, and much embarrassed to look up and find that two men were watching him narrowly. They were big fellows, fashionably if not elegantly dressed. The taller of the pair smiled sympathetically. Vespa nodded and hurried into the coffee room, knowing that his limp was pronounced, and dreading that he would be the object of all eyes. Fortunately, only one other table was occupied, the elderly lady and gentleman seated there being too involved in low-voiced but fierce bickering to pay him any heed.

By the time he finished breakfast, he had come to the reluctant conclusion that he must either rest here for another day or hire a coach. He consulted the host, a cheerful little man who had already drawn his own conclusions about this guest. "Home from Spain, are you, sir?" he asked with a kindness that forbade mortification. "Ar, I reckoned as much. I'll send my youngest over to the Green Duck. It's a nice house no more'n five miles west of here,

17

and they've got a post-chaise for the hiring that's likely gathering dust. Not what you're accustomed to, I don't doubt, but it'll get you where you're going, and easier than riding in this weather."

It developed that the host had a young cousin who had served with the Fourth Division at the Battle of Salamanca, and while Vespa waited, the two men spent a congenial hour discussing the war in general, and Lord Wellington in particular. A sullen-faced youth arrived at last, with an ill-matched team harnessed to an equipage which had indeed seen better days. The host was embarrassed and said he hadn't remembered its being quite this shabby, and that perhaps the captain would be better advised to drive into Andover and secure a more suitable vehicle. Jack was eager to reach Alabaster Royal before the sun went down, however, and in no time Secrets was tied on behind and the antiquated chaise rattled out of the yard.

The miles slipped away, and far from springing his team the postilion had all he could do to keep them to a steady trot. By mid-afternoon the weather closed in and the view from the windows was obscured by misting rain. Despite the poorly sprung coach and lumpy cushions, Vespa felt relaxed and drowsy and eventually slipped into a doze.

He was awoken by an outburst of shouts and curses. Starting up in confusion he thought for an instant that he was back in Spain, but then a large coach loomed up dangerously close to his own. The post-boy screamed with fear and fury. Vespa reached for the window, but he was too late. He had a fleeting glimpse of small, dark eyes in a coarse-featured face that grinned at him from the other coach. A violent shock was followed by screams, a sense of falling, and the swift fading of sight and sound. His last thought was that the man in the big coach was one of the two who had stared at him this morning when he came down to breakfast. . . .

2

*H*e was cold and uncomfortable. His leg was even more painful than usual and his head throbbed so spitefully that he didn't want to wake up. In addition to all the rest, it was most unfair that he should have this heavy weight on his chest. Reluctantly, Vespa opened his eyes.

He was lounging about in somebody's garden, evidently, and it must be getting foggy because it was hard to distinguish who bent over him. He blinked. A remote voice spoke unintelligibly. He began to sort out his unknown companion's features. It was an odd face. Small, and heavily bearded, and with a long nose that looked almost like— He gave a gasp and opened his eyes wider. A small bedraggled dog was sitting on his chest and peering at him hopefully.

"What the deuce!" he exclaimed, and sat up abruptly, which was a major error.

The voice, which he now recognized as belonging to the dog, growled distantly. Gradually, the world stopped spinning and he was able to breathe normally again. His surroundings drifted back into focus. The dog had retreated to a safe distance from which to watch him. Instead of the garden hammock he had at first assumed, his couch was a weedy ditch. When he saw the overturned post-chaise that lay nearby, he remembered. He crawled to the wreck and used the wheel to drag himself to his feet.

The narrow road was deserted. A chill wind moaned across a sweep of equally deserted moorland fringed by distant hills that loomed like grey-blue humps on the horizon. His gaze shortened and held on a dead horse. His heart seemed to stop, then gave a leap of relief as he saw that the poor creature was one of the postilion's mismatched team. The other horse was gone. If the occupants of the big coach had stopped they would surely have made an effort to revive him, or at least had the decency to convey him to a doctor or an apothecary. It seemed likely therefore that the conscienceless clods had not stopped and that the post-boy had ridden away on the surviving hack in search of help.

"Blasted rogues!" Vespa peered about anxiously in search of Secrets. There was no sign of his beautiful black mare, but when he whistled, she trotted from a nearby hollow and came straight to him. She was favouring her right front leg. He ran a practised hand down it and found the knee slightly swollen.

"Nothing too serious, old lady," he told her, and she snorted into the hollow of his neck and lipped at his ear, only to whicker and prance away as the dog rushed up, barking shrilly.

"That'll be enough from you," said Vespa. "Be off! Go home, sir!"

The dog was apparently disinclined to go anywhere. It sat down again, and resumed the role of an interested bystander.

Vespa took stock of the situation. He could wait for the post-boy to return, or ride on alone. There was the risk, of course, that the boy, who had been none too alert, might have presumed him to have expired and would see no need to hurry back, in which case he could have a long wait for rescue.

The papers from Mr. Jermyn, Grandmama Wansdyke's solicitor, were still in his pocket, and he took out the rough map and scanned it. The last time he'd looked out of the chaise window before falling asleep, he'd seen in the distance the great spire of Salisbury Cathedral. How much farther they'd gone before the crash he didn't know, but the last leg of the journey seemed to be pretty straightforward, and he judged that if he stayed on this apology for a road he should eventually reach crossroads and a signpost that would point his way to Gallery-on-Tang. The solicitor had said that the Alabaster Royal preserves had at one time encompassed the village, the quarry providing the major source of local employment. The manor itself stood atop a low hill about a mile east of the quarry, and could be seen from the road.

He was pleased to find his valise half hidden by some shrubs in the ditch and apparently relatively undamaged. He was reluctant to ride Secrets, but his own gait was worse than hers, and his aches and pains were increasing rather than lessening. He apologized to the mare and promised they would take it slowly.

In Spain, Wellington's aides-de-camp had been renowned for the speed and agility with which they mounted up. Today, even utilizing a nearby boulder as a mounting block, it was all Vespa could do to haul himself into the saddle. The little dog watched with interest. Vespa told the animal what his brother officers would have thought of that performance, and added some lurid comments on the insensate bird-brains who had thought it great fun to run his coach off the road and kill a perfectly good horse.

As he rode off, the dog lay down and ignored him, but when he looked back a few minutes later, it was following. He repeated his earlier advice more forcefully, and the dog scuttled away, but his next backward glance revealed it prancing along in the rear again. It was shaggy and unkempt, poor little creature, but perhaps it lived nearby and was homeward bound, in which case he need not worry about it.

An hour later, he was decidedly worried. The crossroads had not yet materialized. He was relieved to encounter a lone shepherd who advised that Alabaster Royal was "just a wee bit further on", and to be sure to skirt it if he was going to the village.

21

"Thank you," he said. "But I'm not."

"If ye bean't going there-aways, why ask full-ish questions?"

"I mean I'm not going to the village. I'm going to Alabaster Royal."

The shepherd gawked at him with his mouth at half cock. Vespa nodded and rode on, trying not to hear the hoots of laughter and some shouted warnings about 'accursed' old houses.

Considerably more than "a wee bit further on" he did come to a crossroads, but there was no signpost. The clouds were heavy and leaden, and a drifting mist made it impossible to tell east from west. The grey afternoon was fading and it would be dusk all too soon. He swung around to the crossroads again just as a dirt clod flew up from the high point of the bank that edged the road. Curious, he urged Secrets towards a steady shower of earth and rocks. Closer investigation revealed a deep hole and the hind-quarters of a familiar and busily excavating dog. As Vespa approached, the little animal paused in its work and sat down, panting at him in a satisfied fashion.

"What are you after, I wonder?" Vespa rode closer, and muttered, "Be damned!" Beyond the bank the ground fell away into a narrow ditch. Lying there, invisible from the road, was the signpost, one arm pointing at the sky and proclaiming with rather forlorn inaccuracy: TO GALLERY-ON-TANG.

He stared down at it, his aching head puzzling at the matter sluggishly. If the post was rotted and had broken off of its own accord, it would not have left a hole in the ground. Even if he'd dozed off in the saddle and Secrets had slowed her pace, it was unlikely that the dog had outrun her and undermined the signpost in so short a time. Nor could such a small creature have dragged it over to the ditch and pushed it in. It must, he deduced, be a case of malicious vandalism.

A gust of wind chilled him and he pulled his wits together. He was tired, bruised and hungry, and there was nothing to be gained by sitting here scowling at a slain signpost.

Turning Secrets onto the left-hand fork of the road, he reflected that this had not been an auspicious start to his "quiet and peaceful" stay in the country.

Soon, he came into more rolling country. The gorse bushes and tufty grasses gave way to greener turf. Clumps of trees were dotted about. He was heartened when the scenery and the road continued to improve, and he saw signs of human habitation again: cultivated fields and low rock walls, a barn, and then a small farmhouse with smoke curling from the chimney. He turned off to approach the house, and as he rounded some tall poplars a low hill came into view, about three miles distant. Along its crest the chimneys and roofs of what must be a very large house were silhouetted against the darkening sky.

His heart leapt. He had found Alabaster Royal at last!

———⟡———

It was almost dark when Vespa followed the rutted track that had once been a drivepath and passed through sagging and rusted lodge gates, one of which stood partly closed, the other having fallen off to lie half buried in mud. The small gatehouse was deserted, the windows broken, and weeds rioting in what had once been flower beds.

The drivepath disappeared into the overgrown grasses of a wide park. He gave up trying to follow it and struck off in a straight line towards the house. He crossed a hump-backed walled stone bridge over a swift-flowing stream and found the path again, leading through rose gardens that had gone wild, and between a double row of yew trees so in need of pruning that he had to bend low in the saddle to avoid being swept out of it by trailing branches.

The manor loomed ever larger; two storeys high, long, dark, and forbidding, the entrance flanked by twin round, conical-topped towers that soared upward like impregnable stone guardians. Most of the tall windows were shuttered, but a few stared out like black eyes that followed his progress suspiciously. The early evening was unseasonably chill, and a rising wind moaned among the chimneys and rattled gates and shutters.

Vespa shivered, but refused to be intimidated. At least he had procured some food. The motherly farm wife had been appalled when she learnt of his destination, but she had very kindly sold him some thick slices of roast pork, cheese, bread and a jug of ale, all of which were packed into the box he balanced on the pommel before him. Even if there were no provisions in the manor, the caretaker could get some fires burning, and with luck he would soon dine for the first time in his life in a home of his own.

Alabaster Royal!

Gad, but it was enormous!

Secrets clattered into a cobbled courtyard. Mr. Jermyn had advised that the caretaker, one Hezekiah Strickley, would see to it that there were livable quarters in the house, and oats and hay in the stables. Vespa halted the mare, and shouted, "Hullo? Strickley?" There was no response. Secrets sidled nervously, but he promised to see to her wants as soon as he'd found caretaker and kitchen. With an effort that racked him, he swung his leg over the pommel and slid from the saddle. He was so stiff he could hardly walk, but he felt triumphant; he'd managed not to drop his precious box.

Among the keys in his pocket were two, both gigantic, labelled FRONT. Tethering the mare to a post, he limped up the eight deep steps and discovered that the doors stood slightly ajar. Frowning, he pushed them wider and walked into a great gloomy high-ceilinged hall. His shouted hail was no more productive inside than it had been in the courtyard, save that his voice echoed lingeringly. The fellow couldn't be far away if he'd left the front doors open. Vespa started across the hall, peering through the dimness in search of the kitchen. The air was musty and icy cold. If Strickley didn't appear by the time he'd taken care of the mare, he'd have to see about lighting a fire.

There arose a faint whispering sound, as of leaves drifting across the stone-flagged floor. At the same moment he sensed that someone had crept up to stand just behind him. In the chill, hushed immensity of Alabaster Royal it was an eerie feeling and he whipped around, his nerves taut.

The small dog raced past and disappeared into the gloom.

⁓❧⁓

Vespa awoke when his elbow slipped from the chair arm. The fire on the hearth of what had evidently been the breakfast parlour was almost out, and the candles had burned low. He stretched, yawning. His homecoming hadn't been quite as dismal as he'd begun to fear, although the caretaker had not yet put in an appearance. It was disgraceful that Strickley should have gone off—to the nearest tavern probably—without securing the front doors, but so far as he could tell, the man was not in the house. He'd found the kitchen, which was predictably enormous, and a very large pantry, the shelves bare except for a bowl containing four eggs, a dish of butter, a loaf of bread and a jug of milk. Gourmet fare, he thought cynically.

Having lighted candles and left his box of food on the long table, he'd unearthed some towels and gone out to tend to Secrets. The barn and stables were located behind a line of cypress trees, and as solicitor Jermyn had promised, there was an ample supply of hay and oats and a lantern, which fortunately contained oil and a usable wick. There were many stalls, one of which had been occupied recently. The absent Strickley's hack, no doubt. He'd wrapped wet cloths around the mare's knee and promised himself to put a flea in the caretaker's ear. The emptiness of the stables and the rather odd whispering voice of the wind had made him feel peculiarly solitary, so that he'd been glad to finish his tasks and return to the house.

At least fires had been laid on several hearths, and there were baskets of logs. He'd settled down here because it was the smallest room he'd been able to find and the table and chairs were clean. He was almost too tired to eat, but he kept awake long enough to enjoy some excellent cheese, bread that he toasted before the fire,

25

a slice of the cold pork and a mug of ale. Yawning, he packed the rest of the food into the box, and deposited it on one of the shelves in the pantry beside the 'provisions' Strickley had laid in. He took up his valise and a candlestick, and with a grim lack of enthusiasm embarked on a search for the master bedchamber, which solicitor Jermyn had advised was prepared for him.

Making his way back to the main hall, he saw many doors farther along the wide, flagged corridor, some standing wide, but he had no least desire to explore tonight. Perhaps because he had so recently known the cacophanous uproar of the battlefield, by the time he reached the loom of the massive staircase, the quiet seemed to press on his eardrums.

At the top of the stairs he was confronted by another wide corridor, stretching off to either side. He turned to the right. The first door was so warped he was unable to force it open. The next was in better condition, and he went on with more success, peering into rooms that yawned in a black emptiness, or were cluttered with dusty furniture, but none that could be judged 'ready for occupancy'.

The master bedchamber was discovered at last, situated on the north-west corner of the house. It was extremely large, and furnished with a great tester bed untidily made up, a wash-stand, some ugly old chests and presses, and a more modern dressing-table. The room was frigid; in fact it seemed much colder in here than it had been in the stables. He undressed, scooped a spider out of the water pitcher, washed hurriedly, and shrugging into his nightshirt even more hurriedly, climbed into bed. The sheets were like ice, but he was inured to frosty nights under the Spanish stars and was asleep almost before his head hit the pillow.

～∞～

Why was he wide awake? He lay very still, listening intently, and heard a soft scampering sound. He'd completely forgotten that scruffy little mongrel! It was probably wandering about, trying to find a way outside. On the other hand, perhaps the errant 'care-

26

taker' had at last deigned to return. Probably he had a key to one of the outer doors and had let himself in. At least, he could let the dog out. Vespa grunted, and closed his eyes again, only to open them very wide.

Faintly, but distinctly, someone was laughing: the soft, provocative laughter of a woman.

"Why, that slippery damned rascal!" he snarled, climbing out of bed and throwing on his dressing-gown.

He found his tinder-box and re-lit the candle, then carried it along the corridor, his bare and cold feet making no sound on the boards. There was not a glimmer of light other than his own, nor any sound except for the whisper of the wind. Beyond the stairwell the corridor made a right turn. Taking it at speed, he all but fell down three unexpected steps. The sudden jolt sent a vicious jab through his injured leg, and the swirl of a woman's skirts disappearing into a nearby room exacerbated his already frayed temper.

"*Strickley!*" he roared.

Not a sound. Not a movement.

Seething, he hobbled to the room the woman had entered. If he surprised the pair cavorting on the bed, they'd cavort out of his house, *rapido*! A soft laugh faded as he tore the door open and lifted his candle high. He had a brief impression of a big room furnished only with sparsely stocked bookcases. Even as he realized it was completely empty, for no apparent reason his candle went out.

"Confound it!" he muttered, then shouted again, "*Strickley! Come out at once, you blasted makebait!*"

The silence was absolute. The wretched caretaker undoubtedly knew every nook and cranny of this very large old house, and had rushed his woman into hiding. Well, she'd been seen— and heard! So just let Strickley try to deny the business in the morning!

Meanwhile, he was shivering with cold and did not intend to play Hunt the Caretaker. His eyes had become accustomed to the darkness, and shafts of moonlight were now slanting through the occasional recessed windows. He was almost to his bedchamber when he felt something brush past. It must be that miserable mongrel. "I suppose I've got to go down and let you out," he grumbled, trying unsuccessfully to see the little creature.

There was neither an answering bark nor the patter of paws. He heard instead an unexpected sound: the throaty purring of what must be a very large cat.

"Just what I need," he groaned. "A house full of immoral servants, uninvited mongrels and now a trespassing moggy. Where are you, cat?"

The feline declined to respond, but with a sudden frenzied rush of paws the little dog scampered over his feet and into the master bedchamber. When Vespa limped in, re-lit his candle and peered under the bed, the dog's eyes reflected the candle flame, and the scrawny tail made a few spasmodic attempts to wag, but neither threats nor promises of some of the pork convinced it to move.

Vespa made a grab, but the dog wriggled out of reach. He told the little pest in French, Spanish and German all about its ancestors, and crawling back into bed once more, grumbled himself to sleep.

Waking to a brisk and radiant morning, Vespa tugged on the bell-pull. Tugs and curses went unanswered and he resigned himself to the fact that his careless caretaker was either in a drunken stupor or had left the house once more. He washed and shaved uncomfortably in the ice cold water of the wash-stand jug, and went in search of sustenance, the dog emerging and padding busily after him. En route he discovered many rooms in various states of disrepair and also realized that the house had been several times added on to during its long life. His first impression had been that it was built in a long two-storey rectangle, but he soon found that some sections were constructed at different levels to follow the contour of the land, with resultant varying roof lines. Parts of the interior woodwork were very fine, but several rooms showed the ef-

28

fects of damp. There were chambers with magnificently carven or painted ceilings, others with fallen plaster, or mantelpieces and ceilings darkened by the smoke of centuries of fires. The windows throughout were mullioned, and he came upon several odd little octagonal-shaped ones placed at jogs in the passage, not designed to open, but set with stained glass, dimmed by dirt now, but that he thought would be charming when cleaned.

The great staircase creaked and some of the rails were broken, neither of which he'd noticed last night. The downstairs floors were stone-flagged and chill, but there was as much to charm as to appall. He went into the kitchen and let the dog out, thinking optimistically that when he set the place in order he could close off the rooms that were past hope and there would still be far more space than he would ever need.

His decision to breakfast on the food remaining in the farmwife's box was thwarted when he discovered that the box was empty. His first irate conclusion that the mongrel was responsible had to be abandoned. The pantry door had been closed all night. His anger mounted when he saw that the bowl of eggs was also empty. "That *damnable* Strickley!" he snarled, and having set out a bowl of water for the dog, limped over to the stables. Secrets greeted him affectionately. The knee was still slightly swollen, but she was not favouring it. He saddled up, watched with interest by the dog.

Riding across the bridge, he glanced back at his inheritance and felt a glow of pride. Alabaster Royal was very old, decaying and decrepit in part, but on this bright morning he thought it as proud and as regal as its name implied, and he could not see how anyone could judge it less than a splendid old place. A coat or two of paint and some cleaning would work wonders. For instance, there was a marked contrast between most of the murky windows and a few at the far south end of the first floor that had been washed, and sparkled in the sunlight. Probably, he thought, scowling, the quarters of the soon-to-be ex-caretaker who had made off with his breakfast!

"Well, sir," said the Reverend Mr. Castle, folding his hands upon his ample stomach and beaming at Vespa. "Welcome to Gallery-on-Tang. You must own you could search the length and breadth of this green and pleasant land and find no prettier village."

The priest had been doing some early weeding in the cemetery of St. Paul's Parish Church when this ill-looking, yet oddly ferocious young man had come riding up on a superb black mare and asked where he might buy some breakfast. One glance at the clean-cut but scarred face had given him the stranger's identity.

Vespa agreed tersely that the village was delightful and extended an equally terse invitation that the clergyman join him, if he could spare the time. Overlooking the none too cordial tone, Mr. Castle accepted gleefully, saying that he would remove his dirt first and directing the newcomer to the Gallery Arms, "a very clean hostelry", farther along the street.

Despite his black humour, Vespa couldn't fail to admire the village. Bathed in the morning sunlight, Gallery-on-Tang was a charming picture of rural England, its winding lane fringed by whitewashed, thatched cottages, a few small shops and the inn. There had been only two people on the street when he'd started along it, but by the time he reached the inn the front doors of almost every cottage held interested spectators, and Secrets was followed by several small boys, a boisterous spaniel who frolicked around the stray dog that had followed Vespa to the village, and a small girl clutching a teddy-bear.

The Gallery Arms was a fairy-tale half-timbered inn set back from its cobbled yard. Hollyhocks nodded beside the door, latticed windows gleamed, and the wagon-wheel thatched roof was home to several romantically twisted chimneys. The very sight of it caused Vespa's mood to mellow, and he smiled at the children who hung back, watching shyly. The smile brought them crowding around, augmented by a small girl who hobbled up with the aid of a crutch and halted some distance from the others.

The eager questions of two boys about eight years old faded to silence as they watched his awkward dismount, his cane and his limp.

An ostler ran to lead Secrets away, and a tall, gaunt, stoop-shouldered man with flaming red hair appeared in the door of the inn and nodded to Vespa, a grin on his freckled face.

One of the boys said audibly, "Crumbs! *He* can't play cricket!"

His friend hissed, "Quiet, you silly dunce! Me Pa says he's just out of hospital!"

The little girl, who'd been watching Vespa wide-eyed while nibbling on the teddy-bear's ear lisped, "Doth you fight Mithter Napoleon, thir?"

Vespa said, "Well, I did. But they're keeping me at home for a while."

At once they pressed closer and three more boys from miniature to tall and gangly galloped to join the crowd. Their questions came thick and fast. Had he ever seen Napoleon? Was he really one of Lord Wellington's famous 'Family' what Aids the Camp? How many French heads had he chopped off with his sabre? Was Lord Wellington as fierce as folks said?

Laughing, Vespa held up his hand for quiet. "I'm hungry and I want my breakfast, so I won't answer all your questions now. But—yes, I was one of his lordship's aides-de-camp, which means that I did whatever he asked of me, such as carrying despatches from him to the various commanders. He can be fierce when he needs to be, but he's a very great man, and Britain's lucky to have him."

Amid whoops of excitement, he held up his hand again and nodded to the crippled child at the edge of the crowd. "Did you want to ask me something, mistress?"

Her thin little face flushed, and she shrank back and shook her head.

One of the boys said impatiently, "Oh, she don't never say naught, sir. Did you ever play cricket?"

"I did. And I can still umpire, but we'll talk about that later." He gave them the sketch of a salute. "Troops—dismissed!"

31

Squeals, whoops, sharp answering salutes—except for the teddy-bear, whose salute was given clumsily and with the left paw—and they dispersed, all talking at once, passing the crippled child who hobbled painfully after them. Vespa was watching her sympathetically when the clergyman came up. "You'll have to forgive the rascals, sir. We've all been waiting for you, you see, and rumours have been flying."

They walked across the yard and the red-haired man who'd awaited them said, "Welcome, sir. It ain't every day the lord of the manor comes home!"

"Thank you." Amused, Vespa said, "Lord of the manor? Glory! I have no title and my poor old house is closer to being a ruin than a manor."

"Well, you're here now," said the priest, "and that's the important thing. We'd so hoped Mr. Sherborne would come last year, but—" He slanted a look at Vespa and added quickly, "We were very sorry to hear of his death, Captain."

Vespa responded appropriately. He could almost hear Sherry's laughing voice after his one visit to the estate: "Of all the grisly old ruins! Grandmama Wansdyke may leave it where she chooses, so long as it's not left to me!"

The priest was introducing him to the red-headed Mr. Ditchfield, proprietor of the Gallery Arms. Vespa pushed away the familiar ache of loss. "You've a fine old place here, Mr. Ditchfield," he said as they shook hands. "Dare I hope you have a fine cook?"

"My missus, sir. I'll let you be the judge."

He led them to a wainscoted dining room with wood settles, beamed ceilings and an enormous fireplace, and seated them at a table before open latticed windows that overlooked the back garden. Flowers were blooming in neatly kept beds, and an apple orchard edged a lawn, the branches laden with ripening fruit. Vespa admired the flowers, and before going off to place their order, Ditchfield imparted proudly that his dahlias had won firsts at the Coombe Hall Flower Show "three years running!"

The cook was indeed fine. After an excellent breakfast of eggs, sausages, warm home-made bread and strong coffee, Vespa felt quite in charity with the world.

Mr. Castle, who'd ordered only a pot of tea and a crumpet, filled his pipe and asked gently, "Feeling better, sir?"

Vespa grinned. "Was I very crusty?"

"No, no. Only when you first rode in you looked a touch—irritated, I thought. Perhaps Alabaster was a disappointment?"

"The disappointment is my so-called caretaker." He stood and the host hurried over. Vespa told him his wife was a splendid cook and assured him that he would be a regular customer. He paid his shot, and they left the host beaming as he hurried to relay the captain's compliments to his spouse.

Accompanying the rotund little cleric across the yard, Vespa said, "I can see why you're so proud of the village. I like the way the cottages are spaced around three sides of the pond and the green. I'd not realized the river is called the Tang."

"It is not, Captain Vespa. It is Moor Stream, merely. Lacking the prestige, as you might say, of a full-fledged river, although I believe it is a tributary of the Avon and can be a major threat when at flood stage. By and large, we are a quiet corner of the Good Lord's universe, and have no wish"—Mr. Castle's round brown eyes slanted obliquely at his companion—"*absolutely* no wish to become—er— notorious."

"Ah, you're thinking of the ruffians I told you about who ran my chaise into a ditch. I've no intention of reporting the matter to the newspapers, if that's what you mean, but I'll certainly lodge a complaint with your Constable."

They had left the inn yard and were walking across the village green. Vespa bowed courteously to a lady taking her dog for a stroll, and she at once stopped and stood staring in that oddly disbelieving way, much as the staff had done at the Gallery Arms. "I collect you get few strangers here," he murmured.

"You are scarcely a stranger, sir, and you're known to favour Sir Rupert Wansdyke."

"Did you know my grandfather, Mr. Castle?"

"Very slightly, sir. His lady didn't care for—er—country living, as you will know, and they spent most of the year in London. I called upon him in Wansdyke House when he was considering awarding me this living. He was nearing seventy then, but a fine-looking gentleman still, and— Oh, here is your dog, sir."

Vespa glanced behind him. The persistent stray sat some ten feet away, watching him. He groaned. "He's not mine, but he seems to have decided I'll do for an owner. I'm ignoring him, hoping to convince him of his error."

"Oh? I thought I heard you tell the host to give him some—"

Vespa interrupted hurriedly, "He's a confounded pest! I thought if the ostler fed him, the little brute might decide he'd enjoy life at the inn."

"I see." Mr. Castle's lips twitched. "Why don't you just chase him away?"

"He's too stupid to know that's what I've been doing."

Two small boys rushed past, then stopped and gazed at Vespa solemnly.

"Come here and pay your respects, lads," called the priest.

Instead, they clung to each other, giggling hilariously, then galloped off.

"Dreadful behaviour," lamented Mr. Castle. "And so angelic when they sing in the choir on Sundays! I apologize for them, sir."

They walked on towards the glittering expanse of the village pond. Amused, Vespa exclaimed, "Aha! So you have some vestige of the notorious in your quiet corner, after all!"

They had arrived at the low bridge over the river; a graceful structure, its stone walls extending a little distance on each side of the approach path. Situated at the foot of the bridge were the village stocks, presently occupied by a cadaverous individual whose greying dark brown hair escaped untidily from under a tattered hat. A pair of long gaitered legs stuck out before him, and his back was propped against the bridge wall. He raised a glum countenance and enquired, "Is you come to give me some Christian charity, Mr. Castle? Only right you should, your calling being what it is,

34

and me locked up fer doing nothing more'n defending of me good name."

The priest said sternly, "By throwing Billy Watson out of the tap and breaking his nose?"

"Nose first, sir. Throwed out, after. And don't be telling of me to repent, 'cause I don't. Called me a liar, he done. I got me rights." He turned a pair of embittered dark eyes on Vespa. "Ain't that so, sir? Everyone got rights—even a poor working cove like me got rights."

"Rights to do—what? Poach, perhaps?"

"Cor! If that ain't just like you rich lot! I ain't never done no such thing! And anyone what says I'm a common poacher is looking fer a bang in the eye." He glared at Vespa and added in a snarl, "Puffed-up London dandies, special!"

The idea of being designated a London dandy brought a glint of laughter into Vespa's eyes. Mr. Castle was much shocked, however, and protested, "What insolence! Guard your tongue, man! This gentleman may be able to help you."

"Why?" jeered the prisoner, unimpressed.

"An excellent question," murmured Vespa.

The priest said apologetically, "Perhaps I spoke out of turn, sir. But he is your employee, after all."

"Oh, yus I ain't," snorted the prisoner.

"But of course you are," argued Mr. Castle. "This is Hezekiah Strickley, Captain Vespa. Your caretaker."

3

The he devil you say!" exclaimed Vespa. "Oh, your pardon, Mr. Castle, but this irresponsible hedgebird—"

"I ain't done nothing! I ain't done *nothing*!" screamed the prisoner, cringing back against the wall and throwing both arms over his face. "Don't you let him bash me with that great ugly stick, Mr. Clergyman! Don't you never!"

Flushed with wrath, Vespa said, "I ought to strangle you! Going off and leaving my front doors wide; an open invitation to any thieves or mischief-making vandals!"

"Throw down a red carpet and they wouldn't come in," babbled Strickley. "Sir," he added with an ingratiating leer.

"To say nothing of bringing your woman into my house in the middle of the night—"

"Ow! *What* a wicked thing to—"

"Be still, blast you! And to add to all else, making off with my breakfast! I've a good mind to—"

"Lies!" howled the prisoner, raising his hands in appeal to the sunny heavens. "Only to think as a eddicated flash cove like this would speak such raspers! And don't it say in the Good Book as them what lies belong in deepest Hell? Tell this sinful young nob, Mr. Castle, sir! Tell him!"

Searching his memory for the biblical reference, the priest said hesitantly, "Well, I'm— Er, that is to say—"

"Tell him there ain't a word of truth in the whole perishing lot," demanded the accused, the picture of outraged virtue. "Tell him to repent."

"You know damned well I speak truth," snapped Vespa.

Mr. Castle said cautiously, "I am very sure you—er—*believe* what you say sir. But—"

"What the deuce d'you mean by that? I tell you the front doors of the manor were wide open when I arrived, and this scoundrel was nowhere evident! In the night I heard him frippering about with his woman and *saw* her run into a room and hide!"

"Hah!" snorted Strickley. "Listen to it, willya!"

The clergyman pursed his lips dubiously.

"If you mean to take this rascal's word over mine," growled Vespa.

Mr. Castle wrung his plump hands. "I—I fear, I have no choice, sir."

"What?"

"Strickley threw one of my best customers out the window, about eight o' the clock last evening, Captain, sir."

The new voice brought Vespa's head around sharply. Mr. Ditchfield, proprietor of the Gallery Arms, stood there, a grave expression on his freckled face and the sunlight gleaming on his red hair. He was but one among the small crowd that had gathered to enjoy the proceedings.

A large man whose gory apron proclaimed him the local butcher nodded vehemently and voiced a supporting, " 'Sright, sir. We all on us see it."

"I don't doubt you," said Vespa. "But it doesn't change the fact that Strickley came back to Alabaster later on, and—"

"Couldn't of, Mr. Vespa," boomed a very tall lady wearing a

sagging poke bonnet that completely hid her features. "My mister put Hezekiah Strickley in they stocks at half past eight o'clock."

"Mrs. Blackham," murmured the priest in Vespa's ear. "Our good Constable's spouse."

"And I ain't been out but once since then," asserted the prisoner defiantly. "And then only fer ten minutes account of me bowils, and thanks to Mr. Castle, and no thanks to them as begrudge a man defending of his honourable name!"

"What man would that be, Hezekiah?" called the blacksmith, a sturdy, bright-eyed individual with a round sweaty face, a leather apron, and a long-handled pair of iron tongs still clutched in his hand. "Not yerself, me buck?"

There was laughter at this, and angry protests from the prisoner, but Vespa frowned. If this was truth, then the intruder last night could not possibly have been Strickley.

Watching him, the priest said, "They're honest folk, Captain. It wasn't Hezekiah who brought his—er—lady to your house, or stole your food."

"See?" jeered the caretaker. "All wrong, wasn't yer, Mr. London Dandy?"

Shocked gasps arose from the onlookers.

Vespa said coolly, "It appears that I owe you an apology. And if you use either that tone or that term to me again, Strickley, you and I will have a private discussion."

"Ar, and he were one of Lord Wellington's 'Family'," announced an emaciated little man who walked briskly to join the group. "An Aid-the-Camp what was knocked down at the Battle of Vitoria. You best watch your p's and q's, Hezekiah! Captain Vespa knows how to deal with your kind, I don't doubt!"

Strickley's jaw fell and he gaped at Vespa as if he couldn't believe his ears.

"This is Constable Blackham, sir," imparted the clergyman. "Our minion of the Law."

"And glad I am to welcome you, Captain," said the constable as they shook hands.

The crowd closed in around Vespa; the men eager to meet him, the bonnets of the ladies bobbing to their curtsies as they murmured shy greetings. The excitement seemed to infect even the little dog, who rushed about barking importantly.

Strickley meanwhile had been released, and stood off to one side, stamping his feet up and down and watching the proceedings with a scowl. "You can pay me off, Captain," he grunted when he could get near Vespa. "You won't want me, no more'n I want you."

"I'll pay you after you've told me why you went off and left my house open. And don't deny you did that, at least."

"Aye. I did." His fierce eyes sweeping the crowd, Strickley snarled, "But I wasn't scared, and I see what I seen! And if any man calls me a liar, he can choose his own winder to be throwed out of!"

"If you wasn't scared, why didn't you stay to close the door, mate?" called the blacksmith.

Strickley turned on him furiously.

The constable warned, "That'll do! Any more trouble from you, and I'll lock you up for a week, Hezekiah!"

"I just want my pay," growled Strickley sullenly. "Fair's fair."

"True," said Vespa. "Come up to the house later, and I'll square accounts." He glanced around at the bright, interested faces of these country folk. "I'll be needing people to work for me. If anyone cares to apply, they can talk to me now, or . . . "

The friendly smiles had vanished, the honest eyes were lowered, the cheerful little crowd quieted and began to drift away, and within seconds Vespa stood by the stocks with only Mr. Castle and his ex-caretaker beside him.

The priest gave a nervous little cough. "I'm—er—rather afraid you'll find it difficult to hire servants here, sir."

Perplexed, Vespa said, "I realize the house is old and rather run-down, but— Jupiter! If the local people are that independent, I'll look elsewhere."

"It's—er—certainly worth a try," mumbled Castle.

Strickley laughed. "No it ain't. Whyn't you tell him the truth, Mr. Clergyman? You won't get no one, Captain. Alabaster Royal's knowed for miles around. Ain't no one in his right mind would spend one night in the old place."

Vespa turned to the cleric. "Surely, in this modern age your people don't still think—"

"They don't *think,* mate," interrupted Strickley rudely. "This here clergyman won't say it, but I will. Yer falling-down great manor's *haunted,* Captain! Lotsa folks has heard 'em whispering and rustling about, but I'm the only one what ever see the woman. I were in—ah—such a hurry to tell everyone about it that I forgot to lock the house up." His face darkened. "And then they wouldn't believe me. That's why I throwed Billy Watson out the winder. 'Cause he said I were making it up. I wasn't. I *seen* her! And now, I ain't the only one. You see her too, didn't you, Captain?"

Vespa hesitated. Could he be sure of what he'd seen last night? He'd been very tired. Perhaps he had dreamt the whole thing. Perhaps it had been another of his hallucinations. It was a depressing thought. Rallying, he said curtly, "I doubt a spirit would have stolen my breakfast. Besides, I do not believe in ghosts!"

"Hah!" snorted Hezekiah Strickley.

Gallery-on-Tang's police station and gaol was located in a tiny two-room building next to the smithy, and having accompanied the constable to this establishment, Vespa gave him a report of the coaching accident. Mr. Blackham was horrified. Such deeds were perpetrated by London's amateur coachmen, he said, who were nothing more than a set of hare-brained noddicocks, but he'd never had such a thing happen in *his* district. He took notes, writing slowly and copiously, but gave it as his opinion that without reliable corroborating witnesses there was small chance of prosecution, even if the miscreants were found.

Indignant, Vespa retorted, "I was a witness!"

"Yes, but with all due respect, sir, from what you've told me, you

40

was asleep. Nor a judge wouldn't rule 'gainst the other driver based on the word of a post-boy; 'specially if a gentleman were tooling that coach. He'd be more likely to find the boy at fault."

Vespa had half-expected such a decision. He acknowledged its logic reluctantly, and went into the sunshine with a rather grim look.

Hezekiah Strickley was loitering about the yard of the Gallery Arms, and Vespa hailed him and told him he would include today's wages provided he hauled a load of supplies out to Alabaster. The ex-caretaker agreed grudgingly. Next, Vespa called in at the fragrant little Grocer's Shop/Post Office and enchanted its fluttery lady proprietor by placing a large order. The Widow Davis promised to have it all packed up and ready by the time Strickley had hired a horse and cart.

"I must apologize for the silliness of the local people, sir," she said in her tremulous voice. "I didn't come here till I married. I'm city-bred, as I'm sure you can tell. Canterbury is where I was born, and you may believe it took me a long time to adjust to country folk, so set in their ways as they are. They won't change, I'm afraid. You'll fetch your servants down from London, will you, Captain? You couldn't live in that great house all by yourself, surely?"

He said with a smile that she was probably in the right of it, and went to find Secrets.

The blacksmith, who was known as Young Tom, gave him a leg-up into the saddle and reinforced his belief that the mare had taken no serious hurt, and that provided she was rested for a few days, she would suffer no ill effects. "Looks to me like you won't be doing no long journeys yourself, sir," he added sympathetically. "Got proper stove in whilst you was in Spain, I hear. A proper nuisance it must be to have to limp about like that."

Inwardly, Vespa cringed, but he answered lightly, "Yes. But it's better than being dead, you know."

This caused Young Tom to roar with laughter and agree that was the way to look at it, all right, and having paid his reckoning Vespa turned Secrets into the lane.

On the way back to Alabaster Royal he tried to make sense of what he'd learnt this morning. Of prime interest was the matter of the intruders in his home. As irritating as it had been to believe his caretaker responsible for the night's activities, it would at least have written *finis* to the problem. Now, he was left with no answer at all except that he was convinced the evil agencies at work were of human origin. *Living* humans! Ghosts were nothing more than flights of fancy indulged in by the gullible. Grandmama Wansdyke had been used to talk about the various legends surrounding Alabaster Royal, but Grandmama had been so very superstitious that he and Sherry had thought it all a grand joke, and now he couldn't even remember most of the lurid tales. The woman he'd glimpsed, and her companion, had likely been keeping a tryst in his house, confound their impertinence! And to add insult to injury, they'd wolfed down his breakfast! His lips tightened and he thought stormily that from now on, windows and doors would be securely locked at night.

Next in order of importance was the matter of servants. When he had so blithely told Sir Kendrick of his desire for a quiet life, it hadn't occurred to him that he would be unable to hire local help. Everywhere, people were seeking positions, and he'd taken it for granted that once it was known he was offering employment, he'd be swamped with eager applicants. Thinking back, he could hear himself declaring that he did not mean to become a recluse. His father's response took on a new significance: "What troubles me," he'd said, "is that you may have no choice." If Papa had known what faced him, it would have been kinder to have given him a more substantial warning. On the other hand, he'd been so damned sure of himself. He smiled ruefully. Perhaps Sir Kendrick had decided that he needed a set-down; he'd always taken the line that experience was the best teacher.

Crossing the bridge he experienced again a thrill of pride in the old place, but now pride was tinged with unease because his was not a solitary nature. He'd been accustomed to the easy camaraderie of army life, and before that, to the company of his brother and of his many friends at University and in Town. The prospect of living all alone in such a vast pile was daunting; in fact, it was downright impossible. Much as he hated to admit it, he was not yet up to par, and in no condition to take care of his own needs, much less those of Secrets, and his curricle and coach and the matched greys that would soon arrive from Richmond. There was nothing for it but to hire people from London; unless perhaps Bristol might contain prospective employees less chicken-hearted than the local—

Secrets reared as the small dog rushed past, barking shrilly. Managing to keep his seat, Vespa swore, and sent a brief summation of the mongrel's likely ancestry after it. The summation was brief because he then saw that a large waggon was drawn up in front of the house. The doors again stood wide, and the dog was already racing inside.

Dismounting in his unfortunate stiff slide, Vespa scowled at the waggon, slipped his cane from the saddle holster, and followed the dog.

The house was dim after the bright outer sunshine. He heard male voices and as his eyes adjusted to the changed light he gave an outraged gasp. A large desk stood at the foot of the stairs and two husky workmen were attempting to lift it. The taller of the pair grunted, "Hold it up higher, Perce! You're shifting all the perishing weight to me!"

"No, I ain't," objected Perce, in a whining, high-pitched voice. "If you could just move yer trotters a bit quicker, we could—"

"Indeed, you could not!"

Vespa's authoritative tone brought the pair to an abrupt halt and the desk was restored to the floor with a crash.

"Who might you be when you're at home?" demanded the whiner insolently.

"I *am* at home," said Vespa. "You, on the other hand, are not. What the devil d'you think you're doing with my furniture?"

"But we are returning it, of course, dear sir." A tall, well-built individual strolled down the stairs and confronted Vespa with a dazzling smile. He looked to be about five and thirty, and there was about him the faint swagger of the man who knows his own worth. It was scarcely surprising, for his loosely curling blond hair and well-cut features undoubtedly won him the admiration of most women. Vespa, a keen judge of men, misliked the full-lipped ruddy mouth, however, and mistrusted the heavy-lidded blue eyes that failed to reflect a trace of that ingratiating smile. He noted that the splendidly tailored coat was beginning to show wear and the glossy riding boots were slightly down at heel. 'The fellow's in the basket,' he thought. "Do you make a habit of calling on people when they're out?" he enquired icily, ignoring the stranger's outstretched hand.

The smile did not waver, and the hand was lowered to search for a card case. "But my dear sir, the owner of this—er—house has been 'out' for years. I heard the new heir was expected, so thought to return the desk before he arrived, so as not to cause inconvenience. I take it I'm—er— remiss, Mr. Vespers, is it?" A card was offered with a blandness that brought sly grins from his servants.

Vespa read aloud, "Sir Larson Gentry". He met the mockery in those very blue eyes with a steady stare. "An unorthodox introduction, to say the least. My name is Vespa. Whatever the reason for your intrusion, I would have thought any *gentleman* would know better than to break into another man's house."

Gentry murmured, "I think you will find, sir, that the occupants of this house are more likely to break out, than others are to break in!"

Perce emitted a hurriedly smothered squeal of mirth.

"Is that why it took you two years to gather sufficient courage to . . . *return* my desk? You *are* aware that my grandmother died two years since? How very brave of you to venture upstairs alone just now. You were pleased with what you viewed, I trust?"

Gentry sighed. "To be so misjudged is wounding. I came here to repay a favour, surely a noble ambition, and had not expected to be taken to task, but—"

"Your 'nobility' having extended to making yourself free of my house, uninvited, sir, perhaps it will stretch to instructing your

44

men to replace the desk. You did just borrow the *desk*? Or are there perhaps other articles to be returned?"

A faint flush stained Gentry's cheeks. Straightening his cuff, he said quietly, "You become offensive. I really think you must apologize."

"You've an odd sense of the proprieties, sir. And I've a limited amount of patience. You men—put that desk back where it belongs! At once! Else I'll have Constable Blackham take you in charge for breaking and entering *and* theft!"

Gentry shrugged and said smilingly, "Now fellows, we must be polite to poor Captain Vespa. Especially in view of his unfortunate condition. Perce, swing that end around. *Move,* man!"

Perce sprang into action so suddenly that his boot slammed against Vespa's cane, sending it spinning across the hall. Off balance, Vespa staggered.

Gentry shouted, "Clumsy oaf! Help the gentleman! Both of you!"

Before Vespa could steady himself, they both ran at him, collided, and lurched against him so that he fell heavily. His head struck the end-post of the stair railing and pain ripped through him so blindingly that the scene blurred, but he heard the little dog's shrill barks cut off by a yelp, followed by Gentry's amused scolding of his servants.

"Now look what you've done! I cannot tell you how sorry I am, Captain. I fear my fellows have alarmed your—er—watchdog." There was loud laughter at this sally. " 'Faith," Gentry went on, "but the quality of help one is obliged to hire these days is depressing. Do let me assist you. Accidents will happen, my dear fel—" He stopped, staring narrow-eyed at the small pistol that was trained on him. "No, really! There's no call for this, only because my men were—"

Infuriated because he was still too weak to have properly defended himself, Vespa managed somehow to keep his voice steady. "I merely even the—the odds, Gentry." Gripping the stair railing, he dragged himself to his feet. The effort caused the room to ripple before his eyes again. Vaguely aware that the dog crouched at his side, growling, he gasped out, "Instruct your accomplices to return . . . my desk to its proper place. Now!"

"My *accomplices*? Egad, but you've an unpleasant way with words. And how your hound terrifies me! No, do not look so grim. Only consider, my poor fellow. If you fire that foolish little pistol, how shall you explain matters to the authorities? Of what could you accuse me, save that I returned your property? I have two witnesses to your—ah—brutal and unprovoked attack. You have no one to back whatever statement you might choose to make. Besides, you've only one shot, and there are three of us, and—"

"There's two of us," growled a familiar voice from the open door. "And *I'm* a witness to what's going on here!"

The smile was wiped from features that were abruptly considerably less than handsome as Gentry's nonchalant pose slipped. "You?" he snarled. "Much heed anyone would pay to whatever you had to say, Strickley!"

"Them two'll pay heed to my pop." The big man trained a wide-mouthed blunderbuss on Gentry's men. "If you coves don't wanta taste of this, do what the Captain said. And smart-like. This trigger's none too steady!"

Thwarted, Gentry wandered to the door, only a tightly clenched hand betraying his rage. With the blunderbuss at the ready, Strickley moved aside to allow him to pass.

"The next time you decide to return something of mine, make an appointment first," said Vespa. "Meanwhile, I'll have stronger locks put on the doors!"

Gentry's answering smile was murderous. As he passed Strickley, he said softly, "Be sure that I'll remember you, fellow."

Apparently unmoved, Strickley escorted the two workmen as they puffed and groaned up the stairs with the heavy desk.

Vespa took the opportunity to hobble into the drawing room and pour himself a good measure of brandy. The dog trotted beside him and sat down an inch from his boot. Vespa bent to stroke him, but the little animal shrank away. "Don't quite trust me yet, do you?" said Vespa. "But you stuck by me, like a true friend, nonetheless."

The ratty tail wriggled and the dog lay down again, only to start up as a great clumping of feet announced the hurried departure of the workmen.

Vespa joined Strickley on the front steps.

"It ain't the first time that set of rum touches has come slithering about," grunted Strickley as the unlovely pair set their empty waggon lurching down the drivepath. "I sent 'em packing twice when they pretended to be lost. They musta s'posed there wasn't no one about today."

Vespa said thoughtfully, "Sir Larson claimed to be returning the desk. Said he'd borrowed it from my grandmother."

"What a rasper!" Strickley gave a derisive snort. "No offence, sir, but ain't you never seen his house?"

"I haven't had time to see much of anything around here. What's it like?"

"Big, sir. Not so big as this here, I don't mean. But spread out, like, with gardens all round, very nice and tidy. Wasn't like that when he come inter the property, mind. Spent a fortune fixing it up. Proper elegant it is now, inside and out. I've delivered goods there a time or two, and I can tell yer that Larson Chase is a little palace. There's some as says Sir Larson Gentry's run hisself orf his legs to make it into a showplace, so as to impress all his London friends and please Miss Ariadne."

"What you're saying is that my grandmother's furniture wouldn't fit into such a house?"

"Well, lookit that there desk, Cap'n. Big, solid mahogany, weighs a ton. The stuff out at the Chase is all velvets and brocades and spindly little legs. Your desk would'a stood out like a sore thumb—no offence intended. I'll bring in yer order now, if that suits."

It suited. Vespa wandered to the side entrance where Strickley had drawn up his cart, and watched as the big man, escorted by the dog, unloaded a large box of provisions.

When the box was carried into the kitchen, Vespa leant back against the long table and said, "Wait up a minute. I'm afraid you've incurred Sir Larson's displeasure. Can he do you a mischief?"

"He could. No doubt o' that, him being a 'ristocrat and me a commoner. Not as he'd do nothing hisself. Real brave he is, when it's three to one odds." Strickley checked, then said with an air of defiance, "Which I shouldn't say, but I done, so there!"

"Yes. Well, how would you feel about staying on here as my steward and head groom?"

Strickley's jaw dropped. "You'd take me back? Arter all them things I said?"

"You stood by me when I needed support, and I need help here. Someone who knows the area and can advise me on local matters."

"Cor! And—you really was one of his lordship's aides?"

"Yes."

"Them what was called his 'Family', I mean."

"Yes."

"Cor! Thinka that! And you don't mind being alone in this house a'nights?"

"You have evidently survived here alone."

"Ar. But I don't go in the house arter dark. I got quarters over the barn. And I'd think, sir, arter what you seen last night . . . Cor!"

"I don't believe in ghosts, if that's what you mean."

The awed look faded, and the untidy head flung upward. "Huh! Then you still thinks as I be a liar!"

"I think you believe what you say. You have your convictions and I have mine. If ever I see something to convince me you're in the right of it, I'll have to change my mind. Meanwhile, let me have your answer to my offer."

"I wouldn't have to come in the house arter dark? Not that I'm scared, mind."

"You might, occasionally. To carry in wood or supplies, as you've just done."

"Well, then," a broad grin transformed the harsh features, "I'm yer man, melord! For as long as you stay."

Vespa put out his hand. "No title, Strickley. Captain will do nicely. And I mean to stay for quite a while."

Returning the handshake and finding it a good deal firmer than he'd expected, Hezekiah Strickley nodded. "Quite a while it is, sir."

Going out to collect the last load of groceries, still grinning, he muttered, "I give you a week, Captain Spunky. At the outside!"

Whether Sir Larson Gentry had been returning or absconding with the mahogany desk, there could be no doubting his interest in it. Vespa climbed the stairs, and having found the desk in an already overcrowded room, examined it thoroughly. The drawers were empty except for some yellowed sheets of paper, a faded racing form, a broken quill pen and a dried-up stick of sealing wax. It was actually a fine piece of furniture, with some elaborate inlay work around the top, but there was nothing to indicate that it had any particular antique value; nothing, in fact, to explain Gentry's most unorthodox behaviour. Baffled, Vespa decided that the solving of the puzzle would have to await future developments.

Perhaps as a result of his rough handling, he was woken in the night by severe pain. He lay there for some time, but no matter how he shifted his position there was no relief, and at length he struggled out of bed and began to pace the floor. He tried to concentrate on anything but his misery and after a while became aware that his footsteps had an odd sort of echo. He peered downward. The glow of moonlight enabled him to make out a small shape trotting along beside him. He'd given up trying to keep the dog out of the house and, truth to tell, was glad of its company. Seldom was it far from his side, and today it had demonstrated its affection by bravely charging at Gentry and his hirelings.

"Hullo, there," said Vespa. The dog sat down and gazed up at him. "We'll have to find a name for you," he added, and resumed his pacing, searching about for a likely name. In some ways the little dog put him in mind of his former batman. Corporal O'Malley had been slavishly devoted, utterly ruthless in procuring whatever was needed to ensure his captain some measure of comfort, and ready, willing and able to fight any man in the army at the slightest provocation. Constantly obliged to rescue him from the consequences of his misdeeds, Vespa had been devastated when O'Malley was fatally wounded while rushing to aid him after he'd been knocked from his saddle early in the Battle of Vitoria. Dear old O'Malley had been undersized, unkempt and fiercely loyal; it would seem the dog had similar traits.

"Hum," said Vespa, halting. "How does 'Corporal' strike you?" The small hind-quarters wriggled.

"Then Corporal it shall be." His own anguish easing, Vespa crawled back into bed, but refused the newly christened canine's appeal to join him, saying sternly that he would not be put upon. "Or sat upon!"

For three days all was tranquil at Alabaster Royal. On the third night, however, Vespa awoke to the rustling of windblown leaves, seemingly inside the house. When he got up and carried a lamp into the corridor, Corporal looked up, but did not follow. There was no sign of blowing curtains or of leaves on the floor; no flicker of the lamp's flame. The air was frigid, but still. Vespa experienced a sudden wave of dizziness, then an eerie feeling that someone stood very close beside him. So strong was the sensation that he could scarcely bring himself to look around. The passage was as empty as before; he was quite alone.

Disturbed, he went back to bed, trying not to recall two voices: the army surgeon who'd warned gravely that the head wound might cause more problems than the severe headaches he suffered with unhappy frequency, and Strickley's harsh assertion— "Lotsa folks has heard 'em whispering and rustling about." He did not sleep well for the balance of the night.

Two more days passed peacefully. Never a fussy eater, he cooked himself simple meals on the vast kitchen stove and ate them in the breakfast parlour accompanied only by Corporal. Strickley worked outside, took care of Secrets, kept the house well stocked with logs and started the fires in the mornings. Vespa sent him into the village with a letter to Sir Kendrick reporting on his progress and advising that his curricle and the new phaeton and his matched greys had not yet arrived at Alabaster Royal as expected. He also despatched letters to an old school friend now living in Bristol and another in London, asking that they be so good as to have enquiries made with regard to securing the services of a competent valet. Once he'd found a good man, he could leave to him the business of hiring a cook and other servants. He ignored the awareness that the most logical course would be to turn for assistance to his father's butler at Richmond. Rennett would, he knew, have been only too glad to help, and would, moreover, find an excellent man. Logic, however, played no part in his determination not to admit to Sir Kendrick that he was incapable of handling his own affairs. He might be temporarily uncomfortable and not quite up to par, but be damned if he meant to play the role of a helpless invalid.

His hopes that some of his neighbours might call were soon dashed. The only caller had been the unfortunate post-boy, who'd come with considerable trepidation to the front door, demanding payment of his fees plus damages for the wrecked chaise and the slain hack. Vespa had questioned him about the accident, but had gained only the information that "they was a pair of proper down-the-road gents." When they'd refused to stop, the boy said, he'd been sure Vespa was dead, so he had taken the surviving hack and ridden in search of help. By the time a constable could be persuaded to accompany him to the scene of the wreck, there was not a sign of the coach, the dead horse, or the 'corpse'. The post-boy had been given "a proper bear garden jaw" about telling raspers to officers of the law. "I 'spect gypsies prigged the horse," the boy said aggrievedly. "And the coach." Vespa paid the fees and gave the boy a generous douceur, but he was not, he'd declared, "a flat", and denied responsibility for the damages.

While allowing Secrets to rest her hurt knee, he had began to explore his silent mansion. His first reconnoitre was cursory, involving merely the opening of doors and a quick scan of the dusty, furniture-shrouded interiors. In some cases he discovered rooms leading into connecting rooms. In others, he was thwarted by doors so warped he would exhaust himself in a doomed battle to get them open, prompting a resolve to hire a carpenter as soon as possible. He was continually astonished by the size of the mansion, and stunned when he came upon a good-sized ballroom, hushed and forlorn in its cobwebby emptiness, and flanked by several ante-rooms. In addition to that long-unused chamber, by the end of his preliminary exploration, he had discovered twenty bed-chambers—some with adjoining parlours, dressing rooms or servants' rooms; a once extensive library with many dusty books still on the shelves; a schoolroom, weapons and game rooms; a sewing room, study, morning and breakfast parlours; the very large drawing room; a daunting fifty-foot-long formal dining room; the kitchen, scullery and flower rooms, pantry, butler's study, and quarters for at least thirty servants.

On his second tour, he started out armed with a pad and pencil to make notes of the approximate positions and dimensions of the various rooms, and determine which were in repairable condition and which must be closed off. This proved a more taxing endeavour than he'd anticipated. He was irritated to find that he still tired easily and that to persist after his wounds began to throb was to invite a night of misery.

On a late afternoon at the end of his first week's occupancy, he was pacing off the dimensions of a large ante-room at the south end of the ground floor, accompanied as always by Corporal. Once again his night's sleep had been disturbed, this time by a piercing scream. Once again, he'd limped into the corridor only to find it deserted; and once again, he'd woken this morning wondering if any of it had really happened.

The day had been grey, the skies overcast and the sun never putting in an appearance, which might account for the fact that this end of the house was exceptionally chill, and so quiet that he felt deafened by the stillness. He gathered his sketch-pad and papers together and stared down at them, lost in thought. During this entire week he'd scarcely uttered a word to a soul except for the sulky post-boy and an occasional exchange with Strickley. Grudgingly, he faced the fact that he was becoming bored with peace, and dissatisfied with his Spartan menu. And, although he loved to read, he missed human companionship. It was not that he was tired of Alabaster Royal, or that he believed all the 'ghost' nonsense, but he'd be dashed glad when his friends responded to his letters, or when his coaches and the team arrived.

His introspection was interrupted by an enquiring bark. Corporal sat in the doorway, watching him expectantly. Amused, he said, "Think it's dinner-time, do you? Well, you're likely right, but there's not a banquet awaiting us, I'm afraid." He reached out to the shaggy little creature, and it started eagerly towards his outstretched hand, only to dart away suddenly and race from sight.

"No banquet, no faithful hound, is that it?" Vespa gathered up his sketchbook and limped into the corridor. There was no sign of the dog, but a scampering sounded from the flight of back stairs that led to the first floor. Vespa hesitated, but the light was fading, and he was cold and hungry. Corporal could find his own way down. He wished it was not so far to the livable part of his inheritance.

It was as he turned away that he caught the first whiff. He jerked to a halt and sniffed. It could not be! Onions frying? And— woodsmoke . . . ?

There *was* someone in his house, by George! The woman he'd seen that first night, no doubt. And not content with trespassing, the wretched creature had the gall to be cooking in one of his bedchambers!

"Confound the wench!" he growled, starting awkwardly up the winding stairs. "It's not my stupid head after all! And this time I've caught her!"

4

Steps were difficult, stairs worse, but rage is an excellent stimulant, and Vespa climbed at a quite respectable speed and arrived in a rush at one end of the dusty upper corridor. Breathless, he came to an abrupt halt. A young woman knelt a few yards from him, caressing Corporal, who wriggled and wagged his small tail ecstatically.

"Poor little soul," she cooed. "Does he never brush or—"

At this point Vespa recovered sufficient breath to snarl, "Perhaps you'd be good enough . . . madam, to explain—"

The intruder leapt to her feet and crouched, facing him.

He had a brief impression of a tiny, somewhat plump form, an untidy mass of jet black hair, and wide blue eyes that hurled loathing. Red lips curled back from gnashing white teeth. *"Ora basta! Vada via! Vada via!"* she cried shrilly, and on the words, turned and with a swirl of petticoats and an unseemly display of ankles, ran wildly along the corridor.

Vespa spoke French fairly well and had picked up a smattering of Spanish and Portuguese. These admonitions he could not quite place, but he had the impression he'd been told to do something, and that the something was very probably a demand that he leave.

"Devil take it!" he gasped. "I've got a foreigner in my house, not a ghost! A spy, more like!"

That a foreign agent would dare order him out of his own home brought his rage to the boiling point. He fairly leapt along the corridor and shot around the corner, remembering too late that the manor had been built on different levels. A short flight of stairs shot at him. His fight to retain his balance was doomed, and with a startled shout he plunged down, lost his footing and fell heavily.

For a few seconds he lay there, dazed, the breath knocked out of him.

There came a clicking of claws, and Corporal was licking his face and whining. Vespa opened his eyes, and beyond the dog saw pink skirts and a ridiculously small pair of sandals. Immediately, he closed his eyes again.

"If you are dead," said the spy, speaking English this time and with no trace of an accent, "you deserve to be."

'Vicious little traitor,' thought Vespa. 'Come a few steps closer, madam, or Señorita, or whatever you are, and I'll show you if I'm dead!'

The sandals crept towards him. "Are you . . . really . . . dead?" she asked, seemingly suffering a belated twinge of conscience.

The skirts swished at him. She bent low and touched his face. With a swift pounce, he sprang up and caught her arm. A shriek rang out and he was struggling to hold a wildcat. Small she might be, but she was strong and agile, and as quickly as he secured one arm she freed the other. The sandalled feet lashed out also, and he was the recipient of a torrent of undecipherable and undoubtedly unflattering words.

"Be still, you little termagant," he panted, holding her in a crushing grip.

"Beast! Monster! Typical *male* that you are! Release me at once!"

He yelped and jerked his hand away as she ducked her untidy

head and bit his wrist. "I'll release you all right, my girl!" he panted, tightening his hold on her squirming form. "Into the custody of Constable Blackham!"

Her response was another kick. "Let me go, you—you fiend! Is this how you treat a lady?"

"If you'd try to *behave* like a lady for just a minute, you hoyden, I might—"

"*Brute!* Take that!"

Another voice, even more shrill than that of his captive, entered the unhappy wrangle. Simultaneously, something slammed at Vespa's head. Very hard. And down he went again.

Through a blurred and painful interval, he could hear the girl laughing.

"Bravo! Oh bravo, Grandmama! You got him fairly. And with the frying pan! You have rescued me from the hideous beast!"

The older female voice, having a decided foreign accent, said uneasily, "*Si,* but I trust it is not that I have killed the wretch! He looks very bad, Consuela."

"Pah! He *mauled* me! Only see my poor arm. I shall be bruised. Besides, he is very strong and likely no more than dazed, if . . . Oh, dear. His head is bleeding. You did hit him rather hard, Grandmama. I wonder if he *is* dead this time."

"*Mama mia!* Then I am a *murderess*? Aieee! I shall be hanged, surely!"

"No you will not!" The girl sounded frightened, but she added, "I will lose no more loved ones. We'll—we'll carry him to the quarry and push him in, and—and no one will ever know!"

Indignant, Vespa gasped, "Why, you wicked little flint-heart!" He tried to sit up, but fell back with an involuntary groan.

Something dabbed at his forehead.

The older lady exclaimed, "Ah, but he has been hurt before this, my Consuela. And see, he is no more than a boy!"

"I am five and twenty," protested Vespa feebly.

"Exceeding elderly, in fact, is it not so?"

He could see her clearly now, and judged her to be at least

sixty. She was slight and even smaller than her granddaughter. The years had etched lines into a face that must once have been lovely; the chin was firm still, but the flesh below it was not, and there were deep creases about the eyes. Those dark eyes were bright; Vespa saw kindness there and entered a plea. "Don't let her throw me in . . . the quarry, ma'am."

"Pish! My little meadowlark? Never would she do so evil a thing."

A rebellious murmur sounded from the "meadowlark".

Despite his pounding head, Vespa asked the old lady, "Will you tell me what you are doing in—in my house?"

A twinkle came into her eyes. "Cooking dinner."

"Is it steak and onions?"

"No. It is stew."

He sighed wistfully. "It smells heavenly."

"And you are hungry, *si*? Why then you must join us, and we will make the explainings and all will be comfortable. Now do not scowl so, Consuela, or your pretty face will grow lines before you are old. Come and help the Captain like a good girl. We owe him dinner, at the least."

'At the *very* least!' thought Vespa.

"But of course I am a duchess! Am I not Francesca Celestina of Ottavio? Was not my dear late husband, God rest his soul, Ludovico, Duke of Ottavio?" Ignoring a murmur from her granddaughter, the "duchess" swept on, "It is a small duchy, this I own. On the French border, but—"

"—But my Grandpapa went to his reward before he could inherit," interposed the "meadowlark", ladling a dumpling onto Vespa's plate. "So that his younger brother became the Duke."

"By all the laws of decency," said the duchess, glaring at her, "my Ludovico *should* have become the Duke! Give the Captain more of the meat, do, Consuela. He is skin and bone, and has eaten nothing save bacon and eggs and cheese since he came here!"

57

A cup of strong tea had helped restore Vespa, although his head still ached unpleasantly. Seated at a small table in a stark but immaculate bedroom that had been converted to a makeshift kitchen, he said, "I couldn't get this door open when I was looking over the manor. Now I see why. May I ask for how long you have been enjoying my involuntary hospitality?"

Consuela's head jerked down and she hissed in his ear, "You see good food set before you, Captain John Vespa! Eat, and keep your mouth closed!"

"Difficult of accomplishment," he drawled. "Moreover, although you appear to know my name, madam, I've not been—er, favoured—with yours."

" 'Favoured' being the correct word," she said haughtily. "I will tell you that I am Consuela Carlotta Angelica Jones." And with an airy wave of the long-handled spoon that promptly sprayed gravy in all directions, she sank into a regal curtsy.

Vespa wiped gravy from his cheek. *"Jones?"*

"Certainly, Jones!" Taking a seat at the table, she demanded, "Why not Jones? What, I should like to know, is wrong with Jones?"

"Not wrong, my love." The duchess passed a basket of warm bread that smelled almost as delectable as the stew. "Regrettable, but not wrong."

"About my darling Papa there was nothing regrettable! He was the best man who ever lived! And the most clever and talented, and—"

"And English," put in the duchess.

"That—yes," admitted Consuela. "But how should one blame him?"

"I'd say, rather, he might have been congratulated," said Vespa.

"Yes, you would! Because you are English, which is bad, and a *man,* which is worse," she retaliated fiercely. "And if you had a vestige of manners, you would wait till my Grandmama says grace before you attacked your food like any hungry pig!"

Gritting his teeth, and knowing his face was red, Vespa bowed his head as grace was duly said. "Pray forgive my lapse of manners," he then murmured drily. "I fear I am not familiar with the protocol to be observed when dining in a bedchamber."

"From what I've heard of Lord Wellington's army," riposted the duchess, "you've dined in worse places."

Reminded of nights of freezing rain and 'dinners' of roots or berries, he grinned appreciatively.

"Did I not warn you, Grandmama?" said Consuela. "You are so good as to invite him to dinner and he can make only sarcastic remarks. A fine guest!"

Vespa choked on a mouthful of beef. "Guest, is it! You invade my house! Try to kill me! Threaten to throw my corpse into the quarry!"

Without a sign of guilt, Consuela snapped, "Tit for tat."

Bewildered, he stared at her.

"Now do stop quarrelling, children," said the duchess. "Your stew will get cold. And besides, Consuela, the gentleman—"

"—Gentleman! Bah! Look at the bruises on my poor arms if you think—"

"The *gentleman*—for all of Lord Wellington's aides-de-camp are gentlemen—is right, you know. And before you rage at me, be casting your mind back. Did I want to move into this horrid old house? No! Did I not warn you it was wrong and impossible, *and* illegal? *Si!*"

"But you came, dearest Grandmama," said Consuela, suddenly all loving humility. "Because you knew it was also the only way we could uncover the truth."

After a brief pause during which they all gave their attention to the food, Vespa asked curiously, "What truth?"

Consuela threw him a smouldering look. "As if you didn't know! The truth, my fine gentlemanly Captain, of why you murdered my dearest Papa!"

Vespa dropped his fork.

"I am sorry I was gone so long, ma'am," said a new voice. "But it's so dark and spidery down in the—" A young woman carrying a wine bottle hurried into the room, gave a shriek as she saw Vespa, and threw up her hands.

He lunged from his chair and caught the bottle in the nick of time. "From my wine cellars, I take it," he said drily. "Or I should say, *you* take it!"

The new arrival gave every indication of falling into strong hysterics, sobbing that they were all doomed to be transported at the very least.

Female tears terrified Vespa and he was silent as the ladies strove to calm the distraught girl, who was, it appeared, Violet Manning, maid to the duchess and her granddaughter. Consuela took her off to her 'room,' saying soothingly that she might have supper while her employers and their 'guest' retired to the 'parlour'.

"Jupiter," muttered Vespa. "This wasn't the only suite I couldn't enter. How many more people have taken up residence in my house, I wonder?"

"So very fortunate that you caught the bottle," purred the duchess. "It will nicely follow my stew, which you like, *si*?"

Despite his irritation, Vespa could not deny that the stew was superb, the meat and vegetables tender and the dumplings light as a feather. It was not an elaborate meal, but it was the best he had enjoyed since he left Richmond, and by the time Consuela carried in a lemon tart, fresh fruit, nuts and cheese, he was feeling far less hostile towards these unlikely trespassers.

The duchess decreed that since he was the only guest, they would not leave him alone with his wine. He pulled out her chair, but Consuela disdained his assistance and pushed back her own chair hurriedly. With a mischievous twinkle the duchess ordered him to bring the bottle, and led the way to an adjacent parlour in which several charming sketches adorned the walls, heavy draperies were closed over the windows, and three presentable chairs were drawn up before the empty hearth. "If you will be so good as to pour for us," she went on outrageously, "you will find glasses on the credenza."

Vespa tightened his lips but did not comment as he uncorked the bottle and poured two glasses. "Mrs. Ottavio," he said, offering one to the old lady.

"It is preferred that I am addressed as Your Grace, or Lady Francesca," she corrected. "And you must pour also a glass for Consuela. Now you may sit here beside me and cease to look so shocked. There is nothing harmful about good wine—taken in moderation."

"I am only glad my cellars please, ma'am."

Ignoring his sarcasm, she said that some of the wine was satisfactory. "Though we had a bottle yesterday that was very poor." She gave a trill of laughter. "*Si,* I comprehend that I am being naughty. You have the look of thunder and yearn to strangle me." She leant forward to place slightly gout-twisted fingers on his knee. "You are charming, do you know? And I like it when you smile . . . *si,* like that. Which is goodness of you, considering that Consuela named you a murderer."

He found that he could not resist the twinkle in her eyes. "Thank you. But you must know I am not, ma'am. I've only been here a week, and since neither you nor your granddaughter are in mourning clothes, I presume your son-in-law died at least a year since, whilst I was in Spain."

"In a fall. Down your quarry."

"Then I am sorry for it. But the quarry has not been in operation for several decades, and my steward tells me the area is plainly marked with 'No Trespassing' and 'Danger' signs."

"Which makes it quite convenable that my dearest Papa should have been murdered, eh?" snapped Consuela. "Oh, but you are like all Englishmen. Cold and heartless!"

"If you mean we are not given to rushing about attacking people and making absolutely unwarranted accusations because trespassers fall into abandoned—"

61

"He did not *fall*!" she hissed. "He was *pushed*! No, you need not say that you do not believe me, for your thoughts are written all over your haughty nose!"

"Good grief, ma'am, your temper is as hasty as your tongue! How can I believe such a—"

"Bull and cock story? Go on, say it!"

"Well, I won't, since you got it hind end foremost. But if you did indeed witness such a wicked act, I must presume that the murderer was apprehended and brought to trial."

Consuela's lower lip jutted rebelliously. She sipped her wine, then muttered, "I did not say I saw it."

"Who did?"

"No one, apparently. Or whoever did is too afraid to speak. And if you believe whatever that great stupid Hezekiah Strickley says, you are a bigger fool than he is!"

"Con-sue-la," said the duchess, who had been watching this exchange with faint amusement. "We are not peasants. We are not rudesbys. You must beg the pardon of our host."

The "meadowlark" fixed Vespa with a stormy stare, and snarled, "Pray accept my apologies, sir," as though the words burned her tongue.

He bowed. He was feeling the effects of the fall again, and his head had begun to pound ominously, but he was curious, and said, "Your father, I gather, had many enemies?"

At once, her temper flared. "No such thing! He had not an enemy in the whole wide world! Why must you say bad things like that? Oh, but this 'gentleman' of yours is impossible, Grandmama! Not for another instant can I endure to listen to his—his nonsense!" And with a flounce of skirts and a toss of her dark locks, she was gone.

"Phew!" Vespa, who had risen politely, sat down again. "Is Miss Jones always so volatile, ma'am?"

The duchess raised her brows. "She is Italian."

"But not on her father's side. Surely it is illogical that she should so loathe the English?"

"Only the men, Captain. And the logic, it is there—in her eyes, at the least. But—this, it is another story."

"What of you, Lady Francesca? Do you believe your son-in-law was murdered here?"

For a long moment she gazed into her glass. "I have not decide what to think. But do not arrange it into your mind that my Consuela she is addle-brained. The thing is that she adored her Papa." She glanced up at him and smiled. "You wonder, I think, what were my feelings about him. Well, he was a good man. But you may believe that my daughter's marriage was far from my dearest wish. They met in Rome. My Athena was ravishingly lovely, as is Consuela, you know."

He bit back an unkind comment and poured them both another glass of wine.

"Athena had a great love for art," said the duchess. "She saw some of Preston's work at a gallery and—"

"*Preston* Jones?" interrupted Vespa in astonishment. "Jove! He is very good. My father has one of his paintings. The gentleman was quite famous. I am astonished that he can have left you destitute!"

"You are also mistook. He did nothing of this kind. We have the most agreeable home."

"Then," he shrugged helplessly, "I'm all at sea. Why would you move in here?"

"If you will remind your manners and cease the interrupting, I will tell you this!"

Amused, he said meekly, "Your pardon, my lady. I shall say no more."

"If that is a promise," said Consuela, returning and pulling a chair closer to her grandmother, "I will come back."

"Preston Jones," began the duchess, "was well-born but a younger son. My Athena should have marry a rich man, but—" She sighed and spread her hands expressively. "What can one do when the heart it is given? So I permit the marriage and we leave our warm and golden Italy and come to your cold, grey England.

It is here that Consuela is born. Preston's work was not so very much admired for many years, and we are no longer rich, you understand. But I have my jewels to sell if necessitated, and his elder brother was so kind as to deed him a house near to this place. Preston came here with the reluctance, and—"

"—And he fell in love with the village and the countryside," put in Consuela nostalgically.

The duchess nodded. "And especially did Preston love Alabaster Royal."

"Which is a silly name, however you look at it," said Consuela. "No kings ever lived here so far as I have heard. Pure pomp and snobbery."

"It was the *gift* of a king to my maternal ancestors," said Vespa, stung. "And when a king awards an estate, the owner is entitled to include the word 'royal' in its—"

"La, la, la, la, la!" She yawned behind her hand. "How greatly I am impressed!"

Perhaps because his headache was worsening, he said irritably, "What you are is the rudest female I've ever met! I wonder, ma'am, that you never taught your granddaughter—"

The duchess came to her feet. Her chin very prominent and her eyes flashing, she was so fiercely regal that Vespa sprang up also and, apprehensive, stepped back. "This it is enough of the sufficiency!" she cried. "Consuela, your behavior is unimportable—"

"Insupportable, dearest Grandmama," corrected Consuela meekly.

"Just as I said. This Captain Vespa he is not quite polite either, but he is justified in his suppose that you have never had the governess or going to seminary. You will leave us at once, if you please. Or if you do not please! Go!"

Obviously distressed, Consuela stammered, "But—but dearest, I—"

"*At once!* You have disgrace me! I am shamed for you, *Signorina!*"

At this, Consuela flushed scarlet, her lashes fell, and with a bobbed curtsy, she crept away.

"I'll—er—be leaving, ma'am," said Vespa uneasily.

The old lady sat down and with a magnificent gesture commanded, "You will sit, and you will listen, for I shall not have you carry away a bad expression of us!"

He obeyed, intrigued by this strange little woman who addressed him as though he was actually a guest in her house.

"Now, where am I?" she murmured, "Ah, yes. Preston's portraits and his paintings of the village and the surrounded country began to sell, and soon his name was known. But always his first love is this estate. The country life it does not please me. I prefer London. But I have cared for Consuela since her dear mother died when she had but ten years. The child is wild and of a temperance, but she has also the great heart and carings for others. Our house is a mile north of the village, and a good house, but Preston was seldom there. He is the artist; time, it is forgot when he work. He is often here, for most of the times there is no others about, so he can sketch and paint in peace. Consuela, she come with him— until—" She paused.

"Your pardon, ma'am," said Vespa cautiously. "You said that most of the time no one else was here. Do you say that sometimes others *were* here?"

She nodded. "Men. My Consuela she is fair of face, and her figure it is what gentlemen admire, you will have seen this."

"And these men—er—annoyed her?"

"*Si.* Preston, he off in his other world, but at last he notice and there is trouble."

"Do you know who these men were? And what they were about?"

"One I know. It was the same that you raise your voice to last week. This man who has the name which he is not."

"Gentry? I found him inside this house. He said he was returning a desk he'd borrowed, but it seemed more likely he was taking it. Dashed if I know why. Do you know anything of the matter?"

"I know he came here. With others. But not inside, I think, for Strickley was always about. Sir Larson, he is too pleased by my Consuela. He and Preston have the big quarrel. Gentry, he tell Preston to keep away from Alabaster, and Preston he say Gentry have no business to speak such things."

"So Mr. Jones continued to come here? What about Gentry and his friends?"

"When Preston sees them, he go where they are not, and he paints."

"But he didn't know who the others were? Or why they were on the estate?"

"I think not. No."

"What about Miss Consuela? Did she recognize any of them?"

"Gentry, only. And his friend. The others she only see once, when her Papa stays so late it gets dark and she comes to find him and there is a coach going away. A gentleman's coach of luxury. Preston, he was inside this house. When he sees Consuela, he is very angry and he say she should come here never. That it is a evil place, with evil presences." She met Vespa's eyes levelly. "The very next day, Preston falls into the quarry."

"You've my sympathy, ma'am." Pondering, Vespa said, "But, even if Mr. Jones caught Gentry taking what didn't belong to him, I can't believe the man would have murdered your son-in-law over a few pieces of furniture."

"Perhaps not," said the duchess. "Perhaps Gentry have nothing to do with poor Preston's death." She leant closer, her eyes narrowed and glowing eerily. "Perhaps it was the evil influences of your terrible Alabaster Cat!"

5

It was dusk when Vespa made his cautious way along the upper corridor and the light came but dimly through a few open doors or the window bays. His fascination with 'Lady Francesca' and her granddaughter had enabled him to ignore his steadily worsening headache, but as he limped along the dusty corridor he knew he was in for one of the attacks he dreaded. No doubt his fall had not helped matters, and the duchess' frying pan had added to the damage. If his vision started to narrow he would be in trouble, for he could scarcely see now and he must be on the lookout for the sudden steps up or down.

He forced himself to concentrate on his dinner partners. They were both unhinged, of course. That bloody-minded girl was capable of anything. It was obvious that her father, poor fellow, had met his death due to his own carelessness, and if madness ran in the family, the late Mr. Jones had likely been as ripe for Bedlam as the rest of 'em.

At this point he blundered into a jog in the corridor, and had to cling to the wall for an unpleasant minute before going on. A dulled saw was cutting a path between his temples. . . . But he could still see. He'd be all right. Only . . . Lord, this was an endless walk.

The Italian ladies . . . Yes. Well, embarrassing as it was to admit such gullibility, he'd actually started to give some credence to their tale until the duchess had uttered that final piece of folly. He could still see the glow in her eyes as she'd hissed, "your terrible Alabaster Cat!" If she had started raving about some bloody apparition with its head tucked under one arm—that might have been a touch less ridiculous. But who ever heard of anyone being haunted by a cat? Wait, though. He paused beside an open door. The Alabaster Cat . . . It sounded familiar. Hadn't Mama said something about a cat? And didn't one of the legends have to do with—

Leaves were blowing all about him; at least, it sounded as if they were inside. Perhaps not all the windows were closed, or there might be a hole in the roof. Clinging to the door-jamb, he peered upwards, half expecting to see clouds. The ceiling was miles above him. He could see no holes, although it was weaving about in an odd fashion. He watched it until the door closed on his hand. Anger cleared his head. "What—another one?" he snarled, and pushed the door wide again. The room was like a black cave. Not a glimmer of light showed from the window. Certainly, there must be a window somewhere. "Show yourself, you skulking coward!" he shouted, clenching his fists.

A voice, echoingly far away, enquired, "Can you get up?"

Crazy Consuela . . .

The leaves were pressing in, tightening their hold.

It was, he suddenly realized, not leaves, but an arm around him. He blinked until he could see just the outline of her face.

"Yes, I followed you," she said. "You are ill. I could see you would fall."

She was tugging at him, and he found that he was on his knees. "I wonder you . . . cared," he mumbled, managing to stand.

"I didn't. Grandmama was worried about you."

Irritation was added to his embarrassment, but he asked, "Did you hear the leaves?"

"Try to stand up straight. It's not far now. Lean on me."

Lean on this termagant? Let this tiny bundle of ill manners and hatred help him? Never! He tried to walk unaided, but was mortified to find that he was clinging to her while she struggled to support him.

"I'm . . . so sorry," he stammered. "It's my—head, you see. Doctor—doctor said I'd have—headaches and—and start imagining things."

Instead of answering, she began to grumble, her voice rising in anger but coming from a great distance.

A cup or something was at his lips.

"Proper driv to the ropes, ain'tcha, Cap'n. Take another swig o' this, and you'll look alive."

Vespa swallowed, coughed, and blinked into the lugubrious countenance bending over him. He was sprawled on his bed. A branch of candles brightened the room, but there was no sign of Miss Consuela Jones.

"Strickley?"

"Aye, it's me. Let me give yer a hand up."

Vespa accepted the steadying arm gratefully. "It was good of you to come inside."

"No, it weren't. That there Miss Jones run to the stables screeching and bellering like seventeen nuns! Little thing like her, ordering a cove about something dreadful. Let's have yer boots orf first—that's the barber. . . . " He went on talking, the words coming alternately clearly and muffled to Vespa's ears. "Proper caution . . . got spirit enough fer two . . . inter yer nightshirt . . . Lift yer arm up a bit, canyer? . . . Yi! Caught a nasty one here, din't yer. . . . With a shape like hers . . . "

His voice rumbled into the distance.

By eleven o'clock it was already warm. The sun slanted brightly through the open casements of the breakfast parlour, and the scent of blossoms hung on the summer air. After a long sleep, a wash and shave, some hot buttered toast and a scalding cup of coffee, Vespa felt like a new man. He sat at the kitchen table for some time, pondering the events of the previous day. It had all been so very weird, and viewed in the light of this radiant morning it was hard to tell where reality ended and hallucination began. His head was clear now, thank heaven, but last night—well, it had been a bad attack, that was all. Hopefully the last. Refusing to brood over his erratic mental state, he began to draw up a list of Things to Be Done.

First, he would confront Lady Francesca and demand that she and her granddaughter leave Alabaster Royal at once. After he'd thanked Miss Consuela for her help, of course. He frowned uneasily. Which might be a trifle difficult. Secondly, he'd have a look at Secrets, and if the mare's leg was healed, he'd ride into Gallery-on-Tang, see if there were any letters, and arrange for more provisions to be sent out. After that, he must really inspect his property and find boundary lines and such-like. Strickley could help with that. And there was still the upper floor to be properly gone through.

It was a good list, he decided. But there was no real need to accomplish it all in order. He pushed back his chair and muttered, "John Wansdyke Vespa, you are a craven coward, sir!" And postponing the first item on his list, he went in search of his steward.

Strickley was nowhere to be found and his sway-backed old bay horse was gone from the stables. Corporal, who had been sprawling in the sunshine, woke up and trotted over, his little tail vibrating. He accepted a friendly caress and went so far as to roll over and allow his stomach to be stroked. Together, they went to the paddock. Vespa whistled and Secrets tossed up her head and cantered to him. She was a pretty sight, her coat gleaming in the sunlight. Her leg appeared completely healed, she was full of spirit and greeted him affectionately. He led her to the stable-yard, noting that Strickley had cleaned up several loose boxes and that the barn was markedly neater. Secrets stood politely for him while he saddled up, but the moment he was in the saddle she started to frolic and caracole.

"Show-off," he scolded fondly. When they were clear of the yard, he gave her her head and they were away at the gallop. The warm fragrant air rushed past his face; the sun beamed like a benediction from clear cerulean skies. His spirits rose, and he thought optimistically that, despite last night's little set-back, his health was returning at last. Soon, he would be a whole man again.

A distant summons caused him to rein in the mare and glance back. Far across the park a small shape tore after them at frantic speed. He patted Secrets' sleek neck and told her they must give the little scrap a chance to catch up, and they proceeded at a sedate trot.

It was Vespa's first real look at his acreage. The neglect was marked. Beyond the weedy park the land was overgrown with shrubs and deep grasses. Occasional boundary hedges were shaggy and unrestrained, and the low walls dividing fields were crumbling into disarray. In places the ground fell away into deep crevices, as swiftly to rise into rolling hillocks. Having ridden for some distance, he came into sweeping level meadowland. It looked more promising, and he dismounted, secured the reins to a shrub, and knelt to tug out a clump of dandelions and take up a handful of earth.

The dog came up, panting, and flung himself down beside his adopted human.

"Look at this, Corporal," said Vespa. "Jolly good loam. D'you know, I'm inclined to believe we could farm here and make a dashed fine go of it. I'd like to make something worthwhile of the old place." He sat down and looked over the stretch of countryside to where the chimneys of the manor rose against the sky. There was serenity here, and beauty, with only the calls of birds to disturb the quiet of the summer morning. He felt comforted and at peace. Sherry would have liked Alabaster Royal, if only he'd taken the time to inspect the property. To know that one's family had dwelt here for generations was a warming thought. Made a fellow think that this was where he really belonged. Not that he was forgetting Richmond, of course, only—

71

"Well, well!" A jeering voice shattered his introspection. "Only look, Durward. The lord of the manor, squatting in the dirt like any cloddish ploughman, and chatting with a mongrel!"

Sir Larson Gentry came riding up. He was mounted on a mettlesome chestnut, and accompanied by a pretty girl and a large, dark, coarse-featured man, the sight of whom caused Vespa to stiffen angrily. Clambering to his feet, he drawled, "Trespassing again? I recognize your friend for the lunatic who ran my coach off the road and killed a good horse. I'll require an explanation of the fellow."

It was a calculated insult, but the big man did no more than give a mockingly exaggerated bow.

The girl's blue eyes widened. She was very fair, her features delicate and her hair arranged in loose curls under a pert little hat. Her dove grey riding habit hugged a slim and shapely figure, and she managed her bay mare with graceful expertise. There could be no doubting that she was related to Gentry, for the resemblance was strong, but there was a sweetness to her face and a gentle expression in her eyes that spoke of a very different nature. She said in a soft but dismayed voice, "Oh, Mr. Cramer—you never did?"

"Of course he didn't," said Gentry, grinning broadly. "Now, forgive me, dear sister, but I suppose I must make you known to our unfortunate neighbour. Miss Ariadne Gentry—Captain Vespa, who is, I grieve to say it, quite lacking in hospitality."

Vespa bowed to the girl, who was obviously embarrassed by the ill-mannered introduction. "Your friend and I have unfinished business," he said, looking fixedly at Cramer, "which we cannot discuss while a lady is present."

"I'm shivering in my shoes," jeered Cramer.

"Evidently," said Vespa. "But do your shivering elsewhere. You have no right-of-way across my land, Gentry. Be so good as to leave it."

"With all the pleasure in the world. We must have strayed onto your poorly preserved preserves by accident. How pathetic that you're obliged to resort to that scruffy mongrel for companionship. But it's all you're likely to lure to your ghastly mansion, my poor fellow. Unless you have perhaps managed to hire a butler?"

"I have managed to recall where I heard your name before. Something to do with an unpleasantness at—White's, was it? But—no. Of course, it wouldn't have been White's."

Gentry's handsome features turned brick red and his eyes flashed to the puzzled look on his sister's face. "Come along, m'dear," he said harshly. "Can't waste time here." He spurred his horse to a canter, and Cramer and an obviously bewildered Miss Ariadne followed.

"*Rompé'd* you, by George!" muttered Vespa. It had been a shot in the dark, but a man of Gentry's type was almost sure to leave a sullied trail that would deny him admission to the best clubs. Mounting up again, he resumed his tour of inspection, thinking it a pity that a delectable creature like Mistress Ariadne should be related to the obnoxious fellow.

For a while the lush greenness of the meadow continued, but gradually the grasses became clumps, separated by bare, pebbly soil. Ahead, a great gash in the earth was backed by the starkly denuded upthrust of all that was left of a high hill. There was a rickety-looking rail fence along the edge of the quarry workings. Beyond it, the ground fell away to a deep hollow littered with rock-piles, abandoned picks and shovels and broken carts. A tunnel leading into the hillside was partially blocked by rocks and shale. It was a grim and forlorn sight. Dismounting, Vespa thought it sad that this rape of the land had been permitted, but the family fortunes had probably benefitted, and very likely some of the rock had gone into the construction of his manor house.

He walked to the edge and peered down the sheer drop. Poor old Preston Jones wouldn't have stood a chance if he'd gone over here. The rail fence trembled under his hand. A man would have to be a fool to lean on such a flimsy structure—if that was what Jones had done.

Corporal ran to sit on his boot with a proprietary air, and Secrets came up and nuzzled at his neck. "Jealous," he said, stroking her nose. He dispossessed the dog and walked slowly along the length of the rail fence, Corporal prancing ahead and the mare thudding along behind him. There was a crude gate, and some steep, rough-hewn steps leading down to the quarry floor. Just past the gate the rail fence was splintered and broken, and a length of rope had been tied across the gap as a makeshift safeguard. Perhaps this was where the artist had plunged to his death. Vespa stood contemplating the scene, lost in thought until a drifting hawk drew his attention to the sky, and the position of the sun told him the morning had ended.

He pulled out his watch. It was after one o'clock, and he was hungry. Again rearranging his list of Things to Be Done, he turned Secrets westward. He had come to the boundary of his estates, and the village was conveniently close; just beyond the quarry hill.

At the Gallery Arms he was received with deference and delight. The ostler led Secrets away, and Corporal followed Mrs. Ditchfield and a beef bone to the kitchen garden. Vespa feasted on an excellent chicken pie, followed by fresh fruit and cheeses. Mr. Ditchfield hovered about him from time to time, and when the few customers had gone, accepted an invitation to join him in a glass of ale.

Vespa guided the conversation to the quaint little village church and its impressive stained-glass windows.

"Admire works of art, does ye, sir?" said Ditchfield. "P'raps you've a interest there your own self?"

"No, unfortunately. My brother had a considerable gift, but I'm a perfect dunce with a sketching-pad or palette. I've a great respect for those with talent, however. I hear that until recently quite a famous artist lived nearby."

"Ye'll be meaning Mr. Preston Jones, I expect. Oh, he were a rare one, Captain." Ditchfield glanced around the now empty dining room and gave an amused wink. "In more ways than one."

"The ladies?" asked Vespa, lowering his voice.

"No, not that, sir. Fair devoted to his wife, till she died, poor lady, and doted on his daughter. But . . . " He lifted his glass suggestively.

"Ah. Was that the way of it? I've seen some of his work. His—er—failing doesn't appear to have interfered with his talent. But I do recall hearing that he was three sheets in the wind on the day he died."

Ditchfield looked alarmed. "I can't be held responsible for what a growed man does in my house, sir. And if a gent chooses to live in the bottle, it ain't my fault!"

"Certainly not," said Vespa soothingly. "I've had men like that under my command. Some of them the best and bravest fighters anyone could wish for. But let them get near a bottle, there was no reasoning with them. Of course, I could clap 'em into the stockade—if we had one—but a civilian's got no recourse. Save for the Law, I suppose, if a man becomes violent."

"And that's just it, Captain," said the host, his long face relaxing again. "Mr. Jones, he never knowed what violent meant, I dare swear. Gentle soul he were. Not as I didn't try to stop him often enough, for I liked the gentleman. But he'd just give me his quiet smile, pay for a bottle, and go wandering off with it. I'm glad, sir, as you see the way it was."

Vespa was still thinking about "the way it was" when he went outside. The village drowsed in the afternoon sunlight. Several geese waddled towards the pond on the green, conversing in their guttural fashion. Sporadically, Young Tom's hammer rang from the smithy. Mrs. Blackham boomed, "Good-afternoon, Captain," and Vespa raised his high-crowned hat as she passed by with a shopping basket on her arm.

Lost in thought, he wandered towards the grocer's and sat down on a nearby bench. The conversation with Ditchfield had confirmed his belief that Preston Jones' death had been accidental. The man had probably—

"You, sir, are a disgrace, and should hang your head in shame!"

Startled by the harshly voiced indictment, he looked up. A

shabby coach had halted nearby and a footman was in the act of letting down the steps for the tall, large-framed, elderly man who scowled from the open door.

"Your pardon, sir?" said Vespa, coming to his feet.

"I knew your grandfather, and he was a rogue! Only good thing he ever did was to keep your father away. Had you a shred of decency you'd burn that damnable pile to the ground!" Having descended to street level this fierce individual stood glowering at Vespa, his deeply lined face distorted with passion, faded brown eyes glaring from under bristling grey brows, while he waved a cane about so agitatedly that his high-crowned hat was dislodged and tumbled to the cobblestones.

'Another candidate for Bedlam,' thought Vespa. He said coolly, "I think we have not met, sir, but—"

"D'ye think I don't know it's thanks to you they swarm here? The scaff and raff of the roads! You encourage 'em to come seducing foolish females, stealing and poaching, trampling across my property night after night!"

"The devil I do!" protested Vespa. "I've not—"

"To say naught of that damn fool painter," roared the old man. "Lurking and slithering about. Well, I warned him! Don't say I didn't! 'We want no foreigners here,' I told him. Laughed at me, confound his insolence! 'You'll pay,' I said. And he did, eh?" He grinned in a sudden and macabre gloating. "Him and his stupid dabbling. Ain't dabbling now, is—" The vengeful snarl rose to a scream, and the cane swung upwards again.

Corporal had arrived, and having discovered the fallen hat, was attempting to shake it, not too successfully, since it was almost as big as he was. The footman made a cautious attempt to retrieve the hat and yelped as the flying cane caught him, while his employer advised in a deafening howl that he was a fool and a blockhead.

Snatching up the dog, Vespa eluded the cane, retrieved the hat and offered it to its irate owner. "Whoever you are, you must know that some people believe Preston Jones was the victim of foul play," he said curtly. "If you have something sensible to say about the tragedy, I will listen to you. Otherwise—"

"It ain't *my* tragedy," growled the older man, snatching at his hat. "Yours, Vespa. And, by God, if you stay here, there'll be another 'tragedy', as you call it! You've had enough of 'em in that curst pile, and rightly so, for it reeks of sin and— Oh . . . *Egad!* Your revolting mongrel has *bit* it! Look at the brim! *Tooth marks!* You owe me a new hat, confound you!"

"If my dog—"

"Dog? That miserable tuppence-worth of mange and fleas ain't a *dog*! A gentleman don't have a cur that's the size of a rat and twice as ugly! I want a new hat, Vespa!"

"I put it to you, sir, that what you want is the attention of a qualified physician. Good-day to you."

"*Stop!* Damn your eyes and limbs, do not *dare* walk off till I'm done with you, else I'll lay my cane across your sides!"

Restoring Corporal to the path, Vespa started away, ignoring the gobbling rage of this vindictive individual, his back tingling in anticipation of the threatened blow. In which case, years or no years, he'd have to take away the old maggot-wit's cane.

He glanced around when there arose a sudden outburst of shrill barking. The old gentleman was dancing about trying to avoid Corporal, who darted and snapped at his ankles, while the footman looked variously aghast and hilarious.

Grinning, Vespa called: "Corporal! Come!" and was agreeably surprised when the little dog obeyed, scampering to him with tongue lolling and eyes bright with triumph.

A flood of vituperation followed, but Vespa ignored it and made his leisurely way to the grocer's shop.

Mrs. Davis stood in the open doorway, her nervous hands fluttering. "Oh, dear, oh, dear! What a pity! He has taken you in aversion, Captain Vespa!"

"Not surprising," said Constable Blackham, strolling to join them. "But you want to be careful of his lordship, sir. He's a hard man, and carries a grudge."

"His lordship?"

"Lord Alperson. The biggest landowner in these parts. Outside the county, lucky for all of us, but your nearest neighbour, sir."

"And a mean, cruel old man," said the widow, *sotto voce,* looking cautiously after the departing coach.

"Now you know you shouldn't say things like that, May," scolded Blackham.

"And I wouldn't in front of anyone else. But I'll hold to it, Captain Vespa. I thought the world and all of his poor little granddaughter, and the way that cantankerous old miser cast her off was wicked!" Her eyes widened as if she'd frightened herself, and she scuttled into the shop saying there was a letter come for the captain.

The letter was a brief note from Lady Faith, which Vespa was not surprised to find consisted of a scold for his having left Richmond against her wishes. There was no mention of his long-overdue team and coaches.

Emerging into the golden afternoon once more, he found the constable waiting for him, and as they strolled along together, he asked bluntly, "Is Lord Alperson short of a sheet?"

Blackham grinned, then, obviously choosing his words with care, said, "I wouldn't go for to say that, sir. But there's too much talk for there to be no fire. He's got a—er—very ugly temper."

"And he carries a grudge, you said. Against whom? Me? Or is he another thimble-wit who fancies Alabaster Royal to be inhabited by herds of spectres?"

"Begging your pardon, Captain, but his lordship's got some grounds for complaint. There *are* poachers. And if someone catches 'em at it and takes after 'em, it often seems like they go to ground, as you might say, in your great house. Where no one dares chase the varmints. Strickley claims he never sees 'em, but . . . " He shrugged.

"And because of that, Alperson wants me to level the manor?

Poppycock!" Vespa's eyes narrowed thoughtfully. "Mrs. Davis spoke of his granddaughter. I don't mean to pry, but—Well, yes. I suppose I do." The constable laughed, and Vespa said with the smile that never failed to win him friends, "But you mustn't feel obliged to tell me if it's a confidential matter."

"God love ye, sir, it's a open secret, and his lordship not better loved because of it. Everyone knows he led the young lady a dog's life. He held she belonged to him 'cause he'd taken her in when her Ma died. A pretty little thing was Miss Robina and more'n one gent had a eye to courting of her. But the old lord chased 'em all off, till along come a fine-looking young naval officer what won her heart. When his lordship found out about it, he threw her out. Disowned the poor lass."

"I'd say she was better off without the old curmudgeon. Did her sailor carry her off?"

The constable fixed Vespa with a steady stare. "No, sir. You might say, begging your pardon, as Alabaster Royal did."

"The devil! You'll have to explain that."

"Now don't go up in the boughs, please, sir. Miss Robina's young gentleman was aboard his ship in the Downs, and didn't know nothing about it till it was too late. Miss Robina was penniless and frightened, I expect. It was a horrid night, but the old skinfl— er—I mean, his lordship wouldn't even let her take a horse. So she walked in the rain till she come to Alabaster Royal and it appears as she took shelter there." Blackham sighed and shook his head. "We might never have found her if a peddler-man hadn't of gone inside, not knowing about the legends, y'know."

Aghast, Vespa said, "You mean the poor lady starved? But surely, she could have appealed to you, or to Mr. Castle, if no one else?"

"That she could, and probably meant to. Though his lordship's powerful, and folks be afraid to cross him. Anyway, Miss Robina didn't have time for any appeals. Fell down the stairs, poor creature. Broke her neck."

"Good Lord! What a dreadful thing! Did you—er . . . ?"

"I did, sir. And I wish I could say I hadn't." Blackham shuddered. "I see her poor face to this day. I never saw such a look of terror. Like—like she'd been scared to death! By whatever, or *who*ever haunts Alabaster Royal. Which is why his lordship so hates the place, and—whoever owns it."

"Nonsense! If what you say is truth, then the blame for the poor girl's death may be laid at his door. Not at mine."

"Well, now," said a mocking voice behind him. "There's a bold statement. Can I quote you, Captain, sir?"

Intent on their discussion, neither man had noticed Durward Cramer come up with them. Vespa turned to the big man and drawled contemptuously, "Eavesdropping's about what I'd expect of you, Cramer. Mean to run to your master with it, do you?"

"I call no man master, curse you! Sir Larson Gentry's my friend." The beady eyes shifted. Cramer said with a smirk, "You want to be more careful who you slander, Blackham. His lordship won't like it. Not the least bit."

"I spoke naught but the truth," said the constable, who had become rather pale.

"I wonder why I'd thought you might have summoned sufficient courage to come here and challenge me," said Vespa lazily. "I should have known an insult is only resented by a *gentleman*!" Despite his slim figure and apparent languor, he moved lightning fast, and the malacca cane that Cramer flailed at him hissed past his ear and splintered on a stone bench.

With a shout the constable sprang clear.

Cramer found his arm seized in a grip of iron and his enraged attempt to tear free resulted in a dazed but correct impression that he had flown through the air before he landed on the cobblestones.

"Oh, bravo, Captain!" cried Mrs. Davis, running into the street, clapping her hands.

Several villagers who had seen the confrontation echoed her sentiments, and Young Tom waved his hammer excitedly from the door of the smithy.

"Well done, sir!" exclaimed Constable Blackham, his eyes

alight. "That is to say—ahem! I don't hold with fighting in public, Captain Vespa!"

"Mr. Cramer and I have a personal matter to settle, I grant you," said Vespa, picking up his hat, which had been dislodged during the tussle. "But, as you saw, I was merely giving him a lesson in the art of self-defence."

The constable's mouth twitched. "Ah. Well, that explains it, then. But I hope your 'personal matter' won't come to no duelling, Captain. If that were to reach me ears, I'd have to put a stop to it."

What reached their ears was a flood of breathless profanity from the recumbent Cramer.

Mrs. Blackham approached, and halted.

The constable's demand that Cramer cease his cursing in the presence of a lady was ignored until Vespa jabbed his cane under the man's ribs, rendering him too short of breath to continue.

Mrs. Blackham jerked up her head so that the poke of her bonnet flapped wide and for the first time Vespa viewed a rosy-cheeked face and a handsome pair of smiling dark eyes. "Thank you very much, I'm sure, sir," she said.

He bowed. "My very great pleasure, ma'am."

As he left them, he heard the lady advising Cramer that it was not lawful to sleep on a public street.

Gallery-on-Tang, thought Vespa, was a most satisfactory village.

6

En route to the Gallery Arms, Vespa was captured by two very determined matrons selling tickets to a Flower Show to be held the following week on the grounds of Coombe Hall, a nearby beauty-spot. He purchased two tickets. The ladies were pleased with him, and he was pleased also, because prior to his army days he had enjoyed working with the Richmond gardener from time to time. He looked forward to restoring the grounds at Alabaster. Some well-planned flower beds and shrubs would soften the stark appearance of the old building. Another item to be added to his List of Things to Be Done.

Word of his encounter with Cramer had spread. Several boys ran up and appointed the tallest to ask shyly how he'd managed to overpower a much larger man. Other children pressed in, and before he knew it, he'd admitted to having learned the art of self-defence at Eton and played cricket for Oxford. These glorious distinctions spurred earnest pleas that he help organize a cricket match after Church on Sunday.

The afternoon was waning by the time he at last rode out, with their jubilant thanks ringing in his ears, Corporal's bone in a bag tied to the pommel, and much to occupy his thoughts. When he reached Alabaster, Strickley was repairing the paddock fence. He came over to take Secrets, and Vespa dismounted, tossed the bone to a very tired small dog, and accompanied Strickley into the barn. He watched his steward unsaddle the mare, and asked what he knew of Miss Robina Alperson's death.

"Same as what everyone knows," said Strickley, heaving the saddle over a rail fence. "The old lord ranted and raved fer months about it, he did, laying the blame everywhere 'cept where it belonged. But it ain't none of your bread and butter, Captain, though he'll try and make out different."

"From what he said, I gather Lord Alperson felt animosity towards Mr. Preston Jones, also. Any particular reason?"

Strickley began to rub down the mare. "He don't need no reason, sir. He just plain hates everybody. Miss Consuela was friends with poor little Miss Robina. Stood up to the old lord, she did. Only thing it got her was he ordered her off his property and she weren't allowed to go there no more. Still, his lordship told everyone Miss Consuela had knowed about Miss Robina's gentleman friend, and encouraged her, what led to her death. Mr. Jones went out to Redways and threatened to have Lord Alperson up for slander, and there was a real fuss." Strickley shook his head. "A mighty good brooder is his lordship, and once he gets something in his brain-box, it stays there. You'll hear from him again, Captain. He'll do you a mischief, if he can."

"Then I'm forewarned. Has he ever, to your knowledge, 'done a mischief' to anyone?"

Strickley's big hands paused. "That he has. Though to prove it would be something else again. Above the Law is rich folk, and his lordship's as full o' juice as they come."

Vespa advised him that no man was above the law in these modern times, and left him, wishing he could believe it. He walked around the back of the house, entered by the door at the south end of the building, and climbed the stairs to Lady Francesca's 'apartments'. There was no response to his knock, and when he opened the door and stuck his head inside the impromptu kitchen, it was evident that the ladies were not 'at home'.

He decided to have another look at the room where the door had slammed on his hand yesterday. A peculiar business that. He'd be most interested to see why the curtains had been so tightly drawn that there had been no sign of a window.

He advanced cautiously, thrust the door wide, and stared in speechless outrage. Today, the window draperies were pulled back and sunlight flooded into the spacious, and at the moment unoccupied, room. A four-poster bed was made up. A framed sampler hung above a fine old chest of drawers on which a brush, comb, and male toilet articles were neatly disposed. Before the windows a geranium in a pot graced a small table flanked by two chairs; there was a large clothes-press against the end wall, a mirror hanging beside it and a wash-stand nearby with pitcher, bowl and tidily hung towel. The furniture shone, and the floor was immaculate.

Recovering his voice, Vespa snarled, "Some damned hedge-bird has made himself comfortable!" and stamped inside.

The few items of clothing in the press were rather threadbare but had been carefully patched; a high-crowned hat showed much wear, as did a pair of boots that were nevertheless brightly polished. The sampler which hung above the chest of drawers depicted several bluebirds fluttering recklessly about the head of a lion. The legend, artistically flourishing, read:

> *What you cannot as you would achieve,*
> *You must perforce accomplish as you may.*

"And having accomplished it nicely, you makebait," he said wrathfully, "you've been properly caught!"

Seething, he went in search of a pistol.

As he neared his own chamber, he was astounded to hear a deep bass voice raised in song. The rogue must be quite demented to show such brazen indifference to discovery. The thought gave

Vespa pause. His pistol was in his room, and the voice appeared to be coming from there. The clothes he'd just found had been tailored to fit a large individual—a large madman, apparently. Common sense whispered that he was unarmed, and would be well advised to go in search of reinforcements. "The hell I will," he muttered, and pushed open the nearest door. Luck was with him; a dusty set of fireplace tools still stood on the hearth. Snatching up the poker, he hurried out, prepared for battle, his advance accompanied by the strains of "John Peel".

"I'll give you a 'view, view halloo'!" he growled, and threw open his bedchamber door, holding the poker poised and ready.

It was not the room he remembered. Rich draperies billowed softly at now sparkling windows, on the small table a handsome snuff bottle, pressed into service as a vase, held wildflowers which lent colour and fragrance to a chamber that exuded cleanliness. Furniture and floors glowed with unsuspected richness, and the once murky cheval glass was spotless.

"John Peel" was abandoned. The singer, tall and stout, his black hair worn rather longer than the current style and framing a round, double-chinned face, looked up from brushing Vespa's new riding coat and offered a flourishing bow. "At last I am granted the felicity of meeting you, Captain Vespa," he said in a deep, resonant voice. "You are somewhat taken aback, I perceive. I trust my song did not annoy. Pray allow me to introduce myself. My name is Thornhill, and—"

"Blast your effrontery!" cried Vespa, striding to face him. "What you are is a rascally vagrant who has dared invade my house! I presume you're aware that I've a perfect right to shoot you where you stand!"

The brilliant dark eyes widened and Thornhill said in agitation, "I beg you will not resort to violence, sir. If you do not choose to avail yourself of my services, I shall grieve, but depart. Nor shall I present you with a bill despite—"

"A *what?*" thundered Vespa.

"I have spent some considerable time and effort in restoring this room and another of your bedchambers that had been most sadly neglected. I think you will find, Captain, that—"

"Have done! You *trespassed* and arranged a room to suit yourself, and well you know it! Put down my coat at once!"

"As you wish, sir. Though it stands in sad need of proper pressing." Laying the coat tenderly on the bed that now looked so neat and tidy, Thornhill murmured, "A peerless cut, but not Weston, I think. I would guess it to have the touch of Balleroy, the émigré genius who has hung out his sign in Clapham. You are to be commended on your taste, sir, if I dare remark it. There is a chill on the air. Would you wish me to start a fire before I remove your riding boots?"

Vespa tossed his poker aside and with a swift pounce reached for the pistol case he'd left on the highboy. It was not there. He whirled. The case was in the intruder's hand. He lifted his gaze to meet a velvety smile.

"I took the liberty of cleaning these for you, sir." Thornhill opened the case and offered one of the deadly duelling pistols, butt first. "A fine pair of weapons, although in my opinion, and intending no least criticism, in the hand of a member of the Quality they might be the better for just a touch more chased silver. It is my way, you see, to try and anticipate the needs of my employers, though I'd certainly not have presumed to do so had I been aware that the duchess was mistaken. Will you not be seated, Captain? A glass of Madeira, perhaps?"

"What are you babbling at now?" asked Vespa, taking the pistol and inspecting it carefully.

"Why, her ladyship convinced me that you stood sadly in need of the services of a valet of the first rank, sir. A charming and most persuasive lady. I could not bring myself to deny her."

Vespa sank into the chair Thornhill drew up, but kept the pistol handy. "Was that before or after you'd broken into my house?"

"Oh, but I did not break in, Captain." Setting a glass of Madeira at Vespa's elbow, Thornhill explained, "I assisted the duchess and

Miss Consuela to move here, you see, though I must own I did not think Alabaster Royal a—er—suitable setting for the ladies. At that time they believed this house to have been abandoned, and Miss Consuela was frantic with anxiety to learn why her dear father had been murdered here, so—"

"Rubbish! From everything I've been able to learn, Preston Jones met his death by accident. Besides which, because a house is empty does not give every Tom, Dick or Harry the right to move in and settle down."

"Exactly so, sir." Thornhill's expressive eyes were reproachful. "But I would not presume to make such a remark to her ladyship."

Vespa looked at him levelly. "You've a clever tongue, and you know damned well I was referring to you, my fine charlatan."

"Ah. In that case I make every effort to understand your point of view. My present circumstances being what they are. Shall you dress for dinner, Captain?"

Change clothes before eating a cheese sandwich in solitary state? "No I will not," said Vespa testily. "What I'll do is march you along to find the duchess and discover just what mischief you're about!"

Thornhill smiled kindly. "By all means, sir. No doubt you will wish me to pull off your riding boots first. And—er—perhaps a wash and a change of linen might not come amiss, if you intend to meet the ladies. The duchess, you know, is a stickler for manners."

Vespa restrained a grin, and while Thornhill removed his boots, advised the interloper in barracks-room language exactly what kind of rogue he was. He kept a wary eye on the clearly unrepentant 'valet of the first rank', but had to admit that Thornhill did indeed seem to excel at his calling. His slightest wish was anticipated, the man's movements were smooth and graceful, his manner politely deferential with just a trace of the proprietary air of a long-time retainer.

The duchess, Thornhill imparted, was below stairs. They started down, the valet in the lead, and Vespa following with one hand on the pistol in his waistband. As they went, he became aware of a most heavenly aroma. 'Freshly baked bread, and roasting beef,' he thought. 'They've moved to where there are proper cooking facilities, by Jupiter!'

Thornhill bowed him into the kitchen.

"Well, well," he murmured.

Wrapped in a voluminous apron, the duchess stood at the table, beating vigorously at a bowl of batter. Similarly protected, Miss Consuela sat nearby, shelling peas. And, again, all was neat and radiated cleanliness. And the smells!

"Ah, so you found him, did you, Thornhill?" Lady Francesca paused at her labours, and smiled fondly at Vespa. "How very much better do you look, my dear boy. A capable valet he can do so much for his master."

"If my looks expressed my mental state, ma'am, they would convey at the very least—amazement. Perhaps you will be so kind as to explain what you are doing in my kitchen, and why you would suppose I'd hire this rascally vagrant as my valet."

"I told you, Grandmama," said Consuela, with a dark frown. "You will get no thanks, no appreciation from this one. After all you have done!"

"Hush, child. It is that the good Captain he does not comprehend. Now do sit down, Vespa, though a gentleman he has no business in his kitchen, you know."

"I suppose it is pointless for me to remark that *you* have no business—"

"But my dear, as your housekeeper this is *my* domain, until Thornhill hires us a proper cook, at which time I—"

"*You?* My *housekeeper?* Madam, you cannot be serious! I gave you no encouragement to believe—"

"Encouragement, is it?" burst out Consuela, dashing peas into the bowl. "We are so good as to offer to work for you in this horrid old ruin—"

"In exchange for our—er—temporary quarters," put in the duchess.

"—And you, with your foolish hoity and toity, fling our kindness back into our teeth! So—go!" Consuela tossed a pea pod over her shoulder and stood up, unfastening her apron. "Hire yourself a fine cook and a splendid housemaid, to say nothing of—"

"*You?*" Vespa gave a shout of laughter. "If ever I saw anyone less like a housemaid! No, really, Miss Consuela, you cannot be serious. A duchess in my kitchen? A lady of—of Quality sweeping my floors?"

"You want for gratitude, Captain," said the duchess sadly.

"And do you find it proper that an *unwed* lady should reside under a bachelor's roof, ma'am? It's bad enough you must try to pass off this rascal as a prospective valet, but you haven't thought a flea's leap ahead if you—"

"He is quite right, Grandmama," interrupted Consuela with an alarming display of small white teeth. "Other gentlemen, they may have housemaids, parlour-maids, cookmaids, kitchen-maids, scullery-maids, laundry-maids—and these females may be safe. But *this* one?" She snatched up two cloths and swung open the oven door. "I should not dare to close my eyes at night! So be it!"

"I'll have you know, madam," said Vespa, angered, but with one eye on the divine joint nestling in the pan, "that I have *never* molested any of my father's maids, nor— Hey! Where are you going with that?"

"To throw it to the dog," snarled Consuela, marching towards the scullery, pan in hands. "Open the door, Thornhill. At once!"

The prospective valet threw an enquiring glance at Vespa.

"Do no such thing!" snapped Vespa.

"Pay him no heed," said Consuela. "He doesn't want you. He has ten thousand valets queuing up outside, praying he will hire them!"

"Put down that pan," commanded Vespa. "It doesn't belong to you at all events."

The duchess crossed to take the pan from Consuela's hands and restore it to the oven. "You will burn yourself, my love. Besides, the dog it cannot eat a joint that is bigger than its own self. Now, Captain, you will please to sit down, and we will make the discussing."

"There is nothing to discuss, ma'am. You cannot stay here, and I will not take on a man of whom I know only that he is a trespasser with a silver tongue. I'll wager that Thornhill—*if* that is his name—is no more a valet than is Strickley!"

"You wrong me, sir," said Thornhill, sighing heavily. "It is true that I am the victim of a capricious Fate, and my name sullied through no fault of my own." He put a hand on his heart, cast a sad glance at the ceiling, and declared, "I have worn many hats, as they say, in this journey called Life. I will tell you my story, sir, so that you can judge. I was the youngest of the eleven children of a country vicar. I had my schooling at my mother's knee, but funds were scarce, and at the age of ten I was apprenticed to a London printer. Alas, the *harshness*, the *cruelties,* that were inflicted upon that lonely child!" Dabbing a handkerchief at his eyes, he continued brokenly, "So I ran away—"

"Very likely," interposed Vespa. "But I would be more interested in seeing your references. If any."

"You might at least have the decency to hear him out," said Consuela, sitting down and picking up another pea pod.

"While the joint is cooking." Her eyes full of mischief, the duchess added, "Do not let me forget to put the Yorkshire pudding in, little one."

'Yorkshire pudding . . . ' Vespa pulled out a chair.

From the age of thirteen, when he'd allegedly run away from his cruel master, Thornhill, it would seem, had indeed 'worn many hats'. He claimed to have worked as a link boy, stable-boy, gardener's boy, butcher's assistant, stevedore, millinery clerk and solicitor's clerk. Whilst in that last unlikely position he'd heard of an opening as footman, for which he had at once applied, since he longed for "the wholesome air of the country once again." Having won the post, he'd remained in the household for twenty years, working his way up at length to the position of butler. He'd fancied himself settled for life, and had proposed to and been accepted by "a most unexceptionable young female." This had displeased the mistress of the house, who had, Thornhill declared, modestly lowering his eyes, for some time made it clear that any advances from him would be "welcomed." Only a week after his betrothal, his noble employer had succumbed to a sudden internal disorder. On the day following the funeral, the lady of the house had once again made "romantic overtures" to Thornhill, and upon his respectfully pointing out that he was shortly to be married and could not betray his bride-to-be, he had been summarily dismissed.

"Disgraceful," said Vespa, trying not to laugh at the 'valet's' tragic expression. "But after twenty years of faithful service you must certainly have been provided with references."

Thornhill sighed. "I was promised the very best character, sir. But upon application for other situations, my prospective employers were advised that I had been dismissed for having made improper advances to my late master's wife. I was quite ruined."

"And your fiancée? Did she stand by you?"

"Had she done so, I would have prevailed. I know it. But—alas, she proved fickle, and married the first footman." He drew a hand across his brow and his shoulders slumped. "I was . . . shattered, Captain. You will comprehend that such a series of disappointments can break the spirit of the best of men. In my grief I sold my few belongings and went on a walking tour, which deteriorated with my fortunes into what is known as 'the padding lay'. I've been 'padding' ever since, and will say that I met many kindly folk who valued my superior social standing and erudition, and formed the habit of turning to me for counsel in certain complex disputes. Not an unpleasant way of life, and one I might still pursue had I not chanced upon your grand old house, and found it so neglected that I decided to do what I might for it."

At this point, he folded his hands, clerical fashion, his smile so saintly that Vespa was undone, and to the extreme indignation of Consuela, who had been greatly moved by the sad story, he burst out laughing.

'I was trapped by roast beef and Yorkshire pudding,' thought Vespa, as he lay in bed that night, with Corporal snoring in the padded basket Consuela had provided. 'Truly, I am become a pawn in the schemes of those two devious ladies!'

He smiled faintly into the darkness. Trapped he might be, but he had enjoyed an elegant dinner, excellently served. The table had been spread with snowy damask and gleaming silverware, the flames of the candelabrum reflecting in spotless crystal. The roast beef had been succulent, the Yorkshire pudding just as he liked it, the peas tender, and a fruit compôte topped with custard had formed a perfect complement to the meal. In the immense drawing room, amid stately furniture now charmingly arranged and transformed by the application of beeswax, he had found copies of yesterday's *Times* and *The Morning Herald* on a table at his elbow, and Thornhill had drifted silently to place a glass of port nearby.

When he had come up to bed, Thornhill had been discretion itself, quietly making himself useful before being dismissed.

'The impertinence of the fellow,' thought Vespa, chuckling to himself. He had believed very little of Thornhill's tale of woe. But the rascal's dramatic presentation had amused him, and the combined influences of a superb meal and the urgings of the duchess and her granddaughter had prevailed. He'd agreed to take Thornhill on trial, and if the fellow continued to perform his duties as he had done today, it might well develop into a permanent arrangement.

As for Lady Francesca and Miss Consuela—now that was another matter. The old lady had argued that with herself as chaperone and ostensible housekeeper, there could be no objection to her granddaughter remaining at Alabaster. "We now occupy what were evidently the servants' quarters," she'd pointed out, "which are far removed from your own suite. I have every confidence in your keeping to the line of behaviour—"

"You are too good, ma'am," he'd inserted ironically.

"—And, besides providing you with some very badly needed assistance," she had swept on, "our staying here will allow Consuela to look about and satisfy herself that poor Preston's death was indeed a tragic accident."

Consuela had inserted stubbornly, "Or prove that he was murdered, Grandmama!"

"So, if you will but be sensible, Captain Jack," the duchess had persisted, "you'll own that our remaining here for a little while can harm none, but help us both."

"And what of the gossip-mongers? Surely I need not remind you of how rumours flourish. What will your neighbours—and mine!—make of it?"

She had said with a shrug, "Merely that as an old friend of your mother, I am visiting you to give you the benefits of my advice on the restorative of your manor house."

Vespa yawned drowsily. Beyond doubting she was a splendid cook. And ladies had such a way of bringing order from chaos; already the house seemed so much more welcoming, and livable. . . .

He awoke with a start. Corporal had left his basket and was scratching at the door.

"I took you out before we came to bed," grumbled Vespa, flinging back the covers.

Corporal barked a gruff little bark and sat down, watching his Person expectantly.

The moon was bright, and Vespa pulled on his dressing-gown and slid his feet into his slippers without bothering to light a candle.

Corporal moved his front paws up and down and barked again.

"All right, all right. I'm coming, confound your whiskers."

The dog was out of sight when he reached the foot of the stairs, but a muffled bark sounded from the main hall, and then from farther along the corridor. Puzzled, Vespa made his way to the door that led to the basement steps. Corporal waited there, jumping up and down as if he were on springs, and uttering little yips of impatience.

"I suppose you're after a rat," muttered Vespa, swinging the door wide.

A waft of noxious air made him gasp and draw back. It was very dark inside, but Corporal shot down the wooden steps and out of sight. "Foolish creature," said Vespa, his nose wrinkling at that pervasive odour. "If you want to go hunting in that stinking cellar, you're on your own. I don't intend to—"

His words were cut off as a sobbing scream was followed by frenzied barking. The unearthly sounds, the foetid aroma, the cold air, caused the hair to lift on the back of Vespa's neck. He wasn't suffering one of his murderous headaches this time. . . . Could it be that he was wrong? That ghosts *did* exist and the old place really *was* haunted? The barking became a worrying sound, and a man's voice was raised in an outburst of enraged profanity. Corporal wouldn't attempt to bite a spirit. Someone down there was abusing a woman!

On the thought, Vespa plunged down the steps and turned to the right, following a distant and faint gleam of light. Corporal barked madly. The woman's voice rose in a barely intelligible plea for help.

"Coming!" shouted Vespa.

An alarmed exclamation and the light was extinguished.

Unable to see anyone, Vespa groped his way towards the voices and added, "Let her go, you scoundrel!"

A man bellowed, "Damn and blast it all! Get away, you curst mongrel!"

Corporal gave a yelp, and another voice called urgently, "Never mind about the woman. Come on!"

Once again caught without a weapon, Vespa rushed forward, shouting, "Stop, or I fire!"

A furious curse. Something was coming at him from impenetrable blackness. A violent impact and he was down and struggling with a powerful individual who smelled strongly of lavender water.

He struck out blindly and his fist rammed against something, eliciting a pained howl, followed by a scared sounding, "Lend a hand here! I can't hold him!"

A boot rammed into Vespa's shoulder. He swore, grabbed for the leg, and heaved. There came a shocked yell, the sound of a fall, then a scrambling retreat, and a flood of moonlight brightened an outer doorway.

Vespa got to his feet. "I think they've gone," he panted. "Are you all right, ma'am?"

A muffled sob. "Why should I not . . . be all right? I am accustomed to being—being strangled!"

"Consuela?" He peered through the gloom. "I thought so!"

Her figure loomed against the lighter rectangle of the door. "Oh, if we could just . . . just find their lantern."

"Never mind the lantern. I see you now. Come. The steps are this way."

A moment, then her hand met his. It was very cold and shook convulsively, and suddenly she was clinging to him and weeping.

"Hush," he said soothingly, one arm about her, the other reaching out to the stair rail. "Tread carefully. You're safe now."

"How can I b-be safe," she cried between sobs. "They—they tried to m-murder me! Just as—as my darling Papa was murdered in this—this horrible house!"

7

In the drawing room Vespa lit candles, then tugged hard on the bell-pull that Thornhill had "temporarily repaired" and promised would be heard in "the servants' quarters". The resultant ear-splitting tolling made him gasp and would, he thought, likely be heard in Gallery-on-Tang. A corner of his mind wondered what size bell his new man had found to create such an uproar. He poured a glass of sherry for Consuela, who sat huddled on the sofa. Her hand shook so that she could scarcely hold the glass and two pathetically tear-wet eyes looked up at him from a face that was deathly pale where it was not dirty.

Torn between compassion and vexation, he said as the clamour faded, "Poor child. You are properly terrified."

She took a great gulp, then burst into a frenzied coughing. "I am *not* terrified," she gasped. "What it is—I am *enraged*! I would like to kill that filthy beast who tried to strangle me! Only look at my—my poor throat!"

She pulled aside the collar of her torn gown, revealing livid welts on her neck.

Inwardly appalled, Vespa asked sternly, "How came you to be with them?"

"*With* them?" A tinge of colour came into her cheeks. "You've a nasty way with words, Captain John Wansdyke Vespa!"

"You were certainly with them when I found you."

"This, it was because I saw them. I was watching from my window, for I know that evil men come here and—" She broke off. "Ah, the dear little thing! See how they have hurt him, and he came so heroically to my rescue!"

Corporal limped into the room, holding up a front paw and whining.

Vespa swore under his breath and picked up the animal gently. "My poor fellow! Let me see."

"It is that *I* shall see. Not you!" Two small hands attempted to remove Vespa's hold.

"He's my dog!" he protested, swinging Corporal away. "I will care for him, thank you just the same."

"You! What do men know of caring—for anyone? How to fight and eat, and drink too much—*that,* men know!" She flashed her eyes at him and said darkly, "Besides other things which I am too much the lady to speak of, but that male animals lust after twenty-four hours of the day! You did not even care enough to think of him till now!"

"Of all the— I'll remind you that I was caring for *you,* Miss Graceless! I would certainly—"

"You rang, sir?" Thornhill rushed into the room, a tasselled nightcap on his head, a startling red and purple dressing-gown wrapped about him, and a great blunderbuss clasped in his hands. He checked, looking from the disarrayed Consuela to his employer's torn garments. "Ah—perchance I come, ah—inopportunely."

Vespa said tersely, "Restrain your imagination! Miss Consuela was attacked by would-be burglars. Wake Lady Francesca and desire her to come down here. Then take a lamp into the cellar and find some way to secure the outer door—or doors. You'd best keep that monstrous weapon by you. I believe they've gone, but they're a vicious pair."

Thornhill scanned him uncertainly. "Are you all right, sir?"

Consuela peered into Vespa's face anxiously. "You are damaged? Where? Here? Here?" Her hands were probing his shoulders and arms. "Why do you not speak? Are you a Spartan, or keeping the stupidly stiff upper lip?"

"I am not— Ow!"

"Ah. It is the shoulder. Oh, my! Look here."

"Good Gad, madam!" exclaimed Vespa, attempting to pull away. "Keep your hands to— Stop it, woman! I'm perfectly—"

"Consuela!" The duchess hurried into the room clad in a voluminous gold wrapper, her hair rolled up in little rags all over her head so that she put Vespa in mind of a latter-day Medusa. "Whatever are you doing to the Captain? And in your night-rail! Have you *no* sense of propriety? I declare I was never more shocked!" She glanced at Vespa and her indignation was replaced by alarm. "My heavens! What on earth has been happening here?"

Consuela suddenly burst into tears and rushed into her grandmother's arms. "Oh, dearest, it was ghastly! They tried to . . . murder me!"

Vespa snapped, "Thornhill, do as I bade you. Now!"

Thornhill hurried out.

The duchess drew Consuela to the sofa and held her close. "Were you spying again, my wilful child?"

Scattering teardrops, Consuela nodded. "It was two men, this time. I saw them creep around to the back of the house, and I followed. And they—they went into the *cellar*! And—and, it *smelled*—oh, foul!"

"You might well have been killed," said Vespa, sitting down with Corporal on his lap and examining the damaged paw.

"Wretched girl!" exclaimed the duchess, shaking Consuela gently. "Did I not tell you to come at once to me if ever you saw something of auspicious? How fortunate that I have ask St. Peter to keep his eyes on you! Have they hurt you?"

"They caught me, dear G-Grandmama. And they tried—they tried to *strangle* me! See!"

The duchess inspected the welts on her granddaughter's throat and turned pale. "The villains! My sweet little one! Oh, but I should spank you for being so foolhardy!"

"If your granddaughter had but roused me, ma'am," put in Vespa, feeling very much to blame, "there'd have been no need for her to suffer such harsh treatment. I've pistols and ammunition, and I am perfectly capable of—"

"Had I taken the time to make my way to your bedchamber and interrupt your snoring, and assure you I had no improper designs upon your body—"

"Consuela!" exclaimed the duchess.

"Well, he would have thought it," said Consuela sulkily. "And by the time I enlisted his help—*if* he had believed me, which I doubt—they would have been half-way to London with their booty."

Vespa said, "I doubt there's much in the way of booty in my cellar. Strickley already unpacked the silver and linens that were locked away down there. I fancy they were simple thieves."

"If they are thieves," argued the duchess, "no matter what you say, Captain, there must be something very valuable in your house. This is the third time Consuela has seen men lurking about at night."

"Strickley says he's chased away some varmints during the daylight," admitted Vespa thoughtfully.

"Just so," said Consuela, holding her throat, but speaking in a less shaken voice. "The men Strickley saw came here to ransack the house. The men *I* saw came here with one purpose only. To silence me. Just as they s-silenced my darling Papa!"

"If that were the case," argued Vespa, "they would have come in by the south side door, and gone upstairs; not broken into my odiferous cellar. Besides, what do you know of them that you must be silenced?"

99

"My father knew, and they may think that he told me."

Vespa stared at her. "He *knew*? What, exactly?"

"I don't *know*." She gave a moan of exasperation. "But they killed him because of it!"

"Lord, give me strength," he muttered. "Ah, Thornhill! Any sign of the varmints?"

Thornhill shook his head. "But a most obnoxious odour, sir. I barricaded the outer doors. And I found—this." He held up a small pocket pistol.

"You see?" shrilled Consuela, clinging to her grandmother. "I was to be murdered in my bed!"

"Then you will be very well advised to deny me the benefit of your parlour-maid expertise and return to your own home, post haste." Vespa stood and tucked Corporal under his arm. "In the meanwhile, I suggest you go back to bed. First thing tomorrow morning I'll report our murderous intruders to Constable Blackham."

"You will waste your time. He is a foolish man! I have told him and told him about my dear Papa, and he smiles and says kindly that I am to be brave! Pah! He will do nothing! I learned long ago that if anyone is to ferret out the truth about my father's murder, it will be me! Now"—Consuela crossed to stand close before him, her eyes very soft—"you will permit that I shake your hand and express my thanks for your very brave charge to the rescue."

It had been more of a hop and skip than a charge, he thought wryly, but she had never spoken to him so kindly. Gazing into her piquant little face, he saw the bruising on her throat and rage seared through him. How *dared* they abuse a lady in his house! "I wish I'd come sooner," he said, reaching for her outstretched hand.

"So do I." She whipped Corporal from his relaxed hold. "But this one did, and I will repay him as best I may." She eluded Vespa's snatch and darted behind Lady Francesca, who had also risen. "Good-night, Captain!" she trilled.

"You are a scamp, Miss Consuela," said Vespa.

There were no further alarms in the night. Next morning, Thornhill brought a ewer of hot water to Vespa's room, together with the information that poor Miss Consuela was "a trifle indisposed," but that Manning was assisting the duchess in the kitchen. As a result of their efforts, Vespa enjoyed a hearty breakfast. Later, Thornhill impressed him by setting out his blue riding coat with not a crease in sight, a snowy shirt, three equally snowy neckcloths— "Just in case you might require more than one attempt, sir"—and a spotless pair of cream buckskins.

Before he went downstairs, Vespa handed the valet a bank draft with instructions that he was to order himself a new wardrobe. "Suitable for a gentleman's gentleman."

Thornhill's dark eyes opened very wide and flew to search his face. He said eagerly, "Then—then can it be that you really mean to keep me on, sir? I've not dared hope. . . . "

"I think we shall go along nicely."

Glancing down at the draft, Thornhill gave a gasp. "But— such a sum, Captain! Are you sure—I mean, well, you scarcely know me!"

Vespa smiled. "I called you a rascal, but I've come to think you're an honest rascal, and if you're to stay on as my valet, you must look the part, you know."

"I wish—" Thornhill sounded close to tears. "I don't know what to say. That you'd be willing to take a chance on me— It means so much more than . . . than you can know."

"I have my consequence to consider," said Vespa, with a twinkle. "My father is a stickler, Thornhill. Were he to visit and consider my man not up to snuff—" He shuddered realistically, and when the valet gave him a misty-eyed look and tried to smile, he patted him on the shoulder, and warned, "Never think I'm an easy master. I rely on you to find me an excellent staff, which won't be easy. And if my coaches and my trunks don't arrive soon, you are going to get very tired of restoring these poor overworked garments. Now, I must hurry and report to our good Constable."

Thornhill ran to open the door. "I won't let you down, Captain Vespa," he promised hoarsely. "I swear it! You—you give me back my self-respect. God bless you, sir!"

The morning was overcast and blustery, and after an exhilarating ride, Vespa reached Gallery-on-Tang feeling quite ready to face the world. Two fine coaches were drawn up at the inn, and a boy was chasing a wind-driven hat along the street, a well-dressed gentleman urging him on.

Constable Blackham was chatting with Young Tom in the smithy, and having exchanged cordial greetings with the sturdy blacksmith, Vespa was able to persuade the officer of the law to accompany him to the Gallery Arms. The small dining room rang with the laughter and talk of the travellers, but Ditchfield led the two men to a side table, saying softly that here they would have some privacy. They ordered a pot of coffee, and as the host went off, Blackham said shrewdly, "That's a nasty bruise under your ear, Captain. Trouble?"

"You don't miss much, do you? Yes. We had a break-in at Alabaster last night."

Blackham sat up straighter. "And you tackled the rogue, did you, sir? Any hope that you have him locked up for me?"

"No. And you can make that plural; Londoners, unless I mistook their accents. I didn't see them well enough to be able to recognize them again, more's the pity. It was too dark. Have there been any strangers lurking about?"

Blackham waited while Mrs. Ditchfield brought their coffee, and then answered, "None that I do know of, sir. But if they'd robbery in mind, they'd likely stay least in sight." He took out a notebook. "Can you tell me more of it?"

Vespa gave him the few details he knew, omitting all mention of Consuela until the finish, when he said, "I understand that Miss Jones has seen men lurking about Alabaster on several occasions."

"Aye. So she claims. The poor young lady has it set in her mind

102

that her father was done to death deliberate." The constable shook his head. "There's nothing to show that was the case, but she upsets herself worrying at it, besides doing just what her father done—wandering about where she's no business going. I warned her repeated, but—not meaning to give offence, mind—she's a stubborn woman, and don't like listening to the advice of them as knows better'n she do."

After a pause, Vespa said slowly, "What baffles me is why anyone should bother to break into my house. Now, I mean. It sat empty for two years, at least. If they were after the silver, why didn't they break in then?"

"Might not've been in the neighbourhood then, sir. You said they sounded like Londoners. 'Sides, they might not've been after the silver. There's some fine old pieces of furniture in the manor. Though I'd've said no one would go in after 'em at night. Even Londoners."

"Well, they did. And I know the place has been ransacked by daylight. I myself ran off Sir Larson Gentry and some of his hirelings when I found them slithering about inside the manor."

"My Lor'!" His eyes very round, Blackham gasped, "Sir Larson *Gentry,* sir? But what would he want with—" He broke off as Vespa's eyes lifted to meet his own. "What I means is . . . If ever I heard of such a thing!" He stared hard at the cruet and asked carefully, "Was there—er—anyone else about at the time, Captain?"

"His own men. And Hezekiah Strickley came up after a while."

The constable pursed his lips. "Ar. Strickley. He, er, works for ye, don't he, Captain?"

"Yes. So his word would be unreliable, is that it? I did *not* imagine the business, Constable!"

"No, sir! Oh, no. I never thunk— That is—ah, does ye want to press charges?"

Clearly, the officer of the law was convinced he was mentally unstable. Gritting his teeth, Vespa said tartly, "I am scarcely in a position to do so. Even if I could prove what I say, Gentry claimed he was returning a desk that he'd borrowed from my grandfather."

"Now I must say as *that* ain't likely! First off, your Grandpa's furnishings is not— Ah, what I means is—"

"Don't hide your teeth, man! Sir Larson's home is in the first style of elegance, I understand, and my furnishings are too old and out of the current style to have charmed him. Correct?"

The constable looked miserable. "More'n that, Captain Vespa. Sir Rupert Wansdyke, your Grandpa, sir, had no use for Sir Larson. Wouldn't allow him to set foot on Alabaster Royal, much less loan him so much as a teaspoon!"

"In other words, Gentry could deny the whole thing, and my version of the business would very likely cause me to be put under strong restraint. As I suspected. No, don't look so distressed. I understand your predicament. If it happens again, I'll deal with the fellow myself."

"Now I wouldn't want as you should do that, sir. Nor I don't— er—doubt your word. Exactly. But like you said, it does sound a bit— Well, might I ask what was the upshot of the business?"

The poor man was trying to believe him. Appreciating that generosity, Vespa said in a calmer tone, "We persuaded them to replace my desk, and Sir Larson rode off in a rage, threatening dire reprisals. Even so, I cannot think he'd have his bullies break in again at night. It's a hanging offence."

"That it is." The constable glanced around and lowered his voice. "Just 'tween you and me, sir, I have heard, though I don't know it for fact, mind, that Sir Larson's, er, under the hatches, as they say. And a man deep in debt—'specially a gent what's trying to keep up appearances—why there's no telling what he *might* do, being desp'rit like."

"True. But how would an old desk, or other pieces of my furniture, keep him out of Debtor's Prison?"

"Wouldn't. Not nohow. Unless—might there be perhaps some antique in the manor that you wouldn't think was valleyble? Like a chair as was sat on by poor Anne Boleyn? Or a very old book, maybe? It sounds foolish, I know, but I've heard as some old hand-writ books is worth thousands. Have you searched all through the manor, sir?"

Vespa admitted he'd not as yet had time to do so, and decided to rectify that omission when he returned home. Leaving Blackham, he walked over to the grocer's, exchanging a few shouts en route with the village cobbler, Samuel Carl, who was elderly and very deaf. In the fragrant little shop Mrs. Davis fluttered at him excitedly and trotted to the Post Office side of her establishment, where two letters awaited him: one addressed in Sir Kendrick's bold hand, and the other from the friend in Bristol to whom he'd appealed for help in hiring servants.

As usual, the widow was eager to chat, and he gratified her curiosity about his bruised jaw by telling her of the attempted robbery. She was horrified, declared she was about to swoon and flapped a handkerchief rapidly at her face, but when he apologized for having frightened her and expressed his intention to leave her in peace, she made a rapid recovery and was full of questions about the incident. Yes, she had indeed seen strangers in the neighbourhood. "In fact," she said, leaning over the counter and whispering dramatically, "there is some very strange folks what comes and goes from Larson Chase. *Very* strange! As I'd not trust so far as I could see them!"

Vespa's ears perked up. "Did they impress you as being criminal types, ma'am?"

"I wouldn't go so far as to say that, Captain. But nor was they Quality folk. Not what you'd expect a baronet to cry friends with."

She had seen the men on several occasions, she declared, when she was out gathering herbs. Her grandmother had been a great believer in the benefits to be gained from a regular consumption of such things as parsley, thyme and garlic. In fact, the old lady had never suffered from gout or the ague in all her days, though she'd lived to be ninety-nine and would have reached her century had she not taken a glass too much of wine and tumbled from her bath chair. The widow launched happily into a detailed account of her grandmother's wisdom and it was only the arrival of another customer that enabled Vespa to escape.

He went out onto the street deep in thought. The widow's remarks bore out what Consuela had said, and if the rough characters she'd described were in the pay of Larson Gentry, there must indeed be something at Alabaster Royal that was of great value. Possibly, Gentry hadn't sought it out while the manor had been abandoned to Strickley's rather erratic care because he'd only recently become aware of the value of the object, whatever it was. It wasn't very convincing, but even less credible was Consuela's belief that she had been the intended victim of the intruders. The poor girl was clearly obsessed—

At this point he collided with a lady who was just leaving the church, causing her to drop her reticule. With a hurried apology, he restored her property and found himself facing the lovely Miss Ariadne Gentry. She stammered in a confused fashion that she was not at all hurt and that she would have seen someone approaching had she not turned to close the gate.

"I was talking with Mr. Castle about the flowers for Sunday, you see," she explained.

"Do you provide them, ma'am?"

"Oh, yes. Sometimes. Well, *I* do not, you know. Our gardener cuts them, but he likes to be given notice of what will be needed, and he is rather testy now that we have had to let his helper go. Oh, dear!" she put a hand to her cheek and her big blue eyes widened. "I should not have said that. My brother doesn't like people to know— I mean—"

"I quite understand, ma'am. Lots of us have had to draw the bustle in these difficult times."

"Yes. And poor Larson does hate it, for we was used to live so differently. He holds that it is all because of this silly war, and that Lord Wellington is spending too much money chasing Napoleon all over Spain when we might better let him have it and be done. After all, Spain was our enemy for centuries. Do you not agree, sir?"

Vespa's jaw had tightened during this artless speech. His eyes glinting, he said, "I'm afraid I don't, Miss Gentry. Your brother would feel differently were Bonaparte to invade Britain, as he has boasted he means to do. Lord Wellington fights to keep the wolf from our doors as much as to protect Spain."

Peeping up at him, she said, "Oh, dear. Now I have made you cross. I forget that you were a soldier. I always supposed that his lordship's staff officers would be great big fierce men, whereas you are not very brawny, are you? Indeed, you are rather thin. They say his temper is extreme uncertain. Did you like him?"

Looking into those guileless eyes, Vespa could not hold irritation. Clearly, Miss Gentry was a lovely bird-wit, but there was not a shred of malice in her, and she would very likely die sooner than advise him (as another lady had done) that he was "foolish, hoity and toity". He said with a smile, "I have never met a man who so inspired admiration and respect. We all would have followed him straight to—er, anywhere, without question. Indeed, our one fear was that *he* was fearless and persisted in exposing himself to enemy fire so as to keep up the spirits of the men. Admittedly, one treads lightly around his temper. But his lordship is a splendid soldier, and a very remarkable man."

"His poor wife thinks so, too. But then Kitty so dotes on him. She is unhappy while he is away, and she is as bad as my brother at holding household, which you would think he might take into account."

"You are acquainted with Lady Wellington, ma'am?"

"Oh, yes. She is older than me, of course, but we have known the Pakenhams forever. I last saw Kitty at Brighton. She doesn't like the Regent's Pavilion, and told me she never saw a less inviting house. I thought it very fine, but, alas, I am not a very good judge of such things. Or, indeed, of any thing. Ah, here is my carriage." She put out her hand, and, dimpling prettily, said, "I am

glad to have met you again, Captain Vespa. Perhaps you would—
But, no, you had better not." And with a dazzling smile she tripped
off to where a liveried footman waited to hand her reverently into
the waiting coach.

Waving farewell, Vespa thought her as sweetly natured as she
was lovely. Certainly, any gentleman would be proud to play escort
to such a Fair. But remembering the calm common sense of his
beloved Marietta Warrington, or even the fiery obstinacy of Miss
Consuela Jones, he knew that the beautiful Ariadne would drive
him to distraction in a week.

He was delighted to return to Alabaster Royal and find that his
father's grooms had delivered his team of matched greys, his curricle and the new phaeton, together with several large trunks.
Strickley was overjoyed to have some "real blood hacks" to care
for, and lost in admiration of the coaches. Thornhill was just as
pleased by the contents of the trunks, and was already busily un-
packing. The large portrait of Sir Kendrick that had hung in
Vespa's Richmond bedchamber had been carefully crated, in ac-
cordance with his wishes, and he insisted that Strickley leave
horses and coaches to help with the proper placement of the painting. His first thought, to give it the place of honour in the entrance
hall, was abandoned, and he decided instead that it must be hung
above the drawing-room fireplace.

Lady Francesca came in during this procedure, and approved
the selected location, "for you will be able to visit him more comfortably in this room. What a splendid handsomeness! You are
right to be proud of him. It is good for the son to be proud of his
Papa."

Jack smiled up at that beloved face. Every day the manor had
seemed less cold and formidable. Now, especially, it really felt like
home.

He sought out Thornhill to help in his investigation of the
upper floor. His new man was busied with lining the drawers in his
bureau and highboy and arranging his personal linens, and looked
so tragic when faced with the prospect of abandoning these vital

pursuits that Vespa told him to carry on, and went alone into the long corridor.

He had removed dusty holland covers and thoroughly inspected two bedchambers, even to the extent of pulling out drawers and looking to see if any secret documents were attached to the undersides, when the busy patter of four small paws announced the arrival of Corporal. Vespa had missed the constant companionship of the little dog, but the animal that bounded joyously into his arms was a far cry from the shaggy creature he'd carried up from the cellar last night.

"Only look at you, my fine-feathered friend," he said, stroking a coat that was now sleek and shining. "Why, you are positively elegant. It would seem that I may have been mistaken in naming you a mongrel!"

"You were indeed." Consuela came into the room attired in her 'housemaid uniform'—a large apron tied over her gown. "He was a diamond in the rough, is all."

"He's had a rough time of it, certainly, poor chap. Did you bathe him?"

"Yes. Manning and I were soaked through, but after we'd dried and brushed him, it was very clear that he felt so much nicer. Which is more than I can say for you, sir! Only look at your shirt! Filthy!"

Vespa restored Corporal to the floor and was taken aback to see that his once snowy shirt had indeed been reduced to shades of grey and his coat was liberally decorated with cobwebs. "Gad! And I've only just started. Well, never mind that. How are you feeling this morning, ma'am?"

Consuela said she was much better, thank you, and stayed to watch as he struggled to pull a reluctant drawer from a chest, then turn it upside down. A shower of shredded paper, dust and debris cascaded out, and Vespa sneezed. Corporal barked and began to race about, nose to the floor.

"Why is all that paper in shreds?" asked Consuela, uneasily.

"From the look of the other contents," Vespa answered, dabbing a handkerchief at his eyes, "I'd say mice had taken up residence in here."

She gave a squeal and gathered her skirts tight around her ankles, which were, he noted, very trim. "I'd thought you would have left by this time," he said, trying not to stare. "Before another murderous crew came to do you in."

"I'm not so easily frightened off. I carry my little pistol everywhere now, and it will be under my pillow at night, so I shall be perfectly safe. Why do you turn the drawer upside down? Whatever do you expect to find underneath?"

"I wish I knew. But I'm convinced that Larson Gentry is after something in this house. Besides you, of course."

"Oh, you may mock, sir! But you'll be sorry when my bloody corpse is stretched out at your feet!"

"Sorry, and extremely surprised. But if you persist in pretending to be my housemaid, I mean to exercise my rights and ask you to give a hand here."

She hesitated, then edged forward, still holding her skirts close. "I suppose that is only fair, but you must pull out the drawers and if there are rodents inside, I shall scream."

For the next hour there were no screams. They worked steadily together and cleared two more large bedchambers and an adjoining parlour and dressing room. Corporal thought the project great fun and would retreat, barking excitedly whenever Vespa up-ended a drawer, then dash to investigate the contents. Consuela was alternately revolted by the dirt and neglect, and ecstatic over a fine example of chimneypiece carving, the frame of an old print, and the elaborate bedposts. The way she had of clapping her hands and squeaking with delight when she discovered something she admired amused Vespa, and when they were investigating a well-furnished parlour and she suddenly began to jump up and down in excitement, he could not restrain a laugh.

In a lightning change of mood, she scowled at him. "I am too exuberant, you are thinking. I am very far from being a perfect English lady—like Ariadne Gentry—is that not so? Oh, I know

110

you have met her, and I suppose you will now go mooning about all over the house, and sigh into your dinner, and write silly poems to her beautiful eyes or her golden hair and dainty ways!"

"I was thinking nothing of the sort, Signorina Scratchy! But I agree that Miss Gentry is very beautiful. I suppose it is only natural that other ladies should be jealous—"

"Jealous? Pish and a fiddlestick! As if I would care to be meek and mild and so stupid as any sheep!"

"Some men, Miss Consuela," he said, hiding his mirth and shaking his head at her, "place a higher value on kindness than on a quick mind."

She flushed, but riposted angrily, "You might better say *all* men, for they cannot bear to admit that any female may have a brain in her head. Mama used to say that gentlemen so dislike sensible women that they make up nasty names, like 'blue-stockings', to mock us."

Vespa unfolded an old map and scanned it critically. " 'Us' inferring that you consider yourself and your Mama to qualify for the sobriquet of 'sensible', I take it."

"Of course. My Mama, especially, was of a high intelligence. And she was bright and gay, and charming. And so very *alive!*"

"She sounds to have been a fascinating creature. Did she object when your father mocked her?"

"He did no such thing. He adored her. We all adored her! His poor heart broke when she died. And I missed her so. . . . " Her eyes were suddenly bright with tears. "I still miss her. . . . And now I have lost them both, and you—you must poke fun at her!"

"No, no!" Dismayed, he protested, "I meant no such thing. Please don't cry. I was only teasing because you said *all* men dislike intelligence in a lady."

"So they do." She sniffed and dabbed at her eyes with her apron. "Well, I mean—*most* men do."

"But not your Papa."

"Most assuredly not my Papa! He was proud because he could enter into really deep discussions with Mama and she would defend her point of view and not be browbeaten. He was proud of me, too, and said I had a good mind. But I know he wanted me to be more—English. He tried always to teach me to be less outspoken and—well, he said I was . . . volatile." She peeped at him from around the apron. "Am I? Dreadfully?"

He pulled out the drawer of an armoire and said with a smile, "I'd say rather that you have plenty of spirit, which will help you get over life's rough spots. And I do believe, Miss Consuela, that no matter what you may think, many gentlemen admire a lady with an informed mind."

Brightening, Consuela lifted a cobwebby marble clock from the mantelpiece and set it gingerly on a desk. "Do your parents discuss things like politics, or world affairs?"

Vespa was silent, trying to recall such a discussion, or any discussion between his father and mother. With something of a shock he realized how seldom he had seen them together. Even when they did meet it seemed that they really had nothing to say to each other, Sir Kendrick being invariably distinguished, distant and formal, and Mama lovely, dissatisfied and querulous.

Watching him curiously, Consuela said in an awed whisper, "You don't know! Good gracious! Are you never all together—like a family?"

"Of course we are! Is that what you talked about with your father? Politics and world affairs?"

"Sometimes we did. More often, it was little things. Like—the wonder of a sunset, or the grace of an eagle in flight, or the innocence of a little child. Papa found beauty everywhere, and he taught me to see it also. I think that is why he was such a magnificent artist. He didn't view things the way ordinary people do. Most people would look at Corporal, for instance, and see a little grey and fawn dog. Papa would have seen every slightest variation of colour, every shading in his long coat, the way the tufts in his ears stick out, the sheen on his little nose, every single whisker. He missed nothing." She clenched her fist suddenly, and pounded it on the desk. "That is why I am so sure he meant what he said!"

112

Vespa turned from poking through a shelf of books and stared at her. "But I thought you said you didn't know anything?"

"I don't. But he did! On the very day he died, he was so *excited*! He said, 'I was right, my little meadowlark! I found it. Oh, that such evil exists in a civilized world!' "

"Evil? You never told me that. But what has it to do with Alabaster?"

"I don't know! I don't *know*! But so soon after he said it, my dearest Papa was—was killed."

"Didn't you ask what he meant?"

"He wouldn't tell me. He said better I should not know, and—"

A small grey shape darted across the floor with Corporal in frenzied pursuit, and Consuela kept her promise and screamed.

8

While waiting for luncheon to be served, Vespa read his correspondence. His friend in Bristol was on an extended visit to St. Petersburg, and his country home had been shut down. His steward wrote to say that Captain Vespa's letter had been forwarded and he would no doubt receive a reply within "a reasonable time". " 'Reasonable time' meaning—never," grumbled Vespa. "Not that I need bother you with my difficulties now, I think. What the deuce are you doing in Russia, Brooms?"

A calling card inscribed "Mrs. Martin F. Tidwell" fell from his father's letter, which was longer than his usual hurried scrawls. Jack read it eagerly. Sir Kendrick trusted all went well—or as well as could be expected—in Dorsetshire. He himself was involved in a "sticky international matter" that kept him very much occupied. "I fancy you also are busy and I trust you are not overtaxing your strength. As a most eligible young bachelor you've doubtless been inundated by the County society—especially the match-making mamas, eh? Don't let them exhaust you, my boy." Jack smiled wryly at this, and read on:

Lady Faith spent a few days in London and met an old friend whose uncle has a country seat in Dorsetshire. He's rich as Golden Ball, I hear, and has a good deal of influence. I urge you to cultivate his acquaintanceship. One never knows, John, when a powerful ally may be useful, and you're relatively unknown in the district. On the other hand, of course, you may very well be bored to distraction in your bucolic ruin and ready to return to civilization. I need not say that such a sensible decision would very much please me and delight your mother.

In that connection, Felton—you'll recall my man of business—was surprised to receive a tentative enquiry about Alabaster Royal. Some mushrooming Cit, no doubt, wanting to acquire the prestige of a country seat at low cost. It was all Felton could do not to laugh in his face, and he very properly advised the dimwit to view the property in person before proceeding any farther. That should put a stop to the matter, eh? If anyone does come down and make you an offer over a hundred guineas, I'd snap it up! Ha, ha! Much chance of that!

Well, this is all I've time for, my dear boy. Let me know how you go along, and don't forget to pay a call on this gentleman. The lady says her card, which I enclose, will serve as your introduction.

I am, as ever,
Yr. devoted father to command, etc. etc.

Amused, Vespa thought that the only thing Papa had forgot was to tell him the name of the gentleman he was to call on. He took up Mrs. Martin F. Tidwell's card and turned it over.

The name of his prospective "powerful ally" was written in a neat feminine hand on the back: "Lord Malcolm Alperson."

─────

After luncheon, Vespa and Consuela resumed their search for anything of unusual value in the upstairs rooms. The duchess wandered in occasionally, but soon retreated, sneezing, from the dusty air. Consuela gave it as her opinion that much of the remaining furniture was quite fine and should fetch a good price when the property was put up for sale.

"What makes you think I plan to sell out?" demanded Vespa from the depths of a huge press.

"You never mean to stay here, surely?"

"Why not? The old place has its own charm, and—" He was interrupted by the sudden slam of the open door. He emerged from the press as Corporal shot into it and hid in the corner. The room grew very chill and the daylight dimmed to an eerie glow. Vespa tensed, his heart beating rather fast.

Consuela skipped to his side and whispered nervously, "I think I am very brave to stay in your haunted house!"

"Let's have a look at these ghosts." Hurrying to the door, he wrenched it open. The corridor stretched out in chill emptiness. A murky window in the opposite room revealed a sky covered with dark clouds. He said, "I think your 'ghost' was the east wind, Miss Jones, nothing more. Come—see for yourself."

Standing very close behind him, Consuela whispered, "How can you be so stubborn? Don't you feel how unnaturally cold it is? Haven't you heard—them—at night?"

He argued firmly that an old and long abandoned house was bound to be a trifle damp. "And who do you fancy trots about the passages after dark? Some of my more infamous ancestors, their sinful lives having denied them heavenly admission? The case is, I think, that you have a perfervid imagination."

"Do I so? Then what are you staring at? Oh, Lud!" Her voice squeaked a little. "That door was closed when we came in here!"

"So I thought." Vespa took the pistol from his belt. "More uninvited guests, probably. Stay here!"

He crossed the corridor and gave the opposite door a strong shove. The hinges were rusted and let out a piercing squeak, echoed by a smaller one, and a voice at his ear hissed tremulously, "Why didn't we hear that noise when it was opened?"

"I thought I told you—"

"I'm not going to stay in there all alone!"

"Then keep behind me."

She stayed very close behind him, gripping his coat as he moved into what had at one time been a study. It still held a fine old library table, a cracked leather armchair, several bookcases and three straight-backed chairs. But there was no sign of life.

"*Voilà!*" he said with a stifled sigh of relief. "No spirits, spectres, or visible vagrants. You may release my coat-tails now."

Consuela had already done so, and went over to poke at the clutter atop the library table. "I would have thought—Oh, no! You're doing it again! What is so fascinating about the floor?"

He held her back as she hurried to him. "Look—here, and over there."

"Four clean spots," she said. "Something stood here."

He nodded. "Until it was removed, very recently. And replaced in the wrong room."

"Your Grandpapa's desk, you think?"

"Yes. I had noticed the room Gentry's louts put it into was too crowded." He frowned thoughtfully, then gave himself a mental shake. "Only look at me, reading something sinister into so simple a thing as the laziness of Gentry's hirelings. They simply couldn't be bothered to carry it this far along the corridor. Well, let's get on with this, Miss Housemaid."

Consuela turned to the library table. A corner of her apron caught on a leather-bound book, and it fell, releasing a shower of old bills and notices. "At least, there are no mice," she said, stooping to gather them up. "Most of these are duns, and— Oh! My goodness!"

Vespa looked at her sharply. She stood pale and rigid, gazing at the sheet of paper she held.

He hurried to her side. "What is it? Do not dare to faint!"

She smiled wanly but her hand shook as she gave him the paper.

It was a head and shoulders sketch of an extraordinarily beautiful young lady of India. The dark, long-lashed eyes, the set of the

117

lips, betrayed both hauteur and determination, and her chin was held with a proud upward tilt. A jewel was set in the centre of her forehead, thick dark hair was wound into a rope that hung over one shoulder, and a sari draped gracefully about her. The paper was raggedly torn, and on the lower edge a column of figures had been added up and totalled. But if this had been no more than a preliminary sketch it showed a remarkable degree of skill.

Awed, Vespa asked, "This is your father's work?"

"Yes." She said sadly, "Do you see how clever he was? I doubt this took him five minutes to sketch, yet he has captured both the lady and her personality. So many artists, they portray the face, but it is blank and the nature of their subject is quite lost."

"One indeed senses that this lady must be formidable. Did he know her well?"

"I don't recall that he knew her at all. Certainly, he never mentioned her." She tilted her head and added musingly, "Which is odd, you know."

"How so?"

"Because he delighted to—what he called 'discover' people, and when he met somebody interesting, he could scarce wait to tell us all about them. This lady is so very beautiful, I'd have thought . . . But then, she might be a complete stranger he'd chanced to notice. He could do that. Just a glimpse of someone, and he could sketch them to the life, even weeks later." She sighed nostalgically, looked up, and frowned. "Now what are you thinking? That she was his—his paramour? Well, and you are wrong, as usual! If that were so, I *would* have known it!"

"Miss Jones!" He threw a hand to his brow and cried, "Spare my blushes!"

"Fiddlesticks! Most of the officers I've met could not blush if they tried!"

"Gad, what a harsh judgment!"

She chuckled. "A candid one, I own, but by now you should know better than to take me for a missish widgeon. And *I* knew my Papa."

118

"Poor fellow. Did you allow him no secrets at all?"

"And you speak of harsh judgments. Now you seek to paint me as the tyrannical— Ah, but I see that you are laughing at me again, wretched male that you are!"

He asked whimsically, "Is that any way to address your employer?"

"You are a great tease, Captain Jack Vespa!" Her sparkling smile dawned, and she coaxed, "Come now, be nice and tell me what were you really thinking about?"

"I was wondering why your father's sketch is in here."

"Possibly because there is a charming view of the little bridge from this window and Papa would have—" She broke off, her eyes widening in indignation. "Oh, that has nothing to say to the case, has it? You are vexed because he dared to invade your holy ruin! Why do I trouble myself to help you? *Why?*" Throwing up her hands in exasperation, she flounced towards the door, only to halt abruptly in front of a bookcase and say in a very different voice, "Oh, Captain Jack! Come and look at this!"

She blew dust from the carving of a miniature coach of state. The detail was astonishing, and the removal of the dust revealed traces of blue and gold beneath. "How lovely it is!" she exclaimed. "A fairy-tale coach!"

Moving piles of books aside, he said, "There are more. Jove, but they really are splendid! More of your father's work, do you think?"

She said this was unlikely, although it was possible that having found the wooden miniatures, Preston Jones had decided to paint them. They had found six more coaches, of differing styles and periods, by the time Thornhill came to advise that a work crew had arrived and the men were starting to clear the drivepath.

Consuela gathered up the miniatures in her apron and announced her intention to clean them properly, and Vespa went out to see what kind of crew Strickley had assembled.

Four men were hard at work down by the gatehouse, and Vespa moved among them, having a word with each individual and finding them a cheerful enough lot, apparently quite willing to toil on his property.

"They seem good fellows," he said, when he and Strickley were out of earshot. "How did you persuade them to risk working at Alabaster?"

"Promised they could leave well before dusk, Captain." The steward sniffed, and added glumly, "Be interesting to see how many of 'em keep coming when we gets closer to the house."

"Let's hope their spines will stiffen. It's to your credit you were able to lure them here." Vespa took the sketch from his pocket and held it out. "Have you ever seen this lady?"

The steward peered at the likeness curiously. "Cor! I never see no one like her. Who is she? Some sorta princess from foreign parts?"

"From India, I would guess." Vespa replaced the sketch in his pocket. "As to her rank, I've no idea, but the lady seems to be of high position."

"I reckon Mr. Preston Jones drawed that," said Strickley. "Always drawing or painting something, he were. Some folks didn't like what he done. His lordship, f'r instance."

"Did Lord Alperson sit for Jones? You surprise me."

The steward grinned. "He'd a bin surprised too, I 'spect. It weren't a drawing of his lordship. Miss Robina, it were, poor little lady, and a very nice picture, I heard. Mr. Jones give it to her for a birthday present. After she died, her young gent wanted it. Very desp'rit he were. He went to Redways and offered his lordship every penny he could put together, if he'd just let him buy it. Lord Alperson come out on the steps—he wouldn't let the young gent in the house. He held out the picture, and when the young gent made as to take it, he snatched it back, set it on fire and burnt it in front o' the chap's eyes. Proper mean, I call it!"

Touched by the sad tale, Vespa said frowningly, "I wonder the poor fellow didn't take it by force."

"Couldn't, sir. Two of his lordship's grooms held him, then drove him off. Fair raving he was, so the story goes. Swore he'd come back and get vengeance on them as killed his lady. Went right orf his tibby. 'Least, that's what folks say. Mad as a hatter. They'd oughta lock him away. Never can tell what loobies is going to do, eh, Captain? Not as you needs to worry about him, even though his lady died here."

"Thank you, Job's comforter. Now come and saddle up Secrets. It's turned out to be a nice afternoon, and I'm going for a ride."

Although the clouds had dissipated, the sun was starting its westward journey and there was a nip to the air as Vespa rode towards the quarry. He decided to follow a short-cut through a little vale that Consuela had said would bring him out near what remained of the quarry hill. The vale, a long velvety depression dotted with wild flowers, gradually narrowed as she had told him, the banks rising steeply in places. It was peaceful and remote. Consuela had said she often rode this way so as to stay out of sight until she arrived at a point where she could watch the quarry unobserved. He could not feel easy about a lady riding alone in so secluded a spot, and made a mental resolve to talk sternly to his fiery 'housemaid'.

The wind was strengthening and with typical autumnal perversity the clouds were banking again. He urged Secrets to a canter, and she responded eagerly. The turf was smooth and level, with only a few small trees ahead. The mare was moving faster, her silken gait a joy as always. Exhilarated, Vespa did not check her. They raced between the trees, and in that moment a mighty hand smashed him from the saddle. Briefly, he was astonished. . . .

Somebody was talking, the words puzzling, but the voice vaguely familiar. " . . . that's all very well, but the fact remains, dear boy, that every time we meet you seem to be flat on your back and holding forth about horticulture. Tumbled clean out of the saddle, did you? Not surprised, in view of your bent brain-box. Concussion's like that, so I've heard. They said you had a concussion, remember? Old Rickaby said it. Might need surgery, he said. Nothing new, so don't fret. They've known about it since the cavemen were toddling hither and yon—pretty near, anyway. There's

121

a papyrus dating back to about three thousand five hundred B.C. describing how it's done. They drill a hole in your skull, but—"

"Toby—Broderick!" Vespa looked up into the slightly myopic but earnest blue eyes bent above him. "What . . . the deuce are you doing here?"

"Long story, old lad. Tell you after we get you home."

With the aid of his friend's supporting arm, Vespa managed to sit up, and gasped dizzily, "I'm—perfectly fine."

"But of course. You always take a nap in the grass in the middle of nowhere, and babble about leaves and cats. I'll own you look better than the last time I saw you. But a fellow don't fall out of the saddle on level ground for no reason, and that mare of yours is a beauty, but don't seem the flighty kind."

"She's not." Vespa felt his side experimentally. Aside from being winded and a little shaky, he didn't seem to be badly damaged. "Is she all right?"

"Oh, jolly good. All present and correct. As for you, my buck—"

"I didn't fall out of the saddle, Toby."

"Jumped, eh? Rather rash under the circ—"

"Dolt! Lend me a hand, would you?"

At once Broderick's arm was about him. "Upsy-daisy! All right, Jack? What is it now? Did you lose something?"

"A tree," Vespa muttered. "Or rocks, perhaps."

The supporting arm tightened. "You've lost . . . a tree. Yes. Well—er—why not? Certainly, a tree. Any particular breed, *mon capitaine?* There are some nice little silver birches yonder, and I'm sure we can find some rocks. I believe there's a quarry hereabouts if you can ride—"

Vespa said frowningly, "But—there are no rocks just here. And I don't see a fallen tree. Do you?"

"No, I'll—er, have to own I don't. But we can have one knocked down for you, if you so desire, m'dear old pippin. Let's just get you home, and—"

Glancing at him, Vespa saw the anxiety in his eyes and said

122

with a smile, "Think I've gone off the road again, do you? And small wonder. What a reception I've given you!" He was delighted by the arrival of Broderick, whom he judged the very best type of man, in spite of his tendency to act as a walking encyclopaedia. Seizing his hand, he wrung it hard. "My poor fellow, I do apologize. How very good of you to come all this way to see me. You'll stay, of course, though you might be better served at the village inn than at my great ruin."

Broderick clapped him on the back. "Actually, I already left my luggage at your house, if— Where are you going? Your mare's over here."

"Yes, I see she is. I want to find what knocked me out of the saddle."

"Was that the way of it, then!" Broderick strode along beside him. "Are you saying someone meant to put a period to you?"

"I'm saying I was riding at the gallop one minute, and dozing in the grass the next. I thought a tree had come down on me; or a branch, perhaps."

"Did you hear a shot?" Broderick jerked him to a halt and inspected him closely. "Sure you're not hit anywhere, Jack?"

"*Something* hit me! I'd swear it. And it feels as if . . . " He unbuttoned his shirt and peered downward.

"The deuce!" exclaimed Broderick, spreading the shirt wider to reveal a scarlet abrasion across the upper chest. "You rode right into an *emboscada,* old lad! It's marvellous you didn't break your neck! Anyone would think we were back in Spain, by Jove! What's to do here?"

Vespa buttoned his shirt again. "Let's have a look at those pretty little birch trees, Toby. Then I'll tell you all about it."

Their inspection of the trees didn't take long. Holding up the frayed end of a length of fine rope, Broderick's usually mild eyes were stern. "Stretched between the trees, waiting to welcome you. This was attempted murder, Jack!"

"Yes. But I wonder—" Vespa gave an impatient gesture. "Let's get back to the house."

Broderick's mount was a tall and raw-boned bay with a nasty temper. He made it clear that he didn't want to be ridden, but after a tussle Broderick swung into the saddle. He said apologetically that he wouldn't tolerate the brute save that when he went he was such a grand goer. "But never mind about that. Who wants you dead, dear boy?"

"Any number of people hold a grudge, apparently. What worries me is that I may not have been the intended victim. But I'm putting the cart before the horse. Prepare yourself for a tale that makes no sense, and I'll quite understand if when I'm done you return to Town at the gallop!"

They proceeded at a walk, and Vespa gave a brief sketch of the state of affairs. When put into words, the whole business sounded increasingly unlikely to him, and he slanted several embarrassed glances at his friend, half expecting to find him laughing. Broderick's face still held that unfamiliarly stern expression, however. Finishing his account, Vespa said quietly, "So there it is, Toby. At first I thought it as stupid as you likely do now. But I'm bound to admit there is *something* going on in that house, and I mean to find out what it is."

"Ghosts," mused Broderick. "It's an intriguing subject, and has been studied for a long time. It's world-wide, did you know? The Maoris in Australia have a deep-rooted belief in hauntings; the Celtic peoples have their banshees; Germans their poltergeists; and heaven only knows how many allegedly 'haunted' houses litter the British countryside. There's a nunnery in Lincolnshire where some really remarkable manifestations have been pretty well authenticated. And I knew a young sprout at school who had some fascinating theories about mediums and séances. A very bright fellow, and he means to study the subject in depth. You'd best not dismiss it all too lightly, Jack."

"You mean you actually believe that Alabaster Royal is haunted? By a *moggy*?"

"I'll own I ain't heard of that one before, but I do believe 'there are more things in heaven and earth,' and so forth. And I'd be very glad if you'd let me lend a hand in your—er—spot of bother."

"It may be a very sticky wicket, Toby. You saw that. But if you're sure the legends don't worry you. . . . "

"Say rather, they enchant me! I'd be overjoyed to meet one of your phantoms. Could write a jolly good paper on 'em, probably. Besides, to say truth, civilian life was beginning to be a bore. A little adventure is just what I need."

Leaving the vale, they started across the park towards the manor. Vespa said gratefully. "It's dashed good of you. I'm glad you came. Which reminds me—why *are* you here? I thought you were in the way of becoming an Oxford don."

With a rueful shrug, Broderick said, "That all sort of frippered away. Seems they can do without me. For a while, at least."

"They must be mad! In a revolting way, you're brilliant." Vespa laughed at Broderick's indignation. "No, seriously. I never met a man with such a wealth of facts tucked away in his head!"

"One such fact is that I—er—incurred the wrath of my tutor in my misspent undergraduate days. Nothing serious, you know. But he brooded over the silly prank, and it turns out he's now brother-in-law to the Provost." Broderick shrugged his broad shoulders. "So that was that. The esteemed parent was mad as fire and decreed I must find myself a place in the world without his assistance. Couldn't decide what place I wanted, so I thought I'd find a wealthy friend and poach on his preserves whilst deciding what to do. I remembered you speaking of your inheritance, so—here I am."

"Alabaster Royal must have been a great shock," said Vespa, amused. "I wonder you stayed."

"It is a bit of a let-down. But I'd already heard a few things, so it wasn't a complete surprise. And it's interesting, y'know. What really surprised me was . . . forgive if I jump in where angels fear to tread, but—isn't it a trifle, ah, soon, Jack?"

"For you to pay a visit? Not so! I couldn't be more pleased of some company."

"Be dashed! I'd have thought that, under the circumstances, company would be the last thing you'd want. But—in your state of health . . . Well, she's jolly attractive, and what a shape!"

"My impossible block, whatever are you babbling at?"

"Your—ah—*chère amie,* dear boy. She pretended to be a parlour-maid, which was funny, but I'm not easily hornswoggled, y'know."

"Consuela?" Vespa said laughingly, "She's not my *chère amie*! The saints forfend!" Broderick looked at him from the corner of his eye, and he amended hurriedly. "Gad! Where are my manners gone? That was rude and ungrateful. The truth is— Oh, the devil! It's coming on to rain. Let's get back to the house. I didn't tell you everything, Toby. I'll lay the missing pieces before you over a glass of my grandfather's excellent brandy, and that superior brain of yours will be able to solve my small riddle."

9

Thornhill was at the door to receive them. His shocked eyes took note of his employer's creased, grass-stained, and slightly torn coat, and widened with horror as they rested upon the splendid pair of Hoby's boots that he'd sent out that morning with a mirror-like sheen and were now scuffed and even *scratched*! He said tearfully, "Oh . . . sir!"

Vespa, who was feeling a trifle unsteady, forced a smile. "Come now, Thornhill. I'm not above taking an occasional toss. Don't look so funereal."

"Of all *times,* Captain," wailed the valet, wringing his hands and lowering his voice dramatically. "We have—*company!*"

"Never mind about me," began Broderick.

"I don't, sir," interrupted Thornhill.

Vespa's eyebrows went up, but before he could comment a new voice was heard.

"John? So you're back at last!" Elegant, poised, but with an irked expression in his dark eyes, and Corporal frisking about his heels, Sir Kendrick Vespa strolled into the hall, only to check abruptly. "Good Lord! What on earth . . . ?"

"Father!" Jack limped forward and put out his hand. Sir Kendrick scanned it through his quizzing glass. Jack pulled off his muddied glove hurriedly. "Welcome, welcome! How glad I am to see you!"

"I wish I might say the same." Sir Kendrick shook his hand gingerly. "Since I cannot think you have sunk to going about in such an appallingly dishevelled state, I must assume you've been thrown. You are in no condition, my poor boy, to be jauntering about in this wilderness."

Jack reached out to grip Broderick's arm as that craven individual started to slip away. "Your pardon, sir, but I'll tell you about it later. May I now present my friend?" He performed the introductions. Sir Kendrick was much too well-bred to betray a resentment of the visitor's presence, but his manner was so polite that Broderick wilted and muttering a plea to be excused, fled.

"I'm acquainted with his grandfather," murmured Sir Kendrick, watching the retreat critically. "Poor fellow." He bent to stroke the dog and said with a smile, "But this is a jolly little chap. I'm told his name is Corporal. Named him after O'Malley, did you?"

"Yes. And Toby's a very good man, sir. He served in Spain with great gallantry, and has a most extraordinary mind that—"

"What a pity he did not use it to better purpose. His achievements in England are not enviable. One hopes his stay here will be brief."

"That's a hope I cannot share. Toby only just arrived. I'm very glad of his company."

"Yes. I fancy you've not had much in that line. I believe there are several good families in the locality, however. Have any of them called on you? What about the gentleman Mrs. Tidwell spoke of?"

"I haven't been here a full two weeks yet, sir," said Jack evasively. "Will you excuse me while I remove some of this dirt? I presume Thornhill has put you into a suite, and I can promise you an excellent dinner."

"My regrets, but I can't stay long. I'm promised to the Haverleys this evening."

Disappointed, Jack protested, "But I see you so seldom. Can't I persuade you at least to dine with me?"

"I wish you could, my dear boy." Sir Kendrick shrugged ruefully. "Lord Felix is a dull dog at best. But it's a case of business mixed with pleasure, I'm afraid. I fancy you're glad to have your coaches at last. That's a dashed fine team of greys. You did well to buy them from poor McNeese."

Ushering him back into the drawing room, Jack said, "So I thought. Suffield was hot after them. Luckily I got my bid in first, or he'd have snapped 'em up."

"I don't doubt that. Now I've something to tell you." He glanced around the great room and shook his head despondently. "No, really, my boy, you *cannot* stay in this rotting ruin! As for that alleged 'man' of yours—" He checked as Thornhill came in with decanters and glasses. Watching him pour the drinks, Sir Kendrick said, "I've seen you somewhere, haven't I? What was your last situation?"

"With Mr. Thatchett, sir." Handing him a glass, Thornhill expanded, "A most demanding individual, if I dare say so, but taught me a—"

"Thatchett? Thatchett?" Frowning, Sir Kendrick exclaimed, "Egad! You never mean Jasper Merridew Thatchett? The actor fellow?"

"The very same, sir, I'm proud to say."

"Proud! You might better be ashamed! I saw him perform at a bachelor party last year. Disgraceful behaviour! Why he's half a step above a procurer!"

"True, sir." Thornhill placed a hand over his heart and sighed. "I tried to warn him, Sir Kendrick, for he was born a gentleman. I strove mightily to guide his faltering steps, but—" He shrugged with great tragedy. "Alas, after I left his service, poor Mr. Thatchett fell from grace."

"After you left his service, my eye! That's where I saw you! You were the one who tossed that abandoned Turkish dancing bag-gage over your shoulder and carried her off! I wonder the lot of you weren't arrested for lewd conduct. And this fellow is your *but-ler,* John? My heavens! I know you're far from well, but I'd have thought you retained some measure of discrimination. How come you to have been taken in by such a mountebank?"

"I take leave to remark—" began Thornhill, red-faced and in-dignant.

"Just take your leave," snapped Sir Kendrick.

Vespa jerked his head and Thornhill walked to the door, his back a silent exclamation point.

"No, really, Father," said Vespa with a rueful smile. "You must not rake me down in front of my servants, you know."

"Servants! He's not a servant. A rank-rider is more his line of work!"

"Oh, very likely. But at present he serves me well, and I'm lucky to have him. As you warned me, nobody is willing to work here."

"I thought that ruffian who calls himself your steward was the outside of enough, but if you're reduced to allowing the likes of this hedgebird to serve you—"

"Why is Thorny huffing all over my kitchen, Captain?"

Jack groaned inwardly as the duchess swept in, a ladle in one hand, flour on the end of her nose, and her apron flapping about her.

"My cheese soufflé it will sink with the thud if there is rage in the air." She waved her ladle at Sir Kendrick. "Who is this? Another dinner guest? How many more, I ask? If you expecting to eat a meal of decency, you must let me know those things. Why does he stare at me? If your mouth you will close, sir, the Captain may pre-sent you."

Sir Kendrick rose. From the corner of his eye Vespa saw his parent's sagging jaw snap shut. 'As well be hung for a sheep as a lamb,' he thought helplessly. "Sir Kendrick Vespa, ma'am. My father. Sir, this is Lady Francesca Celestina of Ottavio. My—er—housekeeper."

"And the Duchess of Ottavio," she said, extending her hand regally.

Sir Kendrick was too stunned to do anything but kiss it, flour and all.

"What I cannot understand," he said a few minutes later, "is why the poor woman would agree to work for you. And why she doesn't appear to be afraid of the legends surrounding this unhappy old pile."

Jack added to his sins by declaring that the lady had called and upon discovering him to be without a chef had volunteered to help out. "On a temporary basis, of course. And I doubt she pays much heed to legends."

Sir Kendrick stared at him, his eyes still somewhat glazed. "A duchess," he muttered.

"So she says. But, er, well, the lady is Italian, and—"

"Mad as a hatter, very obviously. It appears that you've managed to surround yourself with a collection of oddities." Sir Kendrick took another generous sample of his Cognac and appeared to pull himself together. "Well, don't say I didn't warn you." He scanned his son worriedly. "I can't see that your stay here has done anything to improve your health."

"Actually, I'm feeling much better, sir."

"Are you now! That's good, then. Unless you're just trying to ease my mind. Have you had any—er—supernatural visitors?"

"Oh, I don't believe in such stuff. It's mostly delusion, don't you think?"

"Hmm. It certainly deluded your Grandmama, and your mother—who is very cross with you, by the way. She wants you home, John. Why not humour the lady?"

"Perhaps I will, eventually. But not just yet."

Sir Kendrick shook his head. "Well, I'll tell her I tried. You're a grown man, and must make your own decisions, but— Good Lord! What's that caterwauling?"

Somewhere, Consuela was singing with enthusiasm.

Jack said feebly, "It's the—parlour-maid."

"So *that's* the way of it!" Sir Kendrick brightened. "She let me in. A tasty morsel, and with not the faintest notion of how to behave like a parlour-maid. Never mind trying to hoax me any more, you young scalliwag! I understand these little *affaires,* and if she'll help you forget your infatuation with the Warrington girl, so much the better." He threw up a hand as his son attempted to speak. "No, no! I don't want to hear any involved fabrications, if you please. None of my bread and butter, anyway. But I see why you hired such a rascal for your man! I hope you pay him enough to ensure his discretion."

"Sir, you quite mistake the matter. The lady is—"

"A lady! I knew it! Got you there, m'boy!"

"But, if you'll just—"

"Oh, enough, enough! We've more important matters to discuss. I'm pleased to say that I've some very good news for you, John. The fellow I mentioned in my letter—the looby who's interested in buying this disaster—has again called on Felton and made what appears to be a bona fide offer of a thousand pounds for the place!" He laughed triumphantly. "Can you credit the luck? Since I was coming into the west anyway, I detoured to tell you of it. Felton says he's some sort of scatter-witted philanthropist. Trying to buy himself a place in heaven by building a country orphanage for abandoned London children. If you ask me, he should be committed, but, his folly—your gain, eh? Well? What d'you say to that, my boy?"

Jack twirled the brandy in his glass and stared at it unseeingly. "He hasn't approached me, sir. I'd think he would at least want to see Alabaster before—"

Sir Kendrick's elation faded. He said irritably, "Apparently he sent his man of business down. Gad, but you're a cold fish! Here I rush all this blasted way thinking how pleased you'll be that I bring you a fine offer for this white elephant, and you display not one whit of gratitude or enthusiasm!"

132

Jack flushed. "My apologies if I seem ungrateful. I know how busy you are, and I appreciate your taking the time to negotiate in my behalf. But—well, I don't think of Alabaster as being a white elephant, you see."

Sir Kendrick stared at him, then grinned. "Aha! You've more horse-sense than I give you credit for! Playing a cagey game, are you? Want him to bring the price up. Very good! We'll try it, at least. I've as good as told Felton we'll accept his offer, and frankly I doubt we'll get a better one, but you'd best give me a figure that will satisfy you."

Jack set his glass aside and looked at his father squarely. "I don't wish to sell Alabaster, sir."

The next few minutes were uncomfortable. Unable to comprehend what he considered to be a foolish and unrealistic attitude, Sir Kendrick was alternately bewildered and impatient, and it took all his son's powers of persuasion to keep him from thoroughly losing his temper. When the baronet stood to leave, however, he was restored to good spirits. In a rare display of affection he embraced his son and said that he was becoming an interfering old curmudgeon, and that if Alabaster Royal pleased John, he must certainly not give it up. "I'll own I was distressed to see you still looking so poorly, but you know best what makes you happy." He added with a chuckle, "If you're sprightly enough to have set up a mistress, you *must* be improving! I fancy both the woman and this place will pall soon enough, but— No! I'll say no more. Let me know when you're ready to come back to civilization, my dear boy. I hope it won't be too long. We miss you. I wish I could stay longer, but it's as well I leave you young rascals to your—er, frolics. Don't worry—I won't tell your mother there's a bird of paradise keeping her son in the wilderness!"

It would be useless, Jack realized, to try and convince him of the true state of affairs. Sir Kendrick would only be annoyed and suspect an attempt was being made to dupe him with "involved fabrications". Besides, if he was believed, the truth might prove even less palatable.

He walked out onto the steps with his father, and as they waited for the coach to be driven round, he asked carefully if Sir Kendrick knew of any antique or object of great value that might be in the manor. The answer was scornful and unequivocal. The only thing of value about Alabaster Royal was the land on which it stood, and as soon as John tired of his *chère amie* and of mildew, dry rot, woodworms, rats and whatever else lurked within its chilly walls, he'd be well advised to tear the manor down and realize whatever profit he could then make from the sale of the property. Having said which, Sir Kendrick asked curiously, "Why? Has some local busybody been telling you tales of buried treasure or such fustian?"

"Not tales, sir. But we've had a couple of attempted break-ins, and one determined effort to make off with some of the furniture."

"*This* furniture? You jest, surely? Who the deuce would want it?"

"Sir Larson Gentry. A most obnoxious fellow who claims Grandfather Wansdyke loaned him a desk and he'd come to replace it. Without bothering to ask my permission. I believe he was in fact stealing the desk."

The carriage rumbled to a halt. Sir Kendrick waved a delaying hand to the footman who climbed down to open the door. Staring at his son, he said, "Larson Gentry? Not the fellow who owns Larson Chase? Why it's a showplace! What the deuce would he want with— Tell me what he had to say for himself."

Jack sketched the episode. When he finished, Sir Kendrick gazed at him in silence, saying at length, "I see. And did you report the matter to the Law—or whatever passes for the Law down here?"

"I did, but I have no proof of any wrongdoing. The most I can accuse the fellow of is trespass, whereupon Gentry would affect to be very much the injured party being punished for seeking to make honest restitution. The Constable had insufficient grounds to press charges."

"I can't fault him for that." Sir Kendrick added gently, "It don't make much sense, does it, John? You're, er—quite sure it wasn't—"

"A mental aberration? Quite sure, sir."

"Yes. Well, don't get bristly. I'd forget the business if I were you. Enjoy your lady and your privacy, my dear boy, and live a quiet life. That's the way to get well." Obviously troubled, he attempted to conceal it with a light-hearted recommendation that John keep "a weather eye out for the Alabaster Cat," and with a fond smile and a firm handshake, left him.

Jack waved from the top of the steps as the luxurious coach rumbled down the drive. For a moment longer he stood there, looking rather grim. Clearly, his father was convinced that his mind was playing him tricks. Not only that, but in the other matter Sir Kendrick had jumped to a conclusion that all too many others would reach. It would not do. He went slowly towards the kitchen, rehearsing his ultimatum.

When he delivered it, the duchess put down her rolling pin and regarded him gravely. "You are sudden, Captain."

"Not really, ma'am. I didn't approve of this arrangement from the start, if you recall. Now, my father has gone off with a false impression. My friend has arrived, and I expect other gentlemen. You surely must see that it just will not do for an unwed lady of Quality to—"

"Rubbish," interrupted Consuela, carrying a large tablecloth and a pile of napkins into the kitchen. "You did not object when we worked together this morning. Oh, yes, I heard you demand that we leave your hallowed halls!" She came with her light dancing step to stand in front of him and peer up into his face. "There is mud in your hair, and your coat is torn and stained. So do not be maligning your innocent friend as an excuse to be rid of us. What has happened?"

Vespa gritted his teeth. "Very well, if you must have it. I was set upon by—by some louts, and my horse took fright and threw me."

135

Consuela's lip curled. "Another fib! I've seen you ride, even when you were feeling badly, and Secrets is a polite lady; she'd never—"

"What you believe or disbelieve carries small weight, ma'am. The fact is that I have incurred the enmity of Sir Larson Gentry, Durward Cramer, Lord Alperson and heaven only knows how many other dim-witted local citizens. This is evidently a most violent area, and I've enough to occupy me without being held responsible for the safety of two ladies who would do better to keep to their own home. Besides which—"

"Who asked you to be responsible for us?" demanded Consuela, her cheeks flushed and her eyes stormy. "Grandmama and I are quite able to—"

"The fact that you are under my roof makes me responsible, as you know very well. Besides which, my father heard you singing, and assumed that you—er, I mean—"

"So that's it! He fancies I am your opera dancer! What has that to say to anything, when you know it is not so? Only think, Captain Jack. Grandmama and Manning are here to shield my reputation. We cook and clean for you, and improve rather than harm your silly old house. We are getting closer all the time to the truth. I can *feel* it! Do not chase us off only because you are afraid of your high and mighty Papa!"

"Con-su-ela," said the duchess warningly.

"Yes, yes. I know I have no right to protest our dismissal, Grandmama! But what does he mean to do next? Have us dragged out in chains?" She tossed the linens onto the table and stretched her hands out to Vespa pleadingly. "Ah, forgive! I am naughty, and say things I do not always mean. But—let us stay, I beg you! The answer to my dear father's death lies in this house. I *know* it! And if I am not here, it will all be forgotten and his murderers go unpunished. He was such a gifted and good man. *Please* let me stay and—"

She looked so heart-broken; but hardening his heart, Vespa cut off those imploring words. "I came here in search of peace and

136

quiet, Miss Jones. Not to hunt about for clues to a non-existent murder! With you gone, I may have some small hope—"

"Ooh, but you are a great *stupid*!" Tears of frustration glittering on her long lashes, she cried, "Very well, we will leave! 'Faith, but I can scarce wait to see the—the last of you!" And with a muffled sob and a swirl of petticoats, she was gone.

Vespa muttered, "Phew!"

The duchess pulled out a chair and sat down. "And now if you please, you will tell me. What really happened?"

He crossed the room to glance up and down the corridor, then closed the door. Returning to lean back against the table beside her, he gave a low-voiced account of what had transpired on Consuela's 'short-cut'.

The old lady frowned, pondering, then asked, "Who knew you meant to ride through the vale?"

"You come to the heart of it, ma'am. No one knew. I didn't decide myself until the last minute."

"Still, you might have been watched. A signal could have been given. Perhaps the rope was loosely tied and hidden from sight until the intended victim approached, and only then drawn taut."

He shook his head. "Unlikely, I think. Such methods would indicate a long-planned scheme. Despite what I said to Consuela about having made enemies, I've only been here a short time and pose no real threat to anyone. I have no wish to alarm you, but—"

"But you think my granddaughter was the intended victim and that you rode into a trap meant for her?"

"I think it the most likely explanation, yes."

"Then you must also believe that Preston really was murdered." A hand trembled to her throat. Paling, she faltered, "Oh, St. Peter, St. Peter! Do you thinking those evil men really come here in the night to put an end to the dear child?"

"My lady, I honestly don't know. But combining that attack with the ambush today makes me wonder if your granddaughter may indeed be suspected of knowing something, or having seen something she was not meant to see. It may have nothing to do with the death of your son-in-law. I may be jumping to the wrong conclusion entirely. Whatever the case may be, this is no place for her. It is too isolated, and her tendency to wander about alone is dangerous. I do urge you, ma'am, to take her home and keep her away from Alabaster Royal. For her own sake. Have you some reliable menservants about the place?"

"My coachman and gardener are faithful and have been with us for years."

"Then I'd suggest you warn them, and never allow Consuela to go about unescorted. And for heaven's sake lock your doors at night!"

"This we will do. And my husband he have intact me how to fire the pistola. Never look so worried, Captain. We're not weak and helpless by any of the means. We know how to defend ourselves, this I promise you."

"Good. But I want you to promise also that if you have ever a cause for alarm, or suspicion, you will send for me at once."

She smiled at him and patted his hand. "You are very good, considering the trouble we have causing you. Thank you. I will take her home at once. Also, I will of a certainty be consulting my patron saint."

"Who is, I gather, St. Peter? Or have you others, perhaps?"

"No! Never! He is the best for me. Not, I remark you, that I have anything against the rest. Matthew and Mark are very fine, I feel surely. And Luke must be a lovely saint, though he was a physician, which is unfortunate. But, Peter, he is—well," she leant closer and dug Vespa in the ribs, saying mischievously, "he is just a little bit like me, you know? He tries. But he makes mistakes. So he will better sympathize with my small dilemmas, I think. Now you must try not to be judging of my Consuela too harshly. She is fiery—her Papa was right to call her his meadowlark—one minute calm and contented, and the next, poof! soaring into the skies. But she has the goodly heart, Captain Jack. She will be guided by me."

138

Lady Francesca smiled and did not voice her qualifying thought: 'In most things!'

With some qualifying thoughts of his own, Vespa left her and went slowly up the stairs.

———

A fire brightened the hearth of the small dining room (which Broderick described as "vast"). From the mulligatawny soup through the salmon served with cauliflower and a potato soufflé, the sliced sausage, raised mutton pie and a light as a feather lemon *gateau,* the food was excellent and the wines superb. Thornhill waited at table with smooth expertise, and at length breathed a suggestion into Vespa's ear that since there were no ladies present, the gentlemen might wish to retire to the drawing room with their port.

The ladies were very much absent. There was not the faintest echo of a feminine voice. Soon after the two men had settled themselves before the drawing-room hearth, Vespa heard some activity outside, followed by the sounds of a departing carriage. Lady Francesca, her intrepid granddaughter and their nervous maid were, he deduced, returning to their own home. Lady Francesca would surely keep a watchful eye on Consuela now, especially after dark, so that she'd not be prowling about where she had no business—

" . . . bother myself, when you haven't heard a word I said," complained Broderick.

Vespa started. "Oh, your pardon, Toby! 'Fraid I was wool-gathering. May I freshen your glass?"

"Thought you'd never ask. Thank you. As I remarked—when I was talking to m'self just now—your sire missed a jolly fine dinner. Has the duchess really gone?"

"Yes. And taken my"—Vespa smiled faintly—"my 'bird of paradise' with her."

Broderick set down his glass and took up the short clay pipe and tobacco humidor that Thornhill had put on the table beside him. "I've been very patient, old lad, but this would seem a propitious moment for the rest of the story you promised me."

He was a good listener and made only occasional startled exclamations while Vespa related Consuela's part in the events of the past few days. At the finish, he was silent.

Watching him, Vespa asked, "Well? What does the great brain make of it all?"

"Nothing profound, Jack. Only, it seems that far from finding peace and quiet, you've stepped into an assortment of unpleasantnesses. If some rascal is determined to scare you off, he could possibly have installed a resident 'ghost' in this great rambling place."

"Perhaps, though I'd like to know how any trouble-maker could create the sounds of leaves rushing about, when there's no wind nor any leaves in sight. Or cause the temperature in a room to go from chilly to positively arctic within a minute. Or—"

Broderick interrupted with a grin, "Thought you didn't believe in ghosts."

"I don't. But . . . there's something decidedly odd about this house, I'll have to admit. Even so, what could it have to do with the other business?"

"The 'other business' being that you were knocked off the road on your way here; the signpost was deliberately concealed; this Gentry fellow and his bosom-bow have been looting your house; some aristocratic old duck who's properly dicked in the nob blames you for his granddaughter's death; two murderous louts broke into your cellars; and today you damn near broke your neck thanks to an involuntary dismount. And you're half-way convinced that the luscious Miss Jones' life is threatened as well."

"Of course her life is threatened! Those two thieves came near to strangling the poor girl, and this afternoon's ambush was set up on a route nobody could have known I meant to follow. It was intended for Consuela. And she would certainly have been killed!"

"Am I wrong in thinking that you have no especial, ah—interest—in the lady?"

Marietta Warrington's beautiful face came into Vespa's mind. His so missed and so yearned for love. More than a year since last he'd seen her. By this time she was very likely betrothed to some other lucky fellow. He suffered a wrenching pang, and thought, 'I mustn't do this. I mustn't keep grieving for Etta and for Sherry. That was another part of my life. It's done.'

Broderick saw the long hands clench, then Vespa said, "Whether or not I have a special interest in Consuela, you may be damned sure I would mind very much indeed if *anyone* was harmed on my land!"

"Yes, of course you would. I didn't mean— Well, never mind that. What about the business of the coaching accident and the signpost? You surely must see that it all ties together?"

"I didn't think so at first. Cramer is the type of boor who finds it jolly good fun to hurt people."

"Charming. But you believe that the lovely Miss Jones stands in danger of being murdered by some unknown conspirators for reasons equally unknown?"

"It sounds unlikely, I know, but . . . Have a look at this, Toby."

Broderick took the sketch Vespa handed him. "I say! This is a jolly fine piece of work. Preston Jones, isn't it? Why ever did you fold it, you uncouth Philistine?"

"I'm no expert on art, but—"

"Small doubt of that! What a *beauty*! Only look at the subtlety of her expression. Jones was truly a master. I've seen several of his works, have you?"

"Very few, but what I—"

His eyes glowing with enthusiasm, Broderick swept on. "D'you know, this puts me in mind of—what was it, now? A sketch. By . . . Hans Holbein, that's it! Only of a man, not a lady. And the Holbein was done in silverpoint, of course."

"Really. Well—"

"Oh, yes. In early days most sketches were made with the brush—they were in the Orient, at least, till fairly recently. Well,

141

recently in the grand scheme of things. I suppose it changed to an extent beginning with the Renaissance when pens came into use."

"Yes, but Jones used pencil, and—"

"Not just pencil, dear boy. One of Monsieur Conte's graphite pencils, I suspect. Only see the firm lines of the jaw and the throat on this side, as opposed to—"

Running out of patience, Vespa groaned, "Toby, will you please stop educating me?"

"Oh, egad! Popping off again, am I? Boring you to tears? Sorry, dear boy. Say on."

Vespa reached across to cuff his shoulder. "Wretch. You're not a bore, and I'm being a surly clod, I know."

"But I'm droning on about trifles when you wanted to ask my opinion of something. I *will* do it, no matter how hard I try. Used to drive poor Manderville to drink, he said. And off I go again! I shall be dumb, mine host. The sketch, was it? Do you wonder if it has any value? Well, in my opinion—" He stopped as Vespa gave a shout of laughter; then with a rueful grin he reiterated, "Dumb!" and put a hand over his lips.

Chuckling, Vespa said, "Only while I offer my probably foolish theory, if you please. Then I shall beg you to become vocal again."

Still holding his mouth, Broderick nodded.

"You're obviously impressed by this sketch," said Vespa. "But according to Miss Consuela, her father very likely completed it in no more than a few minutes. I find that incredible, but the lady insists Mr. Jones did it all the time. She said he had only to get a glimpse of somebody and he could put their likeness on paper, even if there'd been a significant lapse of time between the sighting, as you might say, and the sketch."

Broderick lowered his hand and looked slightly puzzled. "Well, it's a gift, dear boy. A remarkable one, I grant you. But some people can draw or paint, others can write music, or manipulate gigantic sums on 'Change, or— Whoops! That's not your question?"

"My question is, if anyone with the slightest knowledge of

this lady chanced to see the sketch, they would surely recognize her—no?"

"Aha. You mean, did old Jones fripper about with features—did he make dull people look interesting and ugly folk beautiful, or—Whoops, again!"

Vespa sighed in exasperation. "I *mean,* suppose Jones chanced to see someone, perhaps where he or she had no business being?"

"Like—an international secret agent, an émigré spy for Bonaparte, for example? In this country illegally?"

"Something of the sort. And suppose he were to make a sketch of such a person and they learned of its existence. . . . "

"They'd move heaven and earth to come at it! I say, Jack! Old Nosey knew what he was about when he made you a Staff Officer! You've a head on your shoulders! But, surely, they weren't looking for this particular sketch? This is a lady, dear boy. And do you fancy your other newly made enemies—Gentry, and Cramer, and old Alperson—to be spies also? Gets a trifle boggy, don't it?"

"All right, perhaps they're not spies. But *someone's* after something in this house. Suppose that same someone is involved in hanky-panky and doesn't want it to be known he's in the neighborhood, but suspects Preston Jones had made a sketch of him? He could be fairly certain that Consuela saw it. From what I can tell, she worked with her father and it was their custom to discuss the subjects of his sketches and paintings."

His eyes very round, Broderick muttered, "Then she would have to be—silenced."

"As her sire was silenced. And this house searched until the sketch was found and destroyed. Gentry was thwarted when he tried to search Alabaster because Strickley was usually hanging about. Then I came here, so they decided simply to take the furniture from a room they knew Preston Jones had used, but I interrupted them after they'd only filched one desk."

"Unless they brought the desk downstairs to make it look as if they were returning it, while Gentry nipped up there and ransacked away."

"That's possible."

"You searched the desk, of course?"

"Practically took it apart. Couldn't find a thing, but Consuela found that sketch in the room the desk was taken from. What do you say, Toby? Am I being ridiculous?"

"No, by George! I think it makes a deal of sense. Only—if they're after Preston Jones' sketches, wouldn't they search *his* home rather than yours?"

"I asked Consuela if they'd ever had burglars. Her answer was an emphatic no, but then she admitted that they never lock the doors, so it's very possible the Jones house has already been searched. You may be sure I told Lady Francesca to see their doors are locked from now on!"

"Very good. What do you mean to do now? Will the lady be safe at her own house?"

"Safer than prowling the grounds of Alabaster Royal at night, certainly. But I've a mind to get Strickley to hire some reliable ex-soldier to act as guard out there."

"Good idea." Taking up the sketch again, Broderick said thoughtfully, "I wonder if the lady is in the slightest connected with all this. I'd not care to cross swords with her."

"What? Never say you recognize her?"

"No. But you have only to look at her. Actually, I've a pretty fair memory for faces. Take your man, for instance. I've seen *him* before, somewhere."

Vespa sighed. "So had my father—to my embarrassment." He stifled a yawn. "I must tell you the story of Thornhill's alleged background."

"Not tonight," said Broderick. "If you're not tired, I am! You can tell me about your pseudo-valet at breakfast."

"You'll have to suffer my cooking for that, Toby. I am, alas, *sans* chef. Unless we breakfast at the Gallery Arms."

Broderick said solemnly, "Sunday, old boy."

"Jupiter, so it is! I'm bound to put in an appearance in the family pew, and I promised to participate in a cricket practice later. You don't have to come, though."

Broderick was offended. His family had invariably attended Church on Sunday, he declared, whether in Town or the country. He would most certainly accompany Vespa. Always provided, he added with a grin, that he survived breakfast.

10

It was his wedding day, and as he stood at the altar in all the glory of his Regimentals, Marietta came up the aisle to him, her loveliness enhanced by white silk and net, her adoration for him shining in her beautiful eyes. It was, he thought, a trifle odd that she would carry a cat instead of a bouquet; she could surely have managed to at least also hold a Bible . . . But a man did not criticize his beloved on his wedding day. And it was, of course, an extremely large cat. A handsome creature, with distinctive markings of white, orange and black, and enormous yellow eyes that stared at him unblinkingly.

Marietta reached his side and stood there, smiling and dear and adorable. The church, which was crowded, was very quiet. Everyone, he supposed, was waiting for Sir Lionel Warrington to arrive and give his daughter away. The priest, his head bowed low and long hair concealing his face, demanded, "Who giveth this woman . . . ?" It was a troubling question, because it seemed that there was no one to answer. But then the cat yowled piercingly, "I do . . . *not!*"

Suddenly, the aisle was filled with army officers, marching forward, their familiar and once friendly faces grim and condemning. At their head, Lord Wellington, astride Copenhagen, snarled, "Imposter! You are not the rightful heir!" His sabre whipped up. *"Charge!"*

They were all coming at him then, sabres flashing, boots thundering on the floor of the church. Seizing Marietta's hand, he turned to run, but the priest sprang in front of him. It was Lord Alperson, his face contorted with triumph. "She's not for you!" he shouted. "You are accursed, John Vespa! Accursed!"

"That's a lie!" he cried. "Don't listen to him, my love!"

But Marietta recoiled from him in horror, burst into tears, and fled, the cat bounding after her.

Drenched in perspiration, his heart pounding, Vespa sprang up. Corporal was huddled shiveringly against him, and the sounds of a woman's sobs were augmented by a crash outside his door. Her weeping, he was very sure, had brought about his nightmare. "Confound the watering-pot," he snarled, and made a dash for the door. The corridor was very dark and familiarly freezing. It seemed to him that he caught a whisper as of a woman's skirts, from the stairs. "Hey! A word with you, ma'am," he shouted, and leapt in pursuit, only to fall headlong over something on the floor that had no business being there. Swearing, he hauled himself up, then gave a gasp as a moan sounded from the obstruction. He bent closer. "Good heavens! Toby?"

"Help!" croaked Broderick, floundering about feebly. "Didn't— didn't m-mean it! *Help!*"

Lamplight was bobbing towards them. Thornhill called, "Are you all right, Captain?"

"Yes. But Lieutenant Broderick seems to have fallen. Lend a hand here, please."

When they had settled Broderick into a chair in his parlour, it became very obvious that he needed more than a hand; but after a few gulps of brandy, a trace of colour came back into his pallid cheeks and his shuddering was less convulsive.

147

"What happened?" asked Vespa.

"D-didn't real-realize," said Broderick through chattering teeth. "Oh, God! Oh help! I didn't m-mean it! Should never've g-got out of b-bed!"

"My poor fellow." Vespa patted his shoulder. "You must have had a bad dream. You're all right now."

Broderick clutched at his hand and gulped, "Don't—don't l-leave me!"

"We won't leave you. I'm here, and Thornhill's here. What was it that you didn't mean?"

Thornhill threw a blanket over Broderick's knees and murmured, "I think he must have seen the lady, sir."

Vespa looked at him sharply.

"Didn't s-see her in time," moaned Broderick. "Thought—thought she'd gone past so—so I went into the corridor, just—just to peep, and— Oh, Lord! I w-walked right—right *through* her!"

"Carrying research a little far, weren't you?" said Vespa with a grin. "I'm sure you apologized."

Broderick gave him a reproachful look. "Well, I d-did, of course, but . . . Oh, Jupiter! She was polite, but—"

"The lady *spoke* to you?"

"She—she said it w-was all right, but to p-please be more careful in—in future! Egad! I *knew* I should n-never have come here!"

Vespa said blandly, "But only think, now you'll be able to write a learned paper on the subject. Or do you mean to leave us? No, seriously, old fellow, I wouldn't blame you."

"I'll have to—think about it," said Broderick faintly.

When Thornhill appeared with hot chocolate next morning, he answered his employer's question by saying that Lieutenant Broderick was already awake and appeared to be in good spirits. With a fugitive twinkle he murmured, "It's the sunlight, sir. Lifts the—ah, spirits, if you'll excuse the expression." Vespa gave him a level look, and he went on quickly, "I shall do my best with breakfast. Will nine o'clock in the smaller parlour suit?"

It suited, although the eggs were overcooked and the ham

burned. Broderick appeared his usual cheerful self, and Vespa tactfully refrained from mentioning the night's activities. The two young men decided to make their own toast, which turned out to be a riotous pursuit, Corporal joining the hilarity when they both lost slices from the toasting forks and had to "fish", as Broderick put it, among the flames of the breakfast parlour fire. The charred toast, they decided, went "very nicely" with the rest of the meal, and Broderick denied emphatically that he meant to abandon his friend at Alabaster Royal. "Despite the midnight visitation."

The ice having been broken, they discussed that visitation during the drive to Gallery-on-Tang. Vespa had left orders for Strickley to have his curricle at the door by ten o'clock. The dashing open carriage had been polished till it shone, and the greys were fresh and eager to go. Corporal wanted to go, too, but had to be told firmly that dogs did not attend church services. The day was bright, the deep blue of the sky accentuated by occasional billowing white clouds, and an invigorating breeze carried the smells of late summer: warm earth and growing things.

In response to Vespa's question, Broderick said blithely that he hadn't really expected to be disturbed by the apparitions rumoured to haunt the manor. "But, do you know, Jack, now that I look back on it, I think it was just the shock of my first such experience. Actually, it was fascinating. I hope, though, that I'm not destined to meet your famous Alabaster Cat!"

Vespa waved his whip in salute to Farmer Nimms and his wife as he passed their slow-moving dog-cart. "So you know about that legend, do you?" he said.

"Not much. Just that the cat rather hangs over the heads of the Wansdykes—a sort of Cat of Damocles. Would it distress you to tell me of it?"

"It might distress my powers of recollection. My Grandmama was very impressed by the tale, but to be honest, Sherry and I thought her ghost stories hilarious, and I've never had much patience with such beliefs." He frowned thoughtfully. "Let me see, now . . . As I recall, the legend started with some thirteenth-century Wansdykes, who were then poor tenant-farmers. Their daughter was a beauty, and she caught the eye of the Duke who ruled the area at that time. She was shy, and wanted no part of him. He wasn't interested in what she wanted, and he attacked the farm. Her father and brothers were killed during the fighting. The only thing she had left was her pet cat, and when she begged for its life—well, you can guess what the ignoble Duke's terms were."

"Good Lord! What a bounder!" exclaimed Broderick.

"Yes. If those were the 'good old days' I think I'd want no part of 'em. At all events, the poor girl evidently planned to avenge her loved ones, but she was clever enough to bide her time. One night when her captor was more drunk than usual, she locked their bedroom door and set fire to the room."

"I don't blame her a bit, poor girl! Was it this same house, Jack? Alabaster, I mean?"

"No. The first part of the present manor was built about a hundred years later. But it stands on the site of the original farmhouse."

"Did the girl burn with the rapacious Duke?"

"As the tale goes, the servants could hear him screaming for help, and the girl's crazed laughter. When they managed to break in, the cat ran out, unharmed. The Duke's corpse was there, but no trace of the girl was ever found. It began to be whispered that the escaping cat was huge—as big as a good-sized dog, whereas before it had been a small creature. Soon, just about everybody believed that the girl had taken on the form of the cat."

"And the moggy now haunts Alabaster?"

"That's what the legend says. But this particular apparition needn't worry you, Toby. It affects only Wansdykes."

"Affects? Do you mean it is a threat to you?"

"Not directly. A harbinger, you might say—if you believed in it. So long as the cat is quiet and remains invisible, all is well. If it purrs, all is not so well. But if the animal is ever seen—" Vespa paused, uneasily reminded that on his first night at the manor he'd heard a cat purring.

Broderick said, "Death and destruction, and everyone run for the hills?"

"Something like that."

They had turned onto the village street, and Vespa guided the team neatly past a group of people who were walking towards the church dressed in their Sunday best.

"Gad," remarked Broderick, "to judge from the way they looked at you, they were expecting you to arrive in your phaeton with Thornhill suitably liveried on the box."

"He'd carry it off all right," said Vespa, amused.

"Do you mean to keep him? Rather a questionable character, ain't he? Not that I dislike the fellow, mind. But he's taken the Bard too much to heart, I suspect."

Vespa chuckled. " 'All the world's a stage'?"

" 'And all the men and women merely players.' Yes, by Jove! My thought exactly. Only he never leaves the stage, so how is one to know what he's really like? Or, more to the point, what, if any, moral values he possesses?"

"True. But I have to admit his impudence amuses me. I like the way he looks me right in the eye. I can usually trust my first impressions, Toby. And I believe that somewhere in the lusty melodrama he wove me is a vestige of truth."

Broderick said with a smile, "I see now what O'Malley meant. He used to say you could always find the good in a man."

"There was plenty in him, God rest him! And I think there's good in Thornhill. You have to admit that he knows his trade. Perhaps I'll rue it, but despite all his airs and graces I think the fellow really wants honest work. At all events, so far he's the only man willing to come out to Alabaster, which leaves me little choice. Jupiter! Look at all the people who've arrived early!"

He halted the curricle and a boy came running to lead the team to the livery stables.

Quite a number of parishioners had already gathered outside the Parish Church of St. Paul. Vespa wondered if Preston Jones had ever painted the scene. Certainly it made a charming picture;

151

the ancient grey walls of the turreted stone church providing a serene background for the delicate colours of the ladies' gowns and ruffled bonnets, and male attire that ranged all the way from Broderick's magnificently tailored coat to the humble but immaculate smocks of farmhands.

Their arrival created a stir of excitement. Having introduced his friend to the priest and several of the local people, Vespa honoured the shy Broderick's mumbled plea to be spared more embarrassment, and prepared to enter the sanctuary. Perversely, his friend suddenly halted and muttered an awed, "By . . . Jove!"

Vespa turned and came face to face with Sir Larson Gentry, his sister on his arm and Durward Cramer's coarse and scowling countenance behind them.

"Good morning, Captain," said Miss Ariadne shyly.

His bow polite but perfunctory, Vespa attempted to walk on, only to receive a hard jab in the ribs from an insistent elbow. Broderick's ardent gaze was fixed on the beauty, and there could be no doubt but that her own big blue eyes held a matching admiration.

Irritated, Vespa urged his friend forward, but Broderick was an immovable object except for the elbow that again made his desires known.

Gritting his teeth, Vespa performed curt introductions, pointedly ignoring Cramer.

Broderick bowed.

Miss Gentry blushed and lowered her lashes as she curtsied.

Gentry said laughingly, "What, are we blessed with another military man in the district? How do, Lieutenant. Don't believe everything your friend says of us."

Broderick scarcely heard him, but gazed, trance-like, at the fair Miss Gentry.

Vespa clamped an iron grip on his arm and dragged him along by force. "We're holding everyone back, Toby," he said between his teeth. "Do move, there's a good chap."

"I wasn't introduced to the dashing soldier-boy," complained Cramer audibly. "I am hurt, Larson. Positively slighted!"

"Never fear," said Gentry. "You'll likely meet the Lieutenant when he acts for Vespa in your little dispute."

Cramer gave an exaggerated whimper. "I ain't even challenged yet, Larson!"

The strident tones of the duchess rang out: "And if you had a vestige of good breeding within your veins, Larson Gentry, you would know better than to speak such things in God's house. Be so good as to move yourself!"

Vespa pushed Broderick into the family pew at the front of the sanctuary, and glanced back. Several people were grinning broadly. Gentry, flushed and thunderous, had stepped aside, allowing Lady Francesca and Consuela to settle themselves into a pew. Gentry stamped on, but his attempt to sit directly behind Vespa was thwarted when the constable's large lady surged into the other end of the pew and all but ran across its length to plant herself firmly in the aisle seat. Her husband and the Widow Davis followed, and Gentry and his party were obliged to seat themselves across the aisle, behind Lady Francesca and Consuela.

When Vespa took his seat after a silent and respectful word with the Almighty, Broderick whispered, "If ever I saw such a little Fair! You must show me where they live, Jack. By thunder, but I'm glad I came!"

The service began then. The morning sunlight set the rich hues of the ancient stained-glass windows ablaze; the voices of the six choirboys were pure; the familiar old hymns pleasing. A music-lover, Vespa sang out heartily, vaguely aware that Broderick was staring at him. Mr. Castle's sermon was earnest but over-long. Vespa's attention wandered. From the corner of his eye he could just glimpse Consuela. Her gown was a creamy pink, embroidered in white silks, and a white zephyr shawl was draped across her shoulders. The bonnet's high poke concealed her features, but she turned her head suddenly and looked at him squarely. There was no shy blush on her vivid face; no demurely lowered lashes. Her eyes were bright with mischief.

She smiled at him in so frank and challenging a way that he

could not keep from returning the smile before he restored his attention to the priest. The final hymn was "A Mighty Fortress Is Our God." It had been Sherry's favourite. Vespa tried to join the singing, but nostalgia choked him after the first few lines and he stared down at the page silently.

Outside again, the little crowd milled about, chattering happily. The Reverend Mr. Castle introduced Vespa to several local landowners and he received some hearty but vague invitations to "take his mutton" with them whenever he chose. He replied courteously, well aware that each of them had violated the laws of polite society by having failed to call or at least leave cards at Alabaster Royal. That they were also aware of the breach of manners was made apparent by their evasive eyes, and the haste with which they moved on to greet less disturbing acquaintances.

Taken aback by such conduct, Broderick asked, "Whatever have you done, dear boy, to have been reduced from Non-Pareil to pariah in so short a time?"

Vespa grinned. "I think you confuse me with Paige Manderville."

"I might have had I named you a Dandy. And don't evade, Jack. I'm agog to hear the lurid details of the foul sins you've committed in this sylvan spot."

"I've inherited a haunted manor, you dolt, and they're all afraid I might invite them to dinner. Ah, here comes my favourite housekeeper."

Lady Francesca was regal in dove grey, her bonnet topped by three outsize silver feathers that had already become entangled in a parasol and were now caught in a trailing tree branch. She had been favourably impressed when Lieutenant Broderick had presented himself at Alabaster Royal, and was further impressed when he undertook to release her from the embarrassment of her feathers. This struggle amused them both, and they were soon giggling together like a pair of old friends. Nearby, Consuela was chatting with two pretty young damsels. Their bright eyes flirted

154

with Vespa over her shoulder, and it was clear that they desired an introduction, but she ignored him. He had started towards them when someone tugged at his cane.

The lame child looked up at him solemnly, then withdrew the arm she'd kept hidden behind her and held up three wilting daisies, a dandelion and a blown rose, all lashed together with many winds of thick string.

Vespa bent to her. "How charming. For me, mistress?"

She gazed at him with her big wistful eyes and thrust the bouquet at him again. He took it, but before he could thank her she was hurrying away at an awkward limping run, her small figure fast disappearing into the crowd.

Mrs. Blackham boomed, "I think ye've made a conquest, Captain Vespa."

From somewhere close by a man laughed. "Like to like!"

Vespa turned angrily, but high-crowned beaver hats, tossing feathers and poked bonnets obscured his view and he couldn't see who had spoken.

Moments later he did see Toby making his way to the side of Ariadne Gentry. The girl was exquisite in a cream and blue printed gown, the blue feathers that curled over the poke of her bonnet emphasizing the azure eyes she turned shyly to Broderick. Before he reached her, however, Durward Cramer pushed rudely between them. The Reverend Mr. Castle moved quickly to engage Broderick in conversation. Seething, as Sir Larson Gentry led his sister away, Broderick curbed his temper and answered the clergyman's questions.

Vespa came up with them. One glance confirmed his friend's frustration, but Broderick could never resist a debate, and he and the Reverend Mr. Castle were soon deep in a discussion that swept from the humble design of the little Church of St. Paul to the aisleless early parish churches, the splendid barrel vaults of the third church of the abbey of Cluny, Romanesque architecture, Gothic vaulting and flying buttresses, in all of which Broderick was well versed. His observations eventually reduced the priest to a state of wide-eyed awe, but Vespa had by then slipped away to the side of the duchess.

He had brought with him the sketch Consuela had found at Alabaster and took it from his pocket. It was, agreed the duchess, the work of her late son-in-law, but she did not know the lady depicted. "And how could one forget such a face?"

Consuela left the Widow Davis and rejoined her grandmother. With a glance at Vespa's wilting bouquet, she said archly, "If you desire to be alone while the gentleman courts you, ma'am, I'll go away."

"Minx!" exclaimed Lady Francesca. "The blooms are not for me, and well you know it!"

"Really . . . ? If you favour another lady, Captain, you would do well to improve upon that rather sorry collection."

He said coolly, "Do you find it sorry, Miss Jones? I do not. It was given to me, and I value it highly."

Off balance, she glanced at her grandmother, who said, "Little Molly Hawes."

"Ah, the poor mite," said Consuela in a very different voice. "You had best put your bouquet in water at once, Captain. It is very warm today."

Lady Francesca was going to the inn to give Mrs. Ditchfield a promised recipe, and volunteered to see that the flowers were provided with a vase.

Watching her walk off on the arm of an elderly gentleman, Consuela said in a low voice, "I understand that we were banished because you feared for my safety, sir. That is kind, but foolish. You will not stop me, you know. Though it take the rest of my days, I will find out who put so cruel and needless a period to my Papa's brilliant life."

In his heart, Vespa thought this an admirable and loyal sentiment, but such a task should be undertaken by a gentleman's son, not by his young and reckless daughter. He said dampingly, "Whereupon he will doubtless put a period to your own life."

"Aha! Then you believe such a villain exists! You do not still think Papa's death was accidental!" All but dancing in her excitement, she demanded, "Say it! Say it!"

Trying to look stern, he said, "What I will say, ma'am, is that your antics in a churchyard are attracting attention. These people expect you to set an example, you know."

She gave a guilty look round and hid behind her parasol, but riposted with defiance, "Can I help it if the Italian side of me is spirited and alive, not dull and—and starchy as a stuffed owl?"

"If I catch you spiriting about on my property again, the Signorina will be most unceremoniously returned to Lady Francesca's care! I've had my fill of trespassers, and so I warn you!"

She frowned at him ferociously, then gave a sudden giggle. "Do you really think so? In that house one can never tell who may—as it were—pop up, next."

"As you did when you made off with my eggs and capered about the passages squealing in the middle of the night!"

"I did no such thing. What next will you say! We did borrow a few eggs, but as for capering and squealing—I *never* caper! You must have confused me with one of your other—ladies!"

"What other ladies?"

"Come now, Captain. We are not completely cut off from the world down here. Rumours get about. Your name has been linked with—several ladies."

"And I suppose you kept a list!"

"There weren't so many that I would not recollect. Let me see, now. . . . There was Euphemia Buchanan, and Lisette Van Lindsay. . . . Sarah Leith, and Marietta Warrington . . . to name just a few. Oh—and a *very* dashing young widow, whose name escapes me."

Half laughing, half vexed, he exclaimed, "If you aren't the outside of enough, Miss Jones! Of course I know those ladies. Fortunately for lonely bachelors, London is full of such charming creatures. But as for my name having been *linked* with any one of them— Well, one, perhaps, but in a perfectly honourable way." He shut out Marietta's smile, and added, "But Sally Leith was scarce out of the schoolroom when I knew her. And if the very dashing widow you refer to is Mrs. Esmeralda Stokely, she was betrothed—or as good as—to my brother! Furthermore, Miss Jones—"

"Consuela," called the duchess, returning, "I no sooner turn my back than you are teasing poor Captain Vespa. She is naughty, dear boy. Do not regard it. Now, we must leave, Consuela, for we are to take luncheon with Lady Gouderville and you know she becomes so fussed if we are late. I fear we shall miss your cricketing, dear Captain. Look how Watts springs his horses! My stars, but we will reach the Goudervilles in time for tea at that rate!"

Vespa chuckled as four very fat horses pulled a large carriage at a leisurely pace along the lane.

Lady Francesca flourished her parasol and startled the remnants of the congregation by screeching, "Wake up, Watts! You're half-way back to yesterday!"

The elderly coachman whipped up his horses, and they ambled to halt outside the church gate.

Vespa assisted the duchess into the coach and turned to Consuela. As he reached for her hand, he heard a faint crack like a tree branch snapping. The reticule hanging from Consuela's wrist jerked crazily. The horses reared with screaming neighs of terror and the coach plunged forward. The open door flew at them, and Vespa whipped the girl aside in the nick of time.

Consuela screamed, "Grandmama!" but the coachman already had his team under control and the footman ran to soothe the scared horses.

Broderick and several other agitated people hurried up, passing Vespa, who snatched the reins from a stable-boy's hand and was mounted and sending his commandeered mount across the green at the gallop before the boy could protest, "That's Mr. Kestler's horse!"

Straight for the quarry hill, he rode. He had heard snipers too often among the Spanish hills not to recognize a rifle shot. He was too enraged to pay heed to the fact that his flying leap into the saddle had wrenched his injured leg. He was aware only that someone had come damnably close to murdering Consuela. If it was humanly possible, he meant to catch the miserable bastard. He had a fair estimation of the site from which the shot had been fired, and crouched low over the pommel as he sent the frightened mare thundering up the hill to a little spinney where trees and shrubs clustered. To ride in amongst them without a weapon would be unwise, and he had certainly not brought a weapon to Church. Too angry to consider the risk, he sent the mare plunging into the spinney. Scant minutes had passed since the shot was fired; two, at most. If the coward was anywhere near—

There came a clattering of pebbles; a wild scrambling from higher up the hill. Reining the mare around, Vespa spurred her to another effort, and they charged from the trees. The marksman had taken time to reload. Vespa saw a flash; sunlight on a rifle. He flung himself sideways, and the bullet whipped through his hair with a buzz like an angry hornet. Not giving his adversary time to reload again, he galloped the mare up the hill. At the brink, he could look down into the quarry. A closed chaise waited on the road. A man in dark clothing, his hat pulled low and a rifle in one hand, was sprinting towards it at reckless speed. The descent was too steep and too littered with rocks for a horse to follow. Running like a scared rabbit, the man reached the chaise. The door was flung wide, he sprang inside, and the team was away.

"Damn!" said Vespa. He stayed to soothe his borrowed mare and apologize for her rough handling before turning her down the hill and into the teeth of the storm that awaited him.

Mr. Kestler was the local apothecary. A dour individual at best, he was incoherent with rage. Constable Blackham was astonished, and nobody, it developed, had heard a shot. With many an uneasy glance at Vespa, who was known to have come home from the war with head wounds, several people declared that one of Lady Francesca's lazy hacks had been stung by a bee; nothing more sinister than Nature's handiwork. Mrs. Davis had even heard the bee buzz. The duchess had been shaken, and since the captain

159

had evidently, ah, mistaken the matter and gone riding off on a wild goose chase, Lieutenant Broderick had escorted the ladies back to the Jones cottage. Trying to keep his temper, Vespa managed to calm the indignant apothecary and was restraining himself from strangling Constable Blackham when Broderick came into the little gaol building.

He threw a quick look at his friend's face, and noting the thin tight line of the mouth and the flash in the hazel eyes, cut through the constable's argument to ask, "You all right, Captain?"

"Evidently not," snapped Vespa. "The bulk of the population appears to believe that I'm short of a sheet! Don't say you didn't hear the shot, Toby?"

"I did. But just barely, and I can understand why no one else did. They were all too busy jabbering. Because you've ears like a hawk, Jack, you can't suppose others to be so endowed."

"With all due respect, Lieutenant," said the constable, keeping a wary eye on Vespa. "You didn't say naught when we all opined 'twere a bee. Nor you didn't go chasing off—like the Captain done."

"Of course he didn't, you idiot," raged Vespa. "He had sense enough not to frighten the duchess any further, poor lady."

To be addressed as an idiot soothed the good constable's nerves. It was the way of the Quality. Lord Alperson seldom called him anything else. And looby though he may be, this poor young gentleman was Quality, no denying. "Perhaps," he ventured, "the Captain seen the sniper? If he could identify him, the Law would take action, never doubt that."

"Oh, I saw him, all right," said Vespa. "He fired his first shot from that spinney over there. I'd wager a hundred pounds he was using a Baker. When I reached the spinney, he was atop the hill and fired again. I suppose nobody heard that either?"

"Well now, don't go into the boughs again, sir," soothed the constable. "Just tell me if you recognized the villain."

"I didn't. He saw to that. He was wearing dark clothing, a hat well pulled down over his eyes, and a black chaise was waiting for him on the other side of the hill on my quarry road."

The constable shook his head, wondered bodingly what England was coming to when a madman would fire a rifle into a churchyard, and declared he would "take a couple of men and get up there and search that spinney, this very minute!"

"And ten minutes too late," said Vespa disgustedly, when he and Broderick were seated at the window table in the Gallery Arms. "I wish to heaven everyone wouldn't assume I'm wits to let only because . . . Do I generally behave in an alarming fashion, Toby?"

"Only when you sing, dear boy."

"What d'you mean by that? I love to sing."

"I know. Shouldn't. Dreadful. Sorry, but there you are."

"Of all the— My Grandmama delighted to hear me sing in Church! She said the Lord loved to hear a cheerful noise."

"Must've been tone-deaf, poor lady."

Vespa laughed. "It's possible. But never mind my vocal shortcomings. Did you happen to see Gentry or the unappetizing Cramer lurking about after Church?"

"Come to think on it, I didn't."

"Neither did I. So far as I could judge, the pair of 'em vanished directly the service ended."

"And would have had ample time to reach your spinney, eh?"

"Just so. Much chance I have of proving it!" He frowned. "If Consuela hadn't chanced to move . . . I tried to warn her but she's obstinate and irrepressible."

"And high-couraged."

"Too much so for her own good. I pray she won't come to regret it."

"Shall you go ahead with the cricket match?"

"D'you think the children still trust me despite my melodramatic charge after a 'bee'?"

They evidently did, for all the hopeful players, most of the village population, several dogs, and one large and adventurous goose were soon gathered on the green. Longing to play, Vespa elected to be an umpire, with the proprietor of the Gallery Arms, Mr. Ditchfield, serving as second umpire. Broderick, a skilled batsman, offered an awed young audience a lengthy description of the points of law to be observed in the game. "Although," he said in a murmured aside to Vespa, "I doubt we'll see anything resembling the rules of the Marylebone Cricket Club today."

"They'll get a start, at least, provided we can dredge up two elevens."

They had found nineteen boys for their teams and were almost ready to admit three older youths to make up the elevens when their problem was solved by the arrival of two farm waggons in which four likely youngsters, ranging in age from five to nine, begged for acceptance. This created a new dilemma that Vespa solved by telling a rather frail lad that they needed someone with a quick brain to be score-keeper. The tearful seven-year-old, sure he would be dropped, was jubilant and the game began.

As games go, it was a disaster, but it was the kind of disaster that is thoroughly enjoyed by all. The spectators, expecting (and getting) a very amateurish children's game, were indulgent and good-humoured and soon entered into the spirit of the occasion, choosing up sides and cheering on the efforts of the youthful players whether 'their own' team or not, in the best traditions of sportsmanship. With occasional gleams of promise, the play was for the most part clumsy and erratic. Despite Broderick's earnest instructions and Vespa's demonstrations, overly eager batsmen made wild swipes at balls that came nowhere near them. One small boy swung at a low ball with such mighty determination that he spun around three times, his bat sending wicket and bails flying and the wicket-keeper leaping for his life.

In a later over, it being by that time mid-afternoon and very warm, the batsman's hands had become so sweaty that when he plunged forward to meet the ball, the bat flew out of his grasp; Vespa, who chanced to be nearest, had to make a desperate dive to catch it before it hurtled into the squealing and scattering crowd.

Soon afterwards, a very well hit ball enabled the batsmen to complete a run. The fielders galloped madly in pursuit of the ball; so did an energetic spaniel. Amid the excited cheers of the spectators a second run could have been completed had not the batsmen collided head-on in the centre of the pitch. Simultaneously, the spaniel captured and made off with the ball, hotly pursued by all the fielders and the dogs. Spaniel and ball vanished into the distance. Indignant and outmanoeuvred, both teams gathered around the umpires, all shouting at once. The onlookers, Vespa and Broderick were convulsed, and the cricketers, at first resentful, were won to laughter when Vespa reminded them it was a game—to be enjoyed, which everyone had certainly done this afternoon. Wiping tears from his eyes, Broderick declared both batsmen out, thereby ending the game.

Vespa was well pleased, but he was paying a price for his athletics. His leg throbbed so viciously that he was obliged to move away and lean heavily on his cane. Watching the happy boys and trying not to reveal his discomfort, he was reminded of the Richmond team and the hard-fought games he and Sherry had revelled in during their school holidays.

A hand gripped his. The little crippled girl looked up at him. "Don't you never be sad," she said.

He lied smilingly, "I'm not sad, Mistress Molly."

"You say that, but your eyes says different. You're not like me. You'll get better and you'll play better'n everyone, wait and see."

Touched, he said, "We'll get better together, shall we?"

"I wish—" She sighed. "No. It's no use dreaming. I isn't going to get better. Never."

"It's always worth dreaming, Miss Molly. Doctors are finding out new things every day."

"That's what Pa says. But we can't 'ford doctors, and anyways, I knows. And I don't mind so much. I be used to it now. Just . . . if they'd let me be friends." Suddenly, her big eyes were tearful. "If they just wouldn't make—make fun of me. You know?"

He touched her bright hair, and knowing how cruel children could be, said gently, "I know. Will you have this old crock for a friend, my dear?"

Her hand tightened on his. She said eagerly, "Oh, yes." The brightness died from her face again. In a troubled way she muttered, "But I best not tell Pa. He says you're rich folk. He wouldn't like it."

"I'll come and see him, would that be all right?"

Before she could answer, a mellow voice said laughingly, "Another conquest, Jack? 'Faith, but you're a regular magnet to the ladies!"

Mrs. Esmeralda Stokely, a vision in cream and green, was holding out a daintily mittened hand. One of London's most beautiful young widows, she had adored Sherry, who, in his erratic fashion, had returned her affection. Their eventual marriage had been taken for granted. Bright and witty, the widow had not wanted for admirers after his death, but there could be no doubt that she had mourned him deeply, and she had sent a very kind letter to Jack in Spain that had meant a great deal to him.

Pleased to see an old friend, he bowed over her hand and demanded to know what she was doing in this rural backwater.

"Why, I came to see you, of course," she said coquettishly, tucking her hand in his arm. "How well you look! I'd heard you had one foot in the grave, and here I find you officiating at a cricket match! Nothing keeps you down for long, does it, my dear friend?"

"Thank you for that, Esme. Jove, but I'm glad to see you! Do you stay in the neighbourhood? Would you like to have a look at Alabaster? May I beg to take you to dinner? I want to know all that you've been doing, and—"

She laughed. "Mercy! My country home is just north of Salisbury, have you forgot? I have dinner plans tonight, and must leave at once, I'm afraid. Ah, but I disappoint you! I am so sorry. I know! Do you go to the Flower Show on Wednesday? I have my prize roses entered. Perhaps we could meet there and have a really nice chat about old times. And—new times, no? Ah, here is my footman. I must go, Jack! Till Wednesday, then—*au revoir.*"

She was gone, leaving behind a breath of the sweet scent she wore, and the memory of the fondness in her fine green eyes.

He thought belatedly of little Molly Hawes, but when he glanced about there was no sign of her.

11

A light wind came up during the night and by morning the sky was cloudy and the temperature had dropped. Undaunted by the weather, Broderick was eager to look over the property, and Vespa was only too willing to take him on a tour of the estate. They rode out shortly after breakfast. When they dismounted at the quarry site an hour later, the smell of rain was on the air and the wind was blowing in fitful gusts.

Broderick tethered his mount and started towards the pit. "Is this where Miss Consuela's sire met his end?"

"A little farther to the west, I think. Beyond the steps where the rope is tied across—" Vespa paused. The rope was no longer tied across the break in the railing and the gate at the top of the steps was wide open. "What the devil . . . ?" he muttered, limping to investigate.

Corporal caught up with them, tongue lolling, and started to report to Vespa, but then wandered to a nearby clump of shrubs. Glancing after the dog, Broderick called, "I think you have company, old boy. Jolly neat little hack tied over there. Side-saddle."

Vespa had no doubt as to whom the "jolly neat little hack" belonged. His suspicions were soon confirmed. Far below, Consuela hoisted the skirts of her riding habit so as to climb over a pile of rubble by the tunnel entrance.

"She's a spirited chit," said Broderick admiringly. "That's no easy path for a lady."

Vespa's only response was a series of French and Spanish oaths. He started down, but Broderick pulled him back.

"Do try not to be so silly. I'm aware you were—are—a dashed fine climber, but just at the moment you've only one reliable hoof. I'll go. No, Jack! If you mean to persist, I'll deck you, I swear it!"

His usually mild countenance was stern, and one fist was clenched and ready. It was just like Toby to be loyal enough to knock him down. Vespa swallowed his pride and watched in fuming anxiety as his friend scrambled down the steep and crumbling steps. "Hey!" he shouted.

Consuela spun around and stared up at him, obviously dismayed.

"If Toby falls," called Vespa furiously, "it'll be your fault, Miss Bird-wit! Get up here at once!"

What she did was to back away and hold up her hand warningly as Broderick approached. There was a brief and obviously acrimonious discussion, then Broderick grasped her wrist and growled something, and although she wrenched free, she marched to the steps. Broderick followed, ready to catch her if she stumbled.

She reached the top with a swirl of wind-driven skirts, and one glance at Vespa silenced the angry words she'd prepared to utter.

"Are you gone quite out of your senses?" he raged, taking her by the shoulders and shaking her hard. "I *told* you not to come here again! Bad enough you must be so pig-headed as to defy me, but to risk your life by going down those steps was the height of folly!"

Incensed, she fought and struggled, jerking out demands that he remove his "filthy hands" from her person and promising to shoot him dead. A sharp kick from her riding boot sent him staggering, and on the instant her little pistol was in her hand. There were dirty streaks down her face, her eyes were narrowed and glittering with rage, and with her hair windblown and her skirts muddied she looked wild and eager to pull the trigger.

Vespa said unsteadily, "You won't shoot anyone dead if someone murders you first. As you deserve!"

"And you are afraid that if I should be slain on your precious property—as was my dear Papa—you will be blamed! Much you—" She stopped with a squeal as Broderick, who had crept up behind her, reached around and snatched the pistol from her grasp.

"Oh, but that is unfair!" she cried, rounding on him. "Two great rough men against one girl! Besides, I would not really have shot him!"

Broderick said gravely, "I can't know that, Miss Consuela. Anyone who would kick a fellow who just had fifteen pieces of steel cut out of him is capable of anything."

Her gaze shot to Vespa. His face was unreadable, but he was pale and there were beads of perspiration at his temples.

To the horror of both men, she sank to her knees, bowing her face into her hands and weeping so despairingly that they rushed to console her.

"It's all right, it's all right," said Vespa, trying to lift her. "Please don't cry."

"I am a . . . horrid, wicked . . . girl!" she sobbed. "Again, I have h-hurt you! You're right. I d-deserve to be—to be murdered!"

"No, no! I didn't mean that. Really. I'm perfectly fine. You didn't hurt me. Much."

"Look. Here is your pistol." Broderick pressed the weapon into her grubby hand and, in desperation, offered, "You can shoot me, if you like."

She smiled quiveringly, and allowed herself to be guided to a nearby cluster of rocks. Broderick used his handkerchief to dust off a suitable boulder, Consuela sat down, and Vespa dabbed his own handkerchief at her tear-stained cheeks.

She murmured her thanks, and said with a despondent sigh, "What have I become? Oh, *what* have I become?"

"More to the point, Miss Consuela," said Broderick, "what were you about down there?"

"I remembered something." She looked up at Vespa earnestly. "I told you that Papa made many sketches and paintings of Alabaster Royal."

"Yes. You said he enjoyed to paint the old place."

"He did." She took his handkerchief and blew her nose. "Some were of the manor. But there were others. Several of the little bridge, and a very nice picture of that poor child Molly Hawes picking flowers not far from here. And there were a few of the quarry. I never liked those because this place is so stark and ugly. And I think Papa didn't like them, either. They weren't up to the standard of his other works, and one wasn't right at all."

"In what way?" asked Vespa.

She said frowningly, "I don't recollect exactly. It just looked— odd, somehow. Perhaps the canvas was damaged. After Papa— after he died, the owner of the gallery said his works were now much more valuable." She scowled, and added through her teeth, "It was a beastly thing to say!"

"Clumsy, I grant you," said Broderick. "But the fellow was right, you know. Down through the centuries the work of any artist has been much more highly priced after his death. Just think of poor old Raphael, for instance. He did a painting called *St. George and the Dragon,* and I believe he was paid at most forty guineas for it. Today, it would sell for fifty times that amount. Then there's the great canvas by—"

"Yes. Thank you, Toby," inserted Vespa hastily. "I don't quite see, Consuela, what all this has to do with your venturing down into the quarry."

She opened her eyes at him as though he were very dull-witted.

"Why, because we couldn't find it, of course! We've sold some of Papa's paintings—those I could bear to part with. So I decided to let Signor da Lentino at the Salisbury gallery see what he could get for the ugly one of the quarry. Only—it wasn't there."

"You said your father didn't much like it," Vespa pointed out. "Perhaps he painted over it."

"No. I saw it soon after the funeral. And I stuck it at the back, behind the others, because I wanted only to look at the best. Grandmama and I searched and searched, but it has disappeared."

"Any others gone, ma'am?" asked Broderick.

"Yes. The portrait of Molly Hawes. I hadn't finished cataloguing them all, of course. It had gone out of my mind until last evening when I was thinking about the sketch we found in the manor. And I thought that if I came and looked at the quarry again, I might remember what was wrong with that one odd painting." She searched Vespa's face. "It *might* be important—no?"

He nodded. "It might, indeed. But not so important as to risk your life for. What I would like to do, if I may, is come and visit you, and see the paintings you still own."

She agreed to this, and accepted meekly when Broderick volunteered to escort her home.

All the way back to the manor Vespa pondered the business of the missing paintings. He was still deep in thought when he went into the house and struggled up the stairs. It was probably a simple case of the canvasses having been mislaid. Or perhaps they had been shipped to the gallery at a time when Consuela was too lost in grief to remember events clearly. Such things happened. After Sherry was killed he had seemed to lose touch with many details of daily life, as though even in the heat of battle he'd been too numb to be fully aware of what went on around him. He could find nothing that might connect Preston Jones' paintings of a little girl and an old abandoned quarry with the artist's untimely death. Even less to lend weight to Consuela's conviction that her Papa had been brutally murdered. The Salisbury gallery would be worth a

170

visit, though, if only to see more of Mr. Jones' works—especially if there were any views of the manor. It would be rather nice to own such a painting, provided he could find one he really liked, and if the price was not beyond his means.

It came to him that, aside from the occasional clamourings of the wind, the house seemed even more hushed than usual; almost as if it were holding its breath. He shrugged away such a whimsical notion. Naturally, it was quiet. Thornhill had gone to Salisbury to collect a new coat from his tailor. Strickley was in the barn tending to Secrets, and Corporal, worn out from his long run, had curled up in a favourite spot in the kitchen and gone to sleep.

Captain John Wansdyke Vespa was quite alone in his manor.

The deepening sense that he was *not* alone was as foolish as it was disconcerting.

He turned into the upstairs corridor and started towards his suite. Within seconds, soft footsteps were following. He jerked around, his hand dropping to the pistol in his pocket. The corridor stretched out, silent, yet quivering with almost-heard sounds; empty, yet not empty. Perhaps he was to meet the weeping woman, as Toby had done. Perhaps his optimistic belief that he was getting better was unfounded, and this was another manifestation of a condition that was worsening. He thrust that dread from his mind and walked on, trying to blot out the sounds. They were different now; odd rustlings, a whispering as of subdued voices, and the continuing padding footsteps. He wouldn't look back. There was nothing to see. But the rustling became the voices of leaves again, hurried by the wind across a stone floor. The air whirled about him, icy and paralyzing. He clenched his hand hard on his cane, closed his eyes and took a deep breath, fighting an illogical but near overwhelming terror. The wind was very strong today, it wasn't so surprising that—

Something clamped onto his shoulder. His heart bounced into his mouth. His blood seemed frozen, and with an involuntary shout he spun around, the pistol flashing into his hand.

"Se rendre! Se rendre!" The tall and elegant young man behind him made a rapid backward leap and waved a jewelled quizzing glass agitatedly. "A fine way to receive a guest!"

Vespa stared in astonishment at a lean face framed by thickly waving auburn hair and enhanced by high cheekbones, a classic, well-cut nose above a shapely mouth and firm chin, and a pair of green eyes just now full of indignation. "Paige Manderville!" he gasped. "You crazy gudgeon! You damn near gave me a heart seizure, creeping up on me like that!"

"I wanted to surprise you. Though I needn't have crept with the wind making such a commotion. Why is this passage so beastly cold?" The quizzing glass was levelled at Vespa and a magnified eye scanned him critically.

He said eagerly, "You heard it, then?"

"I'm not deaf, dear boy. You're white as a sheet! If you mean to die, I'm off!"

"No, I don't mean to die, you unnatural clod! What a thing to say! Actually, I go along pretty well." Vespa restored the pistol to his pocket and reached out. As they exchanged a firm handshake he said, "What a magnificent coat! Weston, I suppose."

Manderville smoothed an exquisitely cut sleeve of forest green superfine, and said casually, "No. A new man, actually. Set himself up in Clapham."

"Not Balleroy? Gad, to think I patronize the same tailor as the mighty Beau Manderville! Now come along to my room and while I get out of these boots you can tell me what the deuce you're doing here."

"Leaving." Manderville adjusted his pace to Vespa's as they proceeded along the corridor. "I came expecting a luxurious mansion—not a ghost-ridden ruin. You disappoint me, Jack. Really, you do."

Quite aware of the grin that belied the words, Vespa opened the door to his suite. "You don't believe in ghosts, surely?"

"Don't I?" Manderville inspected a chair carefully before lowering his immaculate person into it. "I hadn't thought I did. Now—

I'm not so sure. Where are your servants? I didn't see a sign of life except for your groom. Odd sort of fellow, ain't he?"

"He's my steward. And groom. And general factotum. I'll tell you all about it after I put a glass in your hand. Jupiter, but Toby will be glad to see you!"

"Broderick? *Here?* Now I *know* I'm leaving!"

It was late afternoon before Broderick returned. Following an enticing aroma to the kitchen, he found Vespa seated at the table, Corporal under his chair, and both watching someone shrouded with sheets who labored at the stove. "By Jove!" he exclaimed happily. "Have we found a chef, Jack? I brought—" Momentarily, words failed him and he clutched at Vespa's shoulder for support. "*Manderville?* Mayfair's debonair darling . . . in a *kitchen?* No! It can't be!"

"You're right," said Manderville blandly.

"B-but—well, what on earth are you doing here?"

"Leaving."

"Hopefully, not before he finishes our dinner," said Vespa, and added with a wink, "He can cook, Toby!"

"He—*can?*"

Manderville turned, looking stern and waving a wooden spoon in one hand. "I do not cook, sir! I *create!*"

"It's jolly decent of him," said Vespa, laughing at Broderick's goggle-eyed stupefaction. "Especially since Alabaster Royal has been a great affront to his sensibilities."

Manderville bowed and slanted a glance at Broderick. "You have some comment, surely?"

"I am . . . " gasped Broderick, "speechless!"

Exultant, Manderville exclaimed, "By George! In that case, I'll be able to overnight! You may tell your alleged valet to prepare me a room, Jack."

Suspecting the motive behind the condescending air, Vespa said, "That's good of you, Paige, but I won't hold you to it. You'd likely be more comfortable at the Gallery Arms. And even if you did stay here, we wouldn't expect you to work for your keep."

Manderville stirred the contents of the fragrant pan carefully, put down the spoon and turned to Broderick. "You had to be here! And you've told him, of course."

"He knows Oxford didn't roll out the red carpet for me, and that I've invited myself to his hospitality, if that's what you mean."

"You and your runaway tongue! Now I suppose you're waiting for me to bare my soul."

"Sorry to disappoint, m'dear fellow, but I really haven't the remotest interest in your soul—naked or fully clad! All I'm waiting for is whatever you've got in that pan."

With a resigned sigh Manderville folded his arms and met Vespa's eyes levelly. "Truth is, I'm properly in the basket, *mon capitaine*. I came here to foist myself off on you. Toby knows, else I'd have bluffed it through."

Broderick said indignantly, "Now dash it all, Paige, you know blasted well I wouldn't rat on a friend!"

"And you both should know me better than to talk of foisting, or ratting," said Vespa. "Next you'll be thinking I require a formal application from prospective guests. Still, I'm very sorry about your hard luck, Paige. I thought your future and your fortune were secure."

"So did I. But my father's man of business contrived—to his own good. By the time we realized what he was about, he'd absconded with the bulk of Papa's bonds. There's enough left to keep the family going, but—" He shrugged resignedly.

"Gad! What a rotten show. And—all your lovely prospective brides?"

"Found better prospects. Natural enough."

Reminded of his lovely Marietta and his own shattered hopes, Vespa nodded sympathetically.

"So I started making the rounds of my friends." Manderville turned to his pan again and said a low-voiced, "But they were all so dashed—kind. Couldn't bear it. Everywhere I went in Town—Hell! I decided to get away, and then I remembered you and your windfall, and came here."

"Only to find my windfall was a rotten apple," said Vespa.

Manderville whipped around, his handsome countenance flushed. "No, truly, Jack. I didn't mean—Deuce take it, I came to sponge off you! I hope I'm not so crude as to really look a gift horse in the mouth!"

Vespa threw back his head and laughed. "So I am become a gift horse! And the only people who'll deign to visit me are two impoverished rascals!" Manderville and Broderick exchanged uneasy looks, and he went on with a grin, "You can't know how glad I am to have you here—whatever the reason. And you shall both earn your keep by helping me solve the riddle of Alabaster Royal!"

Long after they had enjoyed Manderville's chicken fricassée and adjourned to Vespa's newly cleaned book room, they were still discussing that riddle. Broderick said in a hushed tone that he acknowledged that such things as wraiths and spectres were abroad in the world. Manderville admitted that his introduction to the manor had been unsettling, but he inclined to the belief that some living intruder lurked about Alabaster and had been paid to frighten people away.

"But—why?" asked Vespa. "The house is half-way decayed; some of the furnishings are not so bad, but—"

"Good enough for your friend Gentry to try to liberate," put in Broderick.

Manderville argued, "But we are talking about attempted murder. With all due respect, on that score I have to agree with Jack. The estate is isolated and a long way from Town. The quarry is no longer producing, and the house itself—well, its reputation alone renders it practically un-saleable and not sufficiently valuable to justify one murder, if Miss Jones is to be believed, and two, if Jack's life is also threatened."

Broderick threw up his hands. "Then if they ain't after the furniture or the estate, what the deuce *are* they after? You don't pop about running coaches off the road, strangling young ladies, rigging up murderous ambushes, and indulging in churchyard target practice for no reason."

175

Vespa said thoughtfully, "Perhaps there's more than one plot."

Manderville nodded. "From what Toby says, you've certainly got more than one enemy."

"Jack's thinking of Miss Jones," said Broderick, yawning. "He's convinced her father really was murdered here, and that it is connected somehow to all this monkey business. Am I right, old chap?"

"What you are is half asleep," said Vespa. "I mean to ride over and see Preston Jones' paintings in the morning. Perhaps we'll know more then."

To an extent, his optimism was justified. Broderick declined to accompany him next day, saying he wanted to "poke about" the first floor and see if he could unearth something of real value. Manderville rode with Vespa. The Jones cottage was large, thatched, whitewashed, and set in pleasant grounds. Manderville found it delightful. He also found Consuela delightful, which caused her to regard him with distrust, whereupon he at once transferred his considerable charm to Lady Francesca. If she was not deceived, she was amused, told him he was a "charming rascal", and led the way to a spacious studio at the rear of the house where Mr. Jones' works were stored.

Vespa had expected to be impressed, but as he discovered scenes of the village, the Church of St. Paul, the old inn, children playing around the pond, several canvasses depicting various local folk and their cottages, he was awed by the talent of the artist and his inspection became less a search than an appreciation.

"If you mean to admire each canvas for half an hour, we'll be here for several days," drawled Manderville, bored.

"And if you had an eye for art, sir, you would be as enthralled as the Captain," riposted Consuela.

"I have, instead, an eye for a beautiful woman." Manderville offered his arm to the duchess. "May I beg that you grant me the pleasure of a stroll in your gardens, ma'am?"

"But you waste your time in this flirting with an old lady," she advised him.

176

"How so, ma'am, when there are no old ladies present to flirt with?"

Laughing, she said he had a glib tongue, took his arm and went happily off with him.

Consuela scowled after them. "A fine rake you have for a friend, Captain Jack."

"Mmm," he said absently. "How splendid these are. Your father painted Gallery at all seasons, I see."

"And Alabaster Royal also." She walked to another stack of canvasses. "I put those over here. I thought you'd like to see them all together. Captain . . . Ah! Have you found something?" She ran back to his side and scanned the painting he was staring at with such an intent expression. It showed the village green in springtime. A pig was roasting on a spit over an open fire-pit, children were dancing and weaving colourful ribbons around the Maypole, and to one side the twisted little figure of Molly Hawes watched them with ineffable sadness.

"Poor child," murmured Consuela. "You have taken quite a liking to her, no?"

"Yes. These people at the tables, are they all villagers?"

"Most, I think." She leant closer. "I cannot identify everyone. Sometimes, on special feast days, there are visitors, you know. Relations from nearby villages, or even from outside the county, who come and join the celebrations."

"What about this fellow?" He pointed to a tall, dark-haired individual who was part of a group gathered around a cask of ale. Most of the men appeared to be enjoying a convivial tankard together, but the tall man had turned away and was gazing off to the east.

Consuela shook her head dubiously. "I cannot recognize him with his back turned. Why?"

"He doesn't seem to be part of that group."

"He's holding a tankard, like the rest. Why do you think he's not part of them? Because he's looking away? Perhaps something caught his attention."

"I suppose your father would leave to the viewer's imagination what it was that had distracted the man in the picture."

"He might. Only look at how many thousands and thousands of people wonder why the Mona Lisa smiles so mysteriously."

He grinned. "Very true, and I'm making mountains out of mole-hills, no doubt. All right, let's have a look at the Alabaster paintings."

She led him proudly to the canvasses, and watched, pleased by his delight as he scanned views of the manor at twilight; bathed in the sunshine of a summer's afternoon; clothed with white in a wintry landscape; stark and sinister under a cloud-streaked moon with trees whipped by wind and a faint greenish glow emanating from a first-floor window.

Consuela left him, saying she would order some refreshments. Engrossed, he scarcely heard her as he looked through the rest of the paintings. There was a charming view of the manor on a bright day in springtime, as it might have looked in its prime. A richly caparisoned war-horse was tethered at the entrance. Fruit trees were gay with blossoms, the yews neatly trimmed, the lawns lush and green, and bluebells, daffodils and tulips splashed their rich hues along the drivepath and beside the stream. He was inspecting three landscapes of the area around the quarry when Manderville, who had sauntered back into the room, said with a laugh, "By Jove! Now these are really worth a look, Jack!"

He had found several canvasses stacked in a far corner. They were all nudes, apparently of the same lady in different poses: one reclining on a sofa, another in a window-seat, the third curled up in a deep chair and the last lying on her side on a purple rug in front of a hearth, the firelight glowing on the rich curves of hip and waist and breast, and awaking a warm shine on the cloud of dark hair that hung past her shoulders.

"*What* a cuddlesome chit," said Manderville. "But he should have shown us her face, and in this one I really think he might have dispensed with that zephyr scarf."

"Ooh!" exclaimed Consuela, hurrying to join them. "I had set those aside!"

"Why?" Manderville took up the fireside portrait. "They're jolly fine. I wouldn't mind owning this myself. The lady has a beautiful body. What d'you say, Jack?"

"I'm no authority, but I'd say his technique was magnificent."

Manderville grinned broadly.

"And if you could afford one of Papa's works," said Consuela, "which would you choose, Captain?"

He hesitated. "Why, it would be a difficult choice, but—I'd dearly love to own the one of Alabaster as it would have looked long ago. I wonder if—"

"It is not for sale," she interrupted, glowering at him. "And if you are quite finished with criticizing my father's work—"

"I wasn't criticizing. They're magnificent!"

"Especially the one of your precious ruin."

"Well—yes, but—"

"I cannot be wasting my time like this. Good-day to you, gentlemen!"

Disappointed, he protested, "But you said you were ordering some refreshments."

"We have none, sad to tell. So nice of you to have paid us a call. And you may wipe that smirk from your face, Lieutenant Paige Manderville, for it does but verify all the naughty things I have heard of you!"

Walking out to the horses, Vespa shook his head. "I'm sorry she took you in dislike, Paige. Truly, that girl has the most shrewish nature I've ever encountered. I suppose she was annoyed because she thought I was criticizing her father, which I certainly hadn't intended."

Manderville chuckled. "Lord preserve me from such single-minded devotion!"

Stiffening, Vespa said icily, "Perhaps you'd care to tell me what you mean by that remark."

"Don't cut up rough, Jack. You're a bright lad, all things considered, but where women are concerned you see only Marietta Warring—"

"Damn your eyes! My feelings for Miss Warrington have nothing to do with you—or Consuela Jones!"

Manderville threw up a protecting arm and implored, "Don't strike me! But they have everything to do with it, you blind dolt. You were scorning her! Miss Jones was the nude model, and instead of admiring her truly voluptuous shape, you admired the old boy's *technique*! Lord love us!"

Vespa stared at him, then mounted up, his anger subsiding. "What stuff! As if an unwed lady of breeding would pose in that fashion. You know perfectly well that Jones would have hired a professional model."

"Why should he, when his own daughter is so well—er, endowed? And where's the harm? His little meadowlark wasn't the first lady to pose *à la naturelle,* and she won't be the last, I'll warrant. Gad, what a shape!"

Amused, Vespa said warningly, "I shouldn't tell her that if I were you. She'd probably shoot you dead!"

12

Josiah Hawes was a giant of a man, well over six feet tall and massively built, with an untidy mop of brown hair, a thickly curling beard and hot brown eyes that glittered from under tangled bushy brows. Standing on the worn step, he made the cottage look too small to hold him as he blocked the doorway and glared belligerently at the snuff bottle in Vespa's hand. "Never did hold wi' folks like us mixin' wi' folks like you lot." His beard thrust outward as he pushed the bottle away. "Nor us don't want no charity! Not from Wansdykes or Vespas nor no one else o' your breed!"

For the child's sake Vespa kept his temper in check. "How can you call this poor gift charity? It's only something I found at the manor and that has probably gone unused for decades. Molly likes flowers and I thought she'd enjoy to—"

"D'ye think I can't give me lass a better thing than that there tin pot? If she wants a—a pot, she'll have a pot, and none o' your castoffs!"

Persevering, Vespa said, "It's enamel, not tin. I'll admit she's a very kind little girl and deserves better, but I thought the painting rather pretty, and—"

"Oh, it *is* pretty!" Molly squeezed past her father and reached for the snuff bottle. "Is it fer me, Cap'n Jack?"

Hawes shouted, "No, it ain't! And you keep away from him!"

The child looked frightened, and drew back.

Vespa said gently, "I brought it to show your father, Molly, and to talk to him because I know how he must love you, and want the best for—"

"She don't need you tellin' her I loves her! Now you get on your way, Sir Vespa or whatever ye calls yourself! Take that ugly pot and leave us be!"

"No! Oh, Pa, *please!*" Tears came into Molly's eyes and she pleaded, "Cap'n Jack's house is so old and ugly, not nice and cozy like ourn. And he's sad there. P'raps he *needs* to sell a few things! How much you want fer it, Cap'n?"

"*Sell* it?" Hawes' bellow of laughter rattled the windows. "He don't wanta—"

"A groat," said Vespa promptly.

Hawes' laugh was cut off. He stared at Vespa, his eyes narrowing. "Now see here—"

"I got it," shrieked Molly, wriggling with excitement. "I *got* a groat saved from Christmas, Pa. You said as I could buy summat wi' it. You *promised,* Pa! I could put it by me bed, and stick some flowers in it, and—oh, it'd be so *pretty, Pa!*"

Without shifting his gaze from Vespa, the big man growled, "Never mind your groat. Fetch me purse, Moll. It's in me grey coat."

Squealing with joy, she was gone in a flash.

Hawes stepped very close to Vespa and said with soft but deadly menace, "Now you jest say straight out, me fine fancy gent—what d'ye want with my little gal? Why're ye slipping round her wi' your fancy talk and fancy ways? If I was to think—for one minute—"

Vespa met that enraged glare steadily. "Then you would have a very ugly mind, Mr. Hawes. Molly took pity on me because she knows what it's like to be crippled, and—"

Hawes gave a snarl and as much of his face as was visible grew near purple. The great hands clenched and started to lift.

Startled, Vespa thought, 'Jove, but he's an ugly customer!' but he said in the same cool tone, "She has the type of gentleness that is very rare, and a heart that is quick to sense pain in others and want to help. Now *she* needs help, and—"

"Not from the likes o' you, she don't!"

Unable to restrain his irritation, Vespa said, "Be proud for yourself, if you must, man, but—think of the child. I know of a fine surgeon. He might not be able to help her, but he was able to help me, and if you'd allow—"

"Help *you*? I seen you walk. Ye're nigh as crippled as what—"

"Here 'tis, Pa! Oh, is ye sure? Can we 'ford—"

Hawes rummaged about in the worn purse his daughter offered, thrust a groat at Vespa, and snatched the vase. "There. Now run along, Moll. Find some flowers for yourself, lass."

In a transport of joy, the child took the vase and held it as though it were the greatest treasure in the realm. "Ooh, *thank* you, Pa!" She tugged at his breeches until he bent and a smacking kiss was planted on his beard.

"Thank *you,* Cap'n Jack!" She beamed up at Vespa, and when he smiled, but didn't lower his cheek for his own kiss, she whispered, "I *knows* as it's reely worth much more'n a groat!"

Starry-eyed, she went off with her treasure in search of flowers.

Watching that painful progress, Vespa was suddenly wrenched around. A hand of iron clamped on his wrist; a hate-filled countenance was thrust within inches of his own.

Josiah Hawes rumbled, "I be a poor man, and I knows as ye could have me transported jest for holdin' ye—like this."

His grip tightened. Vespa knew beyond doubting that with little effort Hawes could crush his wrist. He asked jerkily, "Why the devil do you—so dislike me?"

"I hates all rich folks! Every last one o' the thievin' worthless scum! It was one o' yourn what crippled my gal and—and killed her Ma. Don't pretend as ye didn't know! Comin' round here wi' your smiles and posh ways and yer fancy bleedin' pots. Feelin' guilty, be ye, *Captain*? Well, it's too late. You so much as look at my Moll again, and I'll tear your wicked heart out!"

Despite himself, Vespa winced as the pressure of the brutal grip increased. "You must think I'm worth hanging for. And what would happen to your little girl then?"

"There'd be one less o' your kind in the world," snarled Hawes. "It'd be worth it, I reckon!"

"I've been patient with you," said Vespa, "But I'd advise you to let go. Now."

He had not raised his voice, but in the tilt of the head, the glinting eyes, the jut of the chin, Hawes caught a glimpse of steel and knew he'd misread his man.

For a few taut seconds hot brown eyes challenged cold hazel ones. Then Vespa was released with a force that made him stagger. Josiah Hawes ducked his head and stepped back into the cottage. The door slammed behind him.

Later that afternoon, watching Thornhill inspect the dark bruises on Vespa's wrist, Broderick lounged comfortably on the great bed and said, "What I can't understand is why you didn't haul off and level the insolent lout. Is anything broke, Thornhill?"

"I think not, sir." Elegant in his new and well-cut habit, the valet looked shocked. "But surely we must keep in mind that the Captain has been very ill. In his present state of health no one could expect him to engage in fisticuffs, and his station in life would forbid an encounter with the likes of Josiah Hawes."

Vespa said meekly, "Exactly so, and he's such a big fellow, Toby. If you'd seen—"

"I've seen you fight, which is more to the point. You may not be in exactly plump currant, but you had your cane and if necessary your pistol. You could have handled him. So don't try and hornswoggle me with your meek and milquetoast!"

Vespa laughed. "Thanks for the vote of confidence. But the

child was there, you see, and if it had come to a real turn-up, things might have become rather ugly."

"It sounds to me as if things became *dashed* ugly! I vow, Jack, Town is fairly cluttered with your friends, but down here in the country you collect enemies like a dog collects fleas! It was more peaceful at Vitoria! This Hawes fella sounds like an exceeding ugly customer. Your Constable needs to give him a good sound warning."

"Speaking of which," said Vespa, easing into the dark blue coat the valet held for him, "do you know what happened to Molly Hawes, Thornhill? It was an accident of some kind, I gather."

"So I understand, sir. I was not in the area at the time, but it is still talked of at the Gallery Arms. May I be allowed to brush your hair, Captain? The 'Brutus' would become you far more than the simple style you affect, and it is well to stay in fashion even in the country."

"No, no," said Vespa hastily. "Thanks, but I can manage. What kind of accident?"

Thornhill began to gather up the discarded garments. "A really dreadful tragedy. It was dusk of a November afternoon. Mrs. Hawes was fetching Molly home from a birthday party when a coach and four came around the bend at the gallop. I suppose, in the dim light the coachman must not have seen them in time."

"Jove!" exclaimed Broderick, sitting up. "They were run down?"

"Yes, sir. The lady was killed outright, and the child—I believe she was three years old at the time—almost died, and has since been, er, as she is now, poor little creature. There was a great fuss over it at the time, so they say."

Vespa put down the hairbrush and asked, "Was the coachman held to blame?"

"Oh, most decidedly, sir. Shall I go and see if I may be of assistance to Lieutenant Manderville?"

"By all means. But first tell me, did the coachman receive a heavy sentence?"

With his hand on the door-latch, Thornhill paused. "I expect he would have, if they'd been able to find him."

Aghast, Broderick said, "Do you say the fellow didn't stop?"

"As I understand it, sir, he didn't even slow his cattle."

"If ever I heard of such a thing!" exclaimed Vespa. "Was every man in the village asleep? Did nobody follow the murdering brute?"

"I believe that Sir Larson Gentry chanced to ride in just after the accident. He gave chase, but the coach had too good a start and got clean away."

"Away," qualified Vespa with a grim look, "but scarcely clean. Did anyone recognize the coach?"

"Not that I know of, sir. There was a crest on the door-panel, but it was apparently too dark for it to be identified."

"Could it have been Lord Alperson?"

"A possibility, Captain. Although it would be difficult to imagine his lordship's carriage travelling at high speed. If you've seen it, you'll know what I mean." With a bow he went out and closed the door behind him.

"I know one thing," said Vespa slowly. "If it had been my wife and child—by heaven, I'd have followed that coach to the end of the earth! I surely cannot blame poor Hawes for his bitterness."

"You don't have to blame him, old lad," said Broderick. "Just keep clear of him. Now why that enigmatic look? You *are* going to call on him again!"

"Who's going to call on whom?" The personification of sartorial splendour, Manderville sauntered in and scanned them lazily through his jewelled quizzing glass.

"Jack's trying to get himself murdered," said Broderick. "He needs a twenty-four-hour guard to protect him from himself, is what it is. You're a fine shot, Paige. I nominate you!"

"You are too good." Manderville bowed low. "But my days of military service are done. I am a weary, wounded veteran, and desire only the quiet life. Nominate yourself, old lad. You have nothing better to do with your time."

Vespa said with a grin, "Oh, yes he has! His time is fully occupied. Haven't you noticed that he vanishes for hours at a time, and returns looking properly moonstruck?"

Very red in the face, Broderick exclaimed, "Now, deuce take you, Jack! Because I've been good enough to survey your estate—"

"In the company of the enchanting Miss Ariadne Gentry," put in Manderville.

"So you did notice," said Vespa. "Confess, Toby! The naked cherub landed one of his arrows right on target!"

Manderville leant against a bedpost and proclaimed laughingly, "The don is done! Long live the lover!"

"I trust you're quite finished with your low mockery and your silly alliterations," said Broderick, standing very straight. "But I forget. With your limited mental powers, neither of you clodpoles will know what an alliteration is. I will explain. It is a noun referring to several words used in immediate succession and commencing with the same letter. Simple minds, such as yours, would probably assume this to be a recent literary fashion, but if you were conversant with Latin you'd discover that, to Cicero's displeasure, Ennius wrote: *O Tite tute, Tati, tibi tanta—*"

"I know what 'tibby' means," interjected Manderville proudly. "It's cant for 'head'."

"Jolly good!" said Vespa. "And *tante* is French for 'aunt'."

"I shall ignore such uncouth interruptions," said Broderick loftily. "As I was about to say, even the Bard used the form, not that you would be aware of it. He wrote: 'Full fathom five thy father lies,' and—"

"Not deep enough," said Vespa, snatching up a pillow and advancing on the almost-don.

Manderville snatched up another pillow. "No, by Jove! Not nearly!"

"Now . . . you chaps . . . " said Broderick, retreating.

He was too late.

For a few minutes their various concerns and worries were

forgotten and they were carefree youths again. Whoops of laughter, shouts of indignation, flying feathers and the crash of a falling chair were interspersed with Corporal's excited barks.

Thornhill returned and had to shout his request for instructions about dinner.

Crawling off Broderick's legs, Vespa said breathlessly, "We'll eat"—he removed a feather from one eyebrow—"at the Gallery Arms. Please tell Strickley to have the coach ready by seven."

"If you mean to stand the huff for a good dinner," panted Manderville, kneeling to reclaim his shoe from Corporal, "I suppose I shall have to relent and be your ADC tomorrow. Let go, you savage brute!"

"It's all right, Corporal," said Vespa, picking up the agitated dog and stroking him. "He wasn't really murdering Toby. And you are very good, Paige, but I won't need an aide-de-camp tomorrow. I have important work to do that will keep me far from both Josiah Hawes and Gallery-on-Tang."

Manderville hauled Broderick to a sitting position. "What he means, Toby old man, is that he don't want company."

"Hee—hooo," wheezed Broderick, with rare brevity.

Vespa smiled and said nothing.

As usual, he was the first to leave his bedchamber next morning, and he walked to the stairs noting with pleasure that the day was bright and sunny. He was less pleased to note that Thornhill had left a pile of dirty laundry on the stairs. 'A fine thing if Paige or Toby should trip over it and break their necks,' he thought, and kicked it aside.

His boot encountered something less yielding than unoccupied garments.

A shrill scream rang out.

Horrified, he recoiled, gasping, "Oh—Egad!"

The pile of dirty laundry gathered itself into the form of a stout young woman, clad in a vast apron and a very large and droopy mob-cap that had fallen over her eyes.

"Ow!" she wailed, rubbing the afflicted area blindly.

"Oh, Jupiter! I am so sorry! I am so *sorry!*" he moaned, pulling back the mob-cap gently. "I thought—" ('That you were a pile of dirty laundry?') "I mean, I didn't know—" A pair of brown eyes regarded him soulfully from a broad, rosy-cheeked countenance. "Do let me help you up," he urged, attempting to lift her. With a combined effort they managed to restore the young woman to a sitting position, but since she seemed disinclined to stand, Vespa sat on the stair beside her, holding her hand and asking if she was very much hurt.

She was not unattractive, and had at one time been quite pretty, he thought, but her face showed the marks of a hard life, and the lack of several front teeth resulted in a hissing slur turning some sibilants to z's when she spoke.

"Why'd ye kick me, zur?" she enquired in a broad country accent. "Oi'd've moved over if ye'd asked Oi."

"I'm sure you would," he said, patting her hand anxiously. "I do apologize. I'd no idea. That is—I—er, tripped. Will you tell me please, who you are and—and what on earth you are doing here?"

"Why, Oi do be Peg, a'course," she said, as if this fact was known to the entire population of the British Isles. "Oi works here. Fer Cap'n Vezpa. He be a gert genelman. And Oi be a"—she took a deep breath and looked at him starry-eyed—"a parlour-maid!"

Startled, he thought that she was a very different article from his last 'parlour-maid'. He could well imagine Papa's reaction to 'Peg' and had difficulty restraining a grin, knowing it would injure the poor woman, who clearly regarded her new position as a great achievement. Equally clearly, she had not always been a parlour-maid, and could probably tell a tale to rival Thornhill's lurid life history.

"I see." He released her hand and smiled at her. "Did Mr. Thornhill hire you?"

In response to the smile, her eyes lit up and her plump face became one large beam so that, teeth or no teeth, he thought her a likable creature. "Aye, zur," she hissed. "He told me as the master wants the manor brung up to ztyle, and he be right fusssy 'bout proper cleaning. Zo Oi started on the stairs, being as they're what he zees when he gets outta bed, ain't they? Oi knowed there was guests in the house, but Oi didn't 'zpect any Lon'on gents to get up 'fore noonday."

"We're not all such laggards," he said. "You're not afraid to work in this house, Peg?"

"Oooh, yes, zur! Oi be proper scared. But—" Vespa blinked as she thrust a hand into her bodice and groped about. With some difficulty she drew forth a faded red ribbon on which hung several small and odd objects. "Zee here," she said, leaning against him and holding up a small ring carven from bone. "D'ye zee this?"

"Yes. A—er, child's ring?"

"No, zur! *Lookee* now! Zee the znake wi' its tail in its mouth!"

"Ah. Yes. A charm, is it?"

"Aye. But it be powerful. A *tell-izzmun,* it be." She pursed her lips and opened her eyes very wide. "And here, Oi got another of 'em." She held what appeared to be the tooth of some large animal. "Tiger," she whispered dramatically. "And—zee here. This un's *very* magic, so 'tis!" The magic object was a small pebble with a hole in the middle and two rounded protrusions on one side. "It be a bat as was turned to stone," said Peg, confidingly. "Zee its ears, there?"

"I—do. So you feel safe under the protection of your talismans, do you? How did you acquire them?"

"Oh, Oi didn't do nothing like that, zur! Oi *buyed* 'em, proper and decent, from Mother Wardloe. She be's a witch as lives in Lord Alperzon's wood, only he don't know it." She dug Vespa in the ribs and giggled hilariously. "Mother Wardloe she zays as Oi'll be pertected. And there you are, zur. Oi be zafe as zafe! Oi got the tiger, the znake, and the bat! Bean't many ghozties as would go up 'gainst that lot, be there?"

"Oh, very few, I'd think." He watched, fascinated, as she thrust the collection back in place. "But they don't look to be very comfortable. Doesn't that great tooth scratch your—er—you?"

"Better a scratch than to meet the Alabaster Cat, zur!"

"I'm sure you're right." He stood, and helped her to her feet. "Well, I must be on my way. I'm glad you're to work here, Peg. Though I'm sorry for the way we became acquainted."

She chuckled. "Don't ye never think on it, zur." She dug her elbow in his ribs again and added with a roguish wink, "It were worth it t'zee yer smile. 'Zides, Peg's had worse nor that, Oi can tell'ee, Left'nant."

"I should have introduced myself," he said apologetically. "I'm Captain Vespa."

"*You* iz?" Her eyes round with alarm she said, "But you be too young t'be a Captain, zure-ly? And, oh lawks! Here Oi been talking to the master like—Oh, *zur!*"

In her agitation, she stepped on her dustpan and it went cartwheeling down the stairs, scattering dust. Snatching for the pan, she tripped on the brush and squealed. Vespa made a grab for her, but she half ran, half fell, in a helter-skelter attempt to catch her balance that ended with her plumping down at the foot of the stairs amid her billowing apron, legs stuck out before her, wheezing with laughter, the mob-cap over her eyes once more.

Hurrying to her assistance, Vespa again restored the mob-cap. "Good heavens! Are you all right?"

She said merrily. "That be Peg! If Oi bean't tripping, Oi do be dropping! Don't ye worrit, Captain. Me old Pa uzeter zay as Oi allus come down on me feet, or where there bean't no brains to break! Good thing Oi buyed them there tell-izzmuns, ain't it, zur?"

Vespa agreed, and having helped her to her feet, went in search of breakfast thinking that with Peg in the house they all might be seeking out Mother Wardloe for talismans.

Thornhill waited on him, and announced that he had taken on a parlour-maid, although she was sadly lacking in experience.

"At being a parlour-maid," appended Vespa drily. "Oh, yes, I've met Peg. I wonder you didn't hear all the uproar."

Thornhill poured coffee and sighed. "She appears to be rather clumsy, I'll own, sir. But at least she's willing to work."

"And to work here, eh?"

"Just so, sir. But I am well aware that she is far from being an acceptable servant and in most great houses would be driven away if she dared approach the back door. If it would offend you, or your guests, to have such a—a person in the manor, I will turn her off."

"Oh, don't do that. I think it would break the poor woman's heart. Let's give her a chance, at least. She seems to have a sunny disposition, though I doubt her life has been very bright. With luck, she'll learn fast."

Vespa would very much have liked to witness the reactions of Broderick and Manderville to his new parlour-maid, but already more time had ticked away than he'd planned; having slipped a small pistol into the pocket of his cloak and settled a high-crowned hat on his head, he hurried outside.

It was warm and sunny when he drove the curricle down the drivepath, but an hour later a brisk breeze had come up, and he turned the team off the road and stopped so as to pull the thick rug over Consuela's knees. "My apologies, ma'am. I think I'd have done better to bring my phaeton."

"I don't mind the wind," she said, retying the ribbons of her bonnet. "Shall we have time to visit the cathedral, do you think?"

He glanced at the sky and a line of small clouds along the horizon. "Perhaps. We'll see how the day goes." Easing back into the traffic he asked, "I suppose you've visited Salisbury often? Did Mr. Jones ever paint the cathedral? I didn't see it among the canvasses you showed us."

"He painted three views. I sent them to the gallery. They're beautiful, but I didn't keep any for myself because I knew Papa always preferred Winchester."

"Did he! So do I."

"For any particular reason? In my view, Salisbury is by far the more magnificent. It has the tallest spire in England, you know. Look—already you can see it! And the oldest clock in England is there, besides a copy of the Magna—" She frowned at him resentfully. "Now why must you smirk? Did I mis-use your superior language?"

192

"You mistook a smile for a smirk. And I smiled because you reminded me a little of Toby Broderick."

"What a horrid thing to say! My voice is not in the least—"

"Not your voice, Miss Fiero. Gad, but you're hot at hand! Just that your interest in the cathedral would have properly set Toby off. He's a fount of knowledge on almost any given subject. I'm very sure he could tell you things about the cathedral that you— or almost anyone—never heard before."

"Is that so? He doesn't appear to be a great brain. Is he a dreadful bore?"

"Oh, no. Actually, he's often most interesting. He's rather shy around the ladies, but he's a jolly good man, and was a splendid soldier. It's just that one has to strangle him now and then to bring him down to earth."

She laughed. "Poor Lieutenant Broderick, to go in such peril! I hope you will curb your violent tendencies; he's too attractive to be done to death. Indeed, Ariadne Gentry thinks he's *very* nice-looking. Why do you prefer Winchester?"

So Miss Gentry had a *tendre* for Broderick. Vespa wondered if Sir Larson was aware that they were riding out together, and how he would like Toby as a prospective brother-in-law. The girl couldn't wish for a finer husband, but if Gentry was really in the basket he'd likely insist upon a rich suitor, and send Toby—

"I expect you will answer me when you wake up—yes?" said Consuela drily.

"Oh, I beg pardon! You asked me about Winchester, I think. It's not that I don't agree with you; Salisbury Cathedral is indeed magnificent. It's just so—well, so *very* magnificent that it's a bit overpowering. Winchester's—I don't quite know how to put it—warmer, somehow. Simpler, and more welcoming. But that's just my own foolish notion. I doubt many people would agree."

Watching him gravely, she said, "Papa would have agreed."

They were coming into heavier traffic, and Vespa guided his team with sure hands among coaches and farm waggons, impatient horsemen, dragoons resplendent in their scarlet and gold braid. The traffic thickened and he had his work cut out to avoid destroying reckless pedestrians, darting apprentices and footmen and the barrows of vendors and peddlers. They passed under an ancient arch and a muffin man hurried by with a steaming tray on his head that left behind the tantalizing aroma of hot bread and spices.

Consuela indicated a quieter cobbled thoroughfare where gables almost met over the narrow street. Here, fashionably clad ladies and their attendants rustled in and out of expensive-looking millinery establishments; gentlemen consulted their tailors; and at the far end of the street a sign outside a stately black and white half-timbered house proclaimed in flowing script: *La Galleria*.

They stopped in front. A porter came running to hand Consuela down and drive the coach to a private stable, and a slender white-haired gentleman hurried to welcome "the so delightful Signorina Jones" and ushered them inside. Consuela presented Captain John Vespa to Signor Cesare da Lentino, a studiedly distinguished individual who might be anywhere from fifty to seventy years of age.

La Galleria boasted a spacious showroom in which large and small works in oil or water-colour were displayed on stands or hung around the walls. There were also sketches and sculptures, some bronzes, and a few tapestries. Lacking the trained eye of the connoisseur, Vespa found most of the work interesting, but to his mind the paintings bearing the signature 'Preston Jones' were far and away the most impressive. In heavily accented English Signor Cesare admired the captain's taste. However, the canvasses of the Alabaster quarry had been sold, as had, he hoped, the works depicting the great cathedral.

Consuela gave a squeak of excitement. "*All* of them? Oh, how wonderful!"

Signor Cesare smiled at her exuberance, and regretted that the quarry paintings had not brought the prices he'd been able to get for those of the cathedral, but the former were confirmed sales, whereas the cathedral canvasses were out 'on approval'.

Vespa wandered off on a tour of inspection while da Lentino and the girl discussed financial arrangements. He rejoined them when Consuela exclaimed, "Two? On the same day! My goodness, is that not rather unusual?"

"Is something wrong?" asked Vespa.

She turned to him. "Signor Cesare says there were two prospective buyers for the quarry paintings, and that he wishes he'd not accepted the first offer."

Vespa looked at the proprietor questioningly. "Is that so remarkable? Mr. Jones is quite famous, after all."

Signor Cesare spread his hands and shrugged. "Rather unusual, let us say. For there to be an interest, *si,* that it is not remarkable. But for the second would-be buyer to fly into such a passion—for him to demand the name and direction of the purchaser—this, ah, but it is *indeed* remarkable!"

Prompted by Vespa's significant glance, Consuela asked for the names of the two men. The buyer was a Mr. Leonard Harrison of Tunbridge Wells. The disappointed gentleman, Sir Montmorency Gridden of Shrewsbury.

"Had you a previous acquaintanceship with either?" asked Vespa.

Signor Cesare replied that he had not, and in answer to another enquiry divulged that Mr. Harrison had paid cash, and, yes, but of course he had noted the direction. He crossed to a desk at the rear of the room. "A very well-favoured young gentleman, I may tell you. And evidently exceedingly well to pass, as you English would say, for I recall that his friend remarked the paintings would look well in the Great Hall, whereas Mr. Harrison appeared to favour the morning room in the east wing. . . . I should have it writ down somewhere. . . ." He rummaged among the contents of a handsomely carven wooden box, and took out a card. "*Si,* this it is—Leonard Harrison, Esquire, Partridge Towers, Tunbridge Wells."

Consuela watched in silence as Vespa read the card frowningly.

Signor da Lentino's gaze went from one to the other, and anxiety came into his dark eyes. "Something—it is amiss, Captain? I promise you the money it was paid in full, and the gentleman he is of a consequence. Very fine and his manner most proud."

Vespa muttered, "My aunt lives in Tunbridge Wells, and my brother and I spent several summers there while we were in school. I never knew anyone of the local society by the name of Leonard Harrison. Nor can I recollect a great house called Partridge Towers."

"A newly built home, perhaps," suggested the proprietor hopefully.

Consuela said, "Signor Cesare has a fine eye for detail, Captain. No doubt you could describe the gentleman for us, sir?"

Flattered, he answered, "But gladly. He is the tall young man, with shoulders," he spread his hands, "very fine, like so. His features they are good, but excessively. His eyes—ah! now this I have forget! But of an excellence and filled with pride. His hair—the light shade—how would you describe? Saxon."

"Blond," supplied Vespa rather grimly.

"*Si.* This it is the word."

Vespa asked, "Might Mr. Harrison's eyes have been blue, perchance?"

Consuela glanced at him sharply.

Signor Cesare pondered but could only recall that they were light.

"His friend," persisted Vespa. "Also of large build, but darkhaired and heavier, and less—er, attractive?"

"You know these men?" asked Signor Cesare, increasingly apprehensive.

"You have indeed a fine eye for detail, sir," said Vespa evasively. "As to the disappointed gentleman, you say he was angry. Did you think he meant to seek out Mr. Harrison?"

"This, it is possible, Captain. He is the older man of great violence and not to be denied. I have his name but not his direction, only that he is the aristocrat." He shook his head and looked sombre. "He have eyes that burn right through a man, and *such* a tem-

196

per! I should not care to displease that one! Ah! You will forgive? There is the customer arriving. I must attend him."

His manner made it clear that he would vouchsafe no more information, and Vespa and Consuela left the gallery.

The sky had clouded over, and the temperature had dropped several degrees. Vespa offered his arm and led the way along the street.

Consuela said, "Well, you properly scared him. He'll tell us nothing more!"

"He told us all we may need."

"You surely do not suspect the buyer to have been Larson Gentry?"

"Why not? The description fits."

"Then that is all that fits! In the first place, Sir Larson is so deep in debt there are rumours that he hides down here from his London creditors. He could not afford to buy one of my father's paintings—let alone three! And to have such a sum in cash on his person—no! Most unlikely. Besides, he never seemed even slightly interested in Papa's work."

"What about the men you've seen lurking about Alabaster? Could not Gentry have been one of them?"

She said hesitantly, "It is possible, I suppose. I only saw them at dusk or at night-time, and not closely enough to recognize anyone."

"Well, I saw him! Making off with my furniture!"

She said nothing, but he caught her glancing at him from the corners of her eyes.

"Good Lord!" he exclaimed indignantly. "You don't believe me! Why on earth would I make up such a silly tale?"

"I didn't say you made it up. Only—"

"Only my mind is still playing me tricks, as it did when I chased the 'bee' on Sunday! Just as yours convinces you that your father was murdered, no doubt?"

"You don't believe me. Why should I believe *you*? I suppose you will next say the disappointed buyer was Lord Alperson!"

"Well, that's not impossible, is it? Your Italian friend said the second buyer was an old aristocrat with a horrible temper. Once again, the cap fits!"

"If Lord Alperson wanted my father's paintings, why didn't he come and buy them years ago, instead of waiting till—till they became more costly?"

"It was my understanding that his lordship and your father didn't cry friends—to say the least of it. Mr. Jones would likely have refused to sell to him."

"True. But Alperson could have hired an agent to buy them. No—it's just too foreign to his nature. He's the most clutch-fisted old miser I ever knew, and doesn't give a button for art."

"Lord give me strength! Here I am come all this way to try and help you, and all you will do is argue! I know what it is! Ladies are much too dainty and coy to admit they're hungry, but I shall ask that you indulge me by accompanying me to luncheon. You'll likely feel better after you've had some food."

With not an instant of coy daintiness, Consuela smiled and admitted that she was "ravenous".

13

I were away down to Yeovil, visiting of my mother, else I'd have made myself known to you sooner nor this, sir." The round little man in the shiny frock coat took off his hat, whereupon his thinning grey hair was ruffled by the rising wind. He smoothed his hair, nodded emphatically several times, and exuded good fellowship. He had come upon this fine example of a London beau strolling along the village street. At a safe distance behind, Dicky-Boy followed the beau, doing his best to emulate the graceful walk of the young exquisite. "I am the mayor of this village," announced the little man, thinking that the landowner was so obvious a Dandy that he'd not be likely to enjoy country life. He replaced his hat and thrust out his hand. "George Fletcher by name, sir. And proud to welcome you to your fine inheritance, Captain Vespa. Get away from there, Dicky-Boy!"

Manderville returned the handshake and glanced over his shoulder at the brawny youth, who went slouching off, grinning and muttering to himself.

"Harmless, I promise you," explained the mayor as they walked on together. "But—" He tapped his temple and looked mournful.

"How unfortunate. He has a good pair of shoulders."

"Aye, he's strong in body. But when it comes to the cock-loft . . ." Mr. Fletcher shook his head with such rapidity that he was obliged to re-seat his hat. "Imagines things, he do, poor lad, and goes round giving himself airs to be interesting, as they say."

"It's a failing shared by all too many," drawled Manderville. Perfectly aware of the searching look that greeted his remark, he added, "And lest you judge me as being tarred with the same brush, I must refuse the honour of your identification."

"Ah . . . Er, eh?"

"I am not Captain John Vespa."

"You bean't?" His face a study in disappointment, the mayor exclaimed, "Oh, dear!"

"I contrive to bear up under it. Do not abandon hope, Mayor. Life has its brighter side, and the Captain is a very good man. My name is Paige Manderville. I'm staying at Alabaster Royal."

Brightening, Mayor Fletcher said, "That explains it, then. You'll be a friend of the Captain. I knowed you was the same type of gentleman. So I wasn't far off, was I?"

"Oh, yes. We're not in the least alike. We served in the army together. More or less."

They were interrupted at this point by the Widow Davis, who had decided to sweep the step of her shop when she saw the mayor and the handsome Mr. Manderville approaching. It was some minutes before Fletcher was able to break into her monologue, but they escaped at last, and proceeding to the village green sat on a stone bench and watched the ducks squabble and bustle about collecting their lunch.

The mayor imparted the information that it was going to rain, and Manderville said gently that Mr. Fletcher knew best. Encouraged by this admission, Mr. Fletcher observed that he had mistaken Mr. Manderville for Captain Vespa because he knew that the Captain was not so dark like Mr. Sherborne had been.

"Remarkably astute," drawled Manderville. "The Captain is

from home at present, but if you call at the manor this evening, I'm sure he'll be glad to receive you."

The mayor's eyes fell away. He shuffled his feet and muttered, "Call at the manor . . . Ah. That I must do, er—soon. Very soon." After another series of rapid nods, he enquired, "And—er, what does you think of Gallery-on-Tang, may I ask? Mighty small in your view, eh? But you'll allow as it's pretty?" Manderville allowing that much, he went on, "We've our share of history. Alabaster Royal's haunted, as you'll have discovered, eh?"

He waited hopefully, and was disappointed when Manderville contributed no hair-raising accounts of grisly spectres, but merely asked, "Is Alabaster your only historical spot, Mayor?"

"Lor' bless you, no, sir. Take the church, now. A monastery it were in olden time, only Oliver Cromwell's soldiers tore it down, and when they restored it—after the Restoration that were"—Mr. Fletcher laughed heartily and slapped his plump knee—"and there's a neat play on words, if I says so myself. Interested in history be you, Mr. Manderville?"

Smiling politely at the 'neat' witticism, Manderville said, "Not at all."

Mr. Fletcher was nonplussed, seeing which, Manderville repented. "But I'm being obtuse, I fear. Actually, Mayor Fletcher, I'm in search of the coroner. I presume there is one in Gallery-on-Tang?"

"In-deed, there be! I'm it, sir. When I'm not mayor-ing I'm crownering." Nodding vigorously, he gripped each lapel of his coat and asked with a solemn air, "How might I be of assistance, Mr. Manderville? Crowner Fletcher, at your service."

"Thank you. Actually, I'm interested in a tale I heard, concerning a famous artist who used to live nearby."

"Ah, you'll be meaning poor Mr. Preston Jones. Famous indeed, sir! World-famous, I wouldn't be surprised. Met a sad end, he done. Not to say downright tragic." The 'Crowner' leant closer, glanced about, and murmured dramatically, "*Frighted* to death, he were, poor gentleman! But he shoulda knowed better than to go

201

out there. A evil place is that Alabas—er—not meaning no offence, sir! But—facts is facts, bean't they now?"

"Allowing for the fact that everyone interprets facts differently, yes. I was told Mr. Jones accidentally fell to his death in the quarry, but I fancy you have more information than is given to the general public."

Crowner Fletcher beamed and gave vent to so violent a series of nods that Manderville wondered he did not get a crick in his neck. "Very true, sir," he said. "A sad case it were. There's them as holds"—he glanced around cautiously, and apparently mistrusting the ducks, lowered his voice—"There's them as says 'John Barleycorn' had a hand in that there 'accidental' death. Now Mr. Jones liked to bend the elbow, surely. But I never knowed him to be shot in the neck, as they say. To my mind, if there *was* spirits involved, they wasn't out of no bottle! More likely the poor gent saw . . . the Alabaster Cat!" He pulled in his chin, pursed his little mouth, and opened his eyes solemnly. "Wouldn't take no more'n one look, and you see what happened!"

"Then at the inquest you found no cause to suspect foul play?"

"Depends what you means by 'foul play', Mr. Manderville. If you was to listen to Dicky-Boy, he'd tell you he see Mr. Jones come outta the manor so lushy his friends had to hold him up. Trouble is, poor Dicky-Boy's always seeing things as nobody else do. Mr. Preston Jones, he were a very shy sort of gentleman, and didn't have no particular friends as anyone knows of. He'd have a brew with the apothecary and Mr. Ditchfield now and then, but they're not the type of men as would go out to the manor secret-like and get roaring drunk. No, sir. The fact is that if Mr. Jones hadn't of kept going where he shouldn't oughta have goed, he'd likely never have see the Alabaster Cat!"

Manderville drawled lazily, "Conversely, if John Barleycorn had a—er—hand in the matter, there's no telling what Mr. Jones may have seen."

The whole trouble was, the good mayor later told his buxom little wife, them London dandies was always funning, and one couldn't never tell whether they meant the silly things they said, or whether they was just pulling a chap's leg. "That Mr. Manderville," he added thoughtfully, "he's a proper Non-Peary, as the Frenchies say. He'll have all you ladies in a twitter, I'll be bound. He's got a fancy way with words, surely."

"Such as, Mr. Mayor?"

"Well, he rolled one out on me as I never heard of. Ob-toos, he says. Ob-toos. You know that one, Mrs. Mayor?"

"Of course I does! Really, George Fletcher! A body would think you never got your schooling at your Ma's knee—as I know you done! Ob-tuse means to put on flesh. Which is a word *you'd* do well to heed!"

⸻

It was a rainy early dusk when Vespa turned the curricle into the drive of the Jones cottage. Peeping at him from under the umbrella that Lady Francesca had insisted be placed in the vehicle, Consuela said, "You're soaked. I hope you may not take a cold."

"Don't believe in 'em, ma'am. Does your Grandmama always burn candles in every room of the house?"

"Goodness, no!" Her head jerked around. Light glowed from each window. The front door was flung open, and Manning came onto the steps holding a shawl over her head, wailing, and waving urgently.

Vespa ducked to avoid the whipping umbrella. "Something's wrong!" exclaimed Consuela, preparing to climb from the still-moving vehicle.

"You won't help by breaking your neck!" he said wrathfully. "Wait up!"

He guided the team to the covered *porte-cochère* at the side of the house and flung the reins to an elderly man who hurried to them. He was too late to assist Consuela, who scrambled from the curricle with a flash of petticoats and ran to her obviously distraught maid.

Vespa turned to the groom. "I'm Captain Vespa. I take it you're Lady Francesca's coachman?"

"Aye, sir," the man answered, out of breath. "Name of Watts."

"You've had trouble here, I think?"

"We've had thieves, sir. At least, there's been intruders, though what they took I couldn't say."

"What about the servants? Is anyone harmed?"

"It's Cook's day off, so she wasn't here. The duchess is all right, sir. She were invited to take tea at the Gouderville estate, but when we got there, Lady Gouderville was gone to Winchester, and the duchess not expected. Mistook in the date was Lady Francesca, I fancy."

"And when you came back, the house had been ransacked, is that it?"

"That's it, sir. And a cove lying on the drive with a broke head. He says Hezekiah Strickley paid him to keep a eye on my ladies, but he don't know what hit him, nor he didn't see nobody. Lady Francesca sent him to Apothecary Kestler, along of Bert, our gardener. Bert was to fetch the Constable here. I thought you was him, sir. Will you be staying?"

Vespa said he would stay at least until the constable arrived, and having assured himself that the coachman would take proper care of his greys, he went to the house.

Lady Francesca was in the tastefully appointed blue and gold drawing room, sipping a glass of sherry and being fussed over by her granddaughter and wailed over by her maid. She greeted Vespa politely, but she was pale and her hands trembled. Manning, it developed, had accompanied her to the Gouderville estate, and had not been in the house during the robbery. Her melancholy lamentations were not helping the old lady, as Vespa told her. He patted the maid on the shoulder and sent her off to the kitchen to make some tea. "You, Miss Jones," he said, "may come back after you've changed into some dry clothes."

This resulted in an argument, with Consuela indignantly refusing to leave her dear grandmama's side, Lady Francesca agreeing with Vespa, and Vespa pointing out that with such a "tower of strength" as Manning to lean on, her ladyship did not need Consuela to be laid low by a feverish cold. His threat to carry the obstinate girl to her room finally won the day, and she went hurrying up the stairs muttering about "overbearing males".

"Now, ma'am," he said, sitting on a footstool in front of the duchess' chair, "are you feeling well enough to tell me what has been taken?"

"I feel better now that you are come," she said, giving him a grateful smile. "I can only be thankful that Consuela was from the house gone! You ask what is taken? The silver candlesticks from the dining room, we know, and a fine jade bowl. Other things, I expect, that we do not yet discover."

"What about jewellery?"

"Manning says no. I have not make the thorough search, but I think they do not go upstairs. Perhaps we come back and they have to run away?"

"Perhaps. What about Mr. Jones' paintings?"

She looked at him sharply. "*Si.* Most of them are overturned and scattered about. Some, I feel sure, have been stole. This, Consuela will know."

At this point Constable Blackham arrived with the wiry middle-aged little man who was Bert, Lady Francesca's gardener. The guard Strickley had hired was not seriously injured, said Blackham, but the apothecary was keeping him overnight, in case he'd suffered a concussion. He took out his notebook, asked to have a word with Captain Vespa before he left, and proceeded to take down Lady Francesca's statement.

Vespa waited in the hall and met Consuela when she hurried down the stairs. She wanted to go to her grandmother, but he persuaded her first to accompany him to the back of the house, saying that Constable Blackham would want to know if anything of great value had been stolen.

"Our most valuable possessions are the Ottavio rubies," she told him worriedly. "Grandmama has always said they would rescue us if we ever became poverty-stricken."

"But they weren't taken."

"No. How did you know?"

He drew her back as she reached for the latch to the door of her father's studio, and said grimly, "I don't think your thieves were looking for rubies." He flung the door open. There was no one in the big room, but the sight of the ruthlessly scattered paintings drew a cry from Consuela and she shrank, both hands flying to her mouth, her eyes huge with shock.

He put an arm about her shoulders and she leant against him, half sobbing, "Oh . . . Jack!"

"Poor little soul. I'm so sorry."

She turned to look up at him searchingly. "You knew they were after my dear father's paintings. But—*why*? And if they are even more valuable than I believed, why not take them all?"

"Probably because it would require several coaches or a waggon that would attract attention. Or perhaps they simply didn't have time. Let's try and find out which ones they selected."

They began to pick up the artworks and stack them in groups. Some of the frames were damaged, and two of the canvasses were ripped, apparently having been stepped on. Consuela began to make furious little growling noises, and the sight of such careless and wanton destruction made Vespa fume. He was pleased, however, to find that his favourite, the picture of the manor on that spring day of long ago, was intact.

When the canvasses were sorted into their various stacks, Consuela looked through them carefully. "Oh, but they've taken so many of those you especially liked!" she moaned.

He joined her. The somewhat sinister moonlit scene of Alabaster was here, as were the twilight view and the depiction of the great house mantled with snow, but the summer scenes and the three paintings of the area near the quarry were gone.

Frowning thoughtfully, he said, "Let's see what else they stole."

A painting of St. Paul's Church, and one of the Gallery Arms at sunset that Vespa had thought particularly fine were missing, but Consuela announced with a sigh of relief that those of the village and of various individual cottages and villagers were all safe. Looking over her shoulder, he said, "Are you sure? Where's the May Day picnic on the green? I didn't see that one."

They checked again, and then they searched through the other stacks, but without success. The May Day picture was added to the list of stolen works.

It was full dark by the time Constable Blackham had concluded his investigation, and the duchess insisted that both men stay and dine. Remembering that it was her cook's day off, Vespa declined, but Consuela leant to fill his wine-glass and murmured that her grandmother was feeling better and would be happy to supervise dinner, so he was pleased to accept the invitation.

When both ladies had retired to the kitchen, the constable said quietly, "Now, Captain Vespa, I'd be glad if ye'd tell me what you knows of this here matter."

Vespa said slowly, "I don't really *know* any more than you do."

"But ye *suspects,* don't ye, sir? Else why would you have ordered Hezekiah Strickley to set a guard on this house? You and Miss Consuela went straight away to Mr. Preston Jones' workroom. Nor you wasn't surprised to hear that none of Lady Francesca's jewels was stole. And I'll own as that gave me one to be going on with!"

Vespa smiled. "You don't miss much, do you? All right. I've come to think that Miss Consuela's quite right in believing that her father was murdered."

"Hum." This was not what the constable had wanted to hear. He pursed his lips and looked dubious. "No offence, sir, but I wouldn't be paying too much heed to her fancifying. A very nice young lady, even if a touch hasty—er, spirited at times. But there bean't no reason for such a wicked deed. I looked into the matter proper at the time the poor gentleman passed to his reward. I spoke to everyone what had knowed him. There was no debts owing—money usually being at the root of such dreadful happenings. There was no lady whose husband or father could've felt—er—badly done by, if you know what I means, sir. Why, if Mr. Jones had a single enemy in the world, I never heard of it."

"What about Lord Alperson?"

The constable looked startled. "Why, they wasn't friends, I'll own that. But to think as his lordship would take Mr. Jones' life because his daughter had cried friends with Miss Robina Alperson, why, that's more'n a little far-fetched, sir. And more'n I'd dare do to make such a accusation 'gainst a peer o' the realm! Not without witnesses and some solid proof. And what's it got to do with Mr. Jones' paintings, Captain? And why, I asks ye, with some pretty near priceless jewels in the house, did them silly thieves steal a jade bowl, a few paintings and a silver candlestick holder? Now *them's* the questions I'd like answered, Captain."

Vespa also would have liked to have the answers to those questions, but it was obvious that none of the theories he might advance would be well received. He therefore murmured a few vague remarks about fanatical art collectors who might covet Preston Jones' works but have no knowledge of the famous rubies. The constable thought this far more likely, and occupied himself with his notebook until the ladies returned.

With her usual expertise, the duchess managed to conjure up an excellent meal in a very short time. The log fire blazed up the chimney and it was warm and cozy inside, but the wind was blowing up, the rain was falling steadily, and the moon seldom broke through the clouds. It was no night for someone unfamiliar with the area to be on the roads, and soon after dinner Vespa apologized for leaving so early, but said his farewells.

Consuela accompanied him to the door. She looked calm and unafraid, but scanning her uneasily he asked if Coachman Watts was quartered in the house.

She chuckled. "Watts and his wife live in the little cottage by the coach house. And if you're going to suggest that he move in here tonight, you must not have noticed that he is somewhat advanced in years. A very kind and faithful man, but I shall feel safer with my little pistol to hand, I promise you. Besides, would it not be a case of shutting the barn door after the horse has fled?"

He argued that the thieves might rely on just such reasoning, and made her promise to bolt all the doors and windows before retiring. His team was soon poled up and the carriage lamps lit, and he drove out, guiding the horses cautiously along the narrow, rutted drivepath.

The rain was not heavy, but at times was driven by the wind in chilling sheets. He pulled the collar of his cloak higher and turned his head aside as another gust came at him. And in that instant he saw the white oval of a face peering at him from the hedgerow beside the gate.

He had pulled up the team and was out of the curricle in seconds. The face had disappeared, but he heard a trampling among the undergrowth. Wrenching his pistol from the holster, he roared, "Stop, or I fire!" A squeal answered him, and the sounds of that frantic retreat were stilled.

Vespa saw a crouching shape, and he charged it at a limping run, rage searing through him. "You slippery varmint!" he shouted, pistol levelled as he gripped the collar of the huddled figure. "Meant to go back and finish your dirty work, did you? Well, you'll go back all right!" He hauled the whimpering man back to the curricle and spun him around.

Seen in the light of the lamps his captive was sturdy, but little more than a boy, who cowered before him, drenched, wet hair plastered about his face, and eyes fixed on the gleaming pistol barrel while he gabbled terrified and disjointed pleas that he never done nuthink. "He only come," he whimpered, " 'cause he knowed bad men was hanging about, and Miss Jones be a kind lady what gives him cakes sometimes."

Vespa relaxed his grip. "What's your name? Do you live nearby?"

"He be Dicky-Boy, sir. That's what they calls him. He lives in the village. His Ma died, so Mr. Tom lets him sleep in the smithy.

Mr. Tom's kind. He lets Dicky-Boy swing the hammer sometimes."
Forgetting his fears, he tilted his head and said boastfully, "Dicky-Boy's strong. There's them as thinks he's not clever." He chuckled to himself. "They might be s'prised one o' these days. Dicky-Boy knows more'n what they knows." The eyes that seemed too small for their sockets took on a cunning look. He half whispered, "There's them as'd be proper *scared* if they knowed what he knows."

Vespa thought, 'But for the grace of God, there go I,' and he said gently, "I expect they would. In fact, you might be just the fellow I'm looking for."

The youth brightened. "What sorta thing you want, Cap'n? He knows who you be, and he'll help, if you want. He likes sojers. He's going to be a sojer. Someday. He tried to be. Once. But they said—" The words trailed off and sadness came into the young face.

Vespa said, "Miss Jones and the duchess are friends of mine. I think you're right about bad men coming here. I had a guard watching the house, but—"

"That were George Cobham. He got knocked down. Dicky-Boy, he seen it."

"Did you, by Jove! Do you know who the men were?"

"No. They got masks over their faces. But Dicky-Boy seen it and were going to tell Tom. He's the blacksmith, y'know. But the duchess come back and the bad men run off. Anyways, Tom wouldn't've b'lieved Dicky-Boy. He's tried to tell them, afore this, but they don't b'lieve when he tells 'em things he sees. If Dicky-Boy was to tell you what he seen—you wouldn't b'lieve neither. But he did see 'em. And, one o' these days . . . "

Vespa waited patiently while rainwater trickled down his neck and the wind grew colder. The boy's expression became vacant, and he seemed to withdraw into some shadowy land of his own. At length Vespa said, "I need someone to watch the Jones house. Just until the guard can come back. I expect you know lots of places where you could keep dry but still see if anyone bad chanced to lurk about. I'd like to hire you as a temporary guard. I would pay for your time, of course."

"You *would*? You'd pay him wi' *money*? To be a guard? That's—that's something like a sojer, ain't it, sir Captain?"

"It is, indeed. Here." Vespa pressed a coin into the grimy hand. "This is for tonight."

"Cor!" gasped the boy. "A—a *shilling*? A *whole shilling*? For Dicky-Boy?"

"Yes. But you must obey my orders. If you see anything suspicious, you are to rouse the house. Here, I'll give you my card. Show them this, and tell them I hired you. Is that agreeable?"

"A-agree'ble! Cor!" A jerky salute was offered. "Dicky-Boy's got a sittyation! Just like Ernie what's 'prenticed to Butcher Durham!"

Vespa pulled the rug from the curricle and tossed it to the boy. "Try to keep dry. Good-night to you."

He started to climb into the curricle, then had to pause as pain jolted through his leg spitefully. Probably, he thought, because he'd been driving most of the day.

A strong arm clamped around him. He was half lifted and deposited on the seat of the curricle. He was, he knew, no lightweight, even in his present state of health, and he stared in astonishment at the youth who stepped back from the curricle and saluted again while declaring, "Dicky-Boy strong!"

Vespa thanked him, waved his whip, and drove on. "Dicky-Boy *very* strong!" he muttered.

———❦———

"Strong?" howled Manderville, rushing past Vespa with his handkerchief clasped over his nose. "That's not *strong*! Putrid is what it is! Leave the door wide, Jack, and let some fresh air in, for mercy's sake!"

Vespa's bewilderment lasted only until the waft of interior air assailed his nostrils. He at once complied with Manderville's request. Corporal rushed to welcome him home, but even as he bent to stroke the dog it raced outside, tail between its legs. "What the deuce *is* that?" demanded Vespa, his nose wrinkling.

"It's Toby." Manderville tottered to the open door and leant there, gulping in deep breaths of the clean, rain-swept air. "He's been poking about your cellars all evening. I went down to see what he was about, and the air down there damn near asphyxiated me."

"Gad! I believe you. Is Toby all right?"

"Right as rain—well, not quite, but the stink don't bother him, he says. He's puttering about down there, happy as a flea on a fox. I told him to open the outside cellar door before he suffocates, and I closed the upper door—for our protection! What are you looking for on the drivepath? Is someone else coming? If so we'd best build up the fire and waft some smoke about to clear the air."

Vespa closed the front door and allowed Thornhill to relieve him of cloak, hat, gloves and whip. "Nobody's coming, to my knowledge," he answered. "But as I turned onto the drivepath just now, a fellow ran out in front of the horses. I suppose between the wind and the rain he didn't hear me coming. I damn near ran the blockhead down."

He excused himself and went upstairs, where Thornhill scolded him for getting drenched, and his muddy boots and wet coat were exchanged for slippers and a quilted dressing-gown. The valet was less gregarious than usual, but said he had not seen any stranger wandering about the grounds.

Vespa thanked him and went down to the drawing room. Manderville was standing by the hearth, lighting a cheroot. Vespa poured them both a glass of brandy, lowered himself into a fireside chair and leant back, stretching out his legs gratefully. "A fine fellow I am to desert my guests. My apologies, Paige. I'd thought to get home in time to join you for dinner. Did you go into the village?"

Manderville sank onto the sofa and waved a dismissing hand. "No. I decided to cook one of my specialities. Unfortunately, your new maid—where *ever* did Thornhill find the wench?—assisted me! Do you know, Jack, that Peg is the only maid I ever saw who could drop a gravy boat while picking up a fork. I thought poor Thornhill would faint!"

Vespa laughed. "Did she show you her talismans?"

"No. Gad, I can scarce wait! However, in spite of her incredible assistance, we enjoyed a good dinner. Never mind about that, and I'll be polite and not demand to know where you've been all day. Were you able to identify your wandering blockhead just now?"

"I caught a glimpse of him. He all but banged his nose on one of the carriage lamps." Vespa added thoughtfully, "The only identification I could make was that he is, I think, from the Middle East."

"*Is* he now! Connected with the lady in Preston Jones' sketch, perhaps?"

"If that's the case, then we must assume that this house is being watched."

"Jupiter! And I thought I came here to share your quiet life!"

"Should've known better, dear boy." Broderick wandered towards them with an amiable smile on his dirty face. "Jack's life is never quiet. He was in the thick of things in Spain, and before that, from what I've heard, he and his brother were always up to some merry gig or—"

"Go away!" demanded Manderville, jumping up and wafting smoke at the latecomer. "Be dashed if you haven't brought that confounded stench with you! And besides, you're downright filthy! What's that stuff all over your hair?"

Broderick wiped a handkerchief across his head. "Oh," he said, examining the sullied linen. "It's only ash. What a fuss you make, Paige. If you weren't such a dandified creature—"

"Dandified! I've sniffed six-week-old cracked eggs that smelled better than whatever you were concocting downstairs!"

"Wasn't concocting." Broderick poured himself a glass of Cognac, and sat on the other side of the hearth. "I accidentally tripped over a vat of acid."

213

"What the deuce were you doing with acid?" demanded Vespa, scanning him narrowly. "Did you burn yourself?"

Broderick smiled and waved the glass at him. "It's a very ancient art form," he said.

"Oh, Gad!" moaned Manderville, closing his eyes. "He's going to tell us all about it—as if we'd asked!"

"Well, but you did," Broderick pointed out excusingly. "At least, Jack asked me. Didn't you, dear boy?"

"I did? Er, what did I ask you?"

Broderick explained kindly, "Why, about cloisonné, of course."

14

*D*on't ask him," pleaded Manderville. "You don't know what he's talking about; no more do I. What's more, we don't want to know. And if he starts explaining, we'll be up all night listening to him prattle about something we'd have been just as well off not knowing."

"It wouldn't hurt you, Paige Manderville, to make an effort to improve your mind," said Broderick severely.

"I suppose a fuller knowledge of cloisonné—whatever that may be—is going to secure me a high position in the Diplomatic Corps, or at East India House, or some such place?" Manderville straightened his cuff fastidiously, and said with derision, "Oh, *very* likely!"

"That kind of attitude will get you—" began Broderick.

"Hold up," said Vespa. "Your pardon, Toby, but—let's leave Paige's ignorance for a minute. Are you saying you've been working on cloisonné in the cellar?"

Manderville muttered indignantly, "In this case, ignorance is *surely* bliss!"

Ignoring him, Broderick answered, "Not me, old boy. But

someone has. It's far from a lost art, you know, although it dates back to the Mycenaean period and the thirteenth century B.C. And there are claims that there have been finds in the Caucasus which—"

"All right, all right," said Manderville with saintly resignation. "Omit the history lesson and I'll surrender. It's some type of jewellery, of course."

"Your depth of knowledge amazes," exclaimed Broderick. "Abysmally incomplete as it is."

Vespa said with a grin, "I don't know much about it, either. Save that it's a form of enamelling. But isn't it quite a complicated process, Toby? What makes you think someone—logically, Mr. Preston Jones—was working on that kind of stuff in my cellar?"

"Because I found an agate mortar, a wooden mallet and a small furnace down there, among other things—"

"—Such as a bucket of acid into which you stuck your silly foot," interposed Manderville, yawning.

"If I had, you'd have heard me howl," said Broderick. "I bumped it and some of the acid spilled onto a stack of rubbish. That's what made the stench, so that I realized what it was. The acid is clear, you know."

Intrigued, Vespa asked, "D'you suppose Preston Jones was fashioning jewellery down there? Perhaps as a surprise for his daughter or the duchess?"

"That's entirely possible. He might not have wanted them to be near the acid or the various chemicals. But it's also possible that he was crafting larger pieces for eventual sale. Like dishes, or jars, for example. They'd be costly items, that's certain. Has Miss Consuela never mentioned that her Papa worked in enamels?"

Vespa shook his head. "And there were none at the Salisbury gallery."

"Why do you say they'd be costly?" asked Manderville, becoming interested.

"Because of the acid," said Broderick. "Cloisonné really requires a fine metal base. If copper was selected to be the base, one would employ citric acid; and if a person was working on silver—he'd use sulphuric."

Vespa probed, "And the acid you found was sulphuric?"

"No, dear boy. Hydrochloric acid."

"Which is used only upon vessels of purest gold, *naturelle-ment*," drawled Manderville mockingly.

"Just so," said Broderick.

Manderville jerked upright. "You're not serious!"

"You're the flippancy expert, dear old Paige. Not I."

The last trace of Manderville's langour vanished. Springing to his feet, he cried, "If your cellar is stocked to the gills with pure gold objects waiting to be enamelled, Jack, we'd best find them!" He started to the door, then swung back, saying excitedly, "You do realize that this explains everything? When those louts nigh strangled Miss Consuela, they hadn't come here to murder the poor girl, they were hunting your hoard of gold! Come on, you fellows! Stir your stumps! A hunting we will go . . . !" He all but ran out, singing lustily.

The two remaining exchanged an amused glance.

Vespa said, "I give him thirty seconds."

"If that," qualified Broderick. "Incidentally, I didn't see any golden jars or bowls or such-like pleasantries down there. Sorry."

His words half awoke something at the back of Vespa's mind, but then Manderville reappeared, coughing, and wiping tearful eyes. "You couldn't have planned a finer deterrent for thieves, Toby," he wheezed. "We'll have to postpone our treasure hunt until tomorrow. That cellar air's too dashed foul!"

The evening was comparatively young and Vespa suggested a game of loo. His guests enjoyed the game (and the brandy) so much that they were soon playing very poorly, dropping their cards, which resulted in much hilarity, and by the time Thornhill helped usher them up the stairs at half past midnight, they were singing at the tops of their lungs.

Vespa climbed into bed convinced he'd sleep until morning. He was awakened at half past three o'clock, however, by the now familiar sounds of blowing leaves, but when he also heard a shrill barking he realized that the wind and rain had intensified and that Corporal, who had earlier refused to come back into the house, had now changed his mind. It wouldn't hurt Thornhill, he thought irritably, to go down and let the dog in. He reached for the bell-pull, only to remember the cacophanous tones of the bell. It would be a poor host who selfishly woke his guests in the wee hours of the morning.

Grumbling, he threw on his dressing-gown and staggered downstairs. Corporal was grateful to be reprieved, which he showed by decorating his master's night-rail with muddy pawprints, and then shaking himself, showering Vespa with cold water.

"You're a full-fledged pest," Vespa advised, towelling the little animal vigorously.

Corporal confirmed this opinion by shivering so violently that he was allowed to curl up on the foot of the bed, where he fell noisily asleep almost at once.

His human was not so fortunate. Wide awake, Vespa lay staring into the darkness, his thoughts drifting from the Salisbury gallery and Signor da Lentino to the thefts at the Jones cottage and poor Consuela's distress; his hiring of Dicky-Boy; and Toby's interesting discovery in the cellar. Two details of the crowded day had triggered an almost realized awareness in his muddled head. One had been a remark made by Dicky-Boy, and the other something that Toby had said. Or was it Paige? He turned over and closed his eyes, wooing sleep, and becoming ever more resentful of Corporal's snores. As the first pale light of dawn outlined his window, he was shocked to realize that he'd been so busily occupied he hadn't thought of his beloved Marietta, nor of Sherry, all day long. Memories crowded into his mind only briefly before he fell asleep.

During the long dark hours he had mapped out a busy schedule for the following day, but when he awoke it was already ten o'clock. A habitually early riser, he was vexed to have slept so late, and even more vexed when he remembered that this was Wednesday, the day of the Flower Show at which he'd promised to meet the lovely widow. He could despatch Strickley with an apologetic note, of course, but Esme Stokely was an old friend, and had been devoted to Sherry. No, it would not do. His neat schedule would have to be abandoned. Or, perhaps . . . rearranged?

His friends had also overslept, and he found them lingering in the breakfast parlour. Manderville, looking heavy-eyed, expressed a marked lack of interest in such mundane pursuits as Flower Shows. He had already met Dicky-Boy, and thought it hilarious that Vespa had hired the youth. When asked to help with the schedule, he volunteered to visit the duchess and Miss Consuela this afternoon and find out if there had been any further disturbance at the Jones cottage. First, however, he intended to search the cellar for any golden objects that Preston Jones had planned to decorate with cloisonné. Broderick, seemingly none the worse for last evening's cards and Cognac, agreed to ride into the village and report last night's prowler to Constable Blackham. Vespa thanked them both for their help, and hurried upstairs to finish dressing, pausing with a grin as a crash from the direction of the kitchen was followed by his new parlour-maid's voice exclaiming, between giggles, "Dearie me . . . oh dearie me!"

Thornhill had set out the wine-coloured coat and pearl grey pantaloons that had arrived with his trunks from Richmond, and was brushing his caped driving coat. Lost in thought, Vespa belatedly realized what the valet was saying.

" . . . seems to have disappeared, Captain. I'd not mention it, save that I chanced to overhear Lieutenant Broderick speaking of enamels. I would not for the world have you think I eavesdrop on your conversations, for never has Aldrich Wolfram Thornhill stooped to such common behavior, but—"

Vespa interrupted sharply, "What has disappeared?"

"Why, the old snuff jar, sir. I put it in your room when first you took me on as your man. I noticed it was somewhat scratched, but I thought it rather charming and utilized it as a vase for some flowers. I cannot think what has become of it."

"I can!" *This* was what his mind had been trying to tell him! One of the things, at all events. Toby had said cloisonné was used for several things, including jars! "By Jupiter!" he exclaimed. "I gave it to Molly Hawes!"

It was essential that he retrieve the jar: not because of its possible intrinsic value, for even had it been solid gold it would not have justified the murder of Preston Jones, nor the following violent incidents. But it occurred to him that it might possibly be the object the thieves had sought, and that, failing to find it at Alabaster Royal, they'd searched the Jones cottage again. But what on earth could be so important about a snuff jar on which the surface was damaged? The only way to find out was to inspect it more closely. He might find a clue to the puzzle, such as a miniature map of some kind, or a hidden message.

Convinced that he was on the right track at last, he rejected Corporal's pleas to accompany him, told his friends to dine at the Gallery Arms at his expense, and with a vase of sparkling crystal carefully wrapped and on the seat beside him, he drove out.

The morning was bright but cloudy. Autumn was painting splashes of rust and scarlet on the trees, the air was cool and already an occasional leaf fluttered down. Vespa held his team to a steady pace, the autumnal colour sending his thoughts back to the previous September. He'd been in Madrid then, with Wellington; his lordship in a rare good humour, and his own spirits sunk in numbing despair because Sherry's death had at last been confirmed. It didn't seem possible that more than a year had elapsed, nor that his own circumstances were so changed.

Whoever would have guessed that after all the grief and pain and disappointment that had beset him, he would find a measure of contentment in a run-down and isolated old house. But it was so. He was, in fact, beginning to feel quite at home in what Papa would call his bucolic setting. And if new troubles had sprung up around him, they seemed less formidable as he drove along this peaceful country lane. He encountered only a tinker rattling past in a battered and overloaded cart, who advised him cheerily that it would rain before sunset.

Minutes later, he turned into the lane where the apothecary lived. The cottage was neat, and a bright-eyed maid directed Vespa around the side and into the back garden. Mr. Kestler—a spare, hunched-over individual—was supervising a middle-aged man with a bandaged head who was chopping wood. The apothecary viewed Vespa with suspicion and upon being handed a calling card demanded to know if he was here to "settle accounts".

Vespa eyed him levelly, then turned to the man with the chopper and held out his hand. "I'm Captain Vespa. I'm sorry you were injured in my service. Your name, I believe, is George Cobham?"

A twinkle came into the tired blue eyes, and Cobham shook hands and said humbly that he was grateful to have been sent here to be taken care of.

"You must not have heard me, sir," said the apothecary in his high-pitched whine. "I asked—"

"If I had come to settle accounts," said Vespa coolly. "I heard you, and I had, but now I see that will not be necessary. Climb in, Cobham, I'll drive you home."

"What d'ye mean—not necessary?" shrilled Kestler. "I treated your confoun—your employee's injuries and—"

"And must have found them trivial since you put him to work so soon," said Vespa, with a shrewd eye on the wood pile. "It appears you've had more than your 'pound of flesh', Kestler."

" 'Pound of—of *flesh*', sir? Of all the— How dare you, sir?"

"Good gracious, man, what are you spluttering about? You surely don't mean to stand there and ask for money after you've made my man work for his keep? That's illegal, Kestler! The truth is, you likely owe *me* for his services!"

"I—*illegal,* sir?" gobbled Kestler. "By—by God, sir!"

"Yes, well, I'm glad to see you're a religious man. But since you evidently believe Mr. Cobham to be quite recovered—"

George Cobham was grinning from ear to ear.

The apothecary, realizing he had met his match, and realizing also how the tale would resound through the countryside, got a grip on his temper and pulled together a lip-cracking smile. "Ah, you military men will have your little jokes, Captain. No, to say truth, Mr. Cobham is far from recovered. Concussion, you know. A tricky business. But it ain't good for a fellow to be confined to the house for long periods, and we came out to get my patient some exercise and fresh air. He's going along fairly well now. Another day or so—"

"Of most excellent food and pampering," put in Vespa.

"You may rest assured, sir," said the apothecary, rubbing his hands together.

Vespa smiled. "How does that suit, Cobham?"

"I'd like some of that there—er, excellent food and pamperin', sir," said the patient, with a sly wink.

"Very good. Then assuming Mr. Cobham will receive such at your hands," said Vespa, "you may send me your reckoning, Kestler. Good-day to you. Come and see me when you're quite well, Cobham." With a wave of his whip, he turned the greys and drove out.

The apothecary watched him with grudging admiration, and muttered something about "vest-pocket lawyers".

"You say something, sir?" enquired Cobham, innocently.

Kestler's wolfish grin dawned. "I said there goes a—er, real top sawyer. Now come in the house, my poor fellow. It's time for a nice cup of tea. We can't have you overdoing, can we? Your Captain wouldn't like that."

"No, I 'spect he wouldn't. It's not every gent would go outta his way for his workmen. Very nice of him, I must say."

"Yes, indeed," said the apothecary through his teeth. "Very nice."

Vespa was smiling to himself as he guided the team along the lane. Kestler was probably competent at his trade, but he was one of the grey people of this world. The old pinch-penny would benefit from a wife like—like Peg, who'd bring some sunshine into his life. The contemplation of such a union made him chuckle as he approached the dirt track leading to Josiah Hawes' little house. He would be even less welcome here, he knew, so he stopped the

222

team a short distance from the cottage. Before he could climb from the curricle, his name was called in an eager childish voice.

Molly came up at an ungainly run and welcomed him, her little face flushed with pleasure. "Can I come up in your coach, sir? Please? Just for a minute?"

When she was joyously enthroned beside him and had recovered her voice, she asked, "Did you want to see my Pa? He's at work. He works at Mr. Simms' farm this month." Her eyes clouded. She added sadly, "I 'spect you'll go away now, 'cos you didn't come to call on me."

Vespa assured her that he had indeed come to call on her, and added to her delight by taking her on a short drive around the field. She had never dreamt, she informed him in an awed whisper, that she would ever ride in such a grand coach. When he halted the team, he was thanked repeatedly. Taking up the parcel beside him, he said, "It was my pleasure, Mistress Molly. Now I wonder if we could make a trade, you and I. . . . "

In very short order, with the cloisonné vase safely bestowed under the seat, he turned the team to the south-west, waving farewell to a small girl ecstatic with joy over the prismatic colours she could awaken by turning her new vase in the sunlight.

It was half past one o'clock and the pale sun had disappeared behind thickening clouds when he reached Coombe Hall. It was a charming estate, the well-manicured grounds thronged with ardent horticulturists. He found Mrs. Esmeralda Stokely engaged in a politely fierce dispute over the merits of her 'cabbage' rose, as opposed to a militant old gentleman's 'French' variety. As soon as she glimpsed Vespa, the widow's lovely face lit up, and she abandoned her rival and hurried to give him both her hands.

"Jack! You *did* come! Rogue that you are, you're so late I thought you meant to disappoint poor me."

Her gown was of palest blue-green, the filmy silk clinging to her willowy figure revealingly; the poke of her straw bonnet was adorned with lace of the same shade, the guinea-gold curls shone, and her famous green eyes flirted with him charmingly. As he bowed over her hand he knew that although Sherry had been her first choice, she had a fondness for him and would probably accept if he offered. He was fond of her also, although no more so than of many delightful young ladies he had squired to *ton* parties or danced with at Almack's, or in Spain, or at the balls his mother so happily planned.

With Sherry gone, he knew he'd have to wed someday and provide heirs to the Vespa name. But there was plenty of time; he was not yet thirty. His most immediate task was to win back to health. Besides, even had he been contemplating matrimony, Esmeralda Stokely was a beautiful and much-admired lady, and she deserved better than to be shackled to a man whose heart had been irretrievably given to another.

Today, however, he was glad of their friendship, and he shared her merry chatter, adroitly parrying her more provocative remarks, and grateful for the fact that she did not once refer to his cane or seem repelled by the scar down his temple. When she had consigned her beloved prize roses to the jealous care of her gardener, he accepted her offer to conduct him among the many tables and displays and more elaborate exhibits.

She was quite knowledgeable and instructed him on the various merits of charmingly arranged bowls and vases of chrysanthemums, dahlias, the less exotic wallflowers, daisies, lupins and many fine rose exhibits. In the process, he met several people he knew, all of whom were delighted to find him up and about so soon. They were heart-warming encounters, each resulting in invitations to dine or to visit, which further lifted his spirits.

The young widow murmured with a twinkle, "Popular as ever, aren't you, Jack? Especially with the ladies. Did you notice how jealously they all looked at me? I vow it will be all over Town tomorrow that I'm your new flirt."

He chuckled. "Flatterer! I saw the ladies taking careful note of that dashing gown, and the pretty way you dress your hair. As for the men, they could scarce— Oh, your pardon, ma'am!"

He had failed to notice an elderly lady who turned abruptly

from admiring a tiered display of lilies-of-the-valley. She tottered as he brushed against her, and he took her arm steadyingly.

She slapped his hand away. "Keep your distance, young man!" she snapped in a thin harsh voice. "I know your kind of buck. . . . Not a shred of manners in the whole worthless breed! Shame to your fathers! . . . Disgraceful!"

"Whoops," murmured Vespa, as she went off, grunting anathemas on today's male youth and leaning heavily on her cane.

"There goes a female you didn't charm," teased Mrs. Stokely softly. "To think one of his lordship's gallant Captains would knock down a white-haired old lady! I am most shocked!"

"Oh, gad! Was she white-haired?" He glanced after the frail figure anxiously. "How could you tell under that heavy veil?"

"You can see it poking out under the back of her bonnet, silly. She's been behind us for some time. In fact I'd begun to think she was as captivated by you as"—she peeped at him coyly from behind her fan—"as the rest of us!"

"Do you think I really hurt the poor lady? Perhaps I should go and—"

She caught his arm. "What we should do is go and claim that lovely arbour over there. No, really, Jack, I'm a trifle tired, and would really like to rest for— Oh, bother! My gardener is waving. You must excuse me just for a minute. I'll come back and find you, directly, I promise. If anyone has damaged my roses . . . !"

He bowed and watched her hurry off, amused by her new passion for horticulture and wondering if it would be abandoned as rapidly as the various hobbies which had preceded it. The arbour she'd indicated was at the end of the little winding path they'd been following. It was a pretty spot, roofed by trellised wisteria and provided with three stone benches. He'd been walking for over an hour, and was quite willing to sit down for a short while.

He propped his cane against the bench, thinking that whoever designed this arbour had placed it in an ideal spot; especially for a pair of sweethearts. It was quiet, away from the crowd, and the trailing sprays of blossom provided a nice degree of privacy. Just

225

such a spot as he'd been used to take Marietta in the gardens at Vauxhall before—

"You will be so good as to accompany me, sir."

Vespa started. There was no one in sight, but the male voice had been clear, and the words spoken with the careful precision that so often marks the well-educated foreigner. He said, "Who's there?"

"This way, Captain. The lady awaits."

A man appeared at the side of the arbour, holding back the shrubbery and smiling invitingly. He was tall and dark-skinned, with hair of jet, eyes almost as dark, and finely chiselled features. He wore Western dress, but Vespa judged him to be a well-born Indian. Taking up his cane, he stood and looked along the path uneasily. "Is something wrong? Mrs. Stokely said she'd come here."

"Yes, but there has been trouble. She asks that you come quickly, please. It is quicker this way."

At the mention of trouble Vespa started forward instinctively. The other man nodded, and pulled the shrubs farther apart. Slanting a quick glance at him, Vespa saw a gleam of triumph in the dark eyes, and a warning bell sounded in his head. He drew back and tightened his hold on the cane. "Wait up! We'll go this way, if you please!"

"Ah, but we don't please, sahib! Do as you are told!"

Another Indian had appeared as if by magic, and the small but deadly pistol in his hand rammed into Vespa's ribs.

"Devil I will! You'd not dare fire that thing in here!" Vespa sprang clear and swung his cane hard.

The second man uttered a muffled howl as the pistol was dashed from his grasp. Vespa whipped around to face the first attacker, and levelled him with a flashing upper-cut. The exhilaration of hand-to-hand combat, the knowledge that his strength was returning, made the blood seem to race in his veins. He whirled again, caught a glimpse of a club coming at him, ducked, then lashed out hard.

"Idiots!"

226

It was a new voice, and even as he turned to face the additional threat, he was blinded by a cloth that was clamped over his face. He struggled madly, but strong hands came from behind to grip his arms. A sickeningly sweet smell was choking him, making it hard to breathe . . . his bones were melting away. Someone was swearing . . . those had to be oaths, spat out in such rage in a fading and unfamiliar tongue. . . .

"I did not wish this." A pleasant voice this time, quite different to the other. Soft and feminine. "I told you not to hurt him."

A man said indignantly, "Perchance, mem, you should have told him not to hurt *us*! This Captain fights like two tigers!"

"Had I known it would take three of you to overpower an invalid, I'd have sent my grandfather along to assist you!"

The sally amused Vespa. He opened his eyes, and the hand that held an icy rag to his face was withdrawn. He blinked dazedly as his vision cleared. The lady was tall and slender. She wore a sari of rich turquoise silk embroidered with gold and royal blue thread. Shining black hair framed great dark eyes and delicate features and was loosely coiled into a thick silken rope that hung over one shoulder. A jewel glittered between softly arching brows. The dusky skin was clear, with the faintest blush highlighting her cheekbones. Perfectly shaped lips curved into a wistful smile. He realized he was holding his breath.

The Indian lady of Preston Jones' sketch said in her soft, purring voice, "How may I apologize to you, Captain Vespa? My people have been unforgivably clumsy and foolish, and treated you brutally, but—alas—the responsibility is mine own. Are you feeling very ill?"

He felt sick and dizzy and his head was throbbing again, but the most annoying symptom was that he couldn't seem to recall why he was here. "I've felt better, certainly," he said.

"No, no!" The rings on small, long-fingered hands sparkled and she pushed him back as he strove to sit up. "You must lie still or you will feel very much worse." She spoke in her own language over her shoulder, and somebody hurried away.

Vespa tried to pull his wits together and take note of his surroundings. He must have been unconscious for some time, for lamps were lit in the room. And what a room it was. The tiled floors were spread with richly coloured rugs. Overhead, great billows of pink and purple satin swept from a gilded circular mirror in the centre of the ceiling and were caught up at the tops of the walls to create a tent-like atmosphere. Deep sofas and the chaise-longue on which he lay were magnificently carven, their scarlet velvet cushions trimmed with braided and tasselled gold. There were tall teakwood cabinets embellished with intricate paintings, and little mosaic-tiled tables were set about, atop one of which a miniature jade temple emitted pungent smoke that wreathed slowly into the warm air. In one corner a great golden many-armed statue soared majestically, a large ruby winking in the forehead, an expression of remote indifference on the gleamingly classic features.

He returned his gaze to the lady who sat beside him. She was turning away to accept a glass handed to her by a manservant, and in profile he thought her even more lovely. The man frowned and murmured something that annoyed. The result was startling. For just an instant her lovely mouth hardened, the corners pulling down, the soft lips curling back from bared teeth as she snapped a response. The man looked alarmed, and withdrew. The lady turned, her gentle smile restored, but Vespa had glimpsed what the artist had seen: the ruthlessness hidden beneath that beautiful exterior.

A servant came to assist him to a sitting position and prop him with cushions. The glass was offered, with the information that the contents would soon reduce the effect of the drug. He hesitated only momentarily. If she wanted information from him, there'd be no point in putting him to sleep again. The drink was thick and tasted of cinnamon, and after a few mouthfuls he set it aside. He felt steadier, and said firmly, "Now I want to know to whom I speak, and why I was attacked and brought here."

"Of course, Captain Vespa," her voice seemed to hold a caress. "Ah, but you are angry, and understandably so. I am Nilima Sutanati, but you may call me Mrs. Nilima. I desired only to speak with you, but my servants tell me you misunderstood and became violent. You will say that I could have called on you, but that is not possible." She gave a forlorn little shrug. "I am a stranger here. My appearance causes great curiosity, especially among country people. I am stared at; sometimes laughed at. So I do not go out. You will understand? It is not—comfortable for me. And this is a most delicate matter. If I had written, it would have been not easy to explain."

"This is not comfortable for *me*," declared Vespa coldly. "I am not a wealthy man, and I cannot think what I have that would justify your taking the risk of being arrested for kidnapping."

A wariness came into those velvety eyes. "I will explain, and you will comprehend." She adjusted her sari, her hand drawing his eyes to the shapeliness of her breasts as she fingered the pearl necklet she wore. "My father," she said slowly, "is a Maharajah. A very powerful man in my country. I am his favourite daughter, and he sent me to England to be educated. Always, however, from the time I was a young girl, even until today, I am to have my ayah—my chaperone—beside me. But, you see," she smiled confidingly, blindingly, "I am no longer a young girl. I met a most charming English gentleman. He is not of great wealth, but he has travelled widely, and has many interests. He has a passion for the work of one particular artist, and he taught me to love this man's work also."

'Aha!' thought Vespa.

"One day," Mrs. Nilima went on, "my friend and I slipped away from my ayah, and we came down to this part of your southland. We visited the great artist, and while my friend was admiring some paintings, I spoke to the artist secretly and ordered from him a snuff jar. He was reluctant, for he did not like very much to work in cloisonné, but he agreed. I was worried that the ayah might report my absence, as she was paid to do, and it came to me that if I ordered a suitable gift for my father also, his anger might be appeased."

"I see. So you ordered a jar for your—er, friend, and—"

"And a fruit dish for my father. I told the artist to paint a landscape on the jar, and he said he would use a similar scene on the dish, which was a good size. But he demanded a great deal of money. Payment in advance, he said, because this work would prevent his taking any more commissions for a while." She sighed, and said sadly, "You will think me a very silly lady. But I had little experience of the world."

"Do you say this artist did not live up to the bargain?"

"I know he made the dish and the jar, but then the poor man died, and I never received either piece, nor was my money refunded. My father sent word he was coming to England and that he was most displeased because he had been told I had gone away—alone—with a man. You cannot know what a sin this is in my country, Captain! If he learns I was here in Dorset, so far from London, and alone with my friend, I shall be utterly disgraced, and no one will ever marry me."

"Not even your friend?"

"My friend," her eyes fell, "has betrayed me, and is wed to another lady."

"Ah. But if you were to confess to your father that you came here only to buy a gift for him, surely—"

"Alas, I cannot prove that. I sent agents to the artist's family and they deny all knowledge of such a commission. My people made enquiries at the galleries that handled the man's work, and they do not know of it, either."

"Dear me," said Vespa politely. "I am very sorry, ma'am. But if the artist is dead, and your friend now married, how will your father know you were down here? You could surely bribe your ayah, and there is nothing to prove—"

"But there may be," she interpolated, wringing her hands despairingly. "The artist, you see, was in the habit of sketching people who interested him. I am told he made just such a sketch of me. My ayah is terrified that if she lies to protect me, and my father learns of the existence of such a sketch, her very life would be in peril! And I promise you, in my country the life of a female servant does not count for much."

"Hum. But, surely, Mrs. Nilima, the artist might have seen you anywhere, and would certainly remember such a lovely lady? You could tell your sire he must have caught a glimpse of you in London, for instance."

"No, no! I thought of that, but it will not do. The artist hated towns. He never went to London, or indeed to any city. Which would mean he could only have seen me here. And the other servants *know* my ayah never was here!"

"I see. You're in rather a predicament. But how on earth can I be of assistance? I presume your artist is, or was, Mr. Preston Jones, who lived near my estate. Unfortunately, I know nothing of art."

"But you've become interested in it, Captain, have you not?" She leant closer, half smiling. "No, do not tease me. I know you went to the gallery in Salisbury, looking at his works. And that you are acquainted with his family."

He drew back and watched her, saying nothing.

"I have been honest with you," she said. "Now, I beg you will be honest with me, Captain Vespa. My only hope is to find the pieces I ordered, and to ensure that there is no sketch of me in existence. I implore you— Help me!"

"My dear ma'am, the chances of my finding such articles are remote and—"

"Do not take me for a fool, Captain!" Her voice and eyes hardened. "Preston Jones did much of his work on your estate, as I very well know. He often used your house as his studio."

"Even so, I have no right to his works, and anything I chanced to find would be at once turned over to Mr. Jones' family."

"I see." She sighed. "If I cannot appeal to your gallantry, then I am willing to pay, sir. Handsomely."

"You have wasted your time, ma'am," he said, standing. "I cannot help you."

She was on her feet in a swift, supple movement, her dark eyes blazing at him. "You mean you *will* not! Why?"

"Good-day, ma'am."

"You are not wealthy, this I also know." She darted to intercept him as he turned towards the door. "I heard you have been denied the lady you once hoped to marry. Perhaps you've found another, eh? Five hundred pounds would buy a grand new bridal suite for your old house."

Astonished by the offer of such a sum, he stared at her.

She laughed softly. "That changed your mind, did it not? Come now, Captain. I *know* a sketch of me exists! I *know* my jar was in your possession, but has now vanished! Why—"

"How could you know such things, unless—" His temper flared. "Good God! It was *your* men who broke into Alabaster and tried to murder Miss Jones!"

"Why would my people try to kill the silly girl?"

"For the same reason, perhaps, that they murdered her father! Did you really think to hoax me with that involved gibberish about your threatened dishonour and the Merciless Maharajah? You'd do better, ma'am, to tell me what you're really up to. I might be interested, if the stakes are high enough."

She frowned at him for a long moment, then gestured with one slim hand and said softly, "What do you suppose I am up to, Captain?"

The air stirred behind Vespa. He'd gambled. Perhaps he was about to be struck down for his pains. He gambled again. "Let's say it has to do with the quarry." At this her eyes became so empty that he knew he'd touched a nerve, and he swept on, "I know you're not in the scheme alone, and I know there's a fortune to be—" Interrupting himself, he leapt to the side and the man who'd aimed a cudgel at his head missed and staggered, blundering against his mistress.

"Stop him, you clumsy imbecile!" she shrieked. "He mustn't get away!"

Vespa snatched up one of the small tables and tossed it at a man

232

charging him and the jade incense-burner hurtled to the floor. At the same moment somewhere nearby a shot rang out and there was a chorus of excited shouts.

The door burst open.

A tiny, veiled old lady ran into the room, screeching at the top of her lungs: "So here you are! You wicked, *wicked* boy! I thought you'd been *murdered*! Might have known you'd run off instead with some *doxy* in a fancy house!" She began to belabour the astonished Vespa with her parasol. "How *dared* you leave your poor old great-aunt to fend for herself? I've got half the constables in Dorsetshire following me, *searching* for you! Out, you libertine! *Out!* I'll teach you to abandon your kin-folk!"

Two exotically clad individuals who appeared to be footmen jumped clear of the door as Vespa dodged through it, the old lady in hot pursuit, her parasol flailing in all directions.

"Stop—" began Mrs. Nilima, recovering from her stupefaction.

His eyes alight with laughter, Vespa glanced back. "Your rug's on fire," he advised.

It was.

Neither he nor his 'great-aunt' stayed to help put it out.

15

It was *my* adventure!" Consuela leant forward on the seat of the rocking coach and removed her veil and bonnet. "It all went *marvellously* well," she declared triumphantly. "Now own it, Captain Jack!"

"How can I deny it?" he said, trying to stop laughing. "But it could have been ugly, you little madcap! Gad! To think that a lady would run herself into such danger, only to help me, is—"

"Stop! I command it! You were there for no other reason than that you have been so kind as to interest yourself in my troubles. And also I do not want my thrilling adventure spoilt by silly lectures about gentle ladies and risks and such dull stuff, when I'm fairly *dying* of curiosity to hear all about it."

Vespa watched in fascination as the snowy wig came off and she started to remove the amazing quantities of hairpins which had confined her own thick locks. "Well, I won't lecture you," he said, knowing he should be more stern. "Though if I was your brother—"

"My—*brother*?" There was an odd note to her voice as she turned her head to stare at him.

"Well—your father, then. I'd take you over my knee and—" He laughed. "No, it's no use! I keep remembering how you scattered those bullies with your parasol, and how you sent them all rushing back into that strange house with your screechings of 'Fire!' I wonder I didn't have a seizure when I realized who was my great-aunt! Oh, Consuela, you little rogue! I've a thousand questions. The first being, how ever did you persuade the duchess to permit such a reckless masquerade?"

"Don't be silly. I told her I was going to the Flower Show. Nothing more."

"But, if that's what you thought, why bother with your great-aunt disguise?"

"Oh. Well, I wanted to see"—she scowled at an apparently offensive hairpin, and stammered—"I mean, that is—if I'd gone as Miss Consuela Jones, I'd have been obliged to endure Manning trailing after me all day long, and whining about her feet. You know a *young* lady cannot go out without a chaperone. Besides, Grandmama was upset by that horrid business last night, and I couldn't leave her alone."

"But why go to all the trouble of disguising yourself? If you'd told me you wanted to go to the Flower Show, I'd have taken you."

"But how charming," she said mockingly. "And I could have spent the day watching you simper and sigh over Esmeralda Stokely?"

"I did no such— Jupiter! Esme must think I deserted her!"

"Well, she won't, for she left directly after you went into that little arbour. I—er, chanced to see her drive off, and I thought you must have quarrelled, which is why I hurried to—"

Frowning, he interrupted, "A moment, if you please. Do you say Mrs. Stokely did not go back to her exhibit? That she left the grounds?"

"That is exactly what I said. She rushed off in such a hurry I was sure you'd offended her, and I went to the arbour to find out what had happened. I got there just in time to see those . . . those dreadful men drag you away. For a minute, I thought . . . " Her voice shook, and was suspended.

Vespa took her hand and held it strongly. "But you followed, is that it? How brave of you. But why didn't you try to get help?"

"Because it would have taken too long to convince anyone to follow you. All they were concerned with were their flowers. They'd probably have thought I was just a confused old lady. And even if I had convinced them, by the time we'd set out, we would have lost you completely. I wanted to find out who was behind it all, and why. And I'm *still* waiting! For mercy's sake, *tell* me!"

"I will, but—didn't old Watts raise a fuss about tearing off in pursuit with you in the coach?"

"No, for I didn't tell him until we were well after you, and then he had no choice but to keep going. He is so loyal to me, bless him, and thought my disguise was great fun at first, but— Oh, Jack, it *is* all connected with my father in some way, isn't it? You have found the lady he sketched!"

"She found me, rather," he said thoughtfully. "I suppose she had me followed, and hoped to lure me away without causing an uproar."

"Her people bungled that. You must have put up a grand fight."

"Which might not have answered had you not come at just the right moment." He took up her hand and kissed it. "For which I humbly thank you, Miss Jones."

Consuela's cheeks flamed. She said in a shaken voice, "Well, well, that's—er, better than being scolded for a 'reckless masquerade'."

"I won't scold, but—had you any idea what you were walking into?"

"None. To say truth, I fully expected to face Lord Alperson, or Larson Gentry. I never dreamt a woman was responsible. Do you see what I meant about my father's talent? He had her to the life."

"Yes, indeed. A remarkable likeness of an exquisite and deadly creature. One can but hope she is the only one of her kind!"

"I thought she was lovely in Papa's sketch, but—my goodness! In person, she is incredibly beautiful! When I saw her in that magnificent room, I was so overawed I almost forgot to be your great-aunt."

He chuckled and squeezed her hand. "But you great-aunted perfectly. And you're right about the connection to your father's work. She is after that sketch. And the cloisonné. Though, why—"

"What cloisonné?"

"Oh, that's right. You don't know. We found—well, Toby found— And— Good God! My curricle is still at the Flower Show! We must go there at once!"

"But—but it has been closed for hours. Your horses will be cared for, I'm sure, and you can send Hezekiah for them in the morning. Let's go home now, please. You've had a terrible time, Jack, and must be exhausted."

"What about you, dauntless one? I'm truly sorry to drag you all that way again, but it's devilish— I mean, it's very important! I *must* locate my curricle tonight!"

"But what has your coach to do with cloisonné?"

"I'd given the snuff jar to little Molly Hawes for a vase, and— Excuse me." He let down the window, and shouted, "Watts! Hey, Watts! I don't know where we are, but there's a moon. Can you find your way back to Coombe Hall? Yes—now! . . . Good man!"

Sitting down again, his arm was gripped by two small but strong hands, and Consuela hissed, "If you do not wish to be strangled by a maddened female, Captain Jack Wansdyke Vespa, speak!"

He had no wish to be strangled.

<hr>

"By Gad, but Miss Consuela's a spunky little lady," said Broderick admiringly.

"Too much so for her own good." Vespa nodded to Thornhill, who hurried over to refill his coffee cup. He was trying to wake up, and wished his impatient friends had waited a little longer before forcibly removing him from his bed at half past nine o'clock and demanding to know what kind of Flower Show lasted until almost two in the morning. His moans of a need for more sleep had been ruthlessly ignored, and he'd been dragged down to the breakfast parlour and plied with strong coffee to, as Broderick said, restore him to consciousness. "I'm grateful to her, of course," he went on, selecting a steaming buttered crumpet from the dish Thornhill offered. "But, dashitall, there's no telling what the little scamp will get up to next! And these people, whoever they may be . . . " He paused, not finishing the sentence.

"They mean business," finished Broderick. "See your point, old fellow. Must keep Courageous Consuela clear of 'em, what?"

Manderville, who had been inspecting the cloisonné vase, shook his head and observed that he could find nothing in the least remarkable about the design. "Save that besides being so cracked, it's a view of your western meadow, mine host."

Vespa looked up sharply. "It is? How can you know that?"

"By this unlovely object." Manderville handed the vase to him and pointed out a stunted tree, meticulously detailed. "See how twisted it is? When I rode over to the village for you yesterday, the sun threw its shadow on the grass and my foolish hack was properly spooked. I damn near took a toss."

"You're right, by George," muttered Vespa. "Mrs. Nilima spoke the truth to that extent. Mr. Jones used the estate for his subject. It's a pretty thing, but I don't think that's why she was so desperate to have it. What do you say, Toby?"

Broderick, who seemed preoccupied this morning, stared at him blankly.

"Hey!" cried Manderville. "Where are you, Toby?"

Broderick started. "What? Oh, sorry. Let me have a look."

Vespa passed the vase to him. "I take it there were no further incidents at the Jones cottage, Paige?"

"None." Manderville grinned. "Your faithful watchman reported all serene, and informed me he is a 'downy bird'. I shouldn't wonder if he's good at watching, if nothing else. Came out of the bushes like a shadow when I rode up. He says he'll report here to collect further orders from 'his Captain'. Leered at me sideways as if we shared some very naughty secret, poor chap. Now suppose you spill the beans, Jack. You must have spent some hours with the fabled Stokely before you launched into that derring-do with the Maharajah's daughter, or whatever she is."

Vespa said thoughtfully, "You know everyone who is anyone in the *ton,* Paige. What do you know of Esmeralda Stokely?"

"You ask *me?*" Manderville laughed. "I'd think your brother would have—" He paused as Broderick slanted an oblique glance at him. "Oh," he said awkwardly. "Sorry, Jack. No offence. How can I help?"

"By finding out where the pretty widow went after she left the Flower Show yesterday afternoon. When we reached that wisteria arbour, she told me she must check on her roses for a minute and would come back at once. Consuela said that instead she drove away in a great hurry."

Manderville said, "And you want to know why? By the lord Harry! You don't think she led you into an ambush?"

"Of course I don't, bird-wit," said Vespa, mildly irritated because Consuela had also jumped to that ridiculous conclusion. "We've been friends for years, and the lady was as good as betrothed to Sherry. She'd never do such a thing. I just wonder if something is wrong. She has a country house near Salisbury. You'll have no trouble finding it."

"This isn't scratched," declared Broderick, holding up the vase. "Those little lines are part of the design."

Closer inspection confirmed his remark. Manderville said curiously, "Now why on earth would Preston Jones do such an odd thing? D'you think it's some kind of code, Toby?"

"It's possible." Broderick hesitated. "Or Mr. Jones may have been trying some new technique. Artists are always experimenting with this or that. On the other hand . . . there's an effect that can occur in old paintings, called *pentimento*. I don't know too much about it, but I think it has to do with changes that take place in the lacquer causing something that was painted over to begin to— sort of reappear, in a ghostly kind of way." He tugged at his earlobe and muttered uncertainly, "But—I wouldn't think that would apply to enamelling."

"Aha!" exclaimed Manderville. "The sage is baffled! Our Don Toby don't have the answer for once!"

"No, but Miss Jones might," said Broderick. "Or more likely that art gallery chap you went to see, Jack."

"Signor da Lentino." Vespa nodded. "Jolly good idea. Perhaps you wouldn't mind dropping in to have a word with him while you're up there, Paige? His shop is called La Galleria, and—"

"Am I become a maid of all work?" protested Manderville indignantly. "What are you going to be doing while I toil and slave?"

"Taking a bath," said Vespa. "I must go and see how Consuela is faring after her adventure. The duchess had retired, of course, by the time we got back, but is likely enraged with the poor girl and thinking her hopelessly compromised. I'll have to try and rescue her, and I still smell of Mrs. Nilima's incense."

"Personally," drawled Manderville, "I thought it was an improvement."

He escaped in the nick of time, but with a crumpet flying past his head as he whizzed through the door.

⌦

Vespa was at his dressing-table putting the finished touches to his cravat when Thornhill returned. He met the valet's eyes in the mirror. "Who is it?"

"A person, sir." Thornhill smoothed the set of the newly delivered dark brown coat across Vespa's shoulders. "An excellent fit, if I dare remark it. Though Monsieur Balleroy will have to allow more width here the next time."

"He just took it in for me!" Vespa stood and inspected his reflection hopefully. "This coat fairly hung on me when I came home."

"Aha!" exclaimed Thornhill. "Then you are regaining your health, Captain. I thought I had observed that you looked more fit. Although, of course, I have not been in your service a great time. Yet."

Amused by the demurely uttered last word, Vespa said, "True. Now, who is this unidentified person?"

Thornhill said disdainfully, "I must confess I did not catch the name, although Harper apparently is acquainted with him."

"Harper . . . ?"

"Oh, my! Had I forgot to mention it, sir? I have succeeded in engaging a manservant." The valet smiled expansively. "This house is in sad need of general cleaning, as you are aware, Captain, and Harper is extreme energetic, although, alas, lacking in that certain polish required of servants in a gentleman's home."

Vespa picked up hat and gloves and said with a wry smile, "Another of your—acquaintances from the theatre, perhaps? Must I keep a pistol under my pillow?"

"Certainly not, Captain! We are acquainted only in that he has been—er—residing at the manor for some while, and—"

Vespa groaned. "Where?"

"The, ah, attic, I believe. But a good worker, sir. A former naval tar, I understand, and not dismayed by the—er—apparitions."

"Well, that sounds more promising. Now what about this mystery caller?"

"He said he was expected, so I told him to wait in the kitchen. Corporal stayed with him."

"On guard?"

"Precisely, sir."

"Is Lieutenant Broderick still here?"

"He rode out while you were bathing, sir, and has come home, if I dare to make the observation, very low in spirits. Very low. He waits in the drawing room. It is my understanding that he has something he wishes to discuss with you."

As he entered the drawing room, Vespa saw that Broderick was looking out at the persistent rain with an unusually grim expression. Apprehensive, he sat down beside his friend on the faded brocade sofa that Thornhill had somehow managed to make look presentable. "Trouble?"

With a wry smile Broderick admitted, "I'm in a bit of a pickle, to say truth." He ran a hand through his hair, the nervous gesture at odds with his customary calm demeanour. "Don't like betraying a confidence. Especially this one."

Vespa leant back on the sofa and waited, feeling the muscles under his ribs tighten.

Broderick stood restlessly, and wandered to the window. "You know," he said, not turning, "that I've been—been seeing Miss Gentry."

Vespa's taut muscles relaxed. He said gently, "I suspected you had ridden out with her a time or two."

"Every single morning from the first day I set eyes on her!"

"With the consent of her brother?"

"No—dammit!" Broderick whirled and said harshly, "With *her* consent, which is all that weighs with me! And I've never done more than kiss the hand of that pure little angel. I swear!"

"My dear fellow, you've no need to swear to me. I've naught to say in the matter. But—aren't you rather—"

"Compromising the lady? Go on! Say it! It's what you're thinking!"

"It seems to be what you're thinking, certainly."

Broderick groaned, and turned away.

Clearly, he was hit hard. Vespa said, "Toby, Lord knows I've no right to give advice, except perhaps as one who's walked that path. I know you're an honourable man, but if you're falling in love with her, be sure there's hope before you're both completely—"

"Well, there isn't! None! And I *am* in love with her!" Broderick paced to the end of the room and back, his face strained and his eyes glinting with desperation. "Ariadne tried to sound out her brother, for she feels as I do, bless her. Gentry was in his cups, or he'd likely have realized she wasn't joking. He laughed, she said, and told her his plans for her future don't include a well-nigh penniless half-pay officer! And—and the most *devilish* part of it is that, 'fore heaven, I cannot blame the beastly fellow!" He tore at his hair and demanded an anguished, "*Look* at me, Jack! What have I to offer? Nothing! And her such a—a vision of beauty, and with so pure and trusting a nature!"

'And not a particle of spirit or common sense,' thought Vespa, recalling Marietta's quiet strength, and a 'little old lady' who'd burst into a deadly room and helped him escape at great risk to herself. But he said only, "All right, I'm looking."

He scanned a man who appeared to be utterly distraught and whose fair curls were comically dishevelled; but he saw a gallant soldier and a loyal friend, and he declared staunchly, "You've a great deal to offer! You're young and healthy and good-looking— most of the time. And you're well-born and carry a fine old name. In my opinion your greatest asset is that you've a brilliant mind, and when you decide what to do with it, you can only rise to the top of whatever vocation you choose. If your parent is displeased with you at the moment, he'll come around eventually; you know it. And I'd think Miss Gentry the type of lady whom any prospective father-in-law would embrace delightedly." He thought, 'For any fool could see she'd be utterly biddable and give him not a whit of trouble.'

Broderick stared at him for a moment, then stamped to the window again and with his back turned blew his nose noisily. Still wielding his handkerchief, he wandered behind the sofa and very briefly rested a shy hand on Vespa's shoulder. "My apologies, dear boy," he said in a husky voice. "I'd not meant to drop all that in your dish. It's just—well you're the sort a fellow can talk to . . . you know."

Touched, Vespa said, "Good. I wish I could offer you a sage solution, but all I can suggest is that since you really love the lady, your best course would be to approach Gentry and put all your cards on the table. And you have some damned good cards, no matter what you may think."

"Thank you." Broderick sighed heavily. "But that bird won't fly, I'm afraid. That's what I really meant to tell you. Gentry's leaving."

Vespa came to his feet. "The deuce! Permanently?"

"Ariadne thinks so, and is heart-broken, poor sweet. All her brother will say is that their fortunes are taking a splendid upward spiral and that they'll be ensconced in an Italian villa before the month is out. So, if you really think Larson Gentry is involved in whatever's going on . . . "

"Then their plans must be almost complete," muttered Vespa. "And whatever their plans are, it would seem that success will demand they leave the country. Jupiter! It must be an ugly business, indeed! But—what? You're the one with the brains, Toby. Put 'em to work!"

For a space the room was quiet as they both wrestled with the problem.

Vespa was frustrated by the feeling that he already knew the answer; that the solution was right before his eyes, only he was too dim-witted to see it. He cast his mind back to his arrival here, searching for any incident that might provide a clue to the puzzle.

A tentative cough awoke him to the realization that he was standing before the hearth, and that Broderick had gone.

"Be he interrupting of ye, sir? He waited, but—"

His temporary 'guard' stood in the doorway watching him with that awful grin of fawning servility. Shocked by the realization that this must be the 'person' Thornhill had told to wait in the kitchen, Vespa exclaimed, "Dicky-Boy! Good heavens! I am so sorry to have kept you standing about all this time. I was—er, preoccupied with another matter, I'm afraid."

The youth came forward shyly, nodding his shaggy head, the

244

eyes that seemed too small for their sockets darting from Vespa to the portrait of Sir Kendrick and back again. "Aye. He thought as ye was talking wi' that there gen'leman. Dicky-Boy don't wonder at it, neither. Such a great gent as he do be."

"Yes," said Vespa. "He is, indeed. You've seen Sir Kendrick, have you?"

The youth put his head on one side and giggled. "Oh, yessir! Dicky-Boy sees lotsa folk." He winked in his odd, sly fashion, and giggled again.

Clearly, the poor fellow was not going on very well today. Vespa said briskly, "Yes. Well now, you've a report, I believe?"

At once the slouching shoulders pulled back, the head lifted and at strict attention the report was offered. There had been no further sign of intruders at the Jones cottage. "Not goin' in, leastwise. He seen a old lady go *out* yes'day morning along of old Mr. Watts." His brow furrowed. "Dicky never see her afore, so she might be one o' they magic folks, like Mother Wardloe. Then he see Mr. Durham's boy take some meat to the back door. And then Mr. Castle, the priest, he called. And there was that there Left'nant Mandy-fil." His eyes glowed with admiration. "Dicky-Boy see *him*. *Very* flash he be, and his horse be flash, too! Dicky-Boy goed to sleep then. That were all, Cap'n. Not no one else as shouldn't ha' been there, or Dicky-Boy would've seen. Sharp eyes, he's got. Mr. Castle, he says so."

"I'm sure he's right," said Vespa, handing over two shillings.

The boy's eyes became as round as the coins. "But—but, sir! Ye give him a shilling day afore yest'day."

"Yes. It sounds to me as if you missed a lot of sleep, lad. You get on home now, and rest."

"*Thankee,* Cap'n! Doesn't ye want him to watch no more?"

"Yes. Until Mr. Cobham can work again. Off you go now."

The boy nodded and started away, beaming down at the coins in his palm, and mumbling, "Dicky-Boy'll be ready, sir. He'll have his sharp eyes ready for ye. He sees things what other folk don't see. Secret things." He reached the door, but turned to look back at Vespa, who stood by the hearth, watching him. "Like—coaches," he said, grinning.

His gaze had shifted. Glancing around curiously, Vespa saw that the seven small coaches he and Consuela had found were now neatly arranged across the mantelpiece. "Do you mean these?" he asked, taking one up. "What d'you know of them?"

His answer was a shrill scream of laughter. "He won't tell. Dicky-Boy, that's *his* secret." Still laughing hysterically, he ran into the hall. A moment later, Vespa saw him lurching along the muddy drivepath, his laughter drifting after him.

'Poor little devil,' he thought, and replaced the coach as Thornhill hurried in with his driving coat.

The rain had stopped, although the clouds were dark and threatening. The latest addition to his household staff was in the barn, talking to Strickley. He was a small man, bow-legged but powerfully built, his skin bronzed by years of exposure to wind and water. He spun around when he heard Vespa approach, and knuckled his brow respectfully, a tentative smile lurking in a pair of bright grey eyes.

"You're Harper, I take it," said Vespa, pulling on his gauntlets.

"Aye, Cap'n, sir."

Vespa looked at Strickley. "And you knew this man was trespassing in my house?"

"No, he never, sir," put in Harper, quickly. "I'm very quick on me trotters, y'see, sir. Comes from years of running up and down the rigging of His Majesty's frigates. If I don't want to be seen, I ain't seen. If you mean to have me put in charge, I'll go quiet. But all I asks is work, sir. I'm a good hard worker, and I done no harm while I were here. That I swear!"

Vespa considered him appraisingly, and liked the steady way the man met his gaze. "I try not to interfere with Mr. Thornhill's decisions," he said. "You understand that you'll be on a trial basis?"

A great grin lit the leathery features. "Aye, aye, sir!" said Harper. "Thank ye, sir!"

Strickley led the team forward, jerked his head, and Harper

246

hurried off, pausing en route to the house to turn two fast cart-wheels and shout an exuberant, "Hurrah!"

Vespa asked with a grin, "What d'you think of him?"

"Seems like he's got plenty of energy," said Strickley. "We're gettin' a crew together, ain't we, Cap'n? We'll have the old house bright and shinin' in no time!" He glanced up at the sky. "More'n I can say fer the weather. Don't look none too promising, sir. I put the top up, just in case."

Vespa had a carrot for each of his greys, and having petted them affectionately and agreed with Strickley's remark that they was "prime bits of blood and bone", he climbed into the sleek coach and guided the team into the courtyard.

Manning admitted him when he arrived at the Jones cottage, and took him straight back to the studio. This unconventional treatment of a visitor did not surprise him, and when Consuela hurried in a moment later, he said, "I suppose you've whisked me back here so as to warn me not to say anything to upset the duchess."

"Well, of course. Grandmama was fast asleep when I got home last night, thank heaven. Luckily, I'd told her that I was to meet my old governess at the Flower Show and might be obliged to dine with her. She's the most proper person you could ever imagine, but loves to talk, and goes on forever, so Grandmama wasn't surprised that I was late; though she didn't know *how* late! Now—quickly, tell me, what did you find in the snuff jar?"

He bowed, and said formally, "Good-morning, Miss Jones. Do I take it that you are 'at home'?"

"Yes, and so is Mr. Castle—well, I mean he's visiting us, and he saw you drive in, so don't tease."

Vespa grinned. "All right. I'm only glad you're none the worse for wear after your great adventure."

"You'll be the worse for wear if you don't tell—"

"Nothing to tell, unfortunately. Even Broderick couldn't find anything in or on the jar that might help us. Except that the scratches weren't—"

247

"Sratches? Do you say you gave my sweet Molly a damaged vase? No wonder you didn't want to show it to me last night!"

"*Will* you try not to explode before I've a chance to finish? I couldn't show it to you last night, Miss Pepper-Pot, because for one thing it was too dark for you to have seen it properly, and for another, you could hardly keep your eyes open. To say truth, when I gave it to the child, I thought it was quite charming, and that the scratch marks were only on the surface. But now Toby says they're not scratches at all, but that your father painted the vase in that way. Do you know— Oh, gad! She's doing it again!"

Consuela's eyes blazed with excitement and she sprang to seize his arm and exclaim, "That's *it*! That's what was so odd about that ugly painting! It had *odd little lines* on it! Oh, Jack! Jack! Whatever can it mean? Why would—"

The door burst open and Manning hissed urgently, "Her ladyship's very cross, and she's coming to find you, miss!"

A distant shriek of *"Consuela!"* emphasized her warning, and Consuela hurried into the corridor calling gaily, "Here I am, Grandmama! Captain Vespa wanted to look at one of Papa's paintings."

Lady Francesca was annoyed by what she termed 'unseemingly behaviours', but Vespa was skilled at calming the uncertain humours of elderly ladies and she was soon thanking him for his assistance during the robbery. Mr. Castle, who had obviously been fully informed of the case, expressed his dismay that such things should occur in "our innocent, sylvan countryside" and went on to deplore the increase of crime in Britain as a whole. "I've no wish to alarm you, ma'am. But with you two ladies living alone, and only a part-time footman and an elderly groom and gardener for protection . . . " He shook his head bodingly. "Dear me! It does seem indicated that you should hire an able-bodied man to guard the house."

"Thank you, Mr. Castle, but Captain Vespa has already hired a guard for us," said Consuela.

"But—was not the poor man injured during the robbery?"

"He was, sir," put in Vespa. "But I had another young fellow

248

watching this house for the rest of that night." They all looked at him in surprise, and he added with some reluctance, "I believe you know him as Dicky-Boy."

Lady Francesca's eyes widened. "Why, the poor lad is witless!"

"He seemed very conscientious," said Vespa. "And I believe he watched faithfully and would have raised the alarm if a mischief-maker came near."

Consuela said drily, "He watches everything that goes on in the village. I fancy, were he able, he'd make an excellent biographer for Gallery-on-Tang."

"True," agreed the clergyman. "The only trouble is that one never knows when his word can be relied upon. Only look at that tragic business with Mrs. Hawes and little Molly. Everyone was frantic to find the murderous individuals who ran them down, and Dicky went about giggling and claiming that he'd not only seen, but had recognized the coach!"

"He had?" Vespa tensed. "Who was the owner?"

Mr. Castle spread his hands helplessly. "We never could get any sense out of the boy. He'd just say it was his secret, and that he knew things other folk didn't know."

"And if he had told us," said the duchess, "how could anyone put any—oh, what is the word that they say for *credenza,* my pet?"

"Credence, dear," supplied Consuela. "But only think, if—Captain Jack? What is it? Have you solved our puzzle?"

Vespa stared at her blankly.

Before he could respond Manning flung open the door, her attempted introduction cut off by Paige Manderville's terse, "Your pardon for this rude intrusion, Lady Francesca. Good-afternoon, Miss Consuela, Mr. Castle. Jack, I've an urgent message for you."

Vespa stood at once and made his apologies, and the two men stepped into the hall.

"What the deuce has happened now?" demanded Vespa softly. "Mrs. Stokely is not—"

"The lady has left the country. Allegedly bound for sunny Italy."

Stunned, Vespa stammered, "But—it cannot be! Only yesterday—" He paused. Only yesterday the lovely widow had led him to the arbour, and then deserted him. And now, without a word to him, Esme was going to Italy? Toby had said the Gentrys were going to Italy. He mustn't let himself think . . . He *wouldn't* let himself think . . . He said brusquely, "Are you sure you're not mistaken?"

"Quite sure. The lady has left these shores. I wish," Manderville looked very grim, "that I could say as much for your gallery owner."

"Da Lentino? Is he ill?"

"They found him in his gallery this morning. He appeared to have fallen off a ladder. Smashed his skull on a marble sculpture. Or something."

"Oh, my Lord! Poor old fellow. He's not . . . ?"

Manderville nodded somberly. " 'Fraid so."

16

⚶

 $\mathcal{F}$ ell off a ladder, my eye!" Frying pan in hand, and his sheet 'apron' protecting his elegance, Paige Manderville hurried into the breakfast parlour. He spooned what he claimed were 'sautéed' mushrooms onto the plates of his eager friends, while declaring, "There's not a doubt in my mind but that the poor old fellow was done away with!"

Outside, the rain was pouring down, so a fire blazed up the chimney. The advent of autumn seemed to have whetted appetites, and the three young men lost no time in dealing with the beefsteak, roasted potatoes and green beans their amateur chef had provided with Peg's willing but erratic assistance.

Broderick accepted a roll from the silver basket Peg thrust at him. "I agree," he said. "Jove, but this smells good! What d'you say, Jack?"

"If we're right in believing this is all part of the same plot," answered Vespa, setting down his wine-glass, "then poor da Lentino would certainly have posed a threat to the men who purchased the Preston Jones paintings. He could have identified them."

Manderville, having sent Peg off with his apron, took his place at the table. "Didn't you say one of the rogues sounded like old Alperson?"

"It was not a very close description, but it could well have been applied to—" Vespa checked and glanced up as his valet came into the room. "That will be all, Thornhill. Thank you."

"I made enough extra for everyone," said Manderville.

"You are very good, sir." Thornhill started out, hesitated, and turned back. "Perhaps I should say, Captain Vespa, that I am aware of your present concerns regarding the unhappy demise of Mr. Preston Jones. And I have come into some information which may be of service to you in that regard."

They all turned to look at him.

"Go on," said Vespa.

"I presume, sir," said the valet, approaching the table again, "that when Dicky-Boy called this morning, it was to tell you of his guard duties at the Jones house, night before last? I wonder if he had already given you his tale of having seen Mr. Preston Jones at Alabaster Royal on the night of his death?"

"No! I wasn't aware the boy had made such a claim."

"I was," said Manderville, attending to his beefsteak. "The Mayor told me. Jove, but I'm a fine chef! I hope you appreciate how fortunate you are to have—"

"We will award you the Legion of the Frying Pan for culinary excellence," interrupted Vespa impatiently. "What did Mr. Fletcher say?"

"Eh? Oh—well, he said Dicky-Boy claimed to have seen poor old Jones here the night he died, lushy drunk and being helped by two men."

Irked, Vespa said, "You didn't tell me that!"

Manderville shrugged. "What difference does it make? The poor block will say anything to be interesting. Likely, there's not a word of truth in it."

Thornhill coughed. "Er, well, there just might be, Lieutenant Manderville. Could we have Harper in, Captain?"

252

"Why? Does he also know something about Mr. Jones' death?"

"I couldn't say, sir. The thing is, he knows Lord Alperson."

Harper arrived, as bright and cheery as ever, and apparently undismayed by the deafening clamour of the bell. He had, he admitted upon being questioned by Thornhill, served as groom to his lordship. "Until 'e turned me off wivout no character, Captain, sir. That's when I crep' in 'ere, eh?"

"Why?" asked Broderick. "I mean, why were you dismissed without a reference?"

Harper looked at Thornhill, who interposed suavely, "As is so often the case, Lieutenant Broderick, Harper saw what a servant should never see. In this instance, he was so unwise as to not avert his eyes when Lord Alperson was—ah, fondling his granddaughter. Much against the young lady's will."

"Why, that dirty old man!" exclaimed Manderville, revolted. "His own granddaughter?"

"And not the first time, neither," said Harper, nodding.

"Poor girl," said Vespa. "What a wretched life she must have led, with no one to protect her."

"If ever I heard of anything so disgusting," exclaimed Broderick. "Some men make me ashamed to be male!"

Encouraged, Harper said, "Ain't it the truth, sir! Some of the gents what useter come to Redways—cor! And their ladies no better. If not worse! When a woman goes bad, Cap'n, she's ten times worse'n—"

"Yes, well, Captain Vespa does not require your philosophizing," interrupted Thornhill. "Tell him what you just told me. About the foreigners."

"Ar," said Harper. "You mean them wiv the dark faces, does yer, Thorny— Whoops! I means, Mr. Thornhill." He turned his head, grinning broadly and winking at Vespa. "They wasn't Frenchies, Cap'n," he said. "Nor Eyetalians. Nor Spanishers. I know that lot. *Proper* foreign, they was."

The three men at the table exchanged a tense glance.

Vespa said, "Might they have been from the East?"

Harper nodded vigorously. "Somewhere like that, sir. Inja or 'Rabia. Out that way."

Manderville asked, "Were there Indian ladies, also? One very beautiful lady, perhaps?"

"No, sir. I couldn't say as there was. Not what you might say *ladies*. And I'd 'ave remembered anyone beautiful. 'Course, they never brung no females when they come 'ere."

"When—*who* came here?" demanded Vespa, startled.

"Why, 'is lor'ship, sir. Like I said. Arter I were turned orf, I thought I'd seen the last of the perish— Er, Lord Alperson. Coulda knocked me dahn wiv a feather when I 'eard someone moving abaht dahnstairs arter dark. I thought it were the ghosties, and I come dahn slow and scared, and there they was! The old lord and 'is friends, sitting' rahnd the kitchen table by candlelight, talking so soft and low that I knowed they was up to no good!"

"So you see, Captain," Thornhill put in, "Lord Alperson *did* come here. Just as Dicky-Boy said."

Vespa asked urgently, "When was this, Harper? Do you know what they were discussing? Or who were the other gentlemen?"

"It were afore poor Mr. Jones died, I know that. But"—Harper shook his head—"I didn't dare get close enough to 'ear naught. But I knowed one of 'em were Sir Gentry. Very thick wiv 'is lordship, 'e is. Very thick. And I think Mr. Cramer were another. The third gent, I didn't never see clear. But 'e were a flash cove, that I knows. And they was all afraid of 'im. I 'eard Sir Gentry say once, 'No, by God! I didn't bargain fer no murder!' And the third gent says, 'aughty as be-damned, 'Fool! Keep yer voice dahn! He suspects, I tell yer!' And 'e says as they wasn't to know if 'alf a 'undred vagrants and tramps might be listening. That's when I guessed they might come looking fer me, so I went inter the ghostie business meself, sir. Scared most folks orf. The gents didn't come no more. Leastways, not as I knowed."

"Whew!" exclaimed Broderick when they were alone again. "If old Alperson's in it up to his eyes, he's been very cagey about things. A tricky customer! Perhaps he *was* one of those chaps who

254

bought Mr. Jones' paintings. What did they call themselves, Jack?"

Vespa frowned uncertainly. "Be dashed if I can remember. I think the buyer was Leonard somebody. . . . He said he was from Tunbridge Wells, I know that. And it seems to me that the name of his house had something to do with birds. Roosters, or peacocks or—"

"Partridge, you great silly!" Consuela burst in upon them. She was wearing a dark rose wool cloak over a pink gown, there were roses in her cheeks and her eyes sparkled. "Partridge Towers!" she said, putting back her hood. "And his name was Leonard Harrison."

They had all sprung up at her arrival. Vespa said wrathfully, "Riding alone again! In the rain and after dark! Are you quite demented, ma'am?"

"The lady comes like the very glow of autumn," said Manderville admiringly.

"Here, Miss Consuela," Broderick drew a chair closer to the fire, and took her cloak. "You're likely cold."

"And hungry," she admitted, sniffing. "My, but that smells delicious. Is it?"

"No," frowned Vespa. "Go home and eat your dinner!" He threw down his napkin. "And I suppose I must escort you."

"Not so," said Manderville, offering a gallant bow. "I shall be most happy to volunteer."

Vespa snarled, "Oh, for lord's sake, stop flirting with her, Paige! You know it's not safe for her to be frippering about over here in the daylight, much less after dark."

"Well, before I take the lady home, she shall have some sustenance." Manderville hurried to the kitchen. "Harper, you rogue! Leave some of that for Miss Jones."

Consuela settled herself before the fire, holding out her hands to the flames. "Brrr. Autumn really is upon us. It will rain all night by the look of things. And you will not have to rouse your lazy self and escort me, Captain John Wansdyke Vespa. Watts drove me here in the carriage. And that is a great waste of a good scowl. I

255

knew by the way you rushed off this afternoon that you have found out something, and you are *not* going to shut me out! What has happened? You'll have no peace until you tell me, I warn you."

Broderick glanced at Vespa uneasily. "Well, er—"

"Your friend da Lentino is dead," said Vespa, not mincing words. "We believe it may have been murder."

Consuela came to her feet. Her face paper white, she gasped, "No! Oh—never say so! He is—was such a dear, kind . . . old . . . "

Vespa sprang forward, and caught her as she swayed.

Coming back into the room with a laden plate held high, Manderville said, "A supper fit for a princess, if I say— Jupiter! What have you done to her?"

"Frightened the poor girl half to death," said Broderick, flapping his napkin at Consuela's face. "Really, Jack! Of all the clumsy chawbacons!"

"Monster!" cried Manderville, putting down the plate and rushing forward. "Let me take her! What did you do to so upset the lady?"

Aghast, Vespa held Consuela close and guided her back into the chair, then dropped to one knee beside it. "Let be! I have her! I never meant to—"

"Yes, you did," accused Broderick. "You were cross because she came here, so you tried to frighten her away!"

"I only meant to—"

"Give her a heart seizure," said Manderville, kneeling by Consuela's chair and chafing her hand. "Villian! And after all she's done!"

Remorseful, Vespa patted Consuela's head, and stammered, "I'm truly very sorry, ma'am. I didn't realize—"

"That I have any feelings, no?" Consuela opened tear-wet eyes and blinked at him. "You think you are the only one who may grieve! Did it not occur to you that Signor da Lentino was my good friend? That now I must blame myself because—because, perhaps . . . " She gulped into silence.

"No, no. You're not in the least to blame." Vespa wiped away the tear that crept down her cheek. "Forgive. I'm a clumsy clod, just as Paige said."

"I said it, not him!" argued Broderick.

"Please don't cry," begged Vespa. "We'll tell you everything, if only you'll promise not to go running yourself into danger again."

Consuela sniffed and said unsteadily, "Very well . . . I—I promise not to run into danger."

⁓∾⁓

Vespa guided his curricle through the rainy afternoon towards his aunt's large house overlooking Tunbridge Wells. His thoughts were on his friends and what success they might have had. Two nights ago they'd decided on their plan of action: Broderick would race up to Shrewsbury and see if he could trace Sir Montmorency Gridden, the violent-tempered gentleman who had been so disappointed when he was unable to purchase Preston Jones' paintings. Manderville was to go to Salisbury and learn all he could of the gallery owner's tragic death, and also see if there was any more news of Esmeralda Stokely. He himself was to investigate the gentleman who had actually purchased the paintings: Mr. Leonard Harrison of Partridge Towers.

His search through Tunbridge Wells had been unsuccessful. There was no Partridge Towers to be found. After much enquiry he had at last located a Mr. Leonard Harrison; a very jolly fat man, the proprietor of a fish market, who had never heard of Signor da Lentino and knew nothing of art. He gladly listed numerous male relatives, but there were no other Leonards, nor did he know of a Partridge Towers in the locality. He could however, he said by way of consolation, offer Captain Vespa some fine lobsters at a bargain price.

At first declining this generous offer, Vespa had then decided to accept it. The afternoon was chill and wet, the horses were tired, he was tired, and the headache that had plagued him all day gave every indication of developing into one of the vicious attacks he dreaded and that made the slightest movement unbearable. He

257

knew his aunt would be pleased to see him, and he could rack up at her house for the night and get an early start back to Dorset-shire tomorrow morning, hopefully *sans* the confounded anvil in his head.

The most logical course would have been for him to first ques-tion his aunt, who was well acquainted in the town. But Lady An-tonia Wansdyke, blessed with an amiable temper and a merry sense of humour, could suddenly become extremely lachrymose. She had adored Sherry and the sight of Jack invariably sent her into an orgy of sorrowful nostalgia, culminating in floods of tears. Even so, with the lobsters for companions, he eventually turned his team up the hill and barely missed a high-perch phaeton that came tearing around the corner on the wrong side of the road.

"Imbecile!" shouted Vespa, reining in his animals and bran-dishing his whip at the phaeton.

He was answered by a flood of indignation; the phaeton swung around and pulled up alongside, a scant two inches from his wheels. "Are you daft?" roared the infuriated young army offi-cer who glared down at him. "If I—Good Gad! *Jack?* You old makebait!" A delighted grin lit the 'imbecile's' handsome features, and he reached out a gauntletted hand. "By Jove, you're still alive after all!"

Equally pleased, Vespa slid across the seat and wrung the out-stretched hand. "Leith! What the deuce are you doing on this side of the stream? Despatches again?"

Colonel the Honourable Tristram Leith nodded. "A flying visit, you might say. But never mind about me. I'd heard you were knocked down at Vitoria. I must say you look pretty spry for a corpse!"

"Then say it somewhere else, sir!" roared a red-faced and irate gentleman, leaning from the window of his ponderous travelling coach. "Be damned if you confounded Hyde Park soldiers don't be-have as though you owned the whole blasted country! You're tak-ing up the whole blasted road, curse you! Move, sir! Move, I say!"

"Jove!" muttered Leith, *sotto voce.* "Very sorry, sir! At once, sir!"

The two young men guided their vehicles to a grassy spot at the side of the road and the big coach rumbled past, its owner glaring at them from the window.

Leith climbed down, tethered his horses and swung into the curricle.

"That'll teach you to call me a corpse, Hyde Park soldier," said Vespa laughingly.

Leith, who had seen more than his share of action, grinned, but his dark eyes scanned this good friend's face with obvious anxiety. To Vespa's relief, there was no comment as to his altered appearance. Instead, they exchanged polite enquiries as to their various family members, then Leith asked, "Are you at your town house, or do you stay in Richmond?"

"Neither, actually. I came into a small estate not far from Salisbury, and am enjoying country air untainted by smoke, shell or shot."

"The quiet life, eh? I'll likely do the same when Boney's tale is told."

Vespa laughed. "I wish I may see it! London's *beau idéal,* wrenched away from the fascinations of Town? Gad, how would Almack's survive?" He glanced around and asked softly, "How does his lordship go on, Tris? Bristly, as usual?"

"More so," groaned Leith, who was on Wellington's staff and idolized the general. "He stamped and swore uphill and down because some of the fellows stabled their horses in a churchyard, and I wonder that peculiar barometer he hauls about hasn't melted, the way he glares at it. Stupid thing always points to 'Rain'."

"How he must hate it for proving right. If rumour speaks truth, he's to have Peacocke to replace poor Cadogan. He'll love that!"

"The sparks fly, my boy! Be grateful you're no longer wearing the blue uniform. Nor is he in alt. over that other business. Remember the heated exchange when you and I stood by, trembling, while old Picton ranted and raved because Whitehall was convinced Boney was about to invade England?"

"How could I forget? Picton said that if the great minds at home were so sure we'd fail, they'd best start preparing, before there was fighting in the streets of London. There was some talk of"— Vespa glanced around again—"a subsidiary arsenal in case Woolwich fell into French hands. I take it that notion was tabled."

"Not so." Leith met his eyes steadily. "Strictest confidence, Jack. And his lordship don't like it above half."

"Why? Have they opted for the Scottish Highlands or somewhere equally remote?"

"No. The West Country, in fact. He just thinks it indicates a complete lack of confidence in his ability to put Boney to rout. He has his full quota of pride, you know."

"Doesn't he just! And justified, God bless his irascibility. Any chance of your coming down to my old house for a day or two, Tris?"

"Old, is it?"

"Ancient. And haunted into the bargain."

Leith, who had a fondness for historical houses, groaned. "What a temptation! But alas, I can't. I'm promised to Garret Hawkhurst, and I've to be back in Spain next week."

"Confound it, you'll be passing within a few miles of my house! I could have put you up for one night, anyway. You never hope to drive straight through to Bath?"

"I'm not so stalwart—or stupid! But with luck if I nudge my cattle along I can reach Basingstoke, and I'll overnight there. Wish I didn't have to rush off, Jack. Keep that invitation open for me, will you?"

Vespa assured him it would always be open, and watched the young colonel send his phaeton off, then pull up his horses, turn back, stand, and offer him a sharp salute. He returned the gesture, thinking what a good fellow was the dashing Leith. They had shared some hectic experiences before and during their army days. When he turned his weary team through the gates a few minutes later and waved to the gatekeeper, his thoughts were still with Leith and the hope that he would come home safely when the war was won, and take up his invitation.

Lady Antonia, the relict of his mother's only brother, was a large, untidy woman, who, as Sir Kendrick was wont to remark, always looked as if she had not quite finished dressing. Despite a tendency to absent-mindedness which sometimes resulted in guests arriving to find they were not expected, she had a wide circle of friends, for she liked to have people around her, and exuded warmth and affection. She received Vespa as though he was the answer to her prayers, thanked him profusely for the lobsters, which would be "so welcome" since they were to sit down twenty to dinner tonight, scolded him for not having come straight to her, and hovered over him with barely concealed anxiety.

His assurances that he was feeling "very fit" were received with obvious scepticism. Her two youngest boys were at home, and learning that their magnificent cousin had arrived, rushed to welcome him, their howls of joy augmented by the barking of their three fox terriers. Vespa was fond of the pair, and returned their affectionate greetings, but the uproar seemed to split his head. Lady Antonia had watched him carefully, and five minutes later he was stretched out on a chaise-longue in a quiet bedchamber, a fire licking cosily up the chimney and the window curtains closed.

He awoke some three hours later, when a footman crept in to announce that his dinner would be carried up on a tray. He felt refreshed, however; mercifully, his headache was gone, and having washed and put on a clean shirt, he hurried downstairs to join the dinner guests. His aunt welcomed him, and he was not greatly surprised to find that they were to dine alone, the lady having, as usual, confused the dates, so that her party was actually scheduled for the following evening.

"I am so glad, Jack," she confided, when they were seated at the table enjoying an excellent dinner, "that you have come to me. Though it was such a surprise, I could scarce believe my eyes when you walked in!"

He laughed. "No, Aunt, do not roast me. I am not *that* remiss in my attentions, am I?"

"Never, darling boy." She leant to pat his hand fondly. "Indeed, from the time you and Sherry went off to school . . . " She paused, looking wistful, and Vespa's nerves tightened as he prepared for the recollections of his brother that were so hard to bear. He was relieved when she said briskly, "But never mind about that. The thing is that I saw your poor dear Mama only yesterday, and"—she glanced at the butler and the maid who hovered about the table, and closed her lips suggestively—"well, we can discuss it after dinner."

"But—you said 'poor' Mama. My mother is not ill, I hope?"

Her laugh was a trifle too shrill. "No, no. Though you know how the dear soul does carry on. Now, tell me what brings you to the Wells, for I don't flatter myself you came to see your old aunt. A charming young damsel, perchance?"

Uneasy, he deferred to her wishes and asked her about Partridge Towers and Mr. Leonard Harrison. Lady Antonia searched her memory, but could recall neither house nor gentleman, and her butler and maid having been applied to were no more helpful.

Since he was the only guest, Vespa did not stay in the dining room alone, but took his port in the drawing room with his aunt, and the moment the door had closed behind the servants, asked about her reference to his mother.

"Well," she said, leaning forward in her chair and lowering her voice dramatically, "I was in Town yesterday, my love, and called in upon dear Faith, of course. I found her—devastated!" She leant back and nodded at him, her eyes bright and her chin tucked in as she reiterated solemnly, "Devastated!"

"Good God! About—what? My father is well?"

"Your father—" Lady Antonia's lips tightened. She gave a little sniff. "I always said Kendrick was too handsome for his own good. Or for *her* good! Yes, I know you are devoted, and I should probably not say— I can only be grateful that my beloved Derek was only passably good-looking, and never—"

With an obvious effort she cut off the improper remarks.

Vespa suppressed a smile. So that was it. Mama must have heard some more gossip about Sir Kendrick and Mrs. Omberleigh. Colonel Omberleigh had allegedly perished while serving on the Indian frontier. No one had ever met him or knew the family, and some uncharitable people went so far as to doubt the colonel's existence. There were no doubts about his 'widow', however. A pretty and light-hearted lady, it was an open secret that she had been Sir Kendrick Vespa's mistress for at least ten years. Lady Faith, mortified, would never allow her name to be mentioned, and referred to her obliquely as "that Person".

Vespa's amusement died abruptly, therefore, when his aunt murmured from behind her fan, "All I will say, John, is that Mrs. Omberleigh has called upon your poor Mama."

"The devil she has! Oh, your pardon, ma'am. But—do you say my mother, er, actually *received* the lady?"

His aunt nodded, dislodging the silk rose her woman had placed in her hair. Vespa retrieved it, and as he gave it to her she seized his hand and said urgently, "Truly, Jack, poor Faith is in a terrible state, and told me she had sent word for you to attend her. When I saw you, I thought perhaps you were on your way to Richmond. You must go to her, my dear."

"You may be sure I mean to do so, ma'am. By your leave, I'll tell your grooms to have my team ready first thing in the morning."

"It was dreadful! Just dreadful!" Lady Faith Vespa sobbed into her son's cravat as he shared the sofa in her private parlour and tried to comfort her. "All these years . . . a devoted wife . . . and he has neglected me shamefully, as you must know, Jack, though I try never to lay my burdens on your shoulders. Heaven knows, he has treated you badly also. . . . He could not have made it more clear that Sherry was his favourite. Which was nothing but hurt pride because . . . because your brother took after him, and you do not!"

"Now, Mama," said Jack, tightening his arm about her, "I'm sure Papa did not mean—"

"Not mean?" She pulled back and sat up straight, dabbing a wisp of cambric and lace at her eyes and regarding him indignantly. "How can you say he did not *mean* it? You weren't here to see him rant and . . . and rave like a—a mad *beast*! Indeed, I thought you would never come, and I needed you so!"

"I know, dear. I'm sorry, but I was in Tunbridge Wells, as I told you, and if it hadn't been for Aunt Antonia—"

"Yes, yes. Antonia has felt the sting of his tongue also, and I expect she purred like a great smug cat and extolled the virtues of her angelic Derek, who was the most *boring* man I ever met! She arrived just after poor Mrs. Omberleigh left, and took advantage of my distress to lead me into saying more than I should have. Which is not to be wondered at, under the circumstances. I am not disloyal, Jack. Just bewildered and hurt. And *shocked* that he should cast the poor creature off without a sou! After all her years of—of what I suppose one must call devotion. It is not *done,* Jack! A gentleman does not abandon his—his—"

"Peculiar?" he offered, struggling to conceal his amazement at having heard his father's mistress referred to by name.

"Just so. He should have *provided* for her. You know it. But he is selfish as ever. Not giving a button for anyone but himself. She was not young enough any more, or pretty enough, so he has cast her off, and found someone else! Disgusting! And if you had but *heard* him! *Accusing* me! Raging!"

Sir Kendrick's impatience with his wife was often barely concealed, but Jack had never known his father to shout at the lady. Frowning, he asked, "Of what did he accuse you, Mama? What sins had you committed to make him behave with such violence?"

"Well you may ask! I had done *nothing*! Well—not in a *meaning* way. Rennett brought it up to me, and I opened it, naturally enough. And the card said: 'I thought you would enjoy to have this.' So I thought that he had been kind." She sniffed, and said resentfully, "Though there was a time when if he had been—er—flirting with another lady, I would be given rubies or diamonds as a guilt-offering."

Trying to sort the wheat from the chaff, he said, "Papa sent you a gift and you were not pleased, is that it?"

"No, that is not '*it*' at all! How can you be so slow to comprehend? It was a simple misunderstanding, and if he had set foot in my private parlour any time this past six months and more, he would have *seen* it and need not have made such a fuss! One might have thought I had deliberately *stolen* the stupid thing, and kept it hidden!"

"You mean—the gift was not for you after all, ma'am?"

"Have I not said it! He had it commissioned for *you,* he said!"

"For *me*? Papa had something made for me?"

"Yes. And he was so angry because it never came—or at least, he *thought* it never came. And when he marched in here demanding to know why his—his mistress had come to me, he saw the bowl, and I vow he went—*berserk* because it was scratched, and he said if he'd seen it at once he could have returned it and insisted that the artist do it properly, only now he's dead, and—and he blames *me*!"

Jack stared at her blankly, seeing instead his first day at Richmond after he'd left the hospital; this room, and the bright colours of the sweetpeas as he'd rescued them from the rug. Scarcely able to comprehend this incredible development, he said in an awed half-whisper. "The . . . enamelled bowl! My God! You said it was a gift?"

"Yes, and you were so clumsy as to knock it over. If I'd known Kendrick meant it for you, I would never have—"

"No, of course you wouldn't. Mama, forgive me, but this is very important. Where is it now?"

"How should I know? Sir Kendrick went storming out, saying the most dreadful things about bacon-brained females—which I am *not,* Jack! You know I'm not! If truth be told, this young creature he's found has addled *his* middle-aged brain! Well, I hope she is pleased with herself, the hussy! He's betrayed his poor wife, *and* his faithful—Mrs. Omberleigh. And you may be sure he'll serve the new chit in exactly the same fashion, when—"

"Yes—but, *please* Mama! Did my father say anything about what he meant to *do* with the bowl? Anything at all?"

"No. Or if he did, I cannot recollect. And you are being very rude to keep interrupting, as if it says anything to the matter. It is just a silly old enamel bowl with scratches all over it. Only it was pretty, and they were just little scratches, and I supposed they were part of the design. How was I to know the artist had made a mistake and— Oh, *now* I remember! Your father said he was going down to that horrid house where you will persist in living now. And that you could both take the bowl to the artist's family and demand they make restitution. Though, if the man is dead, I wish you well of the effort, for they'll likely not— *Jack!* Where are you going?"

He bent and kissed her. "Sorry, dearest. I must leave at once. Papa may be stepping onto a very sticky wicket!"

"You ain't a 'preciative cove, is you, Josiah?" The thin man with the thin smile poured another inch of whisky into Hawes' mug and said in his thin voice, "Here I come to your very door, and on such a nasty wet arternoon, bringing me own bottle o'cheer just so as to be friendly-like, and do I get a—"

The part of Hawes' face not covered by beard was flushed, and his eyes were bloodshot. He peered at his visitor blearily, and taking up the mug demanded, "Why? You ain't never been a friend t'me, Bert Ryan. You're what they call a toad-eater. Allus was. I see how you bows and scrapes to his lordship. Well, *I* don't bow an' scrape. Not to no man!"

"I gotta wife and three brats to think of," protested Ryan, injured. "But I'm a working cove, just like you is!"

"Ho, yes you ain't!" Hawes' massive hand shot out, and fast as his visitor ducked back, the front of his plum-coloured livery was seized and he was jerked forward. Hawes snarled, "Look at *my*

266

coat, Bert Ryan! All frayed and n-nigh wore out, ain't it! But look at yourn—fine cloth an'—an' silver buttons, an' good linen in yer shirt, and strong shiny leather on yer feet. Just like me? Hah! What *you* is"—he hiccupped—"is a slave! That's what you is! A slave wearin' of yer master's u-uniform."

Ryan disengaged the big man's grip cautiously, and said with his persistent grin, "True enough, Josiah. I got these flash clothes and I eats good, and I takes care of his lordship's cattle and his coaches. But if you knowed how that wicked old man treats his servants—us grooms 'special—cor! You'd understand why I hates the Quality. Just like you does. So slippery as serpents, they be. Evil, through and through."

Hawes grunted, and glowered at the stove in the small chamber that served as both kitchen and parlour.

Watching him, Ryan said softly, "I were s'prised, Josiah, that you'd let your poor li'l gal be so friendly-like with that there Cap'n Ves—"

"She ain't friendly wi' him!" shouted Hawes, jerking up straight in his chair, his flush darker than ever. "I told him straight not t'come round here no more!"

"Then I'm sorry as can be," said Ryan. "I bin lied to. That's what I gets for paying heed to gossip. Here I was told as your Molly had took a gift from that young 'ristocrat. A jar, I heard." He jumped back in the nick of time as Hawes' fist crashed onto the table, sending the whisky sloshing in bottle and mugs.

"I *paid* for that there flower-pot, Bert Ryan! An' if any man do say diff'rent, I'll wring his greasy neck like—like a chicken's!"

"I commend you, Josiah," said Ryan, drawing away from those great menacing hands. "Here! A toast t'your noble princ'ples! Drink up, man! You d'serve it. I reckon that dandy Cap'n made you pay through the nose for one of his—er—flower-pots. That must've bin hard on you, Josiah, you not being no rich man."

"It were only a groat," mumbled Hawes.

Ryan laughed shrilly. "A *groat*! Oh my! A groat for a 'namelled snuff jar? Oh, he's a downy cove is that Cap'n Vespa!"

"He ain't so bad as some. It were a pretty thing, for all it were a bit scratched, but he come back and give Molly a better one." Hawes' belligerent expression softened. "The little lass says as it be crystal, and she likes the way it sparkles."

"And *he* likes the easy way he got it back, I betcha," said Ryan with a giggle. "Was you here when he come, Josiah?"

"No." Hawes frowned again. "If I had been—" His hand tightened into a fist that made Ryan's cunning eyes widen. "I told him never to come back no more. But Molly says he didn't even get down outta his coach and weren't here above five minutes."

"I'll lay odds he wasn't!" Ryan laughed again. "Druv right off with his prize, I betcha! My, but they're sly, them 'ristocrats! He found out, Josiah, that's what it is! He'd never of give your gal that there vase if he'd knowed it was—solid gold!"

Hawes stared at him, his jaw dropping. "You got maggots in yer cock-loft, Bert Ryan. Gold, indeed! It were just 'namel, is all!"

"Yus, mate. But enamel over gold! Why, that there jar woulda bought you a new cottage, Josiah. And paid for your li'l gal to see a doctor, I 'spect. No wonder he waited till you was gone 'fore he come slipping round and tricked your Molly into trading gold for a piece o' glass! You been proper hornswoggled, Josiah. He's likely still laughing atcha!"

"Laughin' . . . at me?" Hawes' red-rimmed eyes narrowed. He took a deep breath and said softly, "Laughin' at me? That dirty . . . thievin' . . . *varmint*!" His chair went over with a crash, and Ryan jumped up and scuttled like a scared rabbit to a corner of the room.

Ignoring him, Hawes tore his shabby coat from a hook on the wall and took up a heavy club, muttering, "Cheated my Molly, did he? . . . And—and laughed at me . . . Y'see this here?" He turned on Ryan, waving the ugly weapon in the air.

"I—I see it, Josiah," quavered Ryan, easing towards the outer door, his smile quite gone.

"You see them nails in the top?"

"Yus, yus! I—I see 'em, indeed I do, Josiah."

"I driv 'em in," said Hawes in that deadly hissing growl. "I made this here club for the murderin' hell-born devil as run down me dear wife and crippled me li'l gal an' didn't even slow his bloody horses! I warned that Cap'n Vespa! I told him *plain* to keep 'way! Didn't I?"

"Yes, indeed, Josiah. You wasn't to know as he'd come slipping round your little gal while your back was—" Ryan squeaked and fled back to his corner. "Josiah? What you going to do?"

"Find him," growled Hawes. "The rotten slippery weasel! To cheat a crippled li'l child . . . !"

"But—he ain't at the manor," called Ryan, venturing from his corner as Hawes flung open the door. "He's in London, I heard."

"I'll wait till he gets back," said Hawes. "Molly's over to me brother's farm in Blandford fer a week, so she's safe from—from the perisher." He swung back to snatch up the half-full bottle. "I'll wait. And I'll find that cheatin' Captain. And this time one o' they murderin' Quality'll pay for their—their wicked ways! Now— you—out!"

Ryan ran eagerly outside and down the step. He watched the big man march off, saw him pause to tilt up the bottle again, and chuckled. It had been tricky. Like standing in front of a cannon what might go off any second. He'd earned every penny of what he'd been paid. By grab, but he had! Humming to himself and well pleased with his efforts, he walked quickly to the copse where he'd left his horse, and rode into the grey curtain of the rain.

17

Durward Cramer dismounted a short distance from the quarry. Once or twice he'd suspected he was being followed, and as he tethered his horse in amongst a cluster of stunted trees, he peered around keenly. It had rained all day, and now a cold fog was rolling in. The chances of anyone having seen him were remote. The Captain, the Dandy and the Don, as Gentry called 'em, were all off somewhere. Nosing about, probably, much good it would do 'em. Vespa wasn't likely to ride out here on such a miserable day, even if he did come home, and if Ryan had done his work well, the curst busy-body captain would cease to be a nuisance. There were, he reflected, cunning minds at the top of this scheme. Cunning, coupled with a ruthlessness that sometimes was a bit astonishing and that heightened his unease as he emerged from the trees and went to the gate.

The steps looked wet and slippery, which was natural enough after all the confounded rain that had fallen this week. He trod down them with care, then paused, glancing up tensely as his horse neighed. The meeting was tonight, but if the others suspected he was down here now, there'd be hell to pay. He strained his ears, but there was no further sound. He was likely borrowing trouble. They trusted him. Up to a point. Grunting resentfully, he picked his way down. He was just as good as what they were. Maybe he didn't have their finicking ways or their posh talk, but he'd been good enough to risk his neck for 'em. 'Specially in that gallery business. He hadn't seen no cause to risk another Capital act. But it was the fact that the others *had* felt that particular murder justified which had convinced him his suspicions ran in the right direction.

The tunnel loomed up; a gloomy, forbidding hole in the hillside. He clambered over the rubble at the entrance and groped around gingerly, then swore as he disturbed a web and the owner galloped across his glove and up his sleeve. He shuddered as he brushed it away. One thing he couldn't abide was spiders! Horrid, unnatural things! But the lantern was here, just where they'd left it, and there was plenty of oil. He hadn't brought his light-bottle, but with the old reliable tinder-box he lit the wick and turned down the shutters so that a single bright beam slanted away from the entrance. He played the light across the narrow rock passage and the debris-littered floor, his eyes searching.

There was something about this place; something the others knew. What they didn't know was that he was clever enough to guess there was a deal more to the whole business than he'd been told. The clue was in this ugly place—somewhere. And he'd find it, by God, but he would! And then they'd be forced to own that he was a *very* downy bird, and they'd have to treat him like an equal!

He pushed on, following the bright beam as the tunnel drove deeper into the hillside, ever alert for potholes, his eyes straining through the blackness, searching, searching. . . .

At the brink of the quarry other eyes were searching. Consuela had felt trapped in the house, knowing that Captain Jack and his friends were on their various quests while she sat and did nothing. When the fog started to thicken, however, she'd begun to repent her decision to bundle up in her cloak and hood and go for a long walk. It was as she'd approached the Alabaster boundary that she'd heard a horse coming up behind her. She'd hidden behind a gorse bush, guiltily aware that she was breaking her promise to Jack; although she was *walking,* whereas she'd promised not to *run* into danger. She'd crouched lower, holding her breath as the horseman passed by. Durward Cramer! What on earth was that nasty man doing on Alabaster land? She had followed, of course. Her heart had started to race when she realized he was heading straight for the quarry. It had raced even faster when she'd startled his horse and the animal had let out that great neigh of fright.

Now, as Cramer had not come to investigate, she had crept to the quarry, and finding the gate to the steps open, had peeped over the edge.

There was no sign of him. But he was down there, she knew it! She bit her lip uneasily. Did she dare follow? If he caught her, there'd be nowhere to hide except for the pile of rocks near the entrance. If she could just get that far, she could watch, and listen. It was a great risk, for he might reappear at any second, but risks and adventure went hand in hand—no?

She was trembling with nervous excitement when she reached her rocky sanctuary, and crouched behind it. After a moment, she could hear sounds from the tunnel; muffled sounds, as if Mr. Cramer was far away. What on earth could he be up to? Was something hidden there, perhaps? Had he taken part in a great jewel robbery and smuggled his ill-gotten gains here? Was that what Papa had found?

She crept from her refuge and climbed over the tumbled debris at the entrance, taking care not to cause any to fall or rattle. Far ahead, she could see a glow. Cramer had brought a lantern, then. One would need a light, for it was very dark in there. Still, she could see well enough to follow, at least a little way. If she could just get a hint of what the nasty creature was up to, Jack would be so proud—well, at least he wouldn't be too angry. She crept along carefully. My goodness, but Cramer had gone a long way. It would be easy to get lost down here. She'd already passed two side-tunnels, which might be useful as a hiding place if Cramer came back.

The air was getting musty. She brushed a cobweb from her hair and gave a gasp as she heard a faint scurrying sound. Rats! Of course, there would be rats. Every tunnel had rats. And after all, an adventure wouldn't be worthwhile if everything was neat and tidy.

Cramer's light was going downhill. She hesitated. She'd come much farther than she'd intended, and this tunnel seemed to go on forever. All right, just another minute, and she'd turn back. Well within that minute she halted abruptly. Cramer had stopped. She could see him clearly now, shining his light on a great pile of fallen rock where a cave-in had evidently blocked any further progress. She heard him cursing. He must not have known the tunnel ended here. He'd give up now. He'd come back! She must get out. Hurry! Hurry!

She turned, her heart thundering, and gave a squeak of fright as she saw the dark shape towering behind her. Her instinctive scream was cut off as strong hands seized and shook her hard. Struggling, sobbing with terror, she knew that she had found at last the men who'd murdered her father.

<hr/>

The team was at a full gallop now, and the sound of the coach thundering over the bridge and along the drivepath brought Strickley into the courtyard, running.

Vespa pulled up and was out of the curricle almost before the lathered team had come to a plunging halt. He tossed the reins to Strickley, shouting, "Is my father here?"

The steward nodded. "A half-hour ahead o' ye, sir."

Limping rapidly into the house, Jack gave a sigh of relief as Sir Kendrick came from the drawing room with Corporal frisking at his heels. "Thank God you're safe, sir," he gasped, wringing his father's hand. "When Mama told me—"

"Ah. So that's where you've been." Waiting until Thornhill had divested his son of hat, gauntlets and the caped driving coat, Sir

Kendrick led the way into the drawing room. "I spent the night with the St. Alabans in Reading, and when I reached here took the liberty of desiring your new—ah—footman, to start a fire." He settled into a chair by the glowing hearth. "You'd best warm yourself, lad. You look as if you'd been dragged through a gooseberry bush."

Jack ran a hand through his hair. "I expect I do, sir. I left Richmond at eight o'clock."

"Did you, by Jove!" Sir Kendrick patted the adoring Corporal, but refused to allow him to sit in his lap. "Then you made jolly good time! I can but hope such reckless speed has not jeopardized your rather precarious health."

Pouring brandy into a glass, Jack knew with a trace of irritation that his father would attribute his unsteady hand to his 'precarious health' and that it would be pointless to declare his health much improved. He said, "I'd have started out earlier, but the fog was too dense."

"I'm glad you didn't attempt it. Why the desperate haste, or these kind concerns for my safety? Ah—your mother, of course." Sir Kendrick held up his glass and watched his son thoughtfully as Jack limped over to refill it. "I suppose she has told you, with high drama, of my latest misdeeds. Oh dear! You look grim. Am I *such* a villain, my dear boy?"

Jack met the wistful dark eyes and said levelly, "Mother was distressed, which I cannot like to see. My concern for your safety has to do with the bowl you—"

"That *blasted* bowl!" Sir Kendrick's brows met over the bridge of his nose and he said an explosive, "Damme! I will tell you I was never more vexed! Had I known the confounded artist had foisted a damaged article off on me . . . ! Especially since I'd commissioned it as a gift for you! And the *exorbitant* price I paid for the thing! Yes, that's vulgar, I know, but if your mother hadn't kept it hidden all this time, I might have been able to make things right. Whereas now—" He checked abruptly. "It's irritating past permission, but—what the devil has it to do with my safety?"

"Mama said you brought the bowl with you, sir. May I see it?"

"Of course you may see it. Ring for your latest oddity to fetch it here, and you'll soon compre—" He broke off, clapping his hands over his ears. "My dear God! Where did you find that monstrous bell? In Salisbury Cathedral? This house is beyond the pale! I vow—"

His vow was not to be completed, for he was rendered speechless as Peg rushed in, stumbled over her apron, dropped a wobbly curtsy, and pushed back the mob-cap which had fallen over her eyes.

"Yez, zur?" she lisped sunnily.

Managing not to see his sire's sagging jaw, Jack asked quietly for the bowl Sir Kendrick had brought.

"Zur Kendrick?" She stared at the baronet, nonplussed. "I thinked yer name were Zur Vezpa."

"Sir Kendrick Vespa," explained Jack.

"It's in a b-box," said his father feebly. "I left it in the dining room." He watched numbly as she nodded and went skipping and lurching on her way. "I won't ask," he muttered. "I won't even ask! Oh, Jack! My *poor* boy!"

Chuckling, Jack said, "Her name's Peg—"

"A square peg in a round hole, obviously! What happened to her teeth?"

"I understand that another—er, lady knocked them out with a beer bottle. But she's willing, you see, and—"

"*Willing?* My dear fellow, you've that luscious little bird of paradise to please you, why would you—"

"I mean, she's a willing *worker*! And she has charms and talismans to protect her from the ghosts, so—"

Sir Kendrick groaned and held up one hand. "Spare me. Ah." He lowered his voice. " 'Hugged and embraced by the strumpet wind! How like the prodigal doth she return . . . ' "

Jack managed to hide a grin, but glancing quickly at Peg, he was glad that she appeared not to have heard the quotation. She beamed at him, dumped the box unceremoniously in Sir Kendrick's lap, bobbed one of her ghastly curtsies, and hopped and skipped away.

"Well, my boy," said the baronet, lifting out the bowl. "Here is your father's magnificent gift! You will see why I intend to take it at once to this artist fellow's house and demand his heirs make good my purchase price."

Jack inspected the bowl carefully, marvelling that he had held this in his hands on his first day at the Richmond house and not dreamt the painted scene was of his own land. There was the distant loom of the quarry hill, and, on the other side of the bowl, the spreading might of the manor. And there also were the same little marks, that made it seem as if the enamel was scratched. There were no such defects on the painting of the manor. Just on the quarry side.

The fantastic idea that had hovered around the edges of his consciousness since his encounter with Leith in Tunbridge Wells began to take firmer shape, and the need to investigate, to prove or—as he hoped—disprove his theory took on a compelling urgency. Pondering, he looked up.

Sir Kendrick was watching him intently. "You seem more intrigued than outraged," he said with a smile. "You're such a good-natured fellow, John. Do you mean to tell me what is troubling you so?"

"I'm afraid you're not going to like it, sir. But, well, it began when I was on my way here—or at least, I believe that may be part of the peculiar business. . . . "

For the next ten minutes Sir Kendrick listened without interruption, his eyes seldom leaving his son's face. When the tale was told, there was complete silence in the room.

Jack waited uneasily. He had left out a few details, deeming them so bizarre that his father would laugh outright.

Sir Kendrick had shifted his gaze to the fire. He stared into the flames expressionlessly, then said, "I'll be damned! And you really believe that several attempts have been made on your life; that

Jones was murdered; his daughter almost slain; and the gallery fellow done away with? And all by reason of this—*bowl*?"

Jack noted the incredulity in the tone. How could he blame him? But it was as well he'd not mentioned the exotic Mrs. Nilima, and that astonishing house; Sir Kendrick would certainly have thought he'd gone right off the road! He said, "Not the bowl itself, sir. But what's on it, I think."

"What's—*on* it? But the only thing on it is a very damaged painting of your unfortunate inheritance."

"I think the damage was deliberate, Papa. And I think Mr. Jones was trying to leave a message."

"No, *really,* my dear boy! You *must* try to be reasonable about this. If the fellow wanted to leave a message, all he had to do was *tell* someone! Not go about ruining perfectly good bowls and—"

"And several paintings, sir."

"You don't mean it!" Leaning forward, Sir Kendrick asked, "Can we see them if we go to his house?"

"Well, no. They've all been stolen or—sold."

"They have? I . . . see." The baronet sighed and sank back again. "Now, John, don't you think this has gone far enough?"

"There's a snuff jar, sir. I have it, and it bears the same scratch marks. I can show you!"

"Hmm. Well, I'd like to see it—later. But, even if it is similar, what does it prove? And my earlier question still goes unanswered, you know. Why didn't Jones simply deliver his message in person, instead of all this rigamarole and roundaboutation?"

"Perhaps because he wasn't sure of his facts. Or perhaps because he only had part of the puzzle. He told his daughter that there was evil here, and—"

"Oh, for heaven's sake! People have been mouthing that fustian for years! Ghosts and goblins and disordered minds, and—" Sir Kendrick looked embarrassed and said, "I'm sorry, my boy. I don't mean to imply—"

"It's all right, sir. I know that since Vitoria my head has played me false at times. But, suppose Mr. Jones had discovered another kind of evil here? Something that had nothing to do with the supernatural? Something so outrageous that he dared not speak of it or make any accusations until he had all his facts? Which may have been—the very day he died."

"But—*what* facts? What did he suspect? What could possibly be so important about a bowl and a jar and a few paintings, to justify thievery and violence and at least two brutal killings?"

Jack hesitated, then he asked slowly, "Sir, this gentleman who was interested in buying Alabaster. Did you ever meet him?"

"No. Felton did. Twice. As I told you. Why?"

"Has he approached Felton since?"

"Not so far as I'm aware. Probably came down and took a look and laughed all the way back to Town."

"But he wanted to build an orphanage here. Is that correct?"

"I believe that's what Felton said. Why on earth—"

"Sir—forgive me. I know this must sound wild, but—if what I suspect is true, the man's a heartless, scheming murderer."

"Good God!" exclaimed Sir Kendrick, dismayed. "No, really, John! You simply cannot fling such frightful accusations about! Unless— Have you any evidence this time? A shred of proof of what you say?"

"Not really, sir. Enough perhaps to alert my General, but—"

"*Wellington?* Do you count it a—a matter of national importance, then? Something to do with the war? Spying, or such? Or—Jupiter! Have they put you on active duty again?"

"No, no. Never worry, Father. I'm not investigating for Lord Wellington, or for the Horse Guards—not until I can name names."

"Heaven help us! Do you suspect there is more than one of these—er—heartless scheming murderers? And in this rural backwater? Whatever do you envision? A peasant uprising?"

Jack smiled. "No, sir. The men involved are aristocrats, sad to say. I believe I have the identities of at least two of the varmints, and that our would-be buyer is the third."

278

"And you will give their names to Wellington."

"As soon as I have my proof, yes. And I think I know where to go to find it. Please don't look so horrified, sir. I won't disgrace us by slandering innocent gentlemen or making unfounded accusations, I promise."

"I have every confidence in your abilities, but . . . " Sir Kendrick shook his handsome head; sighing, he stood and walked to stand with one hand on the mantel as he gazed down into the flames. After a moment, he said regretfully, "But try to look at the business objectively, my dear boy. Isn't it reasonable to suppose that Jones' death *was* an accident, just as the Coroner ruled? The gallery owner wasn't young, you said, and it's quite logical that he might have slipped on the ladder. As for the other incidents—well, one could theorize and 'what if' and conjecture all night. I'll not dissuade you from doing what you believe is right. I only ask that you consider very carefully before you take action. If what you believe is truth, your life could very well be in danger."

He turned and set his glass gently on a table, his smile holding a trace of sadness. "Now, I came down here to take that wretched bowl back to Preston Jones' family and demand redress. It's almost three o'clock, and I'd prefer not to drive in this fog after dark, so I'll be off."

Jack came to his feet. "I don't think it's wise for you to take that bowl anywhere, sir. I know you think I'm quite mad, but—"

"Of course I do not!" Sir Kendrick gripped his shoulder and shook him gently. "You've gone through hell this past year. It's only natural you should feel the strain. You stay here and rest, my poor fellow. I'll be perfectly safe, I promise you. I've a brace of pistols in the coach, and Riggs is riding guard today; you know that rascal goes nowhere without his blunderbuss. So there's no cause for you to be anxious."

"Less cause if I ride escort, at least part of the way. My errand lies in the same direction."

"What d'you mean—your 'errand'?" Frowning, Sir Kendrick

exclaimed, "Devil take it! You're going after your alleged 'proof'!"

"I am, sir. But it's purely a preliminary search. Nothing that will involve battle and sudden death, I promise you."

"Dammit!" said Sir Kendrick explosively. "Have you heard nothing I've said to you? John, I'll be blunt. You've been very ill. Your imagination has got the best of you. I will *not* have you endangering yourself with—with whatever you mean to maudle about with! You hear me?"

Jack bowed. "If I'm imagining it all, there's no danger, is there, Father? Are you ready? I'll ring for your coach."

Sir Kendrick swore.

Within five minutes the great coach was at the front entrance, the coachman on the box, the horses stamping impatiently at the cobblestones and blowing puffs of steam to mingle with the chill misted air. The liveried guard held the door wide while he waited to assist Sir Kendrick up the step, and Thornhill followed the baronet, carrying the box that held the enamel bowl.

On the upper landing of the old manor, Jack slipped his new pistol into the pocket of his travelling coat, then started down the stairs. Gradually, the silence intruded on his troubled thoughts. It was deathly still; no cheerful voices of his friends to ring out from belowstairs, no blithe birdsongs, no sounds of Strickley hammering in the barn, or the occasional crashes as Peg tripped or dropped things. Indeed, the mists seemed to have penetrated the house so that even the creaking of the treads was muted. And how dark it was getting. One might suppose it to be dusk instead of only a little past three o'clock.

An odd unease touched him. He settled the high-crowned hat at a defiantly jaunty angle on his head, forgetting that Sir Kendrick frowned on what he termed "unseemly frivolity". When he returned his hand to the banister rail, it was like ice. He halted. Few things so irked his father as to be kept waiting, but suddenly he scarcely dared to draw a breath and was straining his ears to hear . . . what? It was *too* cold! *Too* dark! It went against nature. This couldn't be happening. But he could hear something now. It would be stupid to look around. Whatever moved so stealthily on the landing behind him was probably quite normal and ordinary. Corporal, perhaps. But the dog had scarcely left Sir Kendrick's side since his arrival, and was probably there even now.

He tried to walk on, only to be stunned into immobility as a rhythmical grating sound reached his ears. It sounded almost like—but, no! It *couldn't* be purring! How could it be a cat, when he had no cat, and sounding more like the purr of a lion than a house cat! His heart was hammering suffocatingly. If this was all in his mind, the hallucinations were becoming ever more real. The movements, the strange throaty sounds, were drawing nearer. He wouldn't look. He *dare* not look! But nor, when he tried to walk on, could he move. He'd never fancied himself a hero, but he'd hoped he had his share of physical courage. Yet now here he stood, paralyzed with fright! This, then, was what sheer unreasoning terror could do to a man. He gritted his teeth and fought for control. He was a Vespa, and Vespas didn't bow to fear. However ghastly Badajoz had been, he was damned sure Sherry wouldn't have played the coward. If Sir Kendrick could see him now. . . . Lord! He must make his craven legs obey him. He must face whomever—whatever crouched behind him. . . .

It took every ounce of his will-power, but he managed to turn his head.

The landing at the top of the stairs was pitch black. A corner of his mind whispered a dazed 'In the middle of the afternoon?' Against that darkness he saw nothing at first. Then, the hairs on the back of his neck started to lift. Something *was* there! Something that watched him with two great unblinking yellow eyes. It wasn't a cat! It couldn't *possibly* be a cat! What cat ever had eyes of such a size, or stood three feet tall at the shoulders? But whatever it was, it was there! He blinked and it was still there! The need to escape was overpowering. Bathed in a cold sweat, he managed somehow to turn his back. He tottered down the steps, his knees weak under him, praying that terrible creature wouldn't come after him.

At the foot of the stairs, he clung to the end-post and forced himself to look again.

The landing was bathed in the grey afternoon light.

There were no yellow eyes.

There was no giant cat.

Tearing out his handkerchief, he mopped his wet face and tried to force his numbed mind to think rationally.

Distantly, he heard an impatient hail from the coach and reeled forward, hoping he didn't look as unnerved as he felt.

He had one foot on the threshold when the piercing yowl stopped him in his tracks.

Peg rushed out of the kitchen and lurched across the hall, tugging out her precious charms. "What*ever* was that?" she cried, her voice shaking. "I never heard no moggy make a noise like that!"

Vespa knew then.

He had seen the Alabaster Cat.

<hr>

Broderick's eyes were narrowed and stern, and in spite of the drifts of vapour that at times became dense, he held his tall horse to a steady canter, driven by the guilty awareness that he should have returned two days ago.

En route to Salisbury, he had turned aside to call on his beloved for probably the last time. The cautious pebbles he'd thrown had brought Ariadne to her window, and she'd hurried to their illicit trysting-place in the shrubbery. It had been a wrenching meeting. His impassioned vow to obtain a special licence had been to no avail; she was under age. Abandoning honour, he'd begged her to accompany him to the Border; they would be married in Gretna Green. Ariadne had said tearfully that if he really loved her, he wouldn't ask her to invite such shame and condemnation. Besides which, she'd added with her adorable naïveté, she planned to have a very pretty wedding. Obviously believing herself deliciously wicked, she had shared his embraces and declared her undying love, but had remained immovable. She adored her brother and would not marry without Sir Larson's blessing. Heartsick, he had been left with no recourse but to bow to the inevitable, and wish her happiness.

His despair had reduced his darling girl to tears, but she'd overcome her grief bravely. In fact, as they'd said their farewells, she had seemed so restored to her usual sunny spirits that he'd been rather taken aback, until he'd realized she was making a truly noble attempt to conceal her grief. She had even enquired as to his plans and when he meant to return to Town, and, trying to match her courage, he'd told her of his quest. Ariadne was well acquainted in Salisbury and, eager to help, she'd given him the names of several ladies who were, she said, "the leading gossipmongers of the town."

He had left her then, and made his way to Salisbury, where he'd spent the night drowning his sorrows, and the next day paying the price. Not until this morning had he visited Ariadne's 'gossips'. His belated efforts had borne fruit. True to Mr. Congreve's famous observation regarding 'a woman scorned', the lovely Esmeralda Stokely had allowed fury to get the better of discretion until self-preservation had stilled her reckless tongue and she had fled, leaving the old town reeling with shock and scandal.

Broderick didn't like scandal, and he didn't like the looming consequences. He did like Jack Vespa, who was a good man and had enough in his dish just now. Still, it was better he should hear this from a friend than—

His horse gave a scared snort and shied wildly. Only Broderick's splendid horsemanship saved him from taking a toss. He roared a demand that the rapidly disappearing individual he had almost run down come back at once. He was ignored. Furious, he reined his mount into pursuit, shouting, "Stop, damn your eyes! Are you gone daft to—"

The fugitive crouched as he was overtaken, and turned a white and terrified countenance.

Broderick's anger faded. "So it's you! What were you thinking, boy, to dart out like that? You came curst near to getting yourself killed! Didn't you hear me coming?"

The shaggy head was shaken violently. Pale lips mumbled an incoherent flood of words, and Dicky-Boy sank to his knees, clearly half-crazed with fear. Broderick dismounted and went over to pat the cringing shoulder and say compassionately, "Be easy, lad. I won't hurt you. Whatever has thrown you into such a pelter?"

"He knows," whimpered the youth. "He's coming fer Dicky-Boy now. He knows Dicky-Boy seen." He grabbed Broderick's hand convulsively and pressed it to his cheek. "You tell him! *You* c'n tell him, sir! Dicky-Boy's kept it secret. He's *never* told. He'd've told Mr. Hawes, but—but Mr. Hawes he's allus cross and he don't like Dicky-Boy talking to Molly. He shouts. So Dicky-Boy didn't never tell no one. And now—" He began to sob. "*You* tell him, sir! Won't ye? Please? Tell him Dicky-Boy won't never, *never* tell no one."

"Tell who? Tell about—what? Be dashed if I know—"

The youth made a frantic surveillance of the foggy landscape and said urgently, "Why, the *murder,* o'course! Dicky-Boy seen it *done!* And he knows who done it! And the coach never stopped! But he *never* told, sir! It's his secret. Dicky-Boy *never* told! You tell him that. Do—please, sir! Afore Dicky-Boy gets dead too!"

"Jupiter!" muttered Broderick. "Are you talking about that tragic Hawes accident?"

The youth uttered a strangled scream and clapped a hand over his mouth, his eyes dilating.

"All right," soothed Broderick quickly. "I'll tell him. But first I'll have to know who he is."

Another furtive scan of the surroundings, then the boy scrambled to his feet and on tip-toe leant to whisper in Broderick's ear.

Five minutes later Hezekiah Strickley was again responding to approaching hoofbeats. "Arternoon, Lieutenant," he said, his keen gaze on the big bay. "Your hoss throw a shoe?"

"No, curse it," said Broderick, swinging from the saddle. "He shied and I think he's got a sprained hock or pulled a tendon. I'd not have ridden the poor fellow but I had no choice." Starting for the house, he called over his shoulder, "Take care of him, will you? Is Captain Vespa at home?"

"No, he ain't." Strickley started to lead the bay around to the barn, but halted when Broderick practically sprang at him.

"The devil! Where is he, then?"

"Why—I dunno, sir. Not 'fficial, I don't. Him and his Pa went orf in Sir Kendrick's coach. I gotta say me Cap'n looked so sick as a horse!"

Broderick swore under his breath. "I must come up with them. What d'you know—*un*officially, you rogue?"

The lieutenant seemed uncommon grim. Strickley said, "Peg says Sir Kendrick had some sorta bowl in a box, and he were powerful put out and were taking it back. Though it don't seem—"

"To Preston Jones' house?" interrupted Broderick harshly.

"S'what she thinked, sir. But how—"

Striding toward the stables, Broderick snapped, "Is Lieutenant Manderville back yet? No, well, I didn't expect he would be. Dammit! Are there any decent goers here?"

"Cap'n Vespa's hack ain't no creeper, sir, but I dunno as he'd want ye to take Secrets without—"

"Well, he would! Stir your stumps, man, and saddle her up! If Mr. Manderville comes in before I get back, tell him where I've gone and that there's the very devil to pay!"

Two minutes later, Strickley watched him ride out, the pretty mare only too willing to gallop.

Thornhill walked out to join him.

"What you do, mate?" enquired Strickley with heavy sarcasm. "Die on the perishin' vine?"

"Well you may ask." Thornhill's confused demeanour surprised Strickley, who had expected a sharp reprimand. "I sat down in my parlour chair for a minute, and dozed right off," the valet went on.

"Which I *never* do, not being able to kip in the daytime. More to the point, is Peg completely ripe for Bedlam? She's gone! Says she won't stay in the house another night."

Strickley turned his thoughtful gaze from Broderick's now vanished form, and demanded, "Why? She likes the guv'nor. Said she'd stay as long as he'd keep her. Has Harper been messin' about?"

"Not that I know of. Though he went with her. They said"— Thornhill paused, then finished uneasily—"they said they heard the—the Alabaster Cat! And Peg said she was sure Captain Vespa had *seen* it!"

Strickley turned pale. "Gawd!" he said. "I mighta knowed!"

Josiah Hawes blinked in bewilderment at the leaf which had sent an icy droplet onto his face. He felt cold and his head wasn't thinking proper. It felt even more befuddled when he'd managed to sit up. Why in blazes was he sleepin' out under the bushes. . . ? He saw it, then, a dim upthrust through the drifting fog. Alabaster Royal! *That's* why he'd waited here! To avenge hisself on the curst Quality! To beat the mighty Cap'n Vespa's 'ristocratic brains out! He shouldn't never have gone to sleep, waitin'. But he was awake now, and if the thievin' Cap'n had got back, he'd finish what he'd set out to do.

He found his club and used it to help him get onto his feet. He felt a bit fuzzy for a minute, but he was pleased because of the fog. That'd keep him hid so Vespa wouldn't see him till it was too late. Starting towards the manor, Molly's sweet little face came before his mind's eye, and he paused, troubled by the thought that she wouldn't like this. He felt the weight of the bottle in his pocket, and was gratified to find it still held a couple of inches of whisky. He drank as he went on, and was soon feeling warmer and sure of his rights. Molly didn't understand. She would, when she got older. When he reminded her of what had happened to her Ma, and how that cheatin'—

286

A horseman was comin' this way. Ridin' fast. Just the way that bloody coach had gone when it struck down his dear wife and his li'l gal! The rider was comin' from the manor. He'd have to cross the bridge. The path was narrow there.

Hawes ran. He reached the foot of the bridge and crouched down as the horse approached the far side. Vespa's horse—he was right! Gauging his moment, he sprang out, club flailing.

Secrets reared with a scream of pain and fright. Caught by surprise, her rider was hurled from the saddle to crash against the bridge wall.

Shouting his triumph, Hawes ran forward, club swung high, only to stop and stare in dismay. His club lowered. Catching his breath, he bent over his inert victim. The hat was gone; blood streaked the still face and welled from under the fair curls. John Vespa's hair was light brown, but not this light. "Oh, crumbs," he moaned. "I've gone and killed that Lef'nant fella!" And the Lef'-nant hadn't never done him no harm! Lor', oh Lor! What was he to do? And—someone was comin'. Runnin'!

In desperation, he also turned to run, and came face to face with Dicky-Boy.

18

For the third time Sir Kendrick's velvety dark eyes scanned his son obliquely. He must, he knew, choose his words with care. He said in a very gentle voice, "I know you do not like me to comment on the state of your health, John. But really—forgive a father's concern—does your head trouble you?"

"No, no." Jack's attempt at a reassuring grin was a dismal failure. Aware of it, and knowing he dared not tell the truth, he answered, "Thank you, but—it's just . . . I have had a shock, is all. I am quite well, I assure you."

After another pause, Sir Kendrick said, "Would it help to talk about it? I haven't always been by you when you needed me, I know. But I'm here now, boy, and if you choose to confide in me, I'm a good listener."

"I promise you it's nothing of import. Just—something I've always been very sure about, and—and now I find I may have been mistaken."

"I see. It must have been a great shock, indeed. When you climbed into the coach you looked appalled."

Jack said nothing, and Sir Kendrick began to talk easily about commonplace events. Jack responded politely, while his mind struggled to comprehend what he'd just seen. Never afterwards could he remember what they discussed on that journey, although he knew he'd made his father laugh once or twice. It seemed a very short while before the coach was slowing for the turn onto the narrow lane leading to the quarry.

He said, "I must leave you now, sir. Riggs knows the way to Preston Jones' house, I think? May I hope that this time you will overnight with me before you head back to Town?"

"It will be my pleasure, John." The coach stopped, and the guard opened the door and let down the step. As Jack alighted, Sir Kendrick followed. "And if you think to fob me off," he said, "you may forget it!"

Jack said uneasily, "Fob you off? Sir, I don't—"

"Oh, yes, you do. You want to send me on my way while you search for your proofs. Well, you won't succeed! I don't know what you're after, but," Sir Kendrick clapped his son on the back fondly, "you're not going down there alone!"

"But, sir, it's more than good of you, but I don't know what I'm looking for, either. I might poke about for hours, and there's no need for you to—"

"To do what? Risk getting some mud on my shoes? I'm not the fop you take me for, my boy! Nor am I in my dotage! As old Heywood wrote, 'Two heads are better than one', and I might be of some use to you."

"Of course you would, sir, but—"

"I'm perfectly capable of negotiating those steps, if that's what's making you look so anxious."

"I know that, but—"

"For Lord's sake, stop protecting me! It looks a dismal hole, but you very obviously are intrigued by something in the place, so let's go and have a look. I want to see for myself. Make my mind easy, as it were."

Jack's mind was far from easy when they reached the quarry floor. He was in fact bathed in a cold sweat. Sir Kendrick had thrown him into a panic by twice slipping on the treacherous steps, so that he'd only caught him in the nick of time. They had detached one of the carriage lamps before starting down, and now, undaunted, his father was holding it high and peering into the darkness of the tunnel.

"What d'you think is in here, lad? A vein of silver perhaps, or—What the devil!" He plunged inside. "There's someone here! I saw a light, I swear it! You were right, John! Come on!"

"No!" Jack caught his arm and pulled him back. "Sir, you insisted on coming with me, but this is my responsibility! You really must let me go first."

Sir Kendrick frowned at him for a moment. "It's not my way to follow, John."

"Nor mine, sir."

Cool hazel eyes met annoyed brown ones levelly.

Sir Kendrick's lips twitched. "Your men could attest to that, I don't doubt. Very well, Captain, sir. You command, and I obey!"

They smiled on each other, and Jack stepped into the tunnel. It was much longer than he'd expected, the floor uneven and littered here and there with fallen chunks of rock. The farther they went, the more obvious was the deterioration. They passed a branching passage, the opening half-blocked by debris. The air was stale and musty, the darkness ever more intense, and the awareness that countless tons of earth hung over them was oppressive. Sir Kendrick's ankle turned on a rock and he blundered into one of the supporting beams. At once dirt and litter showered from the roof, and Jack pulled his father back in the nick of time from the large slab that crashed down and shattered at his feet.

"By God, that was close!" exclaimed Sir Kendrick, breathlessly. "I owe you, lad!"

Jack kept a tight hold on his arm. "Then pay me now. This tunnel's not safe, you see how rotten the beams are. I see no light; you must have been mistaken. Let's get out of this, sir!"

"You just want to get me safely out and then you'll come back! Be damned if I— Look there!"

Far ahead a bright glow bobbed and then vanished. Astounded, Jack raised no more objections and they went on, walking more carefully now so as not to betray their presence.

They reached a great pile of rubble where the roof must have come down, blocking the passage. A space had been cleared, and recently, for there were boot prints in the muddy ground.

Sir Kendrick swore softly. "Someone's been busy down here," he whispered. "Like a fool I left my pistol in the coach. I'd feel a sight easier with it in my fist!"

Jack exchanged his new duelling pistol for the lantern. "Now you may be easy, sir. But have a care, it has a hair-trigger."

"Then you shouldn't carry it in your pocket, you young mad-cap!" Sir Kendrick grinned. "But I'm glad you did, even so. Let's find out what the deuce is going on in here."

Jack climbed over the pile of rocks and assisted his father into a wider section of the tunnel that branched off in several directions. They held to the main passageway, which sloped ever downward until the rough-cut walls began to gleam wetly in the rays of the lantern, and drops trickled down the support beams.

"Lord! This place is like a honeycomb," whispered Jack. "I don't see the light any more."

"Nor I. They may have branched off."

"We'll go on a little further, then try a side-passage."

After another minute or two, Sir Kendrick murmured, "Do you notice how damp the walls are? I'll warrant the river rushes through here when it's at the flood. Or perhaps it meets up with an underground tributary."

"Gallery-on-Tang!" exclaimed Jack, mortified. "Lord, what a clunch! I wondered why it wasn't called Moor Stream Gallery, and my mind stopped there. I should have connected the two."

Sir Kendrick slanted a curious glance at him. "In what way?"

"The village, sir. It was established in Norman times. And in

French, *Galerie* would mean tunnel, or even mine tunnel; and *étang—"*

"Pond!" said Sir Kendrick. "Tunnel under the pond! By Jove! I never thought of that!"

"Let's hope it doesn't refer to tunnel *in* the pond! That may well be why mining had to be abandoned here. I've seen no more of the other light. We'd best turn back, sir, and make another cast."

"Yes, confound it— No! See there!"

An intersecting passage lay ahead and light glowed from the entrance.

"Got the bounders!" whispered Sir Kendrick, his eyes glinting wrathfully.

They crept closer and soon could hear voices. Two men by the sounds of it, engaged in an acrimonious dispute, the one voice harsh and commanding, the other full of blustering defiance.

"Cramer!" muttered Jack. "I knew—" He checked, appalled by a third voice.

"Why did you drag me down to this horrid place? You are great fools if you expect to murder me as you did my dear Papa! Captain Vespa knows—"

"Consuela!" gasped Jack, and plunged around the corner.

One sweeping glance revealed Lord Malcolm Alperson and Durward Cramer facing each other angrily, and Consuela sitting on a pile of debris against the wall, her dress torn, her face dirty and bruised.

A blazing rage wiped out sanity, and he charged forward.

The two men jerked around. Cramer swung up a long-barreled duelling pistol. Jack leapt and kicked out. The pistol exploded deafeningly as it flew from Cramer's hand, and a shower of silt poured from the roof. Cramer screamed a curse and springing to the attack was met with a flashing upper-cut that sent him sailing backward.

Consuela screamed, "Look out!"

Jack turned, crouching.

Lord Alperson, wielding a large chunk of rock that was clearly

292

intended to brain him, was being foiled by Consuela, who had jumped onto his back and was beating frantically at his head. The peer cursed and wrenched the girl away, sending her sprawling.

"You filthy swine!" roared Jack, and levelled his lordship with the right that was so much admired by his fellow officers.

"I don't like to hit an old man." He slipped an arm around Consuela, who had flown to cling to him, laughing and weeping in a paroxysm of joyous relief. "But you deserved it."

"He more than deserved it," drawled Sir Kendrick. "Perhaps you two—charming gentlemen will be so good as to explain your presence here?"

Cramer struggled to his feet, holding onto the wall for support. "I was just curious, is all," he said sullenly.

"And you," said Sir Kendrick, waving Jack's long-barrelled pistol towards Lord Alperson, "were you also overcome by—curiosity?"

"I'll overcome your damned bastard," howled Alperson, dabbing a bloody handkerchief at his mouth. "He's curst near knocked out one of my teeth!"

"And you have not answered my question," purred Sir Kendrick.

"They can answer our questions in Constable Blackham's gaol." Jack scanned Consuela anxiously. "Did they hurt you, Miss Meadowlark?"

"That horrid old man choked me," she said.

"Horrid old man, is it," snarled Alperson stuffily. "Vixen! You're damned lucky I didn't—"

"And I am still waiting," said Sir Kendrick.

"The chit was following Cramer," growled his lordship. "The everlasting idiot led her straight here!"

"To—what, exactly?" asked Sir Kendrick. "What did you think to find, Cramer? Gold and gems, perchance? The hoard of some old-time pirate?"

"I didn't know 'cause I wasn't told," said Cramer. "So I came to see. But I didn't find nothing."

"Because there was nothing to find," said Sir Kendrick sweetly.

"Except a tool for blackmail, perhaps," said Jack.

Sir Kendrick's smooth brow wrinkled. "Blackmail? I am lost, dear lad."

"These tunnels, sir. They evidently run for miles underground. Perhaps they were worked centuries ago. Perhaps most people had forgotten how extensive they are. I think that's why the main tunnel was sealed off and made to look as if all mining had ended there. Lord knows where these branches lead, and I agree with you that there are probably other levels."

Bewildered, Consuela drew back from his arm and looked up at him. "This, I do not find at all important. Why should anyone care?"

"Someone cared enough to murder your father. That's what the marks on the paintings, and the bowl and the vase, should have shown us. They were not scratches, but cracks. Mr. Jones found out about all these unsuspected tunnellings. He realized that the ground above would be unstable. Perhaps he began to entertain suspicions that he dared not speak of until he had proof, so he portrayed the ground as being cracked, only we were too blind to see it. At the end he must have learnt, too late, that he was right; something was to be built here." He looked up at his father. "Not an orphanage, I think, sir."

Sir Kendrick glanced at Lord Alperson and raised one enquiring eyebrow.

"Didn't I tell you?" growled his lordship, dragging a pistol from his pocket and aiming it steadily at Jack. "I *said* he knew!"

It struck home like a physical blow. The bits and pieces, the half-formed and angrily rejected theories came together and formed a near-complete pattern. A terrible pattern, because the wrong man was the leader. With a choked gasp, Jack whipped around to confront his father.

Sir Kendrick sighed. "I had to be sure," he murmured.

"Oh—God!" Jack searched the handsome features in desperation. "*No!* No, you *can't* be in league with these—jackals?"

"Hey!" Offended, Cramer sprang at him and backhanded him across the face, so that he reeled back until the wall supported him; and still his eyes never left his father.

Sir Kendrick said mildly, "There is no call for that, Durward. Had you not bungled your every opportunity, this ugly mess could have been avoided. I really am sorry, John. It was a simple case of my being in desperate need of money. A great deal of money."

Jack wiped blood from his lips mechanically, conscious only of the deeper hurt that seemed to be tearing him apart. "You have funds," he said, striving to comprehend. "The houses—the coaches—"

"None of which can be disposed of without time and a fuss," said Sir Kendrick, with a rueful smile. "And I am eager to leave these delightful but so—ah, constricting shores."

"Because of your new woman?"

The smile was wiped away. Sir Kendrick's glare caused Cramer to step back nervously. "Do not *dare* to use that tone in connection with my dear lady! She is the most glorious creature who ever lived! A far cry from the wailing, snivelling fool who mothered you! Stay back—or by God, I'll shoot you where you stand!"

Jack had started forward, but that such a threat should be levelled at him was past comprehension, and it rendered him so sick at heart that he stood silenced and motionless.

"I didn't know what love was until I met her," went on Sir Kendrick, his voice softening. "Beautiful, clever, courageous, loyal; with a shape like Venus and a nature passionate beyond the ken of our cold-blooded English women!"

Consuela stepped to Jack's side and said brokenly, "I am so sorry, dear Captain Jack! I am *so* sorry!"

Jack's eyes were strangely blurred. None of it could be real. The gracious and noble gentleman he had loved and admired all his days was not really standing here looking at him with such amused contempt. Anguished, he thought, 'Please, *please,* God, let it be another of my hideous hallucinations! Let me wake up now.' But he did not wake up, and as from a great distance he heard his own voice: "And for—her you are willing to turn your back on your country? To abandon my mother and—and your mistress . . . all your friends? To murder and lie and cheat?"

"You must try to understand, dear boy," said Sir Kendrick. "I cannot live without my love. And I cannot live in England *with* her."

"Nor—in India?"

Consuela gave a startled exclamation.

"How perceptive of you." Sir Kendrick bowed. "In the eyes of her people or mine, our alliance is unthinkable. Much I care for their stupid shibboleths. But she cares, and I won't have her humiliated. So I've bought us an island. Our own small paradise, where I shall build my lady a palace so that she may live in the setting she deserves."

Wearily, Jack muttered, "Which will cost great sums of money. So you planned to sell Alabaster Royal. You knew Sherry wouldn't stand in your way."

"Of course he wouldn't. He was the one with the looks, as you once said. Looks and charm. But he lacked my ambition. He was careless and easily swayed." Sir Kendrick strolled to the pile of rocks Consuela had left, and seated himself with his customary grace. "I always knew that you were the one to be reckoned with," he said. "The one who thought things through and who led. When he was killed, and you came home alive, I knew you would be difficult. I was right. Only look at how you persisted in your search for those confounded canvasses! When you started inspecting the snuff jar, I knew you were getting very close, and that if you ever saw the bowl Jones had fashioned, you'd surely put two and two together."

"The bowl you commissioned for me, sir?" said Jack ironically.

Sir Kendrick chuckled. "Well, it wasn't, of course. I commissioned it from Jones thinking to present it to my love as a reminder of how we won our island, and I instructed him to deliver it to me. It never dawned on me that he'd actually finished the curst thing, nor that he'd included those indications of faulted earth. If I'd had the remotest notion that the stupid fool had actually sent it to Richmond and that it had fallen into your Mama's greedy clutches, I'd have had it destroyed at once. Alas . . . " He shrugged. " 'The best laid schemes of mice and men . . . ' "

Jack drew a hand across his eyes. "If you'd only *asked* me! I'd have done—anything you wished."

"You forget, when I asked you to stay in Richmond, you refused. How could I believe you'd be willing to give me Alabaster without so much as coming down here to look it over? When you'd found out its true value, would you have handed to me the whole proceeds of the sale? The leases? The rights-of-way? And if you had caught just a whiff of a suspicion that I meant to take the funds and abandon your foolish Mama? What then? No, no. My hope was that you would come down here and be as revolted as any sensible man would be and allow me to—shall we say—dispose of the property. When it became clear to me that you liked the place, I knew you'd start sniffing around, and that sooner or later, you'd come at the truth. And I was right, wasn't I? I suppose you recognized my back in Preston Jones' confounded May Day painting."

He should have. His mind had been trying to tell him, but he hadn't wanted to hear. . . .

Sir Kendrick chuckled. "I thought so. And the half-wit told you about the coaching accident, no?"

Lord! How could he have been so blind? This morning Dicky-Boy had been staring at his father's portrait—not at the miniature coaches! The reason behind the lad's sly giggles, the knowing winks, was clear now, and so tragically different from what he'd supposed. He said wretchedly, "Couldn't you at least have helped the little girl?"

"I wanted to. It was a sad affair. But I couldn't risk being involved in such a murky business at that particular time. And now here I am in another murky business. I swear I didn't want things to take this turn, John. I tried very hard to dissuade you—one way and another. But you have that miserably dogged Scots streak in your make-up. You would persist. And tonight, when you were so damned determined to come here, on the very night we'd planned a meeting, I could see that you'd already put most of it together. You tried, but when you came out to the coach just now, you couldn't disguise the fact that you were hit hard. Poor lad. You were always so devoted."

"Aah!" Consuela tore her eyes from Jack's haggard, stricken face and turned on Sir Kendrick in a fury. Ignoring Lord Alperson's shrill cackle of mirth and Cramer's cheer, she raged, "How can you hurt him so? Does it matter nothing that he loves you? You are a wicked, wicked man, and that you destroyed my dear father is beyond words vile, but—to plot the murder of your own *son*? Faugh! You would disgust even a savage!"

Indignant, Sir Kendrick exclaimed, "Good gracious, I should hope so! As if I would do such a thing!"

Consuela stared at him in bewilderment, but her response was halted by Jack's upraised hand.

He said in a flat colourless voice, "Why bother to deny it, sir? Was it not at your instigation that Cramer ran me off the road that first day? Didn't you arrange the ambush that would hopefully break my neck? Were you ignorant of the fact that I was shot at in the churchyard, or that your—your beautiful lady intended my death?"

"Let us say," replied Sir Kendrick, demurely, "that it was a—er—combined effort. As for having plotted the murder of my son—never! I loved Sherborne."

Despite himself, Jack flinched.

Consuela hissed, "*Canaille!* You have another son!"

"Oh, no," said Sir Kendrick mildly.

Lord Alperson chuckled. Interested, but mildly confused, Cramer frowned.

Jack's bowed head shot up and he met the long-lashed dark eyes that were now so openly laughing at him.

"Do you know," said Sir Kendrick, "it never ceased to baffle me that you, such a very clever fellow, never guessed. Did you not once look at yourself and then look at me and at Sherborne, and wonder? Our colouring alone should have told you that your brother inherited my noble Norman lineage. What is noble about you, John? Your nondescript Saxon brown hair? Your hazel eyes? Didn't you wonder why you stand an inch under six feet, whereas Sherborne and I are three inches *above* that mark? Good God! Were you quite blind to your hopeless inferiority?"

Consuela whispered, "He is *not* your son?"

"The Lord forbid," said Sir Kendrick. "Oh, I grant you I kept up the illusion. Though at first, I was so enraged I wonder I did not strangle Lady Faith—who was, of course, faithless."

Jack said sharply, "As you were?"

"*Touché!* But she drove me to it, my dear boy. You know she did. And when she learnt I had set up a mistress, she avenged herself by taking a lover. I know it is a familiar scenario in our social order. But I have my pride, you know, and your mother was so embittered as to dally with the one man I loathed above all others! A top-lofty fool of a hypocrite, judged by the ignorant to be *sans peur et sans reproche,* and who turned my stomach! Our mutual dislike was well known. So to avoid providing the *ton* the joke of the decade, I frightened your mother into keeping her silly mouth shut—on this subject, if on nothing else. And I played the part of your proud and fond father. No mean task, when you became more and more like him, so that each time I looked at you—which was as seldom as possible— I saw *him!*"

For an instant, Sir Kendrick's eyes flashed rage. Then, he smiled his brilliant smile and said, "I marvel at my forbearance, no, really I do. The only thing that made it endurable was that everyone thought you such a credit to me. My friends admired your athletic achievements, and even that fool Wellington took a liking to you. Besides, Sherry was fond of you, so—"

"Sherry—knew?" asked Jack, the knife in his chest turning again.

"Unfortunately, he did. He saw your father once, and damn near fell off his horse in the middle of Hyde Park!"

Lord Alperson said in his sneering voice, "I must admit that these familial revelations have been very entertaining, Kendrick. But it's cold down here, and damp. Let's have done with it."

"What d'you mean—'have done with it'? What are you going to do?" The new voice startled them all. Very wet, but still elegant, Sir Larson Gentry stood in the mouth of the passage, a dismayed expression on his handsome face.

"Enter one drowned rat," sneered Alperson. "You've kept us waiting long enough, Larson."

"I arrived in time to have heard this," said Gentry. "You surely don't mean to kill them both? Lord! I didn't bargain for all this violence!"

"Just for a large share of the profits," snorted Cramer.

Sir Kendrick said, "None of us intended that any lives would be lost. And they needn't have been had Jones and my pseudo-heir kept their noses out of our business. We won't have to, ah, dirty our own hands in this matter, however. We'll simply leave them here and brick up the entrance to this section again, and they'll—"

"Starve to death?" said Gentry, aghast. "You *can't*! Not the girl, surely?"

"Don't get into a lather," said Alperson. "From the look of you, my buck, it's coming down cats and dogs again. The river's been getting higher for days. Another good storm and it'll rush through here like a cataract. They won't have to wait for starvation."

Jack felt Consuela's cold little hand slip into his own, and he held it tightly and made himself put his personal tragedy aside and concentrate on getting her to safety.

There were four of them, and Alperson and his fath- —Sir Kendrick—held loaded pistols. Poor odds. He had just one card. It might throw them off balance, but it must be played carefully.

He said, "May the condemned man be granted a last request?"

Cramer gave a scornful grunt. "Ain't he taking it like the brave little soldier!"

"It would be illuminating to observe your behaviour under like circumstances," said Sir Kendrick caustically. "By all means, John. We're in no great hurry."

"Except," said Alperson, "that my feet are getting wet."

All eyes scanned the floor.

Cramer gave a yelp. "My Gawd! The river's gone over the top! Let's get out of this!"

"Idiot," said Sir Kendrick. "If it reaches our ankles, we'll run to the upper level. Till then—your request, John?"

"It is that I be told the identity of—my real father."

"Request denied. So I'll give you another chance. Ah, but I think I know what you will ask. To what extent was dearest Esmeralda Stokely involved in our scheme? Right? Well, she was not. Exactly. She has been my woman for several years. I shock you, I see. I rather suspect Sherborne might have been a trifle annoyed, but—it is so. After his death she had it fixed in her mind that she was my great love, and that you were a threat to our future happiness. Such ridiculous self-delusion. As if I would marry such a strumpet. But she believed it enough to do as I asked in the matter of your—er—abrupt departure from the Flower Show. There, I've answered your questions, and I'm afraid we must now resort to the crude necessity of keeping you and the girl immobilized. Durward, tie them up."

Cramer stared at him. "With what?"

"Rip up your neckcloth. It should do nicely."

"Devil I will!"

Alperson leered, "The chit wears a petticoat, no doubt. Let's have it off."

Consuela said in a voice that shook, "Filthy lecher! Come near me and I'll claw your ugly face!"

His lordship laughed softly, and moved towards her.

Jack stepped between them. "I should tell you, gentlemen, that I know why Alabaster became so very valuable, and why you all expected to make a fortune with your rights-of-way and leases and so forth."

Alperson checked and turned his head to look at Sir Kendrick narrowly. "You *told* him? Are you gone daft? If he's passed it to his friends—"

"I told him nothing!" Sir Kendrick frowned. "And he knows nothing."

"I know why Preston Jones was willing to risk his life to find out what you were up to," said Jack.

Consuela put in, "He said it was evil! Is it?"

"It would be, if it succeeded. It will not."

"He's bluffing," growled Alperson.

"Even if you managed to sell the property to the government," said Jack, "how can you think their surveyors would not find these tunnels?"

Alperson let out a howl of rage.

Gentry gasped, "By God! He *does* know! Then—who else has he told?"

As flushed as Gentry was pale, Sir Kendrick said softly, "I really think you must answer that, my dear boy. As you will see, I've turned your pistol on Miss Jones. No—don't move! If you do not at once explain yourself, I will put a bullet in the lady. I mean it."

Jack hung his head. The water was rising over his boots. As if utterly defeated, he sighed, "Very well. You know that I was an aide to Lord Wellington. In that capacity I was present when his lordship and other officers were discussing Napoleon's threat to invade England. Wellington said that, among other things, plans were under way to build a subsidiary arsenal far from Woolwich. Yesterday, I met a military friend in Tunbridge Wells, and a chance remark he made set me wondering about the alleged philanthropist who wanted to put an orphanage on my estate." He looked up. "You—gentlemen—have evidently used your influence to provide Alabaster Royal as a logical site for the new Arsenal."

It was a shot in the dark, but the outburst of cursing confirmed his suspicions and caused Consuela to clap her hands over her ears.

"Have done!" shouted Sir Kendrick, his voice a whiplash. "Very well, *mon capitaine.* So you know. Who else knows?"

"What difference does it make? You'll never get away with it. The instant government surveyors find these tunnels, they'll know the ground above is unstable, and your scheme will fail."

"What a trusting nature." Sir Kendrick shook his head. "Commendable, I suppose. But so very unrealistic. The truth is, John, that many of our government 'servants' are wealthy men. Some, I grant you, had personal fortunes before they got into the game. As for the rest, did they amass their riches from their puny salaries? Of course not. It is done with the aid of graft, my boy. Graft and corruption. And there are palms in Whitehall today that have been so well greased, your beloved Alabaster Royal might be the Rock of Gibraltar!"

Consuela cried in horror, "But—but you *cannot*! To build great storehouses on this land would be to invite disaster! What if the tunnels should cave in under the weight?"

"They probably will," said Alperson with a shrug. "But we'll be far away by then, m'dear. And richly rewarded! Oh, we all share in the bounty, as the gallant Captain said."

"A share with which you two greedy vultures could not be content," murmured Sir Kendrick, shaking his head at Gentry and Cramer. "I cannot but wonder, my dear Larson—or Mr. Harrison, was it?—just what you planned to do with those wretched paintings had I not come up with you."

His face red, Gentry said airily, "Exactly what you did. Destroy them. As I told you. What did you suppose?"

"To my sorrow, I supposed that you meant to keep them hidden and at some future time either attempt to sell them, or, in the unhappy event we should ever be found out and arrested, use them to turn retribution away from yourselves and towards me."

"I protest!" Gentry drew himself up, and trying to appear outraged succeeded only in looking very nervous. "Damme, but you've a nasty suspicious mind, Vespa. I am shocked and—and most offended."

303

"And dear Signor da Lentino is dead," said Consuela. "You must count on large returns, Lord Alperson, to allow murder to besmirch your fine old name!"

"Very great returns!" Alperson rubbed his hands and chuckled. "Trust a woman not to see it. There will have to be roads built, you see, across my lands, and Gentry's. The rights-of-way will be extreme costly. They may even have to buy us out. Lovely."

"But—you can't have *thought*," persisted Consuela. "If explosives are stored here—if heavy cannon and shot and black powder are massed, and there is a cave-in and an explosion—My God! It could wipe out the entire village! How could you live with yourselves if—"

Cramer shrieked, "Look at the water! We've got to get out!"

Startled, they all looked down.

It was the moment Jack had waited for. He shouted, "Consuela, *run*!" and hurled himself at Cramer as the man made a lunge for the main tunnel.

Consuela hesitated, then obeyed.

Jack and Cramer collided violently. Cramer was flung against Sir Kendrick, knocking the pistol from his hand and sending him staggering. Jack steadied himself against the tunnel wall and whipped around to find Alperson before him, a large horse-pistol aiming steadily, and a lusting grin distorting his unlovely features.

"Don't fire that blasted great cannon!" howled Sir Kendrick. "You'll bring the roof down on us, you fool!"

"Well, this won't!" Gentry sprang forward, his clenched fist flying.

Jack dodged aside and Gentry mouthed shrill curses as his knuckles made contact with the wall.

Alperson's pistol butt flailed viciously. Jack's vision blurred and he reeled to the wall, sickened with pain, feeling blood streak down his cheek.

Someone was shouting, "Catch that damned chit! If she gets away we're all ruined!"

"I'll get her," yelled Cramer. "But I'll need a lamp!"

Dimly, Jack saw the approaching light, and as Cramer rushed past he kicked out with all his strength. The lantern flew into the water, hissed, and ceased to glow.

"Damn and blast!" raged Sir Kendrick. "*Hold* him, you idiots! Get *after* her, Durward! The doxy can't see, either! We'll finish here!"

Cramer swore and ran out.

Gentry lunged at Jack.

Snarling with fury, Lord Alperson aimed his horse-pistol.

The knowledge that this time he would fire lent Jack the strength of desperation. As Gentry's fist flew at him, he dodged, seized the man's arm, and sent him spinning into collision with Alperson.

His lordship's *"Whoof!"* was deafening, and his eyes seemed about to pop from his head.

Jack sprang forward, seized the horse-pistol and whirled about.

Gentry had started for him again, but shrank back as the large muzzle waved his way.

"Well, well, well," murmured Sir Kendrick. "One has to admit that Lord Wellington chose wisely. His stellar aide-de-camp has bested the lot of us! But I would point out that you've only the one bullet, dear lad." Smiling, he stepped forward.

Jack clenched his teeth. "Sir, don't make me fire."

Another sauntering step. "Never hesitate, John. You're a crack shot, as I recall. Shoot straight if you please, and spare me the disgrace of"—his eyes darted to the tunnel entrance—"Aha! You caught the wench!"

Jack jerked his head to the entrance.

The shot and the impact were as one.

He was smashed back. The horse-pistol, suddenly too heavy to hold, slipped from his numb fingers.

He was on his knees, leaning against the rockpile, bitterly aware that he'd been taken in by a very old trick.

Alperson let out a triumphant howl.

Gentry looked faintly aghast.

Sir Kendrick sighed. "What a pity. But I do believe we must say adieu, dear boy. You won't be disturbed, I promise. We'll seal the upper tunnel carefully before we leave."

Watching dully as Alperson groped around and found his pistol, Jack knew that he should try to stop them, but he was so tired now . . . so very tired. The water was icy cold, and it was rising fast. He wondered absently where he'd been hit. He couldn't feel much yet. But he was getting weaker. He wouldn't be able to hold on to the rocks much longer . . . and once he fell into that black, surging water, he'd never get up. . . . They were leaving, taking the light with them. It was very dark. He'd always hoped he would die out under the sky somewhere. Not that it really mattered. He coughed, and his head sank onto his arms.

There seemed to be a lot of noise nearby. Puzzled, he looked up.

Light glared. Still holding the coach lamp, Sir Kendrick backed into the tunnel. He looked pale and desperate. Someone was following, crouched and muttering softly and swinging a great club, the end glittering as it caught the rays of light.

"You stupid dolt," panted Sir Kendrick, backing away. "You can't prove it was my coach!"

"Oh, yes, I can!" said Josiah Hawes, gloatingly. "I gotta witness, now. But I don't need no witness. I'm judge and jury, melor'! And you're sentenced to be—"

Sir Kendrick turned and fled deeper into the tunnel, and Hawes growled like a hungry animal and splashed after him.

Jack called weakly, "Hawes! No! They'll . . . hang you!"

There came another glow. Paige Manderville, his elegance wet and muddied, waded in, a lantern held high. "This is no time to take a bath, dear boy. Where did they go? Poor old Toby told us— Oh, my Lord! No! Stay out, m'dear! We'll have to—"

Consuela was bending over him. "Dear Captain Jack! You've saved my life again, and— *Paige!*"

"I know." The dark water surged powerfully, and Manderville steadied her, then grabbed Jack's sagging form. "Dammitall! The river must be at the flood! Hey, Strickley, somebody! Lend a hand here, before we have to swim for it!"

It seemed an unreasonable suggestion. Jack registered a protest. "I don't think . . . I care for a swim . . . just now," he said wearily.

A long way away, a man screamed, the sound echoing and echoing into a complete silence.

19

~•~

A soft hand was stroking the hair back from his forehead.
"Consuela . . . ?" He started up eagerly, and pain lashed
out with such fierce intensity that he was sent spinning into darkness again; but not before he heard a girl weeping.

His father and Hawes had gone off somewhere together. . . . Only, something was very wrong . . . if he could just remember what it was. . . .

Consuela gasped, "He is *not* your son!"
   Sir Kendrick's voice: "The Lord forbid . . . The Lord forbid . . . The Lord forbid . . . "

"But Sherry was fond of you. . . . "

Consuela was speaking again, sounding so troubled that he wanted to see if he could help. "He's not *trying,* Toby! He keeps re-living it, over and over again. I think—his poor heart, it is broken! He doesn't *want* to live!"

"Oh, I, er, wouldn't say that." Broderick coughed and sounded miserable. "But, you can, er, see why he might . . . er . . . "

Lady Francesca said softly, "Your tears won't help him, my little meadowlark. Only your prayers . . . "

Consuela should not be unhappy. He didn't want her to cry. . . .

It was terribly hot. Spain was hot, of course. Sometimes. Perhaps he could go for a swim now. Paige had said something about swimming . . . a long time ago . . .

A dog was barking. He opened his eyes, moved restlessly, and caught his breath.

At once Broderick was bending over him. "Well, this is much better," he said heartily. "How do you feel, old pippin?"

Puzzled, he said, "Are we still in Spain?"

Broderick leant closer. "What? Can't quite hear you, dear boy. What is it?"

But he didn't have to repeat his question, because his chest hurt so intensely that he remembered. Instead, he asked, "Who . . . shot me?"

Broderick's hesitation was very brief. Then, "Alperson," he answered firmly.

But Jack had seen his quick glance at someone who hovered nearby, and he knew.

He turned his face to the wall.

This time, Consuela was very cross. "You are a wretched, wretched Englishman!" she scolded. "You have had a great shock and—and disappointment, and you are very sad. This, we all know. And we are sad, too. And your brother, would, I am quite sure, be sad for your sake."

Sherry . . . Yes, Sherry would have understood. Dear old Sherry.

" . . . have lost your lady-love too, I know. And it is all very hard. Life *is* hard sometimes. But that is no reason to make up your mind not to live, because life can also be good, and beautiful, and full of laughter and happiness! God gave you a kind, warm heart, Captain Jack. And a—a very nice body. And"—fingers touched his cheek gently—"and a face that is most good to look upon. You have friends—you would not believe how many have come! And you have family and—and others who—care very greatly for you. The man you loved as your father was bad. I know it is a great grief, but you should think to yourself that it is better he was *not* your father, instead of lying there wanting only to be—" Her voice broke. She blew her nose and sniffed. "What is to become of Corporal, I should like to know? And where will poor Thorny, or Peg, or Harper find anyone to give them employment if you persist in—in leaving us?"

Had Harper and Peg stayed on, then? Somehow, he'd thought they'd left.

"If you had any rumgumption, Captain Jack Wansdyke— Vespa," said Consuela, suddenly fierce, "you would strike back! You would go and find out who your *real* father was! If Sir Kendrick—forgive me for speaking his horrid name!—if he hated him, then your father was probably a very fine gentleman. Indeed, he must be, to have sired such a gallant and . . . courageous, and— and kind-hearted man as—as you." A smothered sob, then a tremulous, "There! I've said all I care to—to say! Good-bye!"

Who his real father was . . . If he had any rumgumption . . . His *real* father . . .

With a great effort, he said feebly, "Please—don't cry."

Consuela squealed.

———⟨∞⟩———

Jack gazed out at the snowy landscape and thought it very beautiful. It was also very cold, but the drawing room was cozy. Logs crackled companionably on the hearth, two branches of candles added their warm glow to the grey afternoon, and a third candelabra shone on the painting that now hung over the mantel, replacing the one he had placed there with such— Replacing the other. Alabaster Royal in some long-ago springtime, with a mighty war-horse tethered at the front steps.

He was grateful, now, that he had survived; that he could be at peace in his old manor house. Consuela's scold had marked the turning point at which he had begun to fight for life instead of desiring only to be done with it. His recovery had been steady, and as soon as he was well enough, his friends had told him what transpired on that fateful day.

Broderick had learnt in Salisbury that Mrs. Stokely was far from being Sir Kendrick's great love, and the widow's discovery of her betrayal, and her impassioned and bitter description of her rival, had left no doubt of that lady's identity. The conclusion had been inescapable: Sir Kendrick must be in some way involved in the attack on his son, and perhaps in the deeper plot. Poor Broderick's race to warn his friend of the new source of danger had ended when Josiah Hawes had mistaken Broderick for himself and smashed him from the saddle. Dicky-Boy, a petrified witness to the attack, had gulped out his long-concealed knowledge of who owned the coach that had brought about the tragic accident. Hawes, maddened with rage, had rushed in pursuit of Sir Kendrick, leaving Dicky-Boy to care for Broderick.

Returning from a fruitless search of Shrewsbury for the 'disappointed' purchaser of the Preston Jones paintings, Manderville had come upon Broderick attempting to mount his horse with Dicky-Boy's help. Their combined explanations had so alarmed him that he'd stayed only to demand that Strickley and Thornhill be despatched to his aid at once, then he'd ridden at the gallop for the Jones cottage. Luckily, he'd caught a glimpse of Josiah Hawes running towards the quarry, and had the presence of mind to follow.

Jack had been carried back to Alabaster. Manderville had lost

311

no time in acquainting a horrified Constable Blackham with most, if not all, of the details of the plot. Blackham had protested that he lacked the authority to deal with so terrible a conspiracy, especially since highly-born and powerful aristocrats were involved. The tale must be relayed to Bow Street, he said, and he and Manderville had journeyed to London for that purpose. Returning, Manderville's infuriated description of his reception at Bow Street had seemed justified when, although there had been a great flurry of activity over the attack on Jack, any mention of the conspirators had been met with a bland assurance that matters were "being looked into".

Peg and Harper had left Alabaster Royal, but had been so shocked upon hearing of Jack's injuries that they'd at once come back again, Peg having convinced herself that the Alabaster Cat had done its duty and was unlikely to return. Her courage was also bolstered by a visit to Mother Wardloe, from whom she had purchased even more potent charms, against which no ghost or goblin might prevail.

When ten days had passed with no further word from Bow Street, Consuela had lost patience, and, judging that Jack was sufficiently recovered to be left in Lady Francesca's charge, had gone to Town herself, accompanied by her maid, and escorted by Paige and Toby.

Jack's heart beat faster as there came the sounds of hooves and carriage wheels crunching on the snow.

Corporal started to twitch in his sleep and make smothered yips and yelps, then sprang up with such a start that he tumbled from his Person's blanketed knees. He cast a quick and embarrassed look at Jack, then raced to the front door, barking importantly as the carriage halted outside.

The bell had been disconnected during the invalid's long convalescence, but Peg responded to Corporal's warning. She trotted across the hall, peered anxiously into the drawing room, nodded brightly at the sole occupant, and dropped a wooden spoon she'd forgotten to leave in the kitchen. There was a brief difficulty when she tried to pick it up while her foot was still on the handle, but she prevailed at last, and went, giggling and breathless, to open the door.

Jack caught a whiff of frosty air, and tensed when he heard the cheerful and familiar voices. Toby and Paige, and the lighter and eager tones of Consuela. His hands gripped hard at the arms of the chair. He mustn't let them see how anxious he'd been, or Consuela would start looking at him worriedly.

Peg collected coats and cloaks and scarves, and went off, laden, and with many "Dearie me's" as she tripped over trailing garments.

Paige moaned, "My new driving coat, Peg . . . !"

Consuela cried eagerly, "Where is he?"

Broderick said, "What—downstairs now? I say!"

Flying feet, and Consuela was at his side, cheeks rosy from the cold, bright eyes searching his face, and her cold little hands going out to him. "Oh, Jack! How *well* you look!"

"Jupiter," said Broderick, coming up to grip his shoulder, but very gently. "We can't call you a skeleton any more, old fellow! You positively radiate health, be damned if you don't!"

Manderville shook his hand and told him that Toby was a liar, but that he did look a lot better than he had done. "Harper!" he shouted. "We're all half froze! Bring us hot cider, you hedgebird!"

"And sustenance!" added Broderick, pulling up a chair for Consuela. "I'm fairly starved!"

Jack said, "Tell me about little Molly. What did Lord Belmont have to say about her?"

"Nothing polite," answered Manderville indignantly. "What a crusty old curmudgeon! Gave me a proper bear garden jaw, only because I—"

"Because you told him to cut to the chase and stop his round-aboutation," interposed Broderick, grinning. "He's a dashed good doctor, Jack. He thinks he can help the little girl, but says it will take time, and she must stay in Town for several months. Hawes didn't like that much."

"No, so then *he* got a bear garden jaw," said Manderville.

313

"And the upshot of it all was that we told him he could stay with her, and that you'd stand the huff, so all was right and tight," finished Broderick, regarding Jack somewhat apprehensively. "That *was* as you wished, I hope?"

"Exactly as I wished. If anyone can help her, Lord Belmont's the man to do so. Thank you, both."

Manderville straightened his cuff and eyed the sleeve critically. "What d'ye think of this coat, Jack? Balleroy made it for me whilst we was in Town. It would look better with a lace cravat, don't you think?"

"Lace cravat?" snorted Broderick. "Good Gad, Paige! Men haven't worn lace cravats for—what? Fifty years, at least!"

"Not so!" said Manderville. "M'father's wearing a deuced fine froth of lace in his portrait, and that was only painted in 'ninety-three. I really think I may reintroduce lace cravats. Devilish attractive with a coat like this, you can't—"

"Oh, *do* hush, Paige," said Consuela, laughing at him. "You're not letting Jack say a word. I want to know how he is feeling, and if he has heard from his Mama."

He assured her that he was feeling "splendid". The last word he'd had from Lady Faith had been a letter, despatched the day before the confrontation in the quarry. His mother had been horrified by the scandal "that wickedly treacherous and immoral Esmeralda Stokely has loosed upon the *ton*." Poor Lady Faith's nerves and hurt pride could stand no more. She was leaving "within the hour" with Cousin Brian as her courier to his father's plantation in South America. She hoped Jack would follow as soon as he could tear himself away from his "haunted ruin", but for herself, she desired not to set eyes on London for at least a year!

Several members of his family had posted down to Dorsetshire when they were advised of his illness, and his eldest uncle had despatched a letter to Lady Faith desiring that she come home at once. As yet there had been no reply or any indication that the lady contemplated a return to England. Having relayed that information, Jack was obliged to restrain his own eagerness for news

314

when Harper carried in fragrant hot cider and toasted currant buns, and Peg arrived with a brimming tray of half-full mugs of hot chocolate.

They all settled down around the fire, with Corporal at the centre of the circle watching hopefully for scraps. When they were warmer, and appetites and thirsts had been assuaged, Jack could wait no longer. "I am much better, as you see. It's quite safe to tell me. What happened? Did you go to the Horse Guards? What have the authorities done about the horrid mess?"

"Nothing," said Broderick, answering the last question first. "At least, nothing we're privileged to know. We went first to Bow Street and then to Whitehall, of course, where we were shunted from pillar to post, and it was very clear nobody wanted to touch the business."

Consuela said darkly, "Constable Blackham's report had likely gone to the very men who were most involved in the scheme!" Her eyes softened. She added, "Except for Colonel Adair, of course."

Jack frowned slightly. "Who's Colonel—"

"When we found that, as you suspected, there'd been little progress, we went to m'father," said Broderick hurriedly. "Most sensible gentleman I know."

Dusting crumbs from his breeches, Manderville nodded. "Which is the reason we didn't go to mine. Good old boy, you know. But not famed for his needle wit."

"Professor Broderick is *very* learned," put in Consuela. "Though I must say, Toby, he uses the most dreadful language."

Broderick sighed ruefully. " 'Fraid that's right, m'dear. But he's used to talking to students, you see. I remember one lecture he gave—"

"He took us to his solicitor," inserted Manderville.

"Who thought we were all gone demented," said Consuela.

Amused, Broderick nodded. "But he took the case to the Horse Guards again and demanded action, and the very next morning we were all dragged from Claridge's by a troop of dragoons."

315

Manderville appended mischievously, "Under the command of Consuela's prize Colonel."

"He is not my *prize* Colonel," argued Consuela, her cheeks rather pink. "He was very kind and at least he listened to what we had to say. And he told us their preliminary investigations would almost certainly result in the dismissal of two highly placed civil servants."

His gaze turning from her heightened colour, Jack exclaimed, "*Dismissals?* Good Lord above! Two murders, at least! Bribery and corruption! A complete indifference to the safety of the residents of an entire village! And all they can achieve is *two dismissals?*"

Manderville said carefully, "This Colonel fella said warrants have been issued for the arrests of old Alperson—"

"Now believed to be in Ireland," muttered Broderick with a scowl.

"And Gentry—"

"Who took ship for Italy the day after . . . everything," said Consuela.

"But they're wanted for questioning, merely," finished Manderville. "No specific charges. As yet."

Seething, Jack said, "As yet? Are they waiting for the turn of the century?"

Manderville began to examine his fingernails.

Broderick said uneasily, "Well, ah, the problem is, you see, we avoided naming your, er—"

"And anyway, Professor Broderick's solicitor said we could name no names without we had definite proof—or witnesses," explained Consuela.

"They seem to feel that a snuff bottle and a bowl and some vanished paintings ain't enough evidence," said Manderville with a wry look.

Jack said, "Josiah Hawes heard most of it. He's a witness."

"Not a very reliable one, apparently." Broderick tossed a morsel of currant bun to the patient Corporal. "After he had the truth from Dicky-Boy, Hawes followed your coach, as you know, but lost it in the downpour. He stopped several travellers and demanded to know if they'd seen you pass, and declared his intention to murder your—er— Well, you know."

"He's afraid," said Manderville, "that if there's a full-scale investigation, he'll be accused of just such a deed."

Jack said in a controlled voice, "Hawes swears they were separated by the floodwaters and that Sir Kendrick was—swept away."

"Josiah is a poor man," Consuela pointed out gently, "and known to hold a grudge and have a violent disposition. He'd have small chance of being believed."

"What about Durward Cramer? He was in it up to his neck."

"Which got broke in a tavern brawl in Westminster," said Broderick.

"Jupiter!" muttered Jack, shocked. "He was the weakest link. They must have feared he'd talk out of turn."

"You may be sure I will testify," said Consuela with determination.

"And—er, I'm afraid you may have to do the same, Jack," said Broderick. "Sorry, dear boy. But—there 'tis."

"Don't be such a clunch," exclaimed Manderville, revolted. "How can a fellow testify against his own—well, I mean, against the man the world *believes* to be his own—father? He'd be despised by the *ton* for sullying a fine old name, and he'd be damned lucky if he didn't have to leave the country!"

Consuela said fiercely, "Even if his father tried to—"

Corporal burst into a flurry of barking, rushed to the hall door and leapt up and down frantically.

Consuela ran to the window. "Oh, it's Grandmama's coach!"

"Escorted by a whole troop of dragoons by the look of it," said Broderick, peering over her shoulder.

Many hooves were clattering over the cobblestones.

"And Colonel Adair!" exclaimed Consuela, dancing to the door.

"Be damned," said Manderville. "Must've followed us from Town!"

The hall was suddenly full of uniforms. Consuela was gushing something about how glad she was to see someone again. A man's voice remarked with predictable inanity that the pleasure was his. Jack tightened his lips and waited. Lady Francesca demanded to know if "Captain Jack" was well enough today to receive "so many visitings".

The doors were flung wide. Jack was astonished to see that Thornhill—holding a long-handled shoe horn; Harper—armed with a musket; Strickley—hammer in hand; and Peg—gripping a murderous-looking meat cleaver—stood firm in the hall, presenting a united front against the sea of red coats.

Lady Francesca swept in on the arm of a tall colonel who looked too young to have attained his exalted rank.

Preparing to stand, and to dislike this man, Jack was instructed firmly to stay where he was while Colonel the Honourable Hastings Adair was made known to him. The colonel shook his hand, a pair of intensely blue eyes measured him in a swift appraisal, and then glinted smilingly. Bending lower, Adair said, "Very sorry, Captain. But I'll have to request a private word. D'you think you could call off your hound and your faithful retainers? They're frightening my poor fellows to death!"

Jack sighed inwardly, understanding why Consuela was so obviously taken with this gentleman. He was touched to find Broderick standing close to one side of his chair and Manderville equally close to the other.

He said, "Are you here to arrest me, Colonel?"

Adair chuckled. "Gad, I'd not dare! His lordship would have my ears!"

Manderville asked eagerly, "Lord Wellington knows about this?"

"He knows about Captain Vespa," evaded Adair.

Jack reached out, and Lady Francesca hurried to take his hand and pat it affectionately, saying, "Am I to chase these soldier-boys into the snow, my dear?"

He pressed her fingers to his lips and asked that she instead tell his faithful staff that he was not to be rushed off to the Tower for immediate decapitation, and would appreciate it if the military contingent could be offered refreshments in the kitchen.

Five minutes later, alone with the colonel, he watched Adair sample his Madeira and said, "What are you sent to discover?"

"Everything your friends were so careful not to tell us. For instance, where is your father at this moment?"

His smile a little twisted, Jack said, "I haven't the remotest idea."

Adair held his glass up and admired the glow of the flames through the tawny liquid. "That won't do, I'm afraid, Captain Vespa. We've already confirmed a good deal of your story, and thanks to your efforts you may be sure there'll be no more talk of locating a subsidiary arsenal here. But we must know the whole. Even if we appear to do nothing with what we learn."

Jack looked at him thoughtfully. "In confidence? I cannot bring more grief to my mother, you understand."

One of Adair's dark brows lifted. "A confidence for a confidence," he said. "I am here officially as a representative of the Horse Guards. Unofficially, I am here at the behest of your C.O."

"Then Wellington *does* know of this business!"

"Let us say 'whispers' have a way of reaching his ears."

"Through his brother, Lord Richard, perhaps?"

Adair smiled. "I didn't say that. At all events, he has a war to win, but he wasn't pleased with some of the whispers, and I was assigned to investigate. Whatever you choose to tell me will, I must warn you, be relayed to him. An—ah—edited version will go back with me to Whitehall."

Jack was silent through a long, troubled pause. Then, he told Adair everything. When he finished, he was trembling.

Adair took a deep breath, said softly, "My dear God!", took both glasses to the credenza and refilled them. "You've been in a beast of a pickle," he observed, handing Jack his glass and restraining the sympathy he felt. "Shall you change your name?"

"I've thought about it. I'd like to. I cannot. It would shame my mother, you see."

"Yes, of course. It's as well you've decided to let us handle it."

Jack said ironically, "Is that what I've done?"

Adair nodded. "You'll be kept out of it. At least until we've run Alperson and Gentry to earth. As for Sir Kendrick . . . " He shrugged.

"He's—dead."

"Oh, very likely," said the colonel. "But I'm afraid you won't be able to touch the estate until we're sure."

"Devil take you!" said Jack angrily. "I've no intention of touching anything to which I evidently have no right! I've an ample inheritance from my mother's parents to which I've *every* right, and that I *will* claim!"

"I see what his lordship meant about your temper," said Adair, grinning. "Will you strike me if I enquire whether your 'claim' extends to Miss Jones?"

Fortunately, Lady Francesca chose that moment to hurry in, saying that her patient had been sufficiently tired, and that Colonel Adair had better come and take charge of his men before they ate poor Captain Jack out of house and home.

Much later, when colonel and troop had departed, and an excellent dinner had been enjoyed by Lady Francesca and her granddaughter and the three young men, they were all gathered around the drawing-room fire again.

The wind was blustering about outside and Watts had already been told to prepare the carriage to take the ladies home.

Manderville broke a comfortable silence. "I suppose I must say my farewells," he said. "Imposed on your hospitality for long enough, Jack, and you'll be anxious to get back to Town, I expect. This house must hold too many memories for— What I mean to say is—er—nothing."

"Clumsy blockhead," muttered Broderick. "But he's right, dear boy. Time for us to fold our tents, as it were." He quoted rather wistfully, " 'When shall we three meet again In thunder, lightning, or in rain?' "

Perched on a footstool beside Jack's chair, Consuela finished the quotation, " 'When the hurlyburly's done, When the battle's lost and won.' "

With an eye on her granddaughter's pensive face, Lady Francesca said, "I suppose that—it is truth. Your battle was both won—and a little lost. So what do you mean to do with your life now, my Captain? A Town beau, or a country gentleman?"

Vespa stroked Corporal's ear, and said, "A little of both, perhaps. Somebody once said to me that if I had any rumgumption I'd bestir myself to find out who was my real father."

Consuela gave a start and looked up at him guiltily. "Wicked one! You were listening!"

He laughed. "I had a right. I was the one being scolded."

"I say!" exclaimed Toby, brightening. "Now *there's* an interesting prospect. You might need intelligent help, old lad!"

"And expert advice," said Manderville hopefully.

"I thought you'd never volunteer," said Jack.

He insisted on walking out to the front door with Consuela. Snow was falling lightly, and a full moon shone through the drifting curtain and reflected from the white blanket of the lawns. Corporal rushed about biting at the snow and accumulating a small white pyramid on the end of his nose. Thornhill and the duchess had already reached the coach, and Jack drew Consuela to a halt.

She looked up at him, her eyes very tender, and gazing deep into those dark eyes he knew that this valiant girl had become very dear to him, so that life without her bright presence would be a dull business. He touched her cheek gently. "Consuela, you are very lovely tonight."

"Thank you, kind sir."

"I'm not limping so markedly. Had you noticed?"

"Of course. In a week or two you will likely not limp at all. And you are not so thin, indeed you begin to look quite robust, and very like your portrait."

Surprised, he asked, "What portrait?"

"Oh, dear! The one of you and your brother that hangs in Wansdyke House. Yes, yes, I can see the questions boiling up, but desist.

Toby and I called in there, hoping your Mama might be visiting your uncle. She wasn't, of course, but Sir Reginald was most kind, and he gave—er, that is, he gave me permission to see the portrait."

"Ah." He said haltingly, "The fellow in that portrait has no right to the name he bears, it seems. Which makes it impossible for him to—in honour, offer it to a lady."

She stood very still and her long lashes swept down to conceal her eyes. "Does it, Jack?"

"And even if he should discover his—his true identity, he has precious little to offer."

"For instance?"

He sighed. "This old house. An estate I—he—hopes to turn to good account. A comfortable inheritance from his maternal grandparents. Not a magnificent list, I'm afraid."

"No." Still looking down, she murmured, "Is that all he could offer?"

His heart sank. "I fear it is. And I know it would be a paltry prospect for a very special lady, but . . . I'd like to think that, if the time should ever come that he could—improve upon it, he might be—considered?"

"It would take a great deal of—improvement, but," she smiled up at him, "who can tell what the future holds?"

Lady Francesca called peevishly that she was freezing, and Consuela smiled and put out a small gloved hand. "Good-night, and God bless you, my dear Captain Jack."

He kissed her fingers, glove and all, and watched as she hurried to the coach. Strickley assisted her up the carriage steps, and she turned and waved, the lamps lighting her face framed by the snowflakes that clung to the hood of her cloak.

Waving back, he knew he'd had no right to speak at all, under the circumstances. But to the extent he could do so, he had at least declared himself. She'd said his prospects would have to be improved upon. They would be, by George! And then, he'd try again.

He watched the coach rumble away, and turned back to the house. Broderick's quotation came to mind. His own battle had been won—in a sense; but so much had been lost. The brother he'd loved; the 'father' he'd idolized.

Thornhill came up to pull the cloak tighter about his shoulders and tell him with proprietary concern that it was "too cold out here, Captain."

Walking into the warm house with Corporal prancing along beside him, Jack thought, 'And so much gained.' Loyal friends, faithful servants and a pixie of a girl who seemed to get prettier and more desirable every day, who had nursed and cared for him with such selfless devotion. And who was almost certainly going to be courted by a dashing and all too likable Colonel of Dragoon Guards! Deuce take the fellow!

He limped slowly towards the drawing room.

Broderick was saying, "Of course it was Shakespeare! Whom did you suppose it to be? Thucydides?"

"Certainly not," said Manderville. "Never heard of the fellow."

"How could you *possibly* have got through school without having heard of Thucydides? He was an Athenian, who lived about four centuries B.C., and wrote the history of the Peloponnesian War. A bit long-winded, but—"

"Long-winded!" groaned Manderville.

Jack chuckled, and went to join them.

In the carriage, Consuela gave a small sniff.

Lady Francesca reached into her granddaughter's muff and clasped her hand.

"Colonel Adair," she pointed out, "is a man of breeding, my meadowlark."

"Yes."

"And it is that he will inherit a nice fortune. He is, besides, of the handsomeness, do not you agree?"

"Oh yes, I do."

"And the gleam is in his eye for you, I think."

"I thought that, too."

"And you . . . ?"

"Don't be silly, dear Grandmama!"

Lady Francesca sighed. After a minute, she tried again. "Captain Jack, he is the very best of men, Consuela. This I admit it without preservation. The kind that adversity and grief cannot crush, but only refine and make stronger."

"Yes," said Consuela, overlooking the grammatical slip, her voice very tender now.

"Ah, my sweet one, consider! His heart—it is given, and he is not the kind to give lightly, nor forget lightly. He will not love again, child."

"He will! It would have been more difficult had he decided to leave Alabaster, but even so, I would have found a way!"

Consuela turned her head, and the light of the carriage lamps revealed such a troubled expression on the old lady's face that she swooped to kiss her. "Poor dearest one! I know what you fear. That having known grief, I do but invite more. It is not so! He hasn't even seen—her, for over a year, and he loves me a little bit already—he as good as told me so, just now."

"Then this was most improper of him, not having my first permission!"

"I know, and quite unlike such a gentlemanly gentleman, though it was not an offer exactly. The poor dear thinks that, because of his hideous father, who was not a father at all, he is unworthy. Such stuff!"

"Then he should not have spoke!"

Consuela giggled. "I think he did so much against his will. He is afraid, Grandmama. Is it not delicious? Our handsome Colonel inspired him to—enter the lists, as it were."

"And what of you, my poor child?"

"I told him he must improve upon his offer. He did not say he loves me, and I will marry no man whose heart I do not own."

"But—dearest girl, surely—"

"I know. But I shall make him love Marietta Warrington as—as an old friend, only! I shall make him love *me*!" She gave a little trill of laughter. "Did you see how he scowled at Colonel Adair? My poor darling Jack—he is doomed, and doesn't even know it!"

Lady Francesca squeezed her hand, and knew she must talk sternly to St. Peter.